A Shadow on the Snow
A Rae Riley Mystery
A Sequel to "A Rose from the Ashes"

By JPC Allen

M Zion Ridge Press LLC

Mt Zion Ridge Press LLC
295 Gum Springs Rd, NW
Georgetown, TN 37366

https://www.mtzionridgepress.com

ISBN 13: 978-1-955838-04-7

Published in the United States of America
Publication Date: December 1, 2021

Editor-In-Chief: Michelle Levigne
Executive Editor: Tamera Lynn Kraft

Cover art design by Tamera Lynn Kraft

DEDICATION

To my parents, who always encouraged me to chase the next story with my feet firmly planted in reality.

And to my Heavenly Dad—I've learned so much about You as we wrote Rae's stories.

Let's do it again!

FOREWORD

On December 1, 2018, I found out that if I wanted to contribute to the latest anthology from Mt. Zion Ridge Press, I would have to write a 5,000-word story in two weeks. While getting ready for Christmas and a visit from my in-laws. And I don't write fast. At all.

But I discussed it with my husband, and with the Holy Spirit, I wrote *A Rose from the Ashes*, the Selah-finalist, YA Christmas mystery published in *Christmas Fiction Off The Beaten Path*.

I fell in love with Rae, her dad, her extended family, and the characters of fictional Marlin County, Ohio, and wanted to know what happened next to them. You're holding the next episode in the lives of Rae Riley and the Malinowski clan.

Chapter 1

I'M NOT FOOLED, RAE. YOU'RE JUST LIKE YOUR MOTHER.

I stared at the sheet of copier paper in my hand as the note fluttered in a gust of January wind.

Really? It had only taken three weeks for someone to hate me and my mom enough to leave an anonymous insult?

Turning over the envelope, I saw my address was written in the same marker, same all-caps style. It was postmarked. I must have missed it when I grabbed my mail last night.

Shivering on the miniscule landing to my apartment, I blew out a sigh, which formed a little cloud in the freezing air. At least the idiot hadn't crept up to my mailbox in the dead of night. I shivered again, and it wasn't from another gust.

People could hold a grudge in Marlin County, Ohio. I'd learned that in the last three weeks since I discovered Mal was my dad and announced Bella Rydell was my mother. The strained smiles, cold stares, conversations that didn't get much past "hello" and "I'm fine." Mom had made a lot of enemies, but that was twenty years ago. I'd told everyone who asked the story of how she'd been saved and changed her life. Well, most of it.

I shoved the piece of paper back in the envelope, tossed it inside my apartment, and locked the door behind me.

Holding my tripod and a roll of leftover bulletin board paper in one hand, I clutched the strap of my backpack with the other and climbed down the icy steps to the pad in front of the garage. Picking my way across Mrs. Blaney's snow-covered lawn, I pulled the keys to my ancient truck from the pocket of my down vest. The Rust Bucket sat by the curb, draped in a thin layer of snow that couldn't disguise its demolition derby appearance.

After ten cranks of the key, the engine caught. I grabbed the gear shift, and it didn't move. Not a millimeter. I hit the steering wheel. *Not this morning. Why this morning?*

I fished my phone out of the other vest pocket and checked the time. If I walked fast and ran where it was safe on the slick pavement, I'd still make it to the library on time. Although Mal had shown me how, I still couldn't unjam the gears without someone helping.

Grabbing my backpack, and leaving the paper and tripod behind, I slammed out of the truck. Some snow fell off. I wouldn't have been surprised if both bumpers had too.

Avoiding the slick sidewalk, I ran along edges of yards, heading uphill to Main Street. In Marlin County, if you weren't going uphill, you were going downhill, sort of a scaled down version of the West Virginia county Mom and I had lived in when I was in middle school.

The sun shone ice white in a clear sky so blue it looked like an illustration in a hyper-cheerful picture book. But despite the sun's dazzling appearance, not an ounce of warmth made it to the hilly streets. I pulled my scarf over my mouth and nose and held my arms tight against my sides. Maybe I should have taken Mal up on his offer to buy me a proper winter coat.

I zipped my vest to my chin. I hadn't spent the past seven months figuring out who my father was and if he had tried to murder my mom when she was pregnant with me so I could live off of him. I was nineteen. I'd been on my own pretty much since Mom's last round with cancer. If I froze to the bone because my jean jacket and vest only kept me warm above fifty degrees, fine with me. Nobody in Marlin County was going to accuse me of being a manipulator. That's what a lot of people thought the daughter of Bella Rydell would be like.

Whoever sent the note thought manipulation was an inherited trait.

My left boot hit a slippery spot. I flung out my arms, steadying myself. With my camera only wrapped in a towel in my backpack, I didn't want to fall. Avoiding broken bones was a good idea too.

At the top of the hill, I passed the sandstone courthouse, decorated in icicles like a giant wedding cake, glittering in the piercing sunlight. No time for a photo shoot, although if I could capture the way the icicles glistened, it could look like an ice castle in a fairy tale without any filters or photo editing.

I crossed Main Street, striped with white streaks of salt, followed Woodward Avenue down along the side of the library, and turned into the parking lot.

Jill Cerda, second-in-command and my boss when the library director wasn't working, tromped over to the employees' entrance through piles of snow, her unzipped coat flapping in the wind, her fine, graying hair dancing around her face. The cold must not have bothered her. She had plenty of insulation — at least 200 pounds packed onto a body that was a lot shorter than my five-eleven.

I assembled my professional smile, friendly but not too familiar. "Morning."

The slight tilt of her head might have been a nod back. Jill punched in the code on the security keypad and sauntered inside. I hurried in as fast as I could without running her over. Lowering my scarf, I drew in a deep breath of unfrozen air, and my lungs appreciated it.

Jill glanced at her phone. "Leandra is late."

"She's not working today, ma'am. Leandra and Devon switched morning shifts, and Devon won't get here until after her girls head to school."

"I wasn't informed of the switch." Jill made a scolding noise with her tongue. "Did they clear it with Barb?"

"I'm sure they did, ma'am." I took off my hat and fluffed my tangle of dark gold hair.

"That means you're opening alone." Jill aimed a finger at me. "You can't goof off. Keep your mind on your work."

A protest came to my lips, but I clamped them shut. Better to say nothing and get away from her.

In silence, we walked down the hall to the employees' kitchen, flipping on lights along the way. Three weeks ago, she wouldn't have spoken to me like that. Since she'd found out who my mom was, she hadn't had a nice word for me.

I hung up my coat on a rack, changed from boots to loafers, and put my lunch in the fridge. From my backpack, I took out two books on photography I had to return. I placed my backpack inside an empty cupboard. Leaving it by the coat rack seemed a certain way to get my camera broken.

When I entered the two-story lobby, the brilliant sunshine pouring through the tall, narrow windows that faced Main Street almost made the overhead lighting unnecessary. The harsh ceiling fixtures lit the room in a consistent, ugly glare, killing the homey atmosphere the fireplace, overstuffed chairs, and couch gave to the stacks and racks of books, magazines, and newspapers. But I switched them on as part of opening procedures and smiled when they made almost no difference.

Behind the checkout desk, I turned on the computers and pushed the bin with items patrons had dropped off overnight from the slot in the front wall. As I bent over, my hair tried to blind me, and I lifted it up and back. So, it was going to be one of those days when my hair was out to get me. Unless I braided it or secured it somehow, I could never be sure it wouldn't turn on me.

I lifted a mass of books and DVDs from the bin. Could Jill have sent the anonymous note? It didn't seem like something a person in her fifties would do. She would have been in her thirties when Mom lived here and preyed on any guy with a decent bank account. Had Mom had an affair with Jill's husband? But the unsigned note indicated someone afraid of revealing his or her true feelings. Jill had no problem showing me how much she disliked me.

I had almost finished scanning in the materials when Devon Majors and her two daughters, bundled to their eyes, rushed past the windows. I got the keys from the drawer, went to the inner doors, unlocked them, crossed the tiny room with the mat — what was the special name for this little room? — and opened the outer doors.

Devon waved to Liberty and Serenity as they trudged down Main Street. She ducked inside and tugged off her knit hat. The sides of her long, dark brown hair were pulled back in a series of braids, revealing the studs that lined the edges of her ears and a glimpse of the vivid feathered serpent tattooed on the back of her neck, while the rest of her hair poured over her shoulders like molasses.

"Rae." Jill's heavy voice dropped from the balcony overlooking the lobby. "Have you pulled the items for the hold shelf?"

"Just about to print the list." I hurried behind the desk.

"You haven't even printed it?" Jill sounded outraged, like I'd let the toddlers in Storytime make a collage with broken glass.

"Rae's working alone this morning." Devon looked up to Jill, shrugging out her red parka. "I just got here."

"I know that." She planted meaty hands on the black metal railing. "I'm not sure the library can afford to have you come in after your daughters go to school, Devon. Perhaps you'll have to stick to the regular schedule like the rest of us."

A fire leaped into Devon's forest green eyes. She might have been more than half a foot shorter than I was, but she never looked small, especially when she was mad.

She glared up at Jill. "Don't you think—"

"Here's the list." I waved the sheets. "We'll get the items pulled and set aside in no time, ma'am."

"You'd better." Jill disappeared into the shelves of nonfiction adult books, the floorboards creaking under her footsteps.

Devon tossed a braid behind her shoulder. "I owe you. I was about to tell Jill what I thought of her, and I can't afford to lose my job."

One of the million things I liked about Devon was that she didn't filter her words or her feelings. I also liked that although she was thirty-two, she treated me like a friend, not a kid. The only real friend I'd made in the county before I discovered who my father was and that I had about 6,000 relatives.

"I can't afford for you to lose your job either." I handed her half of the list. "You're one of the few people around here who doesn't care that I'm the daughter of Bella Rydell."

"Don't let Jill, or anybody else, get you down." She glanced at the sheets. "Everyone will get used to the truth about you, and most of them won't care. But that's one of the problems of living in a small town or a rural county like Marlin. There's not a lot of new blood moving in. It gives people time to hold on to old wrongs."

"Mom and I usually lived in small towns. It was cheaper and safer than the city. But it was hard getting accepted."

"Wellesville is better than most in that area. I wasn't sure how people would react to two little girls who were half Native American in a county that's ninety percent white. When Shayne and I were traveling around the country, we never knew when someone would take offense to his non-white bread looks. But, except for a few losers, no one has made any nasty comments. The kids at school think it's cool."

Devon stepped closer and added, "Give it time, Rae. It'll get better."

I rolled the hem of my sweater. "I don't like how people treat Mal because of me. Even people at church. I don't want to cause him trouble."

"Your dad knew what a storm he'd stir up if he acknowledged you. He's an adult. He can take it."

I hoped she was right. I prayed she was right. Since early Christmas morning, when Mal and I figured out he was the only one who could be my dad out of the three men my mother had told me were possible candidates, getting to know him and his family had gone better than anything I had imagined.

My stomach tensing, I swallowed hard.

I didn't want to mess things up now.

Chapter 2

Devon had just returned to the desk from unlocking the front doors when the massive frame of Sheriff Walter Reuel Malinowski IV filled the tiny room between the sets of doors. I'd come to expect him on Thursday mornings when I worked late the night before and didn't come out to his farm for supper. Black is supposed to make people look thinner and smaller, but when my dad wore his well-pressed uniform, it made him seem even bigger than around six-six.

Crossing the lobby floor, Mal saw me and grinned. "How's my girl?"

No matter how rotten the morning had started, I had to smile back. Whenever he asked me that question, he always wore this lit-from-within grin that was contagious.

"Not bad." I gestured toward Devon. "Do you know my friend, Devon Majors?"

"Not officially." He offered his broad hand across the counter to her, which she shook. "Your daughters walk by my office on their way to school. They have long dark hair, right? They look about the same age as my two youngest boys—first and fourth grade."

"You're close. Liberty's in fourth grade, but Serenity's in kindergarten." Frowning, she tilted her head to one side. "It's a good thing Rae's been telling everyone you're father and daughter. Nobody'd believe it by looking at you."

"Really?" said Mal. "I thought there was a slight resemblance."

So did I. But not enough to see the similarities during all those months I tried to figure out who my father was. We had the same shade of gold hair and the Malinowski height. He had his mom's dark blue eyes, and I had my mom's dark chocolate brown ones. My face was bony with prominent cheekbones and chin. Mal's boyish face had less harsh angles. The first time I saw him, I thought all he needed to step into the role of Thor was longer hair and a beard.

Devon said, "I'd say more than a slight resemblance. You two move the same. You even stand alike."

We glanced at each other. We both stood with our left leg about an inch ahead of our right one and slightly bent. I'd noticed that before but figured it was because of Mal's bum knee. I hadn't realized I'd adopted the same stance.

"What I mean is that people will think you're brother and sister. Not father and daughter."

Either Mal looked younger than thirty-seven or I looked older than nineteen. Either way, it was a compliment.

The outside door jerked opened, and Mrs. O'Neil marched into the lobby. Skinny as a dead sapling, the elderly woman had a skull-like face and white hair as icy as the sunken eyes she aimed at Mal and me.

My fingers clenched, every muscle going on guard. Since Mrs. O'Neil had decided to hate me, I never knew what she might say, except that at some point, she'd threatened my job. As a member of the library board, she could take it.

Straightening to his full height, Mal said, "Good morning, Mrs. O'Neil. Have you heard that Rae's my daughter?" His booming baritone had toughened into his official cop tone.

"Yes. I've also heard she's the daughter of Bella Rydell." Peeling off her gloves, Mrs. O'Neil delivered a glower that tried to wither me. "And — correct me if I'm wrong — that Rae is the result of a one-night stand." She transferred her look to Mal, and a spark of anger flared in my chest.

"That's right," said Mal.

"And you didn't know Rae was alive until a few weeks ago?"

"Yes. I thought Rae died with Bella in that fire at the old children's home. Bella actually made it out and became a Christian. She started a new life with Rae."

"I also heard you didn't have a DNA test done." Mrs. O'Neil's cold tone implied how stupid she thought that was.

"No need." Mal's voice steeled over. "Bella wasn't sure who Rae's father was, but from the clues Bella left Rae after she died, Rae figured out it must be me. We share a rare blood type."

Mal was always so straightforward when he told how I found him. No excuses, no hedging. Just not the whole truth. But the rest of the story wasn't ours to tell.

Devon said, "You should ask Mal for a job if you like to grill people."

Mrs. O'Neil's sunken eyes snapped to her. "And library employees should display good manners at work, especially to members of the board."

She spun to the staircase that swept up to the balcony and marched up it, her long, black coat swirling around her stick-thin legs.

Devon looked up and up to Mal, sort of like a chihuahua making eye contact with a mastiff. "Why did you answer all her questions? It's none of her business how Rae was conceived."

Rubbing his hand over his crew cut, he said, "The more people who hear the truth from me and my family, the better the chance to kill any rumors before they get started."

Lifting a stack of books, she said, "Nice to finally meet you after all

Rae's talked about you." She headed to the back of the building.

I uncurled my fingers, and my muscles relaxed so much I sagged against the counter.

Mal studied me. "I see you aren't Melissa O'Neil's biggest fan. Most people aren't. That lady has a way of making enemies." He glanced up at the balcony and then lowered his voice. "Has she caused problems for you?"

I twisted the hem of my sweater. I hadn't made Terry O'Neil any promises, but since Mal and I were keeping Rick and Jason Carlisle's connection to my mom a secret, I should do the same for Terry. Mentioning our chats at the library seemed okay.

"Terry liked talking movies with me," I said. "Mrs. O'Neil seemed to think I was flirting with him."

"More like the other way around. Terry O'Neil is known for chasing his female students at the college." He raised an eyebrow. "He never — uh — made you feel uncomfortable, did he?"

"He never acted romantically interested in me. We just talked about old movies. Well, he talked about them. I'd listen and throw in a word when I needed to. I felt sorry for him. He seemed lonely."

"You're using past tense. He hasn't chatted with you lately?"

"Not since Christmas." Whether that was because his wife scared him out of speaking to me or because he didn't want to associate with me after I revealed who my mother was, I couldn't say. Probably both reasons made him avoid the library like it was the lair of a man-eating tiger.

"If Terry O'Neil, or anybody else, makes you uncomfortable, you tell me. You don't have to put up with that."

I smiled up at him. "Thanks. It's nice to know someone's got my back."

His big hand hovered over mine before he lowered it and squeezed my fingers, looking me straight in the eye. "I will from now on."

I put my other hand on top of his and squeezed back.

"Do you want to come to the farm for supper tonight?" He put on his hat. "You don't have to if we're too much family for you. Just tell us. We don't want to make pests of ourselves."

"I was planning on coming over this evening. Although I've gained at least five pounds since I started having most of my meals at the farm."

"You're thin. It wouldn't hurt if you put on a few pounds." Mal sighed. "But I've got to watch myself. That's why I work out every morning."

"You look like you could take to the football field right now and still be a star lineman."

Mal chuckled. "If you believe that, thanks. If you're just being nice, thanks for that too."

"I believe it."

"Are you going to drive out, or do you want to ride with me?"

"I'll drive. It'll save you a—oh, no."

"What's wrong?" Mal's face took on a wary look. "Is the gear shift jammed again?"

I scrunched the edge of my sweater. "It wouldn't shift this morning. I—I haven't been able to unjam the gears by myself. If you come over after work, you can push the clutch, and I'll crawl underneath and loosen the gears."

Mal shook his head. "I'm your dad. Crawling on the frozen ground to fix your truck is my job."

"I don't want to put you to so much trouble."

"I like doing things for you, Rae. I've got twenty years to make up for. I just wish I could have met you and your truck in the summer."

I laughed, and Mal did too.

He stepped toward the doors. "When you're done here tonight, walk over to the office, and then we'll go over to your apartment."

"Sounds like a plan."

After Mal left, I gathered a tall stack of damaged books from behind the counter, hoping I could repair a few in between waiting on patrons. I turned and found Mrs. O'Neil stationed by the desk. Startled, I couldn't stop two teetering books from slipping off the top of the stack as my hair dipped into my eyes.

The older woman's lips pulled back from her teeth into something I would never call a smile. "Done with your visit?"

"Yes, ma'am." I set the stack on the counter and hooked my hair behind my ears.

"You weren't hired to visit with your father. I'll have to report this to Barb. I will also tell my fellow members of the board. Just because you have Jason Carlisle eating out of your hand doesn't mean your job is safe. There are four other board members."

There it was. Right on cue. Threat to my job. Worry compressed my chest. I couldn't get fired.

"You're much cleverer than your mother was." Mrs. O'Neill slipped a glove over her thin-skinned hand. "She appealed to men's animal natures. That led to all sorts of trouble with wives and other relatives of the stupid men she snared. You appeal to their paternal instincts. Much safer."

The spark returned, easing the pressure. Did she think I had conned Mal into believing he was my father?

"Remember, Rae." She straightened the seams on her left glove. "You aren't the only clever woman in the county. Your tricks work on only a small portion of the population." Her deeply sunken eyes met mine.

The spark growing hotter, I didn't blink. "I don't have tricks, ma'am. Mal's my dad, and I'm happy he wants to accept me into his family."

"Oh, I'm sure you're happy. Very happy. But I'm not sure how happy Mal will be at the next election. People in Marlin County have long memories."

The pressure seemed to dent my heart. Mal wouldn't care if he lost the next election because of me. Would he?

The right side of her mouth curving up, Mrs. O'Neil turned and strode out the doors.

Could **she** have left the anonymous note? It didn't seem likely when she was too ready to insult me to my face.

I blew out my cheeks, the pain easing a bit, and stooped to gather the fallen books.

If Mrs. O'Neil would threaten my job when she thought I was flirting with her husband, what would she do if she knew he was one of the three men my mom had tried to blackmail when she was pregnant with me?

Chapter 3

Just because the gas fireplace and comfy chairs and couch looked like a living room, which was especially inviting as the sun slipped to the horizon on a winter evening, that didn't mean the middle school kids could act like they were at home.

I told two of them to quit eating and stalked back to the checkout desk. The clock on the computer said 4:40. Only twenty minutes left. I could keep myself from screaming at those brats for twenty minutes.

Chris Kincaid deposited a stack of books in front of me. "Have you adjusted to the cold here in Ohio?"

"In a way." All thoughts of screaming disappeared as I pulled the stack toward me. "I think my body's finally convinced it's not in North Carolina any more. Mom and I lived near Blackwater Falls State Park in West Virginia for three years, high in the mountains. So I've had some experience with cold winters."

"My body still thinks I'm living in southern California." He sunk his hands into the pockets of his navy blue ski jacket. "I left there almost four years ago. His voice was surprisingly deep. I didn't know why I associated deeper voices with bigger men. Chris was a couple inches shorter than I was, but his rich bass was deeper than Mal's

He had the fiercest face of anyone I'd met—a curved nose like the beak of a hawk; narrow eyes so dark I had to squint to see the pupil; thick, black eyebrows and moustache; and black hair that still looked wavy despite the short cut he wore as a deputy.

Scanning the books, I imagined Chris standing on the deck of a Spanish galleon, ordering pirates to attack. Or leading a cavalry charge of … Arabs? Indians? He'd never mentioned his family's heritage.

"You must be spending a lot of time at Mal's farm." As usual, his black eyes locked on me, giving me his total attention. Or, at least, that was how it looked. "I haven't seen your truck parked by Mrs. Blaney's much lately."

I widened my eyes to clear away visions of galleons and cavalry. "Mal gave me an open invitation to come out to the farm any time." I placed the last book on the top of his pile. "Is my apartment on the way to your place? I thought your house was out in the west side of the county."

"It is. When you first moved here, and Mal learned you were living alone, he told all us deputies to swing by your place when we were coming in and going out of town. In December, he told us to keep an extra sharp look out for you because you were nervous about living alone and had bought a rifle for protection."

I had to smile. My dad was looking out for me even before he knew he was my dad. But I hadn't bought the rifle for protection at the apartment. I had figured I'd need it as backup when I sent anonymous notes to the three men who could have been my father and set up separate meetings with them early Christmas morning. The person who had tried to murder my pregnant mother might have wanted to finish the job, even if it was twenty years later.

Tearing the due date slip from the printer, I said, "Does the sheriff's department patrol in Wellesville with the town cops?"

"No. We can patrol anywhere in the county, but we only patrol in town when they have a gap in their coverage." He tucked the books under his arm, and I ransacked my brain for something to keep the conversation going.

A young town cop hurried through the front door. The few times I'd seen him, he was always hurrying. "I knew I'd find you here. You've got to check your phone, Chris." He even talked fast, his words almost colliding into each other.

"I turned off my phone," Chris said. "I was doing research in the local history room."

"That's why you got to check it." He removed his knit hat, revealing caramel-colored hair. "Houston texted me, saying he saw an ad for a bass, dirt cheap. He's going to meet the guy and try it out and needs your okay to buy it if he thinks it's good enough."

"I'll call him." Chris glanced at me. "Excuse me." Leaving his books on the counter, he stepped into the hall leading to the children's room.

The officer's hazel eyes scrutinized me as if he was memorizing my vital statistics for a report. Then he offered his hand. "I see you with your dad here in town all the time. Probably should have stopped to introduce myself. Garrett Matthews."

"Rae Riley." It still sounded strange to hear someone say, "your dad." I'd wanted one for so long, now it was hard to believe I had one.

Drumming his fingers on the counter, Garrett watched Chris in the hall. He was even shorter than Chris, with a nose and chin sharp enough to slice through paper. Instead of the black-and-gray uniform of the sheriff's department, he wore a white shirt and navy blue pants.

I typed a few nonsense words into the computer catalog, buying time to think of something to say. Small talk was not my strength. "Uh, are you from around here?"

"No, Toledo." He kept his gaze on Chris.

"So you don't have family around here?"

"Nope." He finally looked at me. "My sister lives in Georgia. My parents," he craned his neck in Chris's direction, "my parents died a few years ago."

"I'm sorry. My mom died almost two years ago."

"That's what I heard." His smile was as pointed as his face. "What do I need to get a library card? Might as well apply for one while I'm here."

I had filled out the online application and handed him his new card when Chris rejoined us.

"I told Houston to go ahead," said Chris. "I trust his judgment."

"Is it a bass guitar?" I hoped I didn't sound nosy. "Or violin?"

Garrett chuckled as Chris said, "Bass guitar. Houston plays—have you met him? His real name is Miguel Blank."

"He stopped in and introduced himself a few weeks ago."

"I bet all of Mal's deputies did," said Garrett.

"I bet half the county did." Chris slid his phone into the back pocket of his jeans. "Houston plays guitar. Garrett plays keyboard, and I played bass in high school. So we decided we'd like to jam together, but I don't own a guitar. We've been watching for an ad in the area."

Did they need a drummer? I hadn't played in almost two years, but if I practiced a lot, I might be able to get back in shape.

Zipping his jacket, Garrett said, "I'd better get back on patrol."

"You are on patrol," said Chris. "The library is within the city limits."

"The Chief likes us behind the wheel as much as possible."

"You can't build relationships with people behind a steering wheel."

Garrett held up a hand. "Article one."

"We're not at my house. I said nothing against Simcox. Just his policy."

"I call that a backdoor way to criticizing him." He nodded at me. "Nice to meet you, Rae." Garrett jogged out the front door.

Chris said, "I suppose you're wondering about article one."

"Well—uh—" should I be polite or honest? "—well, yeah. But it's none of my business." That covered both.

"Have I mentioned that Houston and Garrett live at my place?"

"No." Actually, Chris didn't talk a lot about himself, except for the first seven years of his life when he lived in Marlin County with his great-grandfather. We usually chatted about what he was reading, almost exclusively nonfiction.

Chris pulled his gloves from his jacket pockets. "Houston and Garrett stay rent-free in exchange for helping me renovate my house. With Houston and me working for Mal, and Garrett working for Chief Simcox, we came up with a list of house rules, the most important being that we don't discuss our bosses."

"I've heard Chief Simcox was upset about Mal beating him by two votes in the election. But that was over a year ago."

Chris smoothed his moustache with his index finger and thumb, as if he was considering something, but he was one of the hardest people I'd ever tried to read from his facial or body language. His expression rarely changed from one of quiet calm.

"Simcox hasn't made it a secret that he thinks the wrong man won." A muscle flexed along his jaw. "He's said loud and clear he thought his stint in the Marines and work as a homicide detective in Cleveland made him the better candidate."

My fingers tightened around a pencil. "And because Mal's a Malinowski?"

I'd only been in the county a few weeks when I came to understand the long-held prejudice against the Malinowskis. They were no good. Always had been, always would be. Only Gram's kids and grandkids broke the family tradition of hard-fighting, fast-living, and law-breaking. Even then I got the impression some people weren't entirely confident Gram had disciplined all the Malinowski wildness out of her descendants. Which was probably why Mal had won by two votes.

Chris said, "I haven't heard Simcox mention that. But he's not from Marlin County, so he probably doesn't care if your dad is a Malinowski."

Huffing and puffing, Mr. Olsen came up and dropped a pile of DVDs on the counter.

I gave Chris an apologetic smile. "Hope you get your bass."

They probably didn't need a drummer. I didn't have any way to practice unless I went to the church and used the set there.

Gathering his books, Chris said, "I do too. The price can't be beat." He headed out the front door, allowing an icy blast to roar into the lobby and scatter the junior high kids.

At 5:00, I went to the employees' kitchen. Barb Hanson was peering into the fridge. She glanced up and spun, startled. "Oh, hey, Rae." She plastered on a smile.

"Hey." I took my backpack out of the cupboard.

Adjusting her bright blue glasses, she returned her attention to the fridge. I put on my jean jacket and scarf. There was no reason for us to chat. She was busy. I was busy. But we would have found something to talk about before she knew who my parents were.

Barb hadn't turned mean like Jill. Which was good since Barb was the library director. But she acted almost afraid of me. Rick Carlisle must have told her what happened Christmas morning at the children's home. Maybe their relationship had gotten that serious. And maybe she was scared Mal and I were going to blab the truth all over the county.

Holding a plastic container, Barb shut the door to the fridge and pursed her lips, as if weighing her next words. Then she wheeled to the microwave. "See you tomorrow."

That sentence wasn't what she'd been thinking over. I exchanged my loafers for boots. Could Barb have left the note? Had Mom hurt her or someone in her family and that was why she acted nervous around me?

I said good night and stepped into the hall, giving my head a sharp shake. Just because her attitude toward me had changed didn't mean my boss was out to get me.

In the lobby, I waved to Devon and walked out onto Main Street.

The sun hovered above the thickly wooded hills beyond the town limits, outlining them in red light, and the Arctic air tried to freeze the breath in my mouth. I bent my head into my scarf, turning west, and walked by Cervelli's Deli, an antique shop, and a couple empty storefronts.

Cars and trucks ground by on the salt-covered street. More snow must have been predicted.

As I passed the newspaper office, someone popped out of the front door. I swerved in time to avoid a collision.

I lifted my head from my scarf. "Sorry."

"No. My ..." Rick Carlisle didn't finish, his brown eyes widening as he recognized me.

We stood staring at each other for a few silent moments. Fat snowflakes drifted between us.

"My fault." He rushed off in the direction of the library.

That was the second time since Christmas morning I'd seen Rick, and both times he acted like I was a vampire, and he didn't have even minced garlic with him.

Mal had said he'd talked to Jason Carlisle. Maybe Jason hadn't told his brother that Mal and I were keeping to ourselves that Rick had tried to murder Mom when she was pregnant with me.

Chapter 4

Entering the small lobby to the sheriff's department, I said hey to Janice and Liz as they turned off their computers in the off-white reception area with its mismatched chairs. The tilted stairs in the historic building took me to the second floor. There I found the door to Mal's office standing open.

Holding his phone to his ear, Mal grinned and waved me in. I crossed to the worn burgundy couch that rested against a wall covered with framed photos and citations. Photos of Gram's parents, Mal as a little kid with his dad, Mal's engagement photo with his wife. Aside from the people photographed with Mal in a professional capacity, like when he received an award as a deputy, no one in the pictures was living except Mal. That had to be deliberate. Was it to protect the family, like Mal's and Gram's total lack of presence on social media? When I took pictures on Christmas Day, Mal told me kindly but firmly I was not allowed to post any photos of my half-brothers on my pages.

Sinking onto the couch, I took out my phone. Last chance to catch up on posts and messages before we drove into one of the dead zones in the county. I scrolled through comments, checking for any nasty remarks from the note-writer.

Nothing. Just normal, friendly comments from a few online friends and photographers I followed.

When Mal hung up, he unclipped the tie from his collar. "How was your day?"

Getting to my feet, I shrugged. "Nothing special. I bumped into—and I mean literally—into Rick Carlisle when I walked over." I explained how he reacted to me. "You told Jason we weren't telling anyone about Rick's crime, right?"

"I told Jason *and* Rick. His behavior shouldn't puzzle you, Rae. Although he was ready to confess, I'm sure Rick still feels ashamed for what he did. You remind him of what he tried to get away with."

Frowning, I nodded. He didn't need to feel ashamed. I'd explained that at the children's home Christmas morning. Christmas morning …

The crystal cold air and the moonlight gilding the abandoned children's home replayed in my mind. I'd sent anonymous notes to the three men Mom had blackmailed when she was pregnant with me to set up three meetings, so I could figure out who was my father and deliver the notes Mom had written before she died She had apologized or the blackmail and forgave whoever had hit her from behind and tried to burn her up in the children's home.

After telling me his blood type, Terry O'Neil had burnt up his note without reading it and left. Then Jason and Rick arrived, Rick saying he was going to confess to murdering Bella Rydell and her baby. I told him it was only attempted murder and my mom forgave him. To prove it, I'd planned the meetings after the statute of limitations had run out on his crime. Mal, Jason, and I compared blood types, discovering Mal was the only one who could be my father.

Lifting his jacket from a coatrack, Mal muttered, "Took him long enough. Twenty years, and Rick finally couldn't live with trying to murder an unarmed woman and her unborn baby."

After a two-minute drive to my apartment, Mal parked his patrol SUV behind my truck, and we got out. The air was so cold it almost felt solid, pressing against my cheeks. I scooted under the hood. All my effort to make the two gears mesh only resulted in numb fingers. Mal, with a grim look like he expected to find a convicted murderer hiding under the Rust Bucket, crawled underneath the front. Somehow, he positioned his thick fingers to force the gears to interlock, and I shoved the gear shift out of first.

With Mal driving behind me, I headed west out of Wellesville. The dark closed in, the last rays of sunlight fading from the tops of the trees on the heights of the towering hills.

Who could have written the note? Jill? Mrs. O'Neil? Someone from the church who was suddenly cold and distant toward Mal?

Houses grew fewer and more widely spaced as the road plunged and soared between fields and forest. The Rust Bucket followed the asphalt like a ship over the crests and troughs of waves.

If the person was so afraid of me they had to resort to anonymous threats, then he or she was probably hiding their dislike of me.

I tightened my grip on the cracked steering wheel. It could be anybody. The people who were nasty to my face were bad enough, but someone who faked being nice was way worse.

As I drove closer to the state park, tall, bare trees crowded the narrow road, almost forming a tunnel. The black, stripped branches twisted together to make a spider web ceiling. Asphalt petered out, and dirt and gravel took over.

When my headlights revealed trees straight ahead of me, I turned right and smiled. I couldn't help myself. The trees gave way to a little, shallow valley. A barn sat to the left, and the drive dipped down and passed fenced pastures. Then it climbed again to the small farmhouse that sat at the top of the far end of the valley. All the windows lit warmly, the house seemed to say "welcome home" every time I approached it in the dark. A half-moon rose behind it, providing its own bright *hello.*

I braked. After Mom died, I wasn't sure I'd ever feel like any place was home. I had to get a picture. I unwrapped my camera, turned on the cab light, and adjusted my settings. Then I grabbed my tripod.

In front of my truck, I set up the tripod and clicked a few photos.

The images weren't sharp enough. I'd had trouble shooting at night. I changed the shutter speed.

"Rae?" Behind me, Mal stood in the open door of his SUV. "Can you take pictures later? Supper's probably ready."

"Oh, sure." The night would only get darker, so waiting might actually improve the composition. If I could figure out how to work with the dark.

We parked in front of the garage. I carried my backpack, tripod, and the roll of paper, walking through the breezeway to the little screened porch on the side of the house. We took off our boots and went in.

The warmth of the yellow kitchen and the mouth-watering aroma of chili wrapped around me like my favorite sweater. And something else. I sniffed. Something Christmassy was cooking, but I couldn't name the scent.

Gram looked up from the bread she was slicing on the counter. "Hey, you two. The chili will be done in ten minutes. How was your day?" Her relaxed smile and calm, deep blue eyes eased a lot of the day's tension from my muscles.

Mal said, "Not bad."

Aaron shot into the kitchen and greeted his dad—our dad—like he always did, in a flurry of punches.

Chuckling, Mal scooped him up and hugged him. Arms and legs flailing, Aaron yelled, "My spine! My spine!"

Gram said, "How about you, Rae?"

I shrugged out of my jacket. "Normal day at the library."

"How was school today, bud?" Mal lowered Aaron to the floor.

"Okay. I got all my homework done." Aaron hopped from foot to foot. "I gotta show you something upstairs, Rae." His light blue eyes, a shade before white, glowed with their usual excitement.

"Give the girl a chance to hang up her coat." Gram's words meant to scold, but her tone didn't. In the seven months I'd known her, the only time I'd heard her raise her voice was on Christmas morning. After meeting me at the children's home, Mal had called to tell Gram he was still alive. Gram hadn't appreciated his sense of humor.

Keeping an eye out for Micah, I left the kitchen. In the big living-dining room, I stepped around plastic bricks, toy cars, books, and pillows. Mal followed, taking off his black jacket. As we passed an easy chair,

Micah jumped out of it, latching on to Mal's leg. He gave a yelp that wouldn't convince anyone but a first-grader he was surprised.

"Got you again." Micah giggled.

"Yeah, you did, buddy." Mal picked him up in bear hug.

Micah hugged him back, leaped to the ground, and fell in step beside me as I walked into Gram's bedroom. "Can I read to you?"

The left side of my face scrunched into a grimace that I tried to turn into a smile. "For sure." I could stand five minutes of his one-syllable stories before Gram called us to the table.

"You don't have to," Mal said from behind us.

"I don't mind." I placed my jean jacket and vest on the bed.

Micah's smile bloomed, and his strawberry blond hair glowed peach in the light from the ceiling fixture. How could I turn down a request from someone who was as cute as a Christmas elf?

"Rae." Aaron appeared at my elbow as I laid my backpack on Gram's cluttered desk. "Can I show you what I built in the playroom?" He touched the roll of paper. "What's this for?"

"I've been working on family trees so I can learn who all my relatives are."

"She can look at your invention after supper," Mal said. "She's helping Micah with his homework."

"Okay." Aaron frowned. "I guess."

I'd never been so popular in my life. Changing schools so often hadn't given me a chance to make real friends, and, after a while, I gave up trying. Now Aaron, Micah, and their cousin Amber—our cousin Amber—were my devoted followers. And all I'd done to earn their devotion was to be a relative.

Micah and I settled onto the couch. He wiggled in so close I had to put my arm around him. Personal space seemed to be a foreign idea to him and Aaron. I had been used to that, having lived with the assistant pastor's family after Mom died. His twin daughters were either always in my space or attempting to get there. But they had been three, going on four. Micah and Aaron were seven and nine, and only a tiny bit better about giving me breathing room.

A fire welcomed me, each flame waving a greeting, and I stretched my feet toward it. Micah opened a thin, paperback book and read a story about a dog that sat, ate, and ran. Not exciting enough for me to forget the note.

YOU DON'T FOOL ME, RAE. YOU'RE JUST LIKE YOUR MOTHER.

How could someone believe that? I hadn't been on a single date since I moved here in June. Did this person see me like Mrs. O'Neil did? Someone who tricked Mal into believing he was my dad?

Rusty wandered into the living room. "When did you and Dad get here, Rae?"

"A few minutes ago."

He had that super-skinny build a lot of boys get when they hit a growth spurt in junior high. And the most beautiful shade of natural dark red hair I'd ever seen.

Micah was sounding his way through the last page when Gram told us dinner was ready. We sat at the long plank table next to a row of windows overlooking the backyard and frozen fields. Mal came from his bedroom in the basement wearing jeans and a plaid shirt.

"How's the book coming, Rusty?" Mal sat back in his chair.

"I'm kind of stuck." He ladled chili into his bowl. "I want to do a fight scene, but I can't think of a good setting for it." A blush crept up his cheeks, almost darkening them enough to match his hair.

That was the most I'd heard Rusty say about the fantasy novel he was writing. Aaron and Micah told me he sometimes read excerpts to them and their cousin Coral, but never to anyone older than he was. But I got the secrecy. It'd taken me years to work up the courage to show Mom my attempts at art with a camera.

Setting down my spoon, I said, "Would you like to look at some of my photos? Maybe they'd give you inspiration."

Rusty's blush faded against a slow smile. "You used to live near the ocean, didn't you? I've never written a fight scene on a beach."

"I've got tons of beach photos on my phone. I'll show them to you once you get your homework done."

"I'm done already."

Beaming, Mal slapped Rusty on the shoulder. "Sounds like you got a solution."

The rim of my glass covered my smile as I sipped water. Rusty had been the hardest of my half-brothers to connect with. Not that he was mean or cold. He was uncertain, more than anything else, and I caught him studying me all the time. I probably would have done the same thing if a new sibling had just fallen into the family. If he needed time to like me, fine. I wasn't going to force myself on him.

"But, Rae, you're gonna see my invention right after supper." Aaron spoke through cheeks bulging with bread. "You promised."

"Don't talk with your mouth full," said Mal.

"I will. Then I'll help Rusty. After I go outside to take some pictures." I was so in demand I should have whipped out my phone and scheduled appointments.

Helping himself to another slice of bread, Mal said, "Eat your chili, Micah."

Micah pushed his bowl away. "It tastes funny."

"That's the cinnamon," said Gram. "I was trying something new."

Gram was always trying something new with her cooking. She didn't need to. Everything I'd eaten so far had been delicious. She probably experimented here because she couldn't as a cook in the elementary school cafeteria. The school had to have rules about keeping all food as bland as possible.

"You don't like the cinnamon either?" Gram looked to me from across the table.

"Oh, no. It's really good. I knew you'd added something different from the last time you made it. I smelled it when I first walked in. But I couldn't decide what it was. With or without cinnamon, your chili is great."

Which was why I'd gained at least five pounds since Christmas Day. To prove it, I ate another spoonful.

When the boys took their dishes into the kitchen, I gathered up mine.

"Rae," Mal said in a lowered voice, "is something bothering you? You're more quiet than usual. And if you liked the chili, you didn't eat much of it."

Weird. After only three weeks, he could read me as well as my mom. Maybe it was his police training.

I rolled my fork between my fingers. "I got some things on my mind."

"Do you want to talk about it?"

Yes, yes, I did, but I didn't know if it would help.

Mom's words came back to me: "Most people don't really want to know us and our problems. But we can always count on each other and God."

Until she was too sick for me to count on her. And God seemed to have left us on our own.

But Mal was my dad. I should be able to tell him.

"It's totally up to you." He backed toward the kitchen with his plate. "No pressure."

I gave him a quick smile. "I'll let you know."

After depositing my dishes, I almost ran to Gram's room, the memory of when Mom said those two sentences souring the scrumptious supper. Grabbing a few photos would let me forget. I threw on my jacket and vest, grabbed my backpack and tripod, and raced to the porch to get my boots.

Chapter 5

Bitter cold jarred me as I left the house. But in a good way, making me more alert.

I crunched down the drive, a thin layer of broken ice mixing with snow, and stopped right before the road.

Drawing in the icy air, I turned my face to the sky. Orion, the only constellation I could find easily, glittered as gleaming fractures in a sky of black ice. The half-moon sat among the brilliant stars as if the January air had frozen it to the night.

After I got my tripod steady and my camera fastened, I stared a solid minute at the scene—the dark barn in the foreground, the warm house in the back, the moon suspended over the blanketed countryside. I had to match my pictures to what my eye saw as best I could. The camera should be used for revealing the truth. Dressing up photos with filters and other digital tricks, unless you let your viewers know you did it, cheapened the art of the camera.

I tested different settings, trying to focus on my work and the beauty of the ice-still night, but memories of a particular day at our church in North Carolina kept distracting me.

Mom, standing before the congregation during the joys and concerns sharing time, had explained that although she'd had me legally emancipated, she wanted me to live with someone while I finished my senior year and she went into hospice.

And nobody had said a word. Nobody looked at us.

Mom told them we'd wait in the back after the service to talk to anyone who might help.

Then we had sat in that back pew as our church "family" filed past. No words, no looks.

Finally, our assistant pastor offered his basement. Mom made him promise he and his family would go to all my senior events.

Then we had driven home, and I gripped the steering wheel hard enough to shatter it.

Mom had said, "Most people don't really want to know us and our problems. But we can always count on each other and God."

Now, my breath billowing into jagged clouds, I stepped back from my camera. Tears tried to fall, but I clenched my teeth to hold them in. How would Mal react if I came to him with a problem?

Humming sailed through the clear air. Gram strolled down the drive. Even in sub-zero temperatures, she was relaxed and unhurried, moving at the same pace she had in the cozy house. I took photos as she turned into the barn and flipped on the lights. The sound of shifting hooves from the alpacas and guard llama greeted her.

Shaking feeling into my fingers, I bent to my viewfinder and took some more shots with the barn lit, pushing away bad memories and uncomfortable questions with work. My fingers grew clumsier. Even a professional photographer couldn't work with numb hands, so I gathered my equipment and almost made a detour to the barn, but Aaron was waiting, most likely antsy with impatience.

He was right inside the front door, bouncing on his toes. He grabbed my arm. "Can you come upstairs now?"

"As soon as I get my boots off" —I pulled a little, and Aaron released my arm— "and put my equipment away."

Once my camera was safely wrapped in my backpack with the tripod leaning against Gram's desk, Aaron and Micah led me upstairs to the playroom-attic.

The big half-moon window sitting above the front porch let in half-moonlight, but the long, barely finished room, running the length of the house, was really illuminated by the bare bulbs in the ceiling. I squinted against the harsh light, almost as glaring as the lighting in the library.

In the middle of the room sat a three-foot-tall contraption made of plastic bricks, plastic pipes, rubber bands, and a tennis ball. Using his feet, Aaron cleared away vehicles, stuffed animals, and tiny rubber balls to make a path to his latest invention.

"This is it." He circled it, his eyes bright, his grin proud. "Can you tell what it is?"

"Tread-u-shed," said Micah.

Aaron slugged him. "I asked Rae. Anyway, you're saying it wrong."

"No hitting." I did my best version of Mom's warning look. "I was going to say catapult."

"Close. It's a trebuchet." Aaron took in a big breath and watched me.

I knew what the nine-year-old mad genius wanted. "I've never heard of a trebuchet. What is it?"

His grin growing even bigger, Aaron launched into his explanation, pointing out different features.

My memory was pretty good, but Aaron seemed to recall perfectly anything he'd read and told me the whole history of catapult construction.

"You pull back this thing." Micah reached for the machine.

Aaron shoved himself between his brother and his invention. "I made it. I'm going to show Rae."

"Micah," Mal's head appeared as he climbed the stairs, "you haven't finished your math."

"Fire in the hole!" Aaron released the arm holding the tennis ball.

"What?' Mal took the ball full in the eye.

I winced, and Micah gasped beside me.

Slapping a hand over his right eye, Mal shouted, "Aaron!"

His roar could have raised the roof three feet clear of the rafters. It tried to raise me out of my socks.

I hurried over to him. "Are you all right?"

"Oh, sure." Mal dropped onto the top step. "The good Lord, in His infinite wisdom, provided us humans with a spare eye."

"I said 'fire in the hole.'" Aaron ran toward us, skidding in his socks on the varnished floor. "Like you told me, Dad."

"I heard you. But not in time to get out of the way." He glared at him with his good eye. "You've got to check the area for people, then yell to get clear." Mal looked past us. "Micah, I'm okay." His voice dropped a dozen decibels to a reassuring tone.

Micah whispered, "Is your face okay?"

Removing his hand, Mal smiled. "See?" The lid was red and swelling. "I'll have a black eye, but not like before. Just like a bruise you get on your leg. No big deal."

"Dad's tough, Micah." Aaron whacked him on the arm, and Mal mussed up his hair. "A tennis ball isn't gonna hurt him much."

I studied Aaron's face. His confident grin showed he really thought his dad was indestructible. He wasn't faking to reassure Micah.

Kneading his fingers, Micah tiptoed toward us, his eyes focused on Mal's face.

Micah was the most laid back of the three boys. To see him so worried made me want to wrap my arms around him. I held out my hand, and he took it.

A relieved smile crept onto Micah's face. "It doesn't look too bad."

"What'd I tell you?" said Aaron. Regret dimmed his enthusiastic expression. "Sorry, Dad." His face brightened. "But the trebuchet works like it's supposed to."

"Great." Mal stood and rubbed Aaron on the head again. "When you patent it and make millions, you can buy me a seeing eye dog." He headed down the stairs.

I started to follow, but Aaron grabbed my arm. "What do you think?"

Tugging at my ear lobe, I searched for honest but encouraging words. "It's very ... effective. It works exactly like the ones people used to build for wars."

"Maybe I should scale it up."

"No, you don't." Mal's shout flew up the stairs. "No bigger treb-treb-catapult things."

When Mal and I entered the kitchen, Rusty took one look at his dad, set down his book, got a plastic bag, and filled it with ice.

Placing the bag on his eye, Mal grimaced. "I hate going into work looking like a suspect tried to assault me, and here it's just my son's invention. Again."

"Has it happened a lot?" I said. "More than just Christmas morning?"

"Yeah," said Rusty. "Last summer, Aaron made a saddle for an alpaca, and Dad got run over grabbing Micah off it on the test run."

Mal removed the ice pack and touched his sore eyelid. "If one of his inventions is going to malfunction or blow up, it waits until I'm next to it."

"Christmas morning was special, though." Rusty patted his dad's boulder of a shoulder. "Since Aaron had set up Uncle Hank's trail cam to get pictures of Santa coming out of the chimney, we have great photos of you falling flat on your face."

Mal swung at Rusty, and he dodged out of the way.

"Well, that one was my fault," said Mal. "Aaron told me he was setting a Santa trap, but I forgot all about it after finding Rae."

"Was that why Micah was so worried upstairs?" I said. "He's seen you get hurt before?"

"Yeah, but not from Aaron's inventions. It's because of the fight I had with my relatives at Walter's place the fall I got elected. Remember Carrie and me telling you about it? I beat up five of my outlaw relatives, put two in the hospital, and, from my face, you'd think I lost. Scared Micah badly. He was only in kindergarten."

"Is that how you got the scar by your eye?"

Nodding, Mal fingered the white line that ran from his eyebrow to under his left eye. "One of a bunch."

The backdoor squeaked open, and Gram walked in. Her glance swept over us. "Oh, Mal. Didn't Aaron say 'fire in the hole' when he showed you his catapult? He did when he demonstrated it for me."

Mal placed the ice bag back on his eye. "He said it, but not in time for me to get out of the way."

Micah ran into the kitchen. "Is your eye still okay, Dad?"

"Yep." Mal pushed himself off the counter. "Let's go finish your homework."

He broke into a sweet smile. "I don't want to."

"You have to."

"But I don't want to."

I'd never seen a kid fight his parent the way Micah did. No temper tantrums, no yelling. In a pleasant and consistent way, he dug in his heels and refused to do what he was asked.

Bending down to his level, Gram said, "You can do it with me."

"I don't want to."

Turning to Rusty, I said, "Would you like to look at my photos now?"

Rolling his eyes at Micah, he nodded.

I took a seat at the desk by the front door and pulled open drawers. "We should hook up my phone to the monitor, so you can really study the photos you like. Do you know where the cord is?"

Once we found the cord tangled in a drawer in the kitchen, I attached my phone, and my photos filled the desktop monitor. I began scrolling.

"What's that?" Rusty leaned forward. "It looks like a giant mouth, eating the—oh, it's a building with no roof on it. When you were scrolling by so fast, I thought the walls looked like a giant mouth trying to eat the clouds, like you were standing inside the mouth." He peered at the image. "You must have taken that from inside and aimed up at the sky. Is that the old children's home?"

"Yeah, I took that one morning in December when the light from the sunrise outlined the bottom edges of the clouds." I'd gotten that shot just about right, replicating what my eyes had seen. The stone walls were almost black while the clouds were a deep violet rimmed in pink fire.

"You know, I've never done a fight scene in an abandoned building. I set an epic battle in a fortress, but it wasn't abandoned. It would be a great place for a duel. The two warriors wouldn't just be fighting each other, but they'd have to watch out for falling plaster and loose boards and stuff."

"I've got a few more shots of this on my phone. And a lot more on my camera." The enthusiasm in my voice almost surprised me. But I liked helping my half-brothers, especially Rusty, since we were both having a hard time figuring out what to do with each other.

"Fire in the hole!" Aaron shouted.

A crash vibrated through the ceiling.

Growling, Mal got up from his seat. "Micah, keep working." He trudged to the stairs. "Aaron, you'd better fix whatever mess you made. And don't reload the treb-treb—" He turned to Rusty and me. "How do you pronounce that thing he's built?"

"Treb-boo-shay," Rusty and I said together.

Mal mouthed the word and then repeated his warning as he climbed the steps.

Opening a three-ring binder to a clean sheet of notebook paper, Rusty said, "Aunt Jeanine says a writer should put down everything he senses about a setting and then figure out what to actually include in the story. Can you tell me what you heard while you were at the children's home?"

"It does look like a big mouth." Micah held his face only a few inches from the screen.

"You'd better get back to your homework before Mal gets back down here," I said.

Pursing his lips, Micah tilted his head. "Dad said he's your dad, right?"

"Yeah."

"Why else do you think Rae's here?" said Rusty.

Micah leaned a little closer. "Then how come you don't call him Dad?"

A burn rushed up from my neck, and I crossed my arms over my chest as if Micah's question had exposed something very private. "Mal hasn't told me I could."

Rusty said, "But you call Gram 'Gram.'"

"She told me I could." I focused on the monitor. "First thing when I walked in the door Christmas morning, she said I could call her anything I liked, but all her grandkids called her 'Gram.'"

Out of the corner of my eye, I saw Rusty tap his pen against his chin. "I don't think Dad would mind if you called him Dad."

"He's your dad," Micah said, as if I'd forgotten.

I forced a smile. "Thanks, but I'll wait. I think Mal has to get used to the idea of me being his daughter. I don't want to push things." I scrolled to the next photo. "The old home can be really creepy."

I gave Rusty all the details I could think of, like how lonely it was with the wind sighing through the empty windows, and the way the dead leaves and litter from old parties crunched under my feet.

Rusty wrote fast in cursive, surprising me, and Micah plopped himself into my lap.

My skin cooled, but the question lingered in my mind. Why hadn't Mal told me I could call him Dad? He liked me. I could tell. It had to be that he was just getting adjusted to me.

The burn crept back.

That had to be it.

Chapter 6

After Mal finished saying prayers with Aaron and Micah and closed the door to their bedroom, he, Gram, and Rusty settled into their usual before-bedtime, weeknight positions: Gram sitting in the recliner, knitting, Rusty stretching across the couch reading a fantasy book that looked like it could produce a concussion if wielded as a weapon, and Mal occupying the other end of the couch, reading something official. The fire licked at a new log, and a very faint scent of apples drifted through the room.

Hallmark should have copied such a cozy scene for one of their Christmas movies. I hated to break it up, but I did want someone to look at the family trees I'd created. I vetoed asking Mal. After about the fourth night at the farm, I figured out how much Rusty valued this reading time with his dad. I wasn't sure why. They usually didn't talk, just sat on the couch reading together. But if Mal got called out or worked really late, Rusty was disappointed.

"Gram" — I held up the rolled sheet of bulletin board paper — "could you look at this with me?"

"Of course."

I spread the sheet over the dinner table. When it started to curl, Gram took some books off of the shelves by the fireplace, and I laid one on each corner.

"Barb said I could have this after I decorated a bulletin board. I thought it'd be big enough for me to draw the Branson and Malinowski family trees. I wanted you to check it."

"What a good idea." Gram patted my back. "But when it comes to my in-laws, only God can be certain of all the relationships with the way Walter's tomcatted around."

"Ma," Mal said from the couch, glancing at Rusty.

"Sweetie, Rusty knows his great-grandfather's reputation and a lot of stories about the rest of the family."

Rusty shoved Mal with his foot. "I'm not a baby, Dad."

Gram bent over the sheet. "I'm impressed. You remembered every name." She gave me her kind, calm smile. "You must have really been paying attention when I showed you all those albums. I was afraid I was boring you."

"Oh, no." Her compliment warmed me. "I think family history is fascinating. I never had any before." I traced the line from my great-grandparents to Gram. "It's funny, but when I decided I wanted to find my dad, I knew I could have a stepmom and half-siblings. But I didn't think all that much about getting grandparents and aunts and uncles and cousins."

Mal said, "You probably have more now than you ever wanted."

"I've got so many, the only way to keep track of them is to make these trees. I've always been a visual learner."

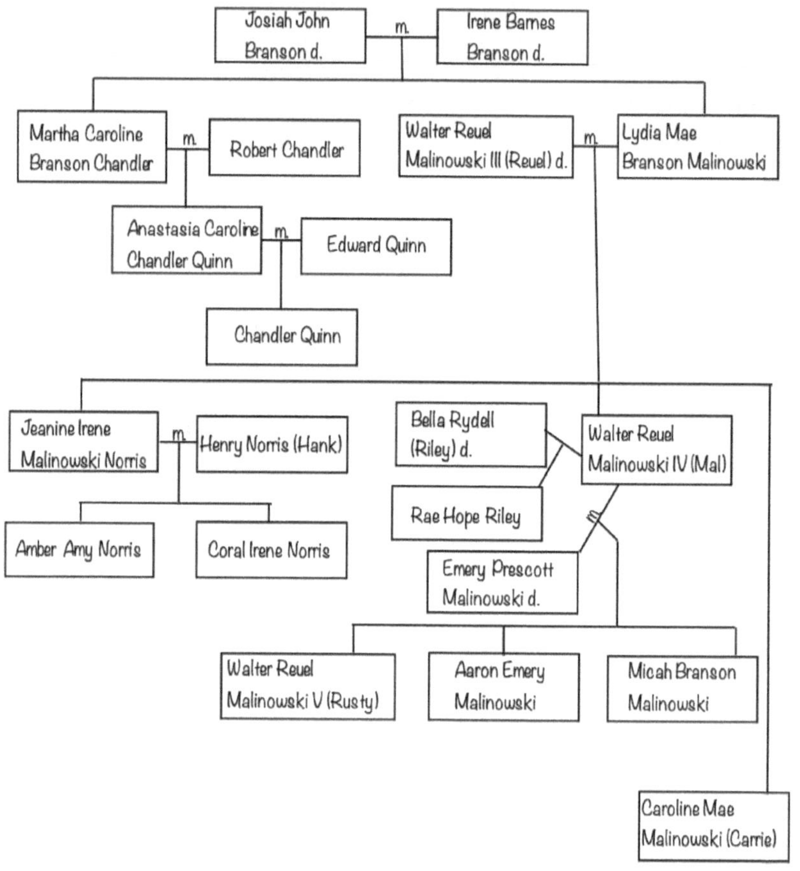

I removed the books from the corners and flipped the sheet over. This side was a maze of erased boxes and lines. "I had trouble spacing everyone on the Malinowski side because of all the marriages and divorces and relationships. So I divided the family tree in two."

"Your memory's as good as your dad's," Gram said. "He knows almost everybody in the county and who their friends and relatives and enemies are."

"You gotta know that," said Mal, "if you're policing a rural community. If someone takes a potshot at Bean Oller, I've got a pretty good idea who to question."

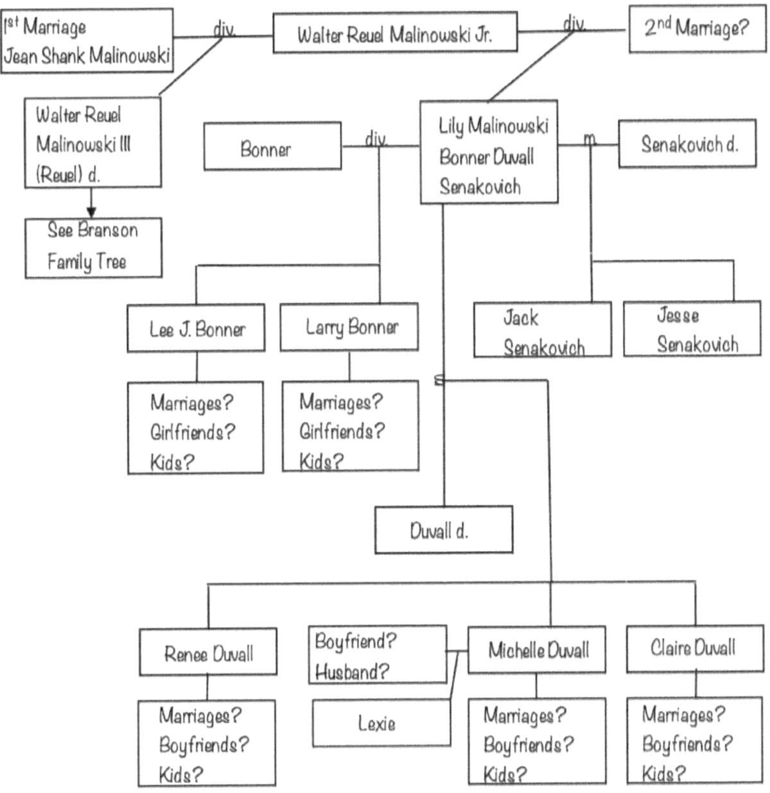

"Bean Oller?" I turned to him. "Is that his real name? Is he a he?"

"He's a man. His real name is Howard. I've heard about fifteen versions of how he got his nickname."

"Howard is about as bad as Walter." Rusty laid his novel on the floor and crossed the living room to the table.

Mal followed him. "You and I are lucky our moms came up with nicknames for us."

"There was no way" —Gram twisted the beaded bracelet on her thin wrist—"I was going to call a son of mine Walter, no matter how badly Reuel wanted to continue the family name. And we couldn't have two Reuels in one house. He suggested we call your dad Wally, but I absolutely refused."

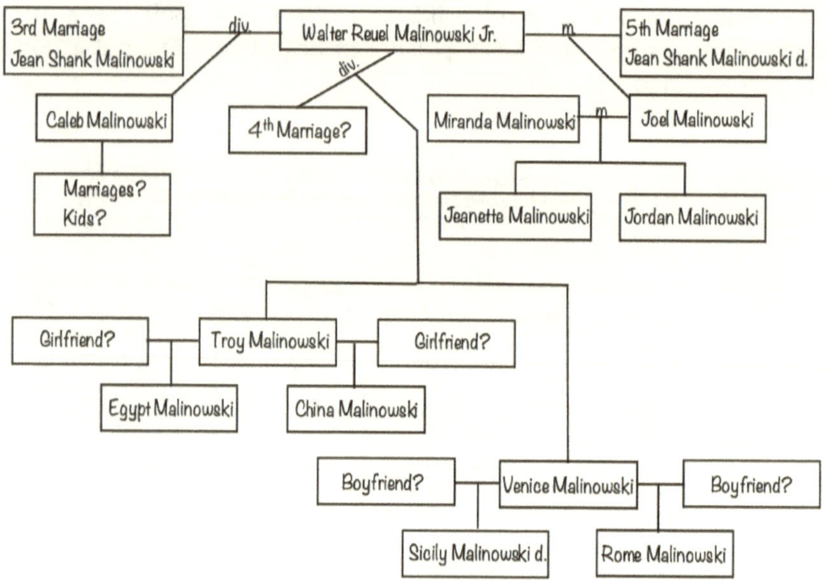

Mal kissed Gram on top of her head. "That's the nicest thing you've ever done for me."

I shook my head. "You do not look like a Wally."

"And that may be the nicest thing anyone has ever said to me."

"I told Reuel we had to come up with a decent nickname." Gram rubbed Mal on his enormous bicep. "But it wasn't until I held your dad that I decided he looked like a Mal."

What did a baby Mal look like? From the pictures I'd seen, and Gram had loads, he looked like your average, pudgy baby.

The landline rang. Gram picked up the receiver from the stand on the counter.

Rusty studied the sheet. "Have I met all these people?"

"No," said Mal, "and you're not going to."

"Why can't you get Cal or some of Lily's boys to help you?"

My head snapped in Gram's direction. Her voice had completely changed. All calm was gone. Now she spoke fast, clipped, like she wanted to end the phone call as soon as possible.

Which gave me a big ol' clue who was on the other end.

"Mal's put in a long day. He shouldn't stay up late helping you."

Stepping over to her, Mal put his hand on the receiver. "I'll take it."

Gram hung on. "You shouldn't go over there." She didn't bother to cover the mouth part. "He can't snap his fingers and —"

"And make me jump. I know." Mal tugged on the phone.

Her lips pressed tight, Gram released it.

Leaning against the basement door, Mal said, "What's the problem, Walter?"

As he listened, Gram walked into the kitchen, opened the dishwasher, took out a few plates, put them away with a clatter, and came back to the table.

"Okay." Mal glanced at the clock on the stove. "I'll be over in twenty, thirty minutes."

He hung up. Crossing her arms, Gram gave him the same look my mom aimed at me when I did something she didn't approve of. "You don't have to go over there."

"You really shouldn't, Dad." Rusty's blue eyes were wide and fixed on Mal.

A tingle snaked up my spine. Was visiting Walter really that dangerous? The tension had been concrete-thick when Mal took me over to introduce me to Walter on Christmas Day. But the relatives who had been visiting my great-grandfather hadn't done anything more than deliver mean looks and nasty comments.

"Rusty, nothing has happened in over a year," said Mal. "And I've gone over a lot."

"I'll go." I pushed the books off the sheet. "Why did Walter call?"

"He needs help getting his old hot water tank out and a new one in. He thought he could do it with Egypt and China—they live with him. But Egypt didn't come home from her job like she said she would, and she won't answer his calls. He already drained the old tank, so he has to put the new one in." Mal went to the coat closet beside the stairs. "You don't have to come."

Heading for Gram's room, I said over my shoulder, "Maybe I can help."

"Walter and I can do it."

When I came back with my jacket and vest, Mal had pulled on his heavy camo coat. His searching gaze bore into me. "You can come if you want. It may take a while."

I flipped my hair out from under my collar. "Fine by me."

He pointed a finger at Gram. "This should prove to you that it's safe since I'm willing to take one of my kids with me."

Rusty planted himself in front of him. "If it's safe for Rae, then it's safe for me too." His newly deepened voice cracked on the last word.

"You've got school tomorrow. I don't know how late we'll be." Mal gripped Rusty's bony shoulder, bending a little to meet his scared eyes. "I'm sorry I have to leave, but nothing bad is going to happen. We'll drive over, exchange the tanks, and drive home. The reason we're going is because Walter only has China to help him. Nobody else is there, so there won't be any trouble."

Rusty glanced back at me. Tears might have been trying to escape. He dashed into the bathroom and slammed the door.

Mal's broad shoulders dropped with sigh.

"Take your gun, sweetie." Gram gave him a patient smile. So that was where Micah got his particular brand of stubbornness.

"I've served warrants on suspected murderers, Ma." He took thick gloves from the pocket of his coat. "I can handle my outlaw relatives."

"But you were carrying your gun those times, weren't you?"

"Ma, only Walter and China are there. Even if Lee J. shows up … fine!" Mal stalked to the basement door. "I could be a decorated Navy SEAL, and you'd still worry about me being able to take care of myself." He stomped down the steps.

I sat on the bench by the front door and picked up a boot. "Are you and Rusty worried because Mal got jumped there?"

Gram nodded. "I know it's the only time any of my kids have had any serious trouble with my in-laws since they were children, and Mal thinks the only reason those five boys picked a fight with him is because of Troy."

"And Troy is …" My memory tried to picture the family tree.

"Walter's son from his fourth marriage. Mal's convinced Troy conned the others into jumping him. Troy left the county shortly after the fight, and Mal hasn't had any trouble since when he's gone over to help Walter." She pulled a hand through her long, gray-white hair. "But when he goes over, he never knows if some relative will decide to take their anger out on him because he's Reuel's son or because he's in law enforcement. The children and grandchildren from Walter's other marriages — well, I don't think 'hate' is too strong a word. They hate the descendants from his marriages to Jean, especially Reuel's."

I pulled my laces tight. Could the note writer be a relative? Someone who didn't like me being a member of the law-abiding branch of the family? I had a ton of suspects to choose from.

The basement door swung open, and Mal marched in. "Okay, Ma. I've got my gun." He kissed her on the forehead. "Don't worry."

Gram pulled on his arm, and he leaned over so she could kiss him on the cheek. "I don't worry. I pray."

I tied my other boot. Rusty darted out of the bathroom and grabbed Mal in a hug.

Mal rubbed him on the head. "Honest, buddy, it's no big deal."

Rusty nodded, though he looked ready to bust loose the tears at any moment.

"C'mon, Rae." Mal opened the front door. "We'll move the cars and take the Beast. Do you have your keys?"

Pulling them from the pocket of my vest, I followed Mal out the door and gave Rusty a reassuring smile.

The tears evaporated in a glare that should have raised blisters through my clothes.

I heaved a sigh. So much for bonding over my photos.

Chapter 7

"If you haven't been able to tell before" —Mal shifted into the next gear as the enormous, black truck rolled down the drive— "Rusty's a worrier." He frowned. "He gets that from me. We had a terrible time with him after Em died because she ..." His Adam's apple bobbed. "Because she walked out the door to go to the store, and the next time he saw her was at the funeral. When I told him being sheriff was a much safer job, he was all for it. Then I got into that fight at Walter's. Upped Rusty's anxiety through the roof."

I turned a vent toward me. "Being sheriff is safer than being a deputy?"

"Patrolling is where the danger lies. I only do that when I need to fill in gaps in the schedule." He eased back into the black bucket seat, getting comfortable in a vehicle that actually fit him. "So, what did you want to talk to me about?"

I drew my eyebrows together. "Why do you think I wanted to talk to you about something?"

"Wasn't that why you came with me?"

No. I came because Gram's concern scared me. I looked out my window. But the sheriff wouldn't like to hear that from his teenage daughter.

"I'm not trying to pry, Rae. Honestly. I just want you to know I'm always ready to listen and help out when I can." He broke into a self-conscious laugh, scratching at an eyebrow. "I'm still trying to figure out how to be a parent of an adult. So I hope you'll excuse me if I treat you too much like the boys."

The Beast ground along the rutted road, passing by woods so dark the tree trunks almost blended into a wall on each side of us.

I looked back to him. "You don't treat me like the boys. I'm sort of in the same boat. I'm not sure—" and my words got hung up. I couldn't admit that I had no idea how to relate to a father. I might sound like I didn't like Mike. "You're doing a great job. It's nice knowing you want to listen. You're not pushy." I sighed. "When I lived with the assistant pastor and his wife after Mom died, they bounced between leaving me to myself and asking—sometimes it seemed like demanding—to know how I was dealing with my mom's death." I set my jaw. "It got so annoying."

"It sounds like they were trying to help but didn't know how."

"Probably. You're much better at it."

That brought a smile to his face. "Well, I see a lot of me in you."

We chatted about our workday, and I sank back into the bucket seat. Hard to believe talking about such ordinary stuff with my dad could be so nice, something I looked forward to.

Eventually, Walter's ramshackle one-story house peeked at us through the black tree trunks, the windows glaring like the eyes of an angry animal. We bounced down the drive and slid to a stop behind a truck that looked even more battered than mine.

Opening his door, Mal said, "How does my eye look?"

"Not bad. Your eyelid's red and a little droopy. The ice must've helped a lot."

Lights from the front windows revealed a sagging porch roof braced with two extra beams. The front door banged open, and a scrawny guy flew off the porch, then spun around in the snow at the edge of the fierce light thrown out into the yard. Charging onto the porch, Egypt ripped off a necklace and hurled it into the snow, screaming at him.

Flinging out his arms, the guy, who looked around my age, screamed right back.

"Nice to see everything's normal," Mal muttered as we crunched through the thin layer of ice coating the snow and climbed the small hill from the drive.

Walter stalked onto the porch. China darted out from behind him, clutching herself against the cold.

"I'm done!" yelled the guy. "You hear me? Done!"

"So am I!" Egypt's long, sepia-colored hair swung into her face.

"Great. And if—" The guy saw us and stopped mid-scream. Beady, dark eyes, like a weasel, glared at us from a narrow face. "Who are you?"

"That's my grandson and great-granddaughter," Walter said in a voice as deep and rocky as an abandoned mine shaft.

"Don't make no trouble for me." The guy backed away from us.

Slipping his hands into the deep pockets of his coat, Mal said, "We're here to put in a hot water tank."

"Get out of here, Harley." Egypt marched down the porch steps. "I only hook up with men. You do a good impression, but you couldn't keep it up for long."

Shaking, Harley fired back his thoughts of her as a woman.

We walked toward the house, Mal putting himself between me and Harley.

"If you talk to Jasmine" —Harley stabbed a finger at her— "you'll be sorrier than you are now. I'll—"

"Boy." The word wasn't a shout or a yell. Walter just put so much force behind it that it would shut up anybody. "I'm gonna do you a good turn and tell you that if you keep runnin' your mouth, the sheriff here'll maybe have a reason to take you in. So shut your trap and get goin'."

"What sheriff?" Harley pointed at us. "You said they're your grandson and great-granddaughter."

"My grandson *is* the sheriff." He grinned, revealing long, strong teeth that appeared powerful enough to bite Harley in half.

Funny. Mal had called them his "outlaw relatives," and Gram had said several times that most of the Malinowskis considered Mal and his younger sister Carrie traitors for going into law enforcement. But Walter sounded almost proud.

"You're lying." Harley's words had punch, but the way his head twitched from the porch to us and back again showed he wasn't all that sure.

From his nasty grin, Walter seemed to enjoy Harley's confusion. So not proud. Just satisfied.

Reaching back to his hip pocket, Mal took out his wallet, his movement slow and smooth as he flipped it open to the badge, like it was no big deal. That's what made it so cool. Like Thor holding Mjolnir as if it were an ordinary hammer.

Harley's beady eyes popped wide enough not to be beady anymore. He tromped across the crackling snow and brought his skinny face within six inches of the badge. He called to Walter and the girls. "How'd a relative of yours get to be sheriff?"

"By the hand of God," Mal said without any hint of sarcasm. "Kid, go home. You haven't broken the law yet. But if you make a direct threat, and Egypt presses charges, I'll have to take you in. A break-up is not worth going to jail for. Same for you, Egypt."

She wheeled to us. "Thanks a whole bunch, Mal. Nice to know you treat family as rotten as everybody else." Then Egypt told Harley where he could go and what he could do once he got there, her insult growing higher and louder until it ended in a screech. She hurtled into the house and slammed the door.

Snow slid off the edge of the roof.

His breath coming fast, Harley stayed rooted in the yard.

Mal said, "Is that your truck in front of me? I can move mine if you can't get out."

Without a glance at us, Harley ran to his truck. He pulled into the narrow strip of grass between the drive and the woods, and, tires spewing clumps of snow, roared past the Beast and into the darkness.

We climbed the porch steps.

Mal said, "Walter, if that kid causes Egypt trouble, she should bring charges against him."

Walter snorted and spat into the snow. "I can take care of my own granddaughters."

"Not if you break the law to do it."

"Malinowskis have always had to take care of themselves. The law around here ain't never gave us a fair shake."

Raising his eyebrows, Mal pointed at his chest. "But *I'm* the law around here now."

"That's right." Tiny China put on a smile so tart it made me wince. "St. Mal will protect us."

China was the perfect name for my—what was she? Since she was the daughter of my late grandfather's half-brother, that might have made her my half first cousin once removed. Her size, along with her coal black pageboy haircut and pale skin, smooth as a porcelain, made her appear as fragile as an old-fashioned China doll. Although China dolls probably weren't painted with mocking smiles and sneaky expressions that made them look years older than sixteen.

Mal rolled his eyes. "China, when someone's doing you a favor, don't rile them."

Standing next to each other, with Mal about eighteen inches taller than China, not only didn't they look like first cousins—no, half first cousins—they didn't even look like they belonged to the same species.

"You get taxed for police services, Walter," Mal said. "You might as well take advantage of them."

Walter lifted his chin up and out. "Did you come here to help me or to lecture me like I was one of your kids?"

He was a smidge shorter than Mal but that only made him look more massive. Anyone could see where Mal got his impressive build and where I got my height.

"If I can keep you out of jail, I am helping," said Mal.

Set in a cinderblock for a face, Walter's eyes, so deep I still couldn't figure out the color, raked me. "Why'd you come? Mal don't never bring his kids over here."

I tried to meet his stare and edged closer to Mal. "I wanted to come."

Walter spat again. "Surprised he let you." Then he trudged into the house. Except for walking a little stiffly, he seemed in pretty good shape for eighty.

We followed Walter into a living room crammed with old furniture but neat, except for a heap of clothes on one chair. The only new things in sight were a smart phone on the dinged coffee table and a row of paperback novels sitting on the shelves dividing the living room from the dining room. The bright, colorful book covers were a complete contrast to the dull, worn easy chairs and wooden end tables. The covers seemed familiar.

Passing the bookshelves, I scrutinized the spines. Yep. They were all mysteries written by Mal's older sister, Jeanine.

Egypt slouched in a doorway to what looked like a bedroom. "Why'd you bring Rae, Mal? I thought we were all too horrible to let your precious, little darlings around." She was taller and heavier than China but shared the same light green eyes with her half-sister. Her mouth seemed chiseled into a permanent frown, a gash across her round face.

"Gyp." Walter barked her name, stopping at a scratched door outside the kitchen.

She still lounged against the doorjamb, but her eyes flicked to him.

"Shut your trap. We need hot water. If you had come home from work like you said you would, me, you, and China could've put that new tank in. But you decided tonight was a fine time to hang out with that idiot."

Her frown deepening, Egypt slumped more.

We descended a rickety staircase. The foundation in the basement was a jumble of irregular rocks cemented together, the concrete floor ribboned with cracks.

"Over here." Walter tromped over to a corner behind the steps where the hot water tank stood.

With me holding open the door out to the garage, Walter and Mal had the tanks exchanged in a few minutes and were connecting the new one.

"Need any help?" I rested against a metal support post.

"Thanks, but we've both done this before." Mal took a wrench Walter offered.

I pulled out my phone. Nothing doing. Walter's house was located in another dead zone.

"By the way, Rae." China took a seat in the middle of the basement stairs. "The next time Egypt and I are going to a party, we'll let you know. We had so much fun the last time."

I lowered my eyebrows. "I didn't. I dropped you and your friends off and left."

"You had a blast." China's forehead furrowed. "Or were you too drunk to remember?"

"China, you've got me mixed up with somebody else." I snuck a peek at Mal. What would he think if he knew I'd been hanging out with China last summer before I knew what she was like? "I went bowling with you and a couple of your friends. Then I drove y'all to that party. When I saw Egypt beating on a girl, and almost everybody else trashed, I left."

Her pale green eyes shifted from me to Mal and back again. "Oh, yeah. That's right. You did just drop us off." Her exaggerated nod and her tone were meant to imply she was covering for me.

Except she wasn't. From the calculating look in her eyes, she knew it.

She was deliberately trying to make trouble for me.

"I remember." Egypt dropped onto a step above her half-sister, fishing pretzels out of a bag. "Rae left right after she dropped you guys off."

Which was true, but Egypt was using the same unconvincing tone.

"I didn't get drunk, and I didn't stay at the party." I watched Mal's profile close to read his reactions, my lungs ratcheting closed.

Mal looked up from the pipe he was working on. "Rae, I believe you. But you're an adult. You don't have to check your behavior with me."

Tension released its grip on my lungs. But it left behind a puzzle.

"So, Mal, you're saying me and China are lying?" Egypt grabbed the railing to the stairs and pulled herself to her feet.

"Yep." His head was bent over the pipe.

Egypt flew down to the floor. "You know all about lying, don't you, Mal? You got a girl pregnant in high school and never told nobody until you had to. Is that how a Christian acts?"

Heat igniting in my chest, I faced her. "That was twenty years ago. People change."

"Not that much." Egypt glared past me to Mal. "I bet all that talk about you not wanting to date since your wife died is a lie too. Who you got your sights set on, Mal? Guys say Liz Mehaffie is hot, even though she's got two kids. She works in your office, doesn't she?"

Twisting the wrench, Mal said nothing.

"Get outa here, Gyp." Walter pointed with his wrench. "I want hot water."

"Hey, I'm only sayin' — "

"We heard what you're sayin'. Git." The last word came out as a snarl.

Although it wasn't aimed at me, I pressed back against the post. If it had been turned in my direction, I'd have probably run.

The bag of pretzels landed by Walter's feet, spraying its contents all over the concrete. Egypt pounded up the stairs, which creaked and swayed under her thudding footsteps, and slammed the door.

Growling, Walter threw down the wrench and stalked up the stairs.

"Perfect," China muttered and followed her grandfather.

Standing, Mal surveyed the tank. "I think we can go in a few minutes, Rae."

As China came back down with a broom and dustpan, screams and shouts ricocheted above us.

"They're swearing, Rae." China placed the dustpan on the floor. "I'm sure you've never heard such language in your life."

"I haven't lived in a cave."

"How about a convent?"

Wiping his hands on an old cloth from a workbench, Mal said, "That should do it. The house is very well-kept, China. I assume you're the one who keeps everything looking so neat."

China held a hand over her heart. "Thank you, St. Mal. A compliment from you just made my year."

Mal set aside the cloth. "All you had to say was thank you and mean it."

"But I did." Her voice breathless, she opened her eyes wide.

Writing anonymous notes seemed the perfect hobby for someone with China's sneaking, trouble-making personality.

The upstairs was quiet when Mal and I came out of the kitchen. Walter shoved another log into the living room fireplace. We bundled ourselves against the weather.

"Appreciate you comin' out," Walter said to the fire. "Surprised Lydia turned you loose."

Mal's hands froze on the collar he'd just flipped up. "Don't." His snarl was just as mean as Walter's. I was glad that one wasn't meant for me either.

Walter squared himself to Mal. "Don't you tell me what to do. I don't care if you're the sheriff or the president."

"Which is why you've done jail time." Mal put his hand on the knob of the front door.

Walter said, "Rae, since you're nineteen, you don't gotta have Mal's permission to come over here. Any of my kids or grandkids or great-grandkids can come over any time they want."

"Thanks." Although I didn't see myself accepting that invitation any time soon.

"Of course she doesn't need my permission," said Mal. "But she's got too much sense to come out here by herself. Egypt and China have given her about a thousand reasons not to."

I followed Mal to the Beast, the cold air as sharp as a thousand papercuts against my cheeks. Once inside the truck, Mal backed down the drive, turned the Beast onto the road, and headed for the farm.

"I really appreciate you believing me about the party," I said. "I met China at the library. When I found out she was a Malinowski, I thought getting to know her might lead me to getting to know you. Although I didn't like her from the start. She looked sneaky and I learned real quick that she doesn't insult you to your face. She has to hide it with hints and insinuations."

"You don't have to explain. I know China. Walter's had custody of her for three years, and she hasn't said an honest or kind word yet."

"Did he have custody of Egypt?" I recalled past conversations with her, before she knew I was Mal's daughter and I knew she was a fiend.

"She's two years older than I am, right?"

"Yep. Walter got custody of Egypt when she was twelve. Her mother went to prison for assault. China's mother OD'd."

"Did Walter have to fight—" another mental peek at the family tree "—Troy for custody?"

Mal barked a laugh. "Troy was only around long enough to get their mothers pregnant and name the girls. It suits him perfectly for Walter to raise his daughters. He can travel around the country, running cons, and doesn't have to worry about getting charged with child neglect."

The Beast hit a slick spot and skidded as we took a turn downhill. Mal guided the truck out of it and onto more reliable ground.

Hooking hair behind my ear, I said, "I've got a question for you."

"Shoot."

I caught my lip in my teeth, then said, "Why do you believe my version about going to the party with Egypt and China? I understand why you don't believe China. But I could be just as big a liar." My stomach doubled over, but I went on. "I did hide my identity while I was figuring out who my father was and if he tried to murder my mom."

"But that was just smart. You were like a cop going undercover." He glanced over at me. "Rae, I don't know many details of your life, like your favorite dessert or movie. But I learned all about your basic personality at the children's home Christmas morning."

Mal braked and swung the Beast around a tight turn. "You are incredibly disciplined and determined. You moved to a county where you knew no one, on a mission to find a murderer, and didn't share that with anybody. Not even on social media. For a nineteen-year-old, that's impressive."

"No, it's not." Closing my eyes, I laid back against the headrest. "I had to do it that way. It was the only way for me to get to the truth. It was just the right thing to do."

"That shows your intelligence. You're also so brave, it scares me. To set up meetings with two men who were possible murderers, and one's a cop, all alone in an abandoned building in the middle of nowhere? It still makes me sick to think about it."

Three men, actually. But Mal didn't need to know that.

"And you're merciful. You didn't have to let the statute of limitations run out on the assault." He looked over to me with that big, lit-from-within grin of his. "You're some kind of wonderful kid, Rae."

Every fiber in me tingled as Mal's compliments sank in. I scooted to the edge of my seat.

Heavenly Father, he likes me. My dad—my dad!—really likes me.

My smile felt like it was about to split my cheeks. "Thanks for believing me. And—and everything else."

"It's just the truth." Mal drove the Beast into the garage.

I ran into the house. Rusty lay on the couch, asleep, a book opened on his chest.

Gram stood up from the recliner, her yarn dropping to the floor. "Everything went well?"

"No problems." I went to Gram's room, slung on my backpack, and grabbed my tripod and the family trees.

As I came out, Rusty stirred, his book sliding onto the floor. "You and Dad are back?" he mumbled, squinting.

"For sure."

At the Rust Bucket, Mal waited as I made sure the gear shift would cooperate.

When it did, he waved and turned toward the house.

Shifting into reverse, I looked over my shoulder and found Mal back by my window.

I rolled it down.

"I wasn't going to ask you this," he said, staring at the ground, "because I don't want to bother you. You're very responsible, so it's not that I don't think you can take care of yourself."

I knew where he was going. "You want me to call you when I get to the apartment."

He looked up. "Do you mind? I'm trying to get used to the idea that one of my kids doesn't live at home. But, I hate to say it, I'm a worrier, and--and—"

And his wife had been killed in a car accident. "I don't mind. It's nice having someone know where I am. Last fall, I went hiking in Hocking Hills to take pictures. I realized I could walk off a cliff, and nobody would ever look for me."

Shoving his hands deep in his pockets, Mal sighed. "I'm sorry you've been so alone. You don't have to worry about that ever again."

The half-moon light revealed his face drooping.

"It's not your fault. You thought I was dead." I made my tone as reassuring as I could. "I'll call as soon as I walk in the door."

A smile tried to lift his sad expression and only partially succeeded.

~~~~~

Clicking on the little lamp sitting on the two milkcrates I'd zip-tied together to make an end table, I braced myself. The dingy beige of my apartment walls did an excellent job of depressing my mood. Even the thrill of Mal's compliments didn't totally insulate me.

I called Mal, then picked up the note from where I'd tossed it on the holey carpet this morning.

So what if some people were rude or insulting? So what if I'd received a mean note? I'd handled a lot worse on my own. No reason to bother Mal.
~~~~~

My dad thought I was wonderful, even if he hadn't told me I could call him "Dad" yet.

Father, please don't let me do anything that would make him change his opinion of me.

I threw the note in the trash can.

Chapter 8

NO ONE WANTS YOU HERE, BELLA

The note, damp from sitting under my wiper blade, lay limp in my hand. The letters had smeared but were still easy to read.

My heart hammering into high gear, I shot quick looks around the library parking lot. Since it was Friday afternoon, just after we'd closed for the day, no other cars were parked in the lot, except for Barb's. I gave my head a sharp shake, a cold breeze brushing my cheeks. Whoever had left this on my truck hadn't waited around for me to spot him or her.

Pulling up beside me in her sports car, Barb said, "Anything wrong, Rae?"

"Uh … uh, no." I crumpled the note with one hand. The third note in nine days, and this time the creep decided not to use the post office.

Barb's wide mouth was caught between a smile and frown. "Okay. See you Monday." She drove out of the lot.

Fumbling my keys, I unlocked my truck, jumped in, got it started, and rocketed onto Woodward Avenue, my truck shifting but groaning as I changed gears. Drawing a long breath, I followed Main Street out of town.

The first note had been mailed last Wednesday, the second one mailed Monday, and now this one left on my truck on Friday. It called me Bella while the other two called me Rae. Why the change? This person couldn't really think I was using men like my mom had when she lived in Marlin County.

The Rust Bucket whined around the turn by a derelict barn at an abandoned farm.

Someone had a grudge against my mom and felt perfectly justified in harassing me because he seemed to see me as the same kind of person she was. Was that the reason behind the name change?

One thing was definite. The stalker had upped his game, taking the risk of being seen while leaving the note on my truck in a parking lot during business hours. What did that mean? My heart revved again, and I exhaled slowly to ease its pace.

Passing the dead-end road that led to Mal's farm, I drove toward Jeanine and Hank Norris's place. Two more turns, and I swung onto the drive to the farm, the truck rocking between potholes. Pulling up to the faded red stable, I parked beside Jason Carlisle's Land Rover.

The sun dipped below a lid of charcoal clouds, finding clear sky just above the horizon. Land and clouds funneled the sunset into a brilliant golden shaft, spotlighting portions of the Norris's patchy yard, stable, and light blue house and leaving everything else in cold shadows.

Squinting, I dug out my camera and took some quick shots. As much as I wanted to do a proper shoot on my tripod, I didn't want to keep Uncle Hank waiting since he'd been nice enough to invite me to ride. I changed into my boots as fast as I could.

Walking into the stable, I drew in the warm scent of horses and hay mixed with a touch of manure, and my heart eased into its normal speed for the first time since I'd read the note. All stables around the world had to smell the same, and I'd feel at home in every one of them, just like I did in my first stable where Mom worked when I was in middle school.

Uncle Hank's big, black stallion, Knight, tossed his head, and the leopard Appaloosa, Smudge, whinnied.

"Hey, Rae." Aaron popped out of the stall used as a tack room.

"Hey." I glanced around. "Did Jason bring the rest of his kids?"

"He brought Richard. He's playing with Micah in the house."

"Where's everybody else?" With the two farms next to each other, it was unusual not to trip over relatives.

"I think Rusty and Amber are in the house. Coral's over at her grandpa's farm. It's across the road. Have you met her grandpa? He's Uncle Hank's dad."

"I've met him."

I went over to the opening at the other end of the stable. Aaron climbed the gate to the corral and straddled the top board.

Jason Carlisle stood at the corral gate, resting his foot on the bottom bar, while he watched his daughter, Allison. The third-grader rode a sleek sorrel horse with a scooped face around Uncle Hank, who guided her horse on a lead line.

Even in a muddy barnyard, Jason managed to be appropriately dressed and perfectly fashionable at the same time. His thick, tan work coat, black jeans, and heavy boots were similar to Uncle Hank's outfit. But Jason's clothes hadn't a stain, hole, or frayed edge anywhere. Despite the thinning light of the sunset, I could see the hole in the elbow of Uncle Hank's jacket and the ragged cuffs of his jeans.

Jason called, "You look great, Alli."

The sunset backlit Uncle Hank and the little girl, making it impossible to read her expression. But her back became rail-straight.

The scene looked so … American. A horse and rider and a cowboy working in the sunset. My hands itched to set up my camera. But I needed to take advantage of Jason's presence.

"Keep your heels down." Uncle Hank turned, keeping Allison in view as she circled him. "Long legs." He waved in my direction.

I waved back.

"How's life with the Malinowskis?" Jason gave me the million-watt smile that made me think of Superman the first time I met him. If he'd been a little taller and more muscular, he could have been cast perfectly in that role with his warm, brown eyes and brown hair that had been sculpted into its precise place with some kind of gel.

"Great." That was lame. "Better than anything I'd hoped for."

Aaron twisted around to us. "Rae's a lot of fun. She likes all of my inventions."

"Could I talk to you, Jason?" I leaned closer. "Privately."

His smile dimming, Jason nodded. I led him back out the door by the vehicles. Already the gold light wasn't as strong. I'd have to capture my American scene some other time.

"Is something wrong?" Jason asked in a low voice. "At the library?"

Shaking my head, I scanned the muddy yard and the front porch to the small house. We were alone.

I whispered, "I've seen Rick twice since Christmas morning. He—well, he acts like he's afraid of me. Mal thinks he feels ashamed. He doesn't need to. I thought I explained that at the children's home."

"You did. But knowing and believing are two very different things. Rick's very confused right now as well as ashamed."

"Confused?"

"Rick thought his life was ending Christmas Day. He was going to Mal to confess he murdered Bella and her unborn baby to protect me. He put all his affairs in order, made me his executor—" Jason's breath came fast as his words came faster "—said goodbye to my kids, called Barb. Rick was prepared to spend the rest of his life behind bars." His eyes grew moist. "Or worse."

My jaw swung loose. "You thought the court would have gone for the death penalty?"

"Rick had carried out what he thought was premeditated murder. There was a possibility." He inhaled, lifting his shoulders. "Since you let the statute of limitations run out, Rick has his life back. He knows he's forgiven, but he's not sure what to do with it. I've tried to persuade him to speak with Father Keir, tell him the whole story. He's finally considering it."

The clatter of horse hooves made me look over my shoulder, past the sliding door of the stable, to where Uncle Hank led Alli's horse into the wide aisle between the stalls.

I whispered, "Let Rick know he can act normal with me."

Sniffing, Jason wiped his eyes and turned on the full power of his smile.

"You ready to ride, Rae?" Uncle Hank latched the horse's halter to a thick rope clipped to a post.

"Whenever you are," I said, reentering the stable with Jason.

Alli and Aaron unwrapped cloths from her horse's front legs. Uncle Hank pulled off the saddle. He would have looked more at home riding the range in Texas than working a farm in Ohio. He had the tall, lanky frame and bowlegs you'd expect of a cowboy.

"Rae, as soon as we get Tornado put away, I'll get Pokey ready for you." Uncle Hank adjusted the battered tan cowboy hat over his wiry, dark hair.

"Tornado?" I said.

"I wanted a tough name for my horse." Alli took off her helmet, only a few wisps of hair, the same shade as her father's, escaping her French braid.

A door slammed, and Mal strode into the stable, nodding toward Jason. "Carlisle."

Aaron darted over to his dad, swinging at him. Mal blocked his flying fists and grabbed him in a one-arm hug.

"My spine!" Aaron wriggled every which way. "My spine!"

An ornery glint came into Uncle Hank's enormous deep brown eyes. He stepped into the aisle between the stalls. "Now keep calm, boys and girls. My brother-in-law is not here to ride any of you. Your backs are safe."

"Like I'd trust you to pick a mount for me." Mal released Aaron.

Hank placed his hat over his heart. "Big Guy, just give me the word, and I promise to get you the gentlest Clydesdale I can find."

Mal rolled his eyes.

Their relationship puzzled me. Hank seemed to sincerely annoy Mal, but several times, I'd seen them remain talking at the dinner table long after everyone else had left.

Mal put an arm around me and squeezed. "How's my girl?"

My shoulder blades met and were in danger of passing each other. Small wonder Aaron squealed about his spine. I smiled around gritted teeth.

Mal jerked his arm away as Hank shut Tornado into her stall.

"See you next Friday, Hank," Alli said, taking Jason's hand and beaming up at her dad.

As Jason and his daughter left, Hank led a palomino into the aisle. "Pokey here should be a good mount for you, Rae. You should find a helmet to fit you in the tack room."

"Rae's riding?" A note of concern notched Mal's baritone a few tones higher.

"She told me she rode in middle school." Hank talked over his shoulder, following me. "I called her today and asked if she wanted to ride since the corral thawed enough for lessons."

Clipping the helmet's strap under my chin, I returned to Pokey.

Worry etched lines on Mal's face. I'd picked up that he wasn't a horse nut like his older sister and her family. But now he looked almost scared.

"Shoot, Mal, I ain't puttin' her on a wild mustang." Hank must have noticed too.

"Oh, hey, Dad. Hey, Rae." Rusty ambled into the stable. "Aunt Jeanine said supper's almost ready."

Hank stopped buckling the bridle. "We'll have your lesson after supper, Rae."

Aaron ran up to the house with Rusty, but Mal and I waited as Hank returned Pokey to her stall.

With the last stray rays of sunlight pulled from the hills, we crossed the yard to the house under a sky of unbroken black.

Mal said, "Are you staying with us tonight, Rae?'

"Yes, if that's okay. I'm opening the Barton branch in the morning."

"You can stay with us any night you like."

On the porch, Hank and I leaned against the railing to take off our boots. A gray-striped cat draped over one shoulder, Coral walked out of the dark with a retriever trotting on one side and a dog that might have had some basset hound in it on the other.

"Hey, there." Coral's freckled face broke into a rare smile, making her look younger than twelve.

Uncle Hank said, "Did you ask your grandpa if he wanted to come over for supper?"

"Yep. He didn't." Coral swung open the front door, and the smell of baked parmesan cheese mixed with the damp night air.

His shoulders slumped, Uncle Hank tore off a boot.

Mal said, "You know your dad'll never accept an invitation when my crew is around."

"He keeps to himself too much since Mom died." Hank whistled for the retriever, which had veered toward my truck.

It raced to him, and Hank moseyed into the house in his sock feet.

I dropped a boot, and Mal whispered, "I am so sorry. The last thing I want to do is make you uncomfortable."

I stared at him. "What're you talking about?"

"When I hugged you in the stable. I'm so used to hugging the boys and Amber and Coral that I kinda forgot myself."

"But I didn't mind. Not at all."

"Then why did you make that face?"

He'd noticed my gritted teeth. "Well, I—I liked your hug. It was just—uh—a bit—uh—powerful?"

"Sorry." His expression turned sheepish. "I forget my strength sometimes. But you don't mind if I hug you? It's okay if you do. You tell me what you're comfortable with, and I'll abide by it."

"Hugging is fine." To prove it, I put my arm around his waist and gave him my version of a one-armer.

His face lighting up, Mal laid his arm across my shoulders.

I looked up at him. "This is how we walked to your SUV Christmas morning."

"Yeah, but we weren't hugging then. You were my crutch." We walked through the front door, the retriever trotting out of our way. "I was very close to passing out from the shock of finding out you and Bella hadn't died in the fire."

We laid our coats on a big recliner. In the kitchen, Aunt Jeanine fanned a pizza that was smoking on the counter.

I said, "You really don't like horses, do you?"

"Not really. I'd better wash my hands." He hurried down the hall to the bathroom.

There was a story there. Since Uncle Hank had grown up with Mal and his sisters and seemed to be the family storyteller, I'd ask him later.

I stayed by the recliner, flicking the zipper on my vest. Could Rick be leaving the notes? Having second thoughts about confessing? But he'd have to scare off Mal too, which he'd know was impossible.

Shaking my head, I walked down the hall. If I didn't watch myself, I'd be suspecting Aaron and Micah.

Chapter 9

"Rae, are you awake?"

Rolling over on the inflatable mattress under the half-moon window in the playroom, I cracked open an eye.

Micah's face was about an inch from my own. "'Cause if you aren't, I'll play downstairs."

Suppressing a groan, I said, "If I was awake, I wouldn't be lying in bed."

"But sometimes I lie in bed when I'm awake, waiting for Aaron or Rusty to wake up."

I fumbled for my phone under my pillow and squinted at the time. It was only ten minutes before my alarm would go off. Allowing a groan, I pushed myself into a seated position on the inflatable mattress in front of the half-moon window and stretched.

Micah dropped down beside me. "You wanna play with me?"

"I've got to work today." I lifted my mop of hair out of my eyes.

"It's Saturday."

"I sometimes work Saturdays. I'm working at the branch library in Barton."

As Micah selected plastic bricks from heaps on the floor, I gathered my clothes and the supermarket bag containing my toiletries and picked my way through the minefield of toys to the stairs. At the bottom, the aroma of baked bread greeted me. Gram was up.

Once I'd showered and made myself look decent enough to wait on the public, I went to the kitchen. The yellow walls and crimson counters seemed as warm as the scones Gram was pulling out of the oven.

"Morning, Rae. Did Micah wake you? He knows not to."

"It's fine." I opened a cupboard and took out a mug. The boys wouldn't stay my fans if I tattled on them.

She faced me. "So he did. He'll pull a chore from the chore jar."

"Really, Gram. It's no big deal." I filled the mug with water and put it in the microwave.

"Yes, it is. He's not listening." She placed scones onto a wire rack. "Would you like a scone for breakfast? They're lemon-rosemary, not that sweet. You can put preserves or jelly on them to make them sweeter."

"You didn't have to get up early and fix me breakfast." But her effort made me feel toasty clear through.

"I know. I wanted to." She gave me her relaxed smile. "I also wanted you to drop off some goodies, if you have time. It's on the way to the branch in Barton."

"Well …" The left side of my face contracted. Since the Barton branch library didn't open until 10:00, I'd wanted to take my time this morning, not feel as rushed as I usually did on a work day.

"Oh — oh, my goodness!" Gram's fingers flew to her lips as she stared at me.

I checked my outfit. Yep. I'd put on leggings.

"Mal makes that same face."

"What face?"

"The left side of his face bunches up, like he's got a sudden pain, when he's asked to do something he doesn't want to do but knows he should. He's made that face since he was little." Gram shook her head. "You hear about nature versus nurture, but it's amazing to see it in real life." She handed me a plate with two scones on it. "You have a lot of your dad's mannerisms."

Since my face had given me away, I put on an eager tone. "Where do you want me to take the goodies?"

"To those three boys living in the old Kincaid place. That reminds me …" Gram opened the fridge.

One eyebrow rising, I bit into a scone. I'd expected the delivery to go to a church member who was ill.

She took a cookie tin from the fridge and put it in a cardboard box sitting on the counter by the back door. "The one boy who works for Eric Simcox — I can't remember his name — his birthday is Monday or Tuesday. I made a pie for him." She stepped back from the box, turning her beaded bracelet. "I'd better write a note, explaining the pie is for him in case you have to leave it without seeing anybody."

"That's nice of you." I dunked a bag of English Breakfast tea into the steaming mug. "How did you know it's Garrett's birthday? He's from Toledo and doesn't have any family around here."

"He said that? I thought he was born in Zanesville and moved away as a child."

"He told me he was from Toledo."

"Must be another one of Eric's officers. Anyway, I bake goodies for all the police in the county on their birthdays. But I like to send extra food to those boys since they don't have family close by." She studied the contents of the box. "It's so nice to see someone living in the Kincaid house. It's stood empty since Dave Kincaid died, and -- and … what's that young deputy's first name?"

"Chris."

Gram returned to the fridge. "It was so sad when Dave died. Chris was sent to live with some relative out of state. There weren't any Kincaids left in the county. I always wondered what happened to him. I'm glad to know he turned out well. Dave would be proud."

"Speaking of birthdays," I said, scooping sugar into my tea, "Mal's is coming up in a few weeks, and I want to get him something special since it's my first gift to him. Got any suggestions?"

"Mal is very hard to buy for." Gram took a scone from the wire rack. "He's very single-minded. He picks a few things and does them very well. Right now, he parents, polices, and fishes, and that's it. Except for reading the rough drafts of Jeanine's mysteries to check for inaccuracies in police procedures. I guess that comes under policing too." She brushed crumbs from her fingers. "He's the exact opposite of Em."

"What was she like?" I sipped tea.

Gram's face softened as she stared into the living-dining room. Wan dawn light picked out the recliner and the assortment of chairs surrounding the plank table. "Aaron's a lot like her. Always enthusiastic and optimistic, except he loves science, and Em loved art and sewing. But she would try anything, always looking for a new experience."

A sigh, barely audible, escaped her lips, and her gaze returned to me. "I'm so glad Mal told her about Bella and losing you. At least he didn't always carry his secret alone." Her mouth tightened along with her grip on a cup of tea.

"I still can't believe he didn't tell me. I know we'd been at war when he was in high school — he let all the attention he received as a star football player go to his head. He didn't think he needed to listen to his mother anymore. Or anybody else, really. But I thought, if he was in real trouble…" Another sigh welled up from deep inside. "It's past. Nothing will change that." Her smile rose into place. "But we're very close now. I didn't dream that was possible twenty years ago."

We drank tea, and I finished my first scone.

"But an idea for a gift …" She peered behind me, then whispered, "Mal would kill me for saying so, but you could give him a pile of dirty socks, and he would turn to mush. It'd be the first present from the Child Who Came Back from the Dead."

A dirty pile of socks would save me money, but … "That's good to know, but I still want to give him something—" I pulled on my earlobe "—meaningful."

"Well, your photos are meaningful to you. Pick one of your favorites. He'll love it."

~~~~~

Glancing at Gram's directions, I turned onto a dirt road, and a pothole nearly sent me to the roof. Fog, piled in heaps and mounds along the road, camouflaged any hazards.
~~~~~

I passed two drives — at least, I saw two drives. I could have missed one if the fog was thick in the right spot. I turned right onto the third. And squealed to a stop. Out of the fog, sitting on a small rise with steeply wooded hills behind it, loomed a peeling, three-story Victorian house. If I hadn't already known who lived here, I'd be worried about disturbing the crazy caretaker who carried a chainsaw or scythe or something equally murderous.

Unable to resist the moody setting, I jumped out long enough to click a few photos, then drove on. To the right of the house sat a barn that looked as if the weight of the fog might collapse it. Lined up in front of it were two county patrol SUVs like Mal's, a Wellesville police car, two other cars, and a truck. I parked beside it.

The porch wrapped around one side of the house, the railing in dire need of repair, but its intricate pattern still evident. And beautiful. On the second story, a turret jutted onto the porch roof. Gram was right. This place could be featured on a home-and-garden show if it was renovated right.

Carrying the box of baked goods, I squished through the muddy yard and around all the vehicles. A tall, very skinny guy in jeans and an orange and blue ski jacket strode onto the porch from the direction of the barn, one arm cradling a load of firewood. He waved a branch at me.

The deputy from Texas. What was his nickname? Dallas? Austin? He hated his real name, Miguel Blank. So why could I remember that and not his nickname?

I slopped to the porch and scraped my boots on the steps.

"What brings you out here, Rae?" His Texas drawl took me back to the little towns Mom and I lived in, where people talked slow, moved slow, and took their time about almost everything.

Holding up the box, I said, "Gram sent goodies and a birthday pie for Garrett."

"He's got a birthday coming up?" Houston — that was it — scratched a sideburn about the color of burnt umber with the branch. "Or has it already happened?"

"Gram thought it was Monday or Tuesday."

Tucking the box under one arm, I opened the door and stepped aside to let Houston in. A nicked but still gorgeous dark-stained staircase twisted up to the second floor in a foyer that was empty except for two chairs — the kind you take to parades — covered in winter coats and other outdoor clothes.

Houston strode into a large room on the right and dropped his load by a fireplace. The antique furniture, like a ball-and-claw table, didn't fit with the outdoor chairs and tables, or with the instruments. Three guitars lay on tables or in their cases while a keyboard stood near the fireplace.

"You know," he said, leading me through the dining room, "Mal should put in his job ads that one of the perks of being his deputy is free baked goods from his mother. He'd have more applicants than he'd know what to do with."

The soft twang of his accent, although not exactly what I'd grown up with, was still soothing. Though his round face needed more chin to be truly handsome, my eyes had no complaints.

We walked into a kitchen with white walls and cupboards and dark blue counters flecked with white. Every inch of it was clean, fresh, and shining.

I set the box on the small, butcher block island. "I see you renovated the kitchen first. It's beautiful." The nautical look of white with navy blue had always appealed to me.

Houston dug into the box. "It should. Chris is a slave driver." He went back to the dining room and yelled, "Chris, Garrett, we got eats!"

Feet thudded down the stairs as I helped Houston empty the box.

"Did you go out this morning?" Chris stumbled in wearing boxers, a sleepy expression, and nothing else.

Our eyes locked for a second, then I became fascinated with the bottom of the box.

Chris muttered something like a curse. "Why didn't you tell me we had a guest?"

"Man, it's just above freezing." Houston's words were tangled in his laughter. "I figured a guy from southern California would throw on a few clothes."

"Who's here?" Garrett's sharp question came from the dining room.

"Rae Riley," Chris growled behind me.

"Dude, give us some warning."

They pounded up the stairs.

"Contrary to present circumstances, we don't usually walk around naked when we're off duty." Houston lifted a pot off the coffee maker. "Want some?"

"No, thanks. I don't like coffee. And I can't stay. I'm opening the library branch in Barton this morning."

"You grew up in the South, didn't you?" He poured himself a cup. "I can hear it in your voice. But not Texas. Where?"

"West Virginia, Virginia, Kentucky, Tennessee, North Carolina, South Carolina, and Missouri—those are the places I remember."

"Did your mom have to move so much for her job?"

No, we moved because she was terrified her attacker would figure out she hadn't died in the fire and come after us. I shrugged. "Mom wanted to move around."

Wearing t-shirts and sweatpants, Chris and Garrett joined us.

"Sorry." Chris picked up the cookie tin and fixed his attention on that.

"No harm done," I said in my most reassuring tone.

Houston took a long sip. "Except she's got PTSD now."

Chris threw him a resentful scowl, and with his fierce features, it looked downright murderous.

"These are still warm." Garrett sank his teeth into a scone.

"This is for your birthday, Garrett." I pointed to the apple pie on the island. "From Gram."

A crumb fell from his lip. "How'd she know my birthday was this week?" He rattled off the question like Gram was a suspect.

"I don't know. She said she makes treats for everyone in county law enforcement on their birthdays. Maybe Mal knows."

"No. The town cops and the county cops are completely separate."

Houston slapped Chris on the shoulder. "Guess that makes you the baby of this establishment."

"I'm still the landlord." Chris chanced a glance at me. "I'll be twenty-three in April. You'll be twenty-four, right, Garrett?"

"On Tuesday."

"I hope now" — Houston's accent become more obvious — "y'all recognize that as the oldest, I have the experience and wisdom you all sorely need. You can rely on me to freely dispense both."

Garrett opened his hazel eyes wide. "Wow, Chris. We're so lucky. Look what we have to look forward to when we're twenty-five."

I checked the time on my phone. I couldn't stay much longer. But I wanted to. Listening to Houston's tenor drawl, Garrett's staccato tones, and Chris's bass rumbles was like enjoying a tune played by jazz musicians, each one improvising off the other.

I wanted to make it a quartet. "Did you buy the bass, Chris?"

"Yeah. It's actually a good guitar, like the ad said."

"You wouldn't know it from the way you play it," Garrett said around a mouthful of apple bread.

"I just need to practice."

Houston refilled his cup. "Fortunately, playing a guitar so it screams like a dying cat is not a crime in Marlin County."

"But singing like one should be." Chris said this in the same composed voice he used when we talked at the library, but he slid me the briefest of ornery looks.

"I gotta go." I sighed.

"How come?" said Garrett.

Tugging on my gloves, I explained I was working, and the guys walked me to the foyer. We passed the instruments in the living room.

Houston swung open the door. "Tell your grandmother we accept any and all donations in carbohydrate form."

"The higher the calories, the better," Garrett added.

"Could you use a drummer?" The question burst out of me like a grenade.

If they'd been dogs, their ears would have pricked to attention.

"I played in high school — in marching band and jazz band. I'm pretty rusty, and I don't have my own trap set, but our church has a praise band with a set. Maybe I could borrow it when they aren't practicing." I ended on a pleading squeak.

Chris smoothed his moustache. "We need a drummer."

Sliding his hands into his back pockets, Houston stared over my head. "I might be able to locate a set. I know a lot of local musicians." He lowered his gaze to me. "You check on the one at your church, and I'll see what I can find out."

I smiled without effort. "For sure. I'll text you if I can borrow it."

The four of us exchanged numbers.

My smile lasted all the way to the truck. Why? We were just jamming together. It wasn't like any of the guys had acted interested in me. Since I was taller than Chris and Garrett, Houston was the only one I had any chance with. Guys in high school seemed to lose interest like a preschooler in church when they realized I could look down on them.

The ignition caught the first time, and I had depressed the clutch when Garrett tapped on my window. I cranked it down.

"Tell your — what do you call Mrs. Malinowski?"

"Gram."

"Tell your gram thanks for the pie." Garrett's knife-blade face turned thoughtful. "If you call your grandmother 'Gram,' why don't you call Mal 'Dad'?"

My heart sagged. "I--I don't know. Gram told me I could call her that. Mal hasn't said anything."

"Oh." Garret drew back. "Sorry. That was none of my business." He tucked his hands under his armpits. "I guess it's my police training. When I've got questions, I just start asking and can't give up until I get some sort of an answer."

Like a terrier digging in and nosing around. A good quality in a cop, but not in casual conversation. I shifted into reverse. "Enjoy the pie."

His question hung in my mind, like the fog, as I drove over and around hills to Barton. Why hadn't Mal said I could call him "Dad" when he liked me so much?

My heart collapsed in on itself, and my breath came short.

It didn't make sense.

Chapter 10

Wednesday night, my backpack bouncing against my back, I limped through the puddles that now made up Mrs. Blaney's yard.

Still no photo for Mal's gift after I'd spent my whole day off Monday and all of this morning, before my shift started at noon, driving around Marlin County, taking pictures. The only thing I'd gained was a sore ankle from falling off a rock outcrop while getting a shot of a cardinal. If I had a zoom lens, I wouldn't have had to crawl so far out. At least my ankle was the only real casualty. My camera escaped with just a tiny scratch on the rim of the lens.

Maybe I should choose an old photo, like my favorite beach in North Carolina. Mounting the steps, I held both railings to take some weight off my ankle. I had to pick something soon so I could get it printed and buy an appropriate mat and frame.

As I opened the screen door, a white sheet of paper fluttered onto the sopping wet doormat. I bent over. What was Mrs. Blaney complaining about now? She had no right to ride me about anything when she hadn't bothered to fix the leaky window in my bathroom and I'd been telling her for over —

My fingers curled above the paper, my lungs constricting. I snatched it up, shoved the key in the lock, and dashed inside the apartment.

Pressing against the locked door, I gulped for air. I turned on the light in the kitchen. Trembling, I unfolded the paper.

LEAVE BEFORE YOU RUIN YOUR FAMILY, BELLA.

He'd been at my door. He'd come to my apartment and touched my door.

For the first time since I'd moved in in June, the one room that made up most of my apartment seemed huge, like every shadowy corner hid an army of stalkers. I switched on my lamp and the overhead light, despite the glare. Lifting the urn with Mom's ashes from the spool I used as a coffee table, I pushed it against my door.

Gasping, I sat on the spool.

Father, what am I going to do? How can I sleep tonight?

I drew in a long, quivering breath. Then another.

Help me think, Father. What should I do?

What facts did I have? Focus on those, like when I was researching Terry O'Neil, Jason Carlisle, and Mal to see which one of them was my father and if one of them had attacked my mom.

The first note had been mailed last Thursday. The second one on Monday. The third one had been left on my truck on Friday. Now, it was Wednesday night and this one showed up at my door. Was there a pattern? In the first two notes, he'd called me Rae. In the last two, Bella. A sure sign he thought I was just like my mom.

Resting my elbows on my knees, I held my head in my hands. He was getting bolder, but not all that much. He left the fourth note when it was obvious I wasn't at home. If my truck wasn't parked on the street beside my landlady's house, then the stalker knew he was safe approaching my door. I hadn't been home since yesterday morning, sleeping over at the farm because I didn't have to be at work until noon today. He could have stuck it in the door at any time between when I left Tuesday morning and now.

My phone rang. I launched off the spool. My heart drumming in cut time, I swiped to answer.

"Sorry to bother you." Mal's baritone boomed, and I pulled the phone away. "But I thought you said you'd call me."

"I -- I forgot."

"Rae, what's wrong?" Concern made the question sharp.

I dragged in a deep breath and pursed my lips, slowing its release. How could he know just from my tone? Did he have some sixth sense because he was my dad?

My gaze slid to the note on the spool. Had the stalker committed a crime yet? The notes were nasty but not exactly threatening. And what would Mal think of his new daughter attracting trouble? Everything was going so great. My dad liked me, the rest of the family liked me. I didn't want to make them regret welcoming me into their lives.

"Nothing. I'm fine. I'll see you tomorrow."

"Good." The concern released its grip on his voice. "Take care."

We clicked off.

I took the second and third notes from a kitchen drawer, picked up the latest one from the spool, and spread all three of them on the card table. Whoever it was wasn't giving up. I couldn't just ride this out.

Opening another drawer, I removed a worn black-and-white notebook and sat at the table.

Since I'd figured out who my father was and who tried to murder my mother, I could solve this mystery. I'd use the same approach. First, I'd check old newspapers for clues. In this case, a divorce or broken engagement could signal someone my mom had hurt, someone who held a grudge. Even an arrest could mean that, if someone blamed Mom for it. Second, trawling through local social media sites, looking for hostile comments toward me and Mom or ones that used the same words in the notes. Third, talking to people, seeing if I could figure out if someone's friendliness was an act or if they could lead me toward other men Mom had been involved with.

On the first clean sheet of paper, I wrote down the dates and the words of all four notes, how they were delivered and when the stalker had opportunity to leave them. On the next page, I began to write "Suspects," but scratched it out and moved four pages ahead.

I'd need more pages for the notes.

Because there would be more.

Chapter 11

The next morning, yawning, I lifted my camera from the card table and wrapped it in its towel. Between staying up late to do research and trouble falling asleep, the yawns kept on coming.

Stepping onto the tiny landing, I looked for another note, but I didn't really expect one. My truck parked on the street sent an unmistakable message that I was home. Was there a way to hide my phone so I could get a video of the creep if he left a note at my door again? The landing wasn't big enough for me to set anything on it to camouflage it.

I descended the stairs. My garbage can and Mrs. Blaney's sat under them. Could I hide my phone here? I might get a glimpse of a face through the steps, but I might not. The bare trees and bushes near the stairs wouldn't hide a sparrow. Even if I did hide my phone, my battery wouldn't last all night with the video function running.

I kicked the bottom step, then limped over to my truck. There had to be a way.

The ignition caught the first time, but the gear shift had gone on strike, refusing to move as if actual shifting was a dangerous demand that needed to be negotiated.

Perfect. I ripped the key out. I'd either have to fix it on my lunch break or after work or call Mal or Gram for a ride. Growling, I slammed out of the Rust Bucket, shouldered my backpack, and headed up Woodward Avenue. Despite icing it most of the night, my ankle hadn't improved much.

The sky had turned a pearly gray so smooth I couldn't detect any contours of the clouds, the pale color taunting me with the hope that the sun might break through at any minute. Trying not to favor my ankle, I inhaled the cold, clammy air. Now that I had a plan, last night's terror seemed ridiculous. I wasn't going to just take it. I was going to solve this mystery. Then, if the notes constituted a crime, Mal would only have to arrest the guy. Or girl.

A blast from a horn spun me around. A rusty red truck that appeared older than Gram slid up to me.

"What're you walkin' for?" Egypt leaned over the steering wheel to look past China, who studied her scarlet nails as if they had to be more interesting than me. "Car break down?"

"Yeah." Why wasn't China in school? I quickened my pace as much as my ankle let me.

"Wanna lift?" said Egypt.

"Gyp, do you really think Rae would soil herself with outlaws like us?" China did an excellent job of sounding astonished while letting on she wasn't astonished at all. "What would her daddy say?"

I skirted a crumbling island of snow on the sidewalk, my focus straight ahead.

"Is that it?" Egypt shouted. "You're too good to sit in my truck?"

It's just noise. Just like the blast from the horn and the wheeze of the engine. Noise that didn't need a response.

"She's not too good to be rude to us," China said in a fake, chipper voice.

"Don't you walk away!" Egypt gunned the engine.

A different horn honked.

My cousin's truck slammed to a halt.

Wheeling around, I brought up my arms in the protective position I'd learned in self-defense classes at my high school.

Egypt banged out of her truck, screaming at the car behind her. It pulled around her and turned onto Main Street. I hurried on, crossed under the light, and had reached the curb in front of the library before my cousins' truck roared by, the right wheels digging into a cinder-clogged drift. Dirty pellets of ice sprayed me, hitting me from ankle to face.

Wiping the cold moisture and gravel from my cheek, I surveyed the damage. My black leggings hid most of the dirt, but my jean jacket looked like I'd hand-applied mud clods for artistic effect.

I blew out my cheeks. At least my camera was safe.

In the employees' bathroom, I wetted a paper towel and cleaned the side of my face.

Egypt and China were already on my list of suspects, but maybe Egypt shouldn't have been. She was so hot-tempered I couldn't imagine her doing something as calculating and sneaky as writing anonymous notes and planting them.

Unless China put her up to it.

My shoulders drooping, I gripped the sink with both hands.

I wouldn't put anything past China.

~~~~~

Chewing a bit of Gram's pepperoni roll, I scrolled through a twenty-four-year-old edition of *The Marlin County Recorder* on the microfilm viewer, looking for some event to link my mom to current citizens.

Resting against the back of the hard, wooden chair, I rubbed my eyes. After Mal met me to fix my truck during my lunch break, I only had twenty minutes for research. I'd read one newspaper and was halfway through the second and still had found nothing. If it took me ten minutes
~~~~~

to go through each edition, and there were six editions each week, and Mom lived in the county for four years ... I pressed my palms into my eyes. A story problem. My least favorite part of my least favorite subject.

"Why'd you eat your lunch in here?" Devon stopped with a book cart at the door to the local history room.

I tugged at my earlobe. I didn't want to lie to a friend. "I'm doing research to figure out why some people don't like me because of my mom. Like Jill." That was the truth, just not all of it.

"Those kinds of grudges don't make the paper." She shrugged. "Just ask them."

My eyebrows lifted. "Ask them?"

"Why not? If they have no problem being rude, they should have no problem with you calling them on it. They might not give you the truth, but at least they'll know that you know they're being ... since you're a Christian, I'll say 'jerks'."

Bringing it all out in the open seemed like a good idea, although I doubted the stalker was one of the people who had no hesitation showing his dislike of me. "I don't know if I could confront Jill. I can't afford to lose my job."

"Jill isn't dumb enough to try to get you fired when Barb and Jason are in your corner."

"But Mrs. O'Neil is in hers."

"I'd still call people on it."

Of course she would. Devon wasn't afraid of anything. She never backed down from Barb or Jill when she thought they were out of line, or from an angry patron demanding "justice" or his rights or something.

Fingering the studs along her ear, she said, "I'm working Saturday. Can you watch the girls?"

"For sure." I turned in the chair. "Would they like to come out to the farm? There's lots they can do. Aaron and Micah are about their ages. I'll drive them out and bring them back when you're done here."

An impatient frown creased her face. "If you want to hang out with your family, just say so."

"I, uh ... no." Where'd that come from? "That's not why I want to take the girls out there. I just thought they'd have fun, something different from your apartment."

Devon's frown turned thoughtful. My muscles tightened for one of her blunt opinions.

"I know your dad's been really good to you. I was impressed at how he answered Mrs. O'Neil's nasty questions. He didn't make excuses or try to dress up the truth. Just the facts." A grim smile came and went. "Like he was reading one of his reports."

Fiddling with the edge of my sweater, I waited. Where was this going?

"But I've had some bad dealings with cops. I don't want my girls around them."

My muscles went as slack as my jaw. "But--but--but a few bad cops don't mean they're all bad. Mal isn't."

"You only know his personal side, Rae. You don't know what he's like on the job. He's worked his way up to sheriff. He didn't get there by being sensitive and cuddly."

"Actually, he got there by two votes."

Her eyes took on that fiery look. "The girls aren't going to your farm." Her tone softened an ounce. "I don't want to offend you. You're a good friend, Rae. I can't tell you know much I appreciate you watching the girls for free on the Saturdays I work. Liberty gets so scared staying in the apartment without an adult, and Serenity—" her voice soured "—might burn down the whole building."

"They're great kids. I like watching them." I knew exactly how Liberty felt. Many, many weekends I had spent alone when Mom had a job that didn't allow her to bring me along. I hated those endless days when every minute was as long as the first day of school.

"Thanks, Rae." Her expression relaxed. "It's a serious burden off my mind to know I don't have to leave my girls alone."

After Devon left, I scrolled at a snail's pace through the next newspaper edition, but I didn't read the articles. What kind of trouble had she had with cops? Nothing in Wellesville since I'd known her. She would have said something to me if the local cops had harassed her or her daughters. Devon had mentioned moving around the country as the girls' late father looked for work as an artist. Maybe they'd run into trouble because of their unconventional lifestyle.

Or maybe she clashed with racist cops because the girls were half Native American and their dad was fully one. She had said she and Shayne never knew when someone would take offence to his ethnicity. Was that what she meant?

But that had nothing to do with Mal. Devon always seemed so sensible, down to earth. Something really bad must have happened to give her such a blind spot.

The clock in the local history room told me I only had a few minutes left to my lunchbreak. Better rewind the film and put it back.

As I reached for the knob, a headline caught my eye: "Woman Stabbed at Illegal Party."

A lot of parties had been held at the abandoned children's home, making all of them illegal, and Mom had used the home as her unofficial rendezvous with her boyfriends.

"Phoenix Moore, 24, was found stabbed in the woods during an illegal party held at the closed Marlin County Children's Home on St. Rt. 15 Saturday night. She was rushed to Good Samaritan Hospital in Zanesville by Sean Ross, 37, and Bella Rydell, 21. Mr. Ross and Miss Rydell say they discovered Miss Moore alone behind the home and saw no one in the vicinity. Miss Moore remains in critical condition. Sheriff Seaver is questioning everyone who attended the party. If anyone has any information concerning this crime, please contact the sheriff's office."

On my phone, I noted the date of the article. It happened twenty-four years ago, in the fall, so Mom had lived in the county about a year. I'd have to dig through later editions and find out if the crime was solved or if Mom had any more involvement. If she had been responsible in some way for the stabbing, Mom would have written a note apologizing, like she had to the three men she had tried to blackmail when she found out she was pregnant. But that didn't mean somebody couldn't blame my mom and vent their anger through threatening notes.

Phoenix Moore. I couldn't remember meeting any Moores, but she could still live in the county or have family here. Sean Ross's age was odd. Why would someone that old attend an illegal party? He could drink without worrying about the cops and should have had his own place if he wanted to get high. This definitely needed more investigation.

I removed the roll of film from the spool and returned it to the appropriate drawer. As I walked to the kitchen, my phone pinged with a text from Houston.

Don't ask how all 3 of us free Sunday night got set can you come around 8ish

For sure

I put my backpack in the cupboard, then took the stairs two at a time up to the main floor. Almost skipping into the lobby, I skidded to a halt under the balcony.

What was I getting so excited about? I was just jamming with three guys. Three cute guys, but that didn't mean anything. Actually, two cute guys and one— well, Chris's face was too fierce to call it cute. But it was handsome. Very handsome.

"Isn't your lunch break over?" Jill snapped at me, pushing a book cart.

"Yes, ma'am. I'm heading for the checkout desk right now." I looked past her and froze.

Jill didn't seem to notice and went on.

Terry O'Neil was chatting with Leandra Hamilton as she passed book after book under the scanner.

I hadn't seen him since Christmas morning when we figured out his blood type prevented him from being my father. And when he told me that even if he was my father, he couldn't acknowledge me.

Act like nothing happened. Sauntering to the desk, I smiled at Terry.

He jerked, like the book he touched held an electric charge, making his bearded cheeks shake. Then he thanked Leandra, slapped his driving cap over his bald head, tucked his stack of books under his arm, and left as if he'd realized he was late for an appointment.

Glancing at the two patrons reading magazines by the fire, Leandra stepped over to me and said in a lowered voice, "I thought he'd talk about movies with you. He always made it a point to chat if you were working."

Studying the hold shelf, I shrugged. "Guess he doesn't want to anymore."

"I bet it's his wife." Leandra whispered, "She seems to think if Professor O'Neil talks to any woman, he's flirting with her. She probably scared him out of talking to you. She scares me."

Scared him out of … from what I'd learned about Terry O'Neil while determining if he was my father or Mom's attacker — that he would hide affairs from his wife and allow her to bully him — he had the perfect personality to be a stalker who wanted to terrorize me and protect himself from discovery as much as possible. And he had the perfect motive. At the children's home, he said if I told anyone he was involved with my mother, he'd say I was lying. But maybe he was afraid I'd talk and people would believe me. Scaring me out of the county could give him protection.

"Does Mrs. O'Neil scare you?"

Leandra's question jarred me out of my analysis. "Yeah" — I stretched out the word, hating to admit it — "she does."

"When I first started working here, I thought she was racist because she was so rude to me. But then I noticed she acts that way with everybody."

"No, she is racist."

Her big brown eyes flew open. "Really?"

"Mrs. O'Neil hates the whole human race."

Leandra stared, then burst into giggles.

Chapter 12

After work, with a powerful puff, I blew a strand of hair off my lips and rolled up to a sitting position on the wood floor of the playroom.

I was related to the biggest hams on the planet.

"How's this, Rae?" Micah gave me a grin that threatened to reach his ears.

"You don't have to smile, Micah. Just play, and I'll take some candid shots."

"What does that mean?" He set aside the plastic brick truck he'd partially built. "Candid?"

"Well, when it comes to photos, it means pictures that aren't posed. The ones I just happen to take."

Aaron hooked a bungee cord to his latest fiendish device. "You told us you were taking pictures of us doing something we like for Dad's birthday gift. So you're telling us how to pose."

"But I don't want it to look that way." I dragged my fingers through my hair. "Pretend I'm not here. Don't look at the camera."

Why was it so hard for little kids to smile naturally? The associate pastor's twin preschoolers were like that. I took hundreds of photos of them while I roomed with the family after Mom died. The best ones were when they didn't notice the camera on them.

"Like this, Rae?" His head bent, Micah snapped a brick onto his truck.

"Perfect." I laid on my side and aimed up.

He really was adorable with his pink cheeks and sweet smile that was only sweet as long as he didn't try to smile.

I clicked as fast as I could. Any distraction could make him start posing again. I sat up, checking the images. "These look good, Micah."

He grinned, totally natural. And if I lifted my camera to capture it, it'd be gone.

"Let me see." Aaron reached over my shoulder for my camera.

I jerked it away. "Don't touch my camera. My mom gave it to me, and I don't let people handle it. I need to get shots of Rusty writing. I'll show you later."

"My mom loved me so much she made me a blanket." Micah peered at a pile of bricks. "I let people touch it."

"A blanket isn't as fragile as a camera." A sad smile twisted my mouth. As hard as it was to lose Mom at seventeen, at least I'd known her.

Aaron had been two and Micah had been just nine days old when their mom died in a car crash. They had to rely on photos, videos, and other people's memories to have any chance of knowing her.

The aroma of cooking garlic reached us, and I followed the smell into the kitchen.

Gram opened the oven, and steam infused with the garlic enveloped the room.

"What's for supper?" I scrolled through photos on my camera.

"Tandoori chicken." Gram closed the door to the bottom oven and opened the one to the small top oven.

"I've never heard of it."

"It's an Indian dish. It's one of my favorites. Mal's too." She flipped a flatbread frying in a skillet. "Although just about any dish is Mal's favorite. He's the only one of my kids who wasn't a picky eater when he was little."

I set my camera on the counter. "Can you tell Rusty it's okay if I take his photo?"

Couldn't catch a break and have one brother who was a good subject. No, two mugged for me, and the third acted like he was afraid my camera would steal his soul.

"He said he hates pictures of himself," I said. "Why? He's a really good-looking kid. I'd probably have a crush on him if I was in his grade. And not his sister."

Gram lifted a lid from a small saucepan. "In the past six months, Rusty's grown much more self-conscious. Did you tell him the photo's a gift for Mal?"

"Yeah. He told me to use one I took of him at Christmas. But I want to take a picture of him writing. I don't have one like that."

"Your idea for a gift is wonderful." She opened the door to the bottom oven again. "But I think that would be a better gift for Father's Day. Mal would prefer your first gift to be just about you."

A sigh slumped me against the fridge. "I don't have any other ideas. I spent all day Monday and yesterday morning, taking photos, trying to come up with an idea. Since Mal likes to fish, I thought a nature picture might work. I got a lot of shots, but nothing that seems right for a first gift to my father."

"Dad'll probably like whatever you give him." Rusty leaned against the counter separating the kitchen from the living-dining room, a notebook and pencil in his hands. "Micah gave him a crumpled piece of paper with scribbles all over it for Father's Day last year, and he almost got choked up." He lowered his voice. "Could I show you something, Rae?"

Odd. He sounded so serious.

I nodded, and he led me to the couch and handed me several sheets of notebook paper. "I wrote a fight," he whispered. "I--I--I wondered if you'd like to read it." He shoved the sheets at me.

Taking them, I tried to cover my surprise. "For sure. Is this the duel in the abandoned building?"

He shook his head. "I'll use that for another scene, but that picture of the children's home and how it looked like a mouth — I couldn't get it out of my mind." Eagerness pitched his newly deepened voice higher. "I thought about a warrior fighting a ginormous creature and almost getting swallowed, but he's able to stay in its mouth. The mouth is opening and closing, and he's battling to get out."

My eyes widened. "I've never read anything like that. Or seen it in a movie. Very original."

A shy smile eased onto Rusty's thin face.

As I read the first page, a surge of excitement made it hard to sit still. Rusty and I were finally figuring each other out.

His cursive writing was difficult to decipher in spots, and the fight seemed to have a lot of repeated moves but ... my half-brother hovered just within my peripheral vision.

I shuffled the sheets together. "It's really good. Lots of action. And good descriptions. I felt like I was inside the mouth of the--the—" I glanced at the top page " —levyrn."

"Aunt Jeanine said that should be my goal—making people feel like they're living the story." His face seemed to grow longer as it became concerned. "Do you have any suggestions on how to improve it?"

His tone implied that he didn't want any suggestions, but I got that. I found it hard to take criticism of my photos. I tugged at my earlobe. Had to be careful. "I think you can add more description about how awful it smells, like the guy's trying not to hurl as he jabs his sword into the thing's mouth."

Inspiration lit his blue eyes. "Instead of fighting his way out, he could throw up, and the taste is so disgusting, the levyrn spits him out." He flipped over a sheet of paper and began writing fast.

"Anytime you want me to read something, I'll be glad to."

He gave a single nod, scribbling faster.

Gram cocked an ear toward the back door. "Your dad's pulled in. Rusty, get the boys. Rae, would you help me?" She had to ask Rusty twice before he could tear himself away from his writing.

I took glasses of water to the table, and Mal trudged in the back door.

"Hey, Ma. Am I late?"

"No." She smiled up at him. "Just in time." Her smile faded. "Rough day?"

Reentering the kitchen, I studied Mal. He only looked a little tired to me. But I hadn't known him all his life.

Mal rubbed his forehead. "Had a long meeting with Simcox. Not the easiest man to work with."

"I've heard he's still mad about losing the election." I picked up glasses of milk.

Mal broke into that big grin that seemed reserved especially for me. "How's my girl?"

I grinned back. "Fine."

Taking off the heavy coat that went with his uniform, Mal said, "Who did you hear that from? About Simcox and the election?"

"Anyone in the county could have told her." Gram placed pieces of chicken, deep orange from the spices coating them, on a serving platter. The aroma flooded the kitchen.

"Don't pay attention to gossip, Rae," Mal said.

Gram lifted the platter. "It's not gossip when it's true, sweetie."

After we finished eating, Gram went to the screened porch and pulled on her long, tan duster, which seemed a better fit for a cowboy, to go down to the barn.

"Would you like some help?" I said, stooping to my boots.

"No." Gram stomped her foot into her boot, then smiled up at me. "But I'd love some company." She covered her long, white-streaked gray hair with a dilapidated, broad-brimmed hat.

The thick cloud cover didn't let a glimmer of starlight through, but we didn't carry a flashlight. Gram could easily find her way down the drive in the dark. The air was so humid we might as well have been swimming through an icy pool to the barn.

Once inside, Gram flipped on the light switch, and the fourteen alpacas hummed and pawed their straw bedding to greet us. Their fluffy heads and big, soft eyes made them look like they were designed by kindergartners. Horace, the guard llama, looked down his long nose at us.

"I've been doing research." I followed Gram to small hay bales stacked in a corner. "Reading old newspapers, trying to figure out why some people don't like me because I'm Bella Rydell's daughter."

She picked up what she called a flake of hay. "I heard a lot of stories about your mom. But I didn't know her personally. I can't know if the stories were true, rumors, or lies." She shoved the flake into the manger for the females.

"I read an article about a stabbing at the children's home. Phoenix Moore was the victim. My mom and a guy found her lying outside the home and drove her to the hospital." I filled a scoop of grain from a bag.

Gram stared over the heads of the milling alpacas. "I sort of remember a stabbing. That seems like a century ago."

"Is Phoenix Moore related to anyone living here now?"

"I can't remember. I have a feeling she belonged to one of the old families. Maybe the Cervellis?" She shook her head. "Would you get the hose?"

Smothering a yawn, I poured the grain in the trough and unwound the hose from the holder on the wall. "Do you know of a connection between my mom and Jill Cerda, the assistant director at the library? She's been really hostile since she found out who my mom was."

Gram adjusted her beaded bracelet. "I only know Jill to see her. She wasn't raised here. She moved into the county when her husband got a job at the high school."

"How about Sean Ross? He might have been a friend of my mom's. Maybe a boyfriend."

"That doesn't ring a bell at all."

Covering another yawn, I stuck the hose in a bucket wired to the wall of the females' stall.

Patting the puffball head of the black alpaca Onyx, Gram said, "Do you want to sleep here tonight? I know Tuesdays and the weekend are your usual nights, but you seem really tired. You can stay any night you want."

"I didn't bring any pajamas or anything, and I've got to be at the library by 8:30." An image of my empty, dark apartment leaped into my mind, and my stomach took a sick twist. "But I didn't sleep well last night. I'll see if I can catch up here tonight. I'll just get up early."

Gram took my hands in hers. "If people's attitudes are bothering you, pray for them. Pray God softens their hearts so they can see how wrong they are. Pray God strengthens yours so they can't hurt you."

She hugged me, and I returned it.

Before I went to bed on the air mattress beside the half-moon window, I gazed into the velvet darkness of the country night, my lined face reflecting back to me.

Father, make the stalker stop. Or help me figure out who it is. I don't want Mal or anybody in the family ever to wish they hadn't welcomed me into their home.

Chapter 13

Sunday night, I whipped my truck around on the one-and-a-half lane road. The rain pelting my windshield had made me miss the turn. I spotted the charred stump that marked the road to Chris's house. My left leg bounced like a rabbit in spring as the truck ground onto the crumbling pavement.

Why was I so excited? In my whole life, the only real friend I'd ever made was Devon. I was just one of those people who had no talent for friendship. Why would this be different? I'd have a good time playing music with some guys and that was it.

I planted my left foot against the mat, driving between the concrete posts that leaned on either side of Chris's drive, and the old Victorian house appeared out of the rain and the night.

As beat up as it was, it should have looked even scarier in this weather. But with almost all the windows lit, the house seemed cheerful, like a poor person who had put his best effort into sprucing up for a party.

I parked at the end of the long line of police and civilian vehicles. Anybody driving by might think the place was getting raided. A giggle escaped, surprising me.

Pressing my lips together, I slid out of the truck with my backpack. I had to bring down my mood and my expectations.

Lowering my head, I dashed and splashed through the yard to the worn porch.

Garrett opened the door. "Glad your schedule worked with ours."

"Me too."

Inside the bare foyer, he pointed into the dining room. "Hang your coat and backpack on a chair."

As I draped my jacket and vest over one of the elaborately carved chairs, Houston ambled in from the kitchen. "Hey, Rae." He held up a can. "Beer?"

"Uh, no." I ran a hand through my damp hair. "I'm nineteen."

Chris appeared in the foyer. "Good job, Houston. If she'd said yes, I'd have to arrest you both."

"You'd never take me alive." Houston looked to me. "Coffee? Soda?"

"That's pop here in Ohio," said Garrett.

"I refuse to turn my back on my Texas roots."

I took my drumsticks from my backpack. "Soda'd be great, especially if it's got caffeine."

In the living room, a fire snapped and popped in a large fireplace. On the heavy stone mantle was a photo of an elderly man with thinning, white hair and the mildest blue eyes I'd ever seen. A little boy, around five years old, sat in his lap. Even at that age, Chris looked fierce, like he'd take out anybody who messed with his grandpa.

"This is your great-grandfather, isn't it, Chris?" I touched the smooth wood frame.

Sitting down in a camp chair, Chris broke into one of his rare smiles that lasted all of a half-second. "Yes. I was in kindergarten then." He picked up his bass and began strumming.

"Gram says she remembers you. She said you and — it's Dave, right? — Dave Kincaid went everywhere together."

His smile came back, sadder than before. "Yeah, we did."

I examined the drum set the guys had placed in a bumped-out bay. It had a lot of wear on it, scratches in the finish on the drums, tarnish on the cymbals. But it looked pristine compared to the set my high school had provided.

"Tyler — he's the guy letting me borrow this set — he loaned me some sticks." Houston handed me a Coke.

I took the can and held up my sticks. "Still had a pair." I placed the can on the floor. Then I thumped the bass, rolled on the snare, and all my preferences for the positions of the instrument came racing back to me. And I hadn't thought about drumming since I'd hit the last beat at my senior concert almost two years ago. Old habits die hard.

Taking his place behind a keyboard, Garrett said, "Is Rae short for something?"

"No." I moved the hi-hat an inch closer. "Mom said I was her ray of hope. So that's what she named me."

His hazel eyes widened. "Your middle name is 'Ofhope'?"

"Just Hope. Rae Hope Riley. I suppose — " I tilted one of the tom-toms another degree " — Mom could have gone with 'Ofhope.' It'd be unique."

His electric guitar in his lap, Houston said, "Before we get started, I gotta ask you a crucial question." His expression grew serious. "Do you like the music coming out of Nashville now?"

Garrett watched me, but Chris settled back in his chair, still strumming.

"I'm not a big country music fan." Actually, barely at all.

"Does that you mean you like some of it?"

"Well ... I don't mind playing it if that's what y'all like."

"We will not ask you to make that sacrifice." Houston held up a long, thin hand. "If you truly hate modern country music, you may join the Fellowship of Country Music Loathers."

"United," Chris and Garrett said.

I grinned. "Do I have to be initiated?"

Houston nodded. "Turn toward Nashville and spit three times."

"What kind of music do you like?" said Garrett.

"Almost anything except rap and country. Although," I scooted back the stool, "I do like some old country. Grandpa Willis liked Charlie Daniels. Mom and I rented a house from a man named Barrett Willis in West Virginia, and he was so nice he let me call him Grandpa. I've heard a lot of Charlie Daniels."

Garrett's eyes grew big, and Chris quit strumming. Houston murmured, "This is too weird."

Had I just made a big mistake? I gulped and said, "But I didn't mean we had to play country music like that."

"No, that's the kind we like to play," said Chris. "It's freaky that you're familiar with outlaw country. A lot of country music fans aren't."

Garrett shook his head. "It must be fate."

"It's got to be. Country music now," Houston said, his tenor voice dropping low with disgust, "is as processed as cheese dip. No character, no art. They compose bland music with bland lyrics because music producers think that will sell the most."

"You've got to admit," Garrett said. "It's popular."

"So are cheese puffs, but you shouldn't have a steady diet of them." Houston's smooth comeback made me assume the guys had had this argument before.

Garrett pressed buttons on his keyboard. "And yes, we do see the irony of being in law enforcement and liking outlaw country."

I played a rimshot.

"In Rae's honor, let's play 'The Legend of Wooley Swamp' by the Charlie Daniels Band." Garrett flipped a switch. "I'd suggest 'The Devil Went Down to Georgia,' but none of us play violin."

"Fiddle." Houston stood, pushing his chair aside. "This is outlaw country. Not Mozart."

Chris led off on the bass, then Houston and Garrett joined him. I listened for several bars before I tried a simple rhythm. But as my hands grew comfortable with the sticks, I complicated the beat. My hair enjoyed the rhythm and danced into my mouth. Chris announced we were near the end, and I added a roll.

The next song Houston suggested was one Grandpa Willis had played many times on his CD player, and I fell into a rhythm easily. My hair had fun with this one, too, and bounced into my eyes. Just like it did in band class when I was dumb enough to play with my hair loose.

Ending the song with a cymbal crash, I said, "I have to get a scrunchy."

As I went into the dining room and rummaged in my backpack, Chris said, "You know, we're a lot better than I thought. All we needed was a drummer to hold us together."

My heart beat in a triplet as I pulled my hair back.

With Houston as lead singer, we played song after song, each growing easier than the last as I dredged up techniques I'd forgotten I'd learned. Then we took a break and played favorite songs from our playlists. I had some really obscure ones the guys might have thought were just too strange. How many people have even heard of "St. Matthew" by The Monkees? So I chose two songs by Mumford and Sons. Houston played some Johnny Cash, and Garrett selected songs by Bruno Mars, possibly for the sole reason of relishing how Houston made puking sounds as an expression of his opinion of them.

Then Chris said, "I'm more of an instrumentalist." He played two tunes, no singing, by a Celtic band from Ohio named Lone Raven. The first was fast-paced, like a jig, but the second had the mournful sound that was unique to Celtic music. As the last note died away, the fire hissed, and the rain drummed on, like it hadn't seen the cut off.

Chris stretched. "I need a break." He set his bass aside. "Rae, would you like a tour?" He sounded almost shy and glanced at me and away.

This was new. Chris always appeared so quietly confident when we talked at the library.

I laid my sticks on the head of the snare. "I'd love to. I love old houses. I guess I'm nosy."

A smile came and went beneath his black moustache. "You're not nosy if you've been invited."

"Have mercy on the girl and don't show her my room." Houston gathered up his can and an empty bag of popcorn.

"Mine's not fit for human eyes either," Garrett said over his shoulder, heading toward the back of the house.

Except for the kitchen, most of the rooms were the same strange combination of heavy, antique wood furniture and camping gear, like folding chairs and tables.

Leading me up the massive stairs, Chris said, "I'm taking my time fixing up the place. I want to do it right."

We stopped at the second floor, but the stairs wound higher.

I craned my neck. "Is the third floor finished?"

"Not really. I hung dry wall in one section. We put exercise equipment up there."

Chris held open a door across from the stairs. The large room was furnished like a real bedroom with an antique chest of drawers and wood nightstands and a double bed, all stained a honey color. A section of the room was five-sided with three windows.

"That's the turret, isn't it? That sits on top of the porch." I followed Chris to the windows, and we looked out on the vehicles, rain streaking the glass. "When I came the first time, I noticed the turret right away."

"This has always been my room. Houston picked Grandpa's, and Garrett chose one of the two bedrooms at the back."

As we passed his desk, I noticed another photo of Chris and his great-grandfather. Chris was even younger, maybe three. He had a mop of black hair and thick eyebrows, but he was too chubby to look fierce. Funny these were his only family pictures. Unlike me, he had to know who his parents and grandparents were to tie him to his great-grandfather.

"Your grandpa must have been a great guy."

"He was." Chris stroked his moustache. "I want to fix up the place like he always wanted to. He didn't have much money when I lived with him. But he told me all kinds of stories about what the house was like when he was a kid."

"Is that why you do so much research in the local history room? So you can restore the house to the way it looked back then?"

"No. I just like history. I'm not trying to restore the house. More like salvaging what I've got, like the staircase, and making improvements."

Chris showed me the empty back bedroom and described his plans to turn a section of it into a second bathroom. Then we mounted the stairs to the third floor.

The space was about the size of Chris's bedroom, but a dormer and soaring rafters made it feel bigger. A punching bag dangled in the center of the room, and a rowing machine, a bench, and weights surrounded it.

Hanging on the only drywall in the room were daggers and swords. Ten total. Some rested in scabbards. Others were displayed next to their sheaths.

I gasped. "Are those yours?"

"Yes." His deep voice sounded proud.

"Wow." I reached for a dagger with a wavy blade. "Where'd you get them all?"

"Don't touch." He put his hand in front of mine. "I keep them sharp. I've collected them from all sorts of places. I got interested when I began studying martial arts."

"I didn't know that. Which one?"

"I've taken lessons in aikido and karate and Hungarian-style fencing. My favorite is the first one I studied, kalaripayattu."

My gaze roved over the slender blades. "I've never heard of that."

"Few people have. Kalaripayattu is an Indian martial art that not many Indians have heard of, let alone Americans. Some people think it's the oldest martial art in the world." He lifted a sword from its display hooks. "When I finish this room, I might make it a study and take the exercise equipment to the basement."

I moved toward the stairs. "I'm sure y'all will make this place look great by the time you're done."

"As much as home improvements cost," Chris said with a frown, "it may take ten years."

"Well, it'll keep you out of … you're a cop. I guess you don't worry about keeping out of trouble."

"A cop's like anybody else." He switched off the light "We can get into trouble like the rest of the population."

Chapter 14

After the tour, we started up again, performing songs and playing from our playlists until a wave of weariness hit me that even the caffeine of a second Coke couldn't fight off.

Laying aside my sticks, I sighed from my shoes. I didn't want to be the one to break up the evening. I'd had the best time of my life.

I pulled out my phone, glanced at the time, and bobbled it. 12:46! "Not good." I swiped in Mal's number.

"What's wrong?" said Chris.

"Mal likes me—hey, Mal." He'd picked up before the first ring had finished. "I'm still at Chris's house. I'll leave in a few minutes and call you when I get to the apartment."

"Sounds good."

"Talk to you later." I clicked off.

Garrett studied me, one side of his mouth turned down. "You've got a curfew?"

"No. Mal likes me to call when I get home. He said he has to get used to having an adult kid. I think it's because his wife was killed in a car accident. I'd told him I didn't think I'd be out later than midnight. I don't want him to worry."

"So he's got a phobia?" Garrett sounded confused.

"Mal's protective." I worked to keep an edge out of my voice. "His dad was murdered, his wife was killed, and he thought I was dead for twenty years. I get it. If it makes him feel better, I don't mind calling. It's not like he makes me. He always asks."

"Yeah, but sometimes his asks are orders." Houston drained his beer can.

"Maybe at work." I smiled, hoping that would prevent me from sounding defensive. "But not at home. Not with me."

Houston laid his guitar in its case. "My father worries about me so much I have to remind him I'm in law enforcement every time I talk to him."

Garrett shot Chris an aggravated look, but Chris was staring at the ceiling, thumbing the strings on his bass.

Houston went on, "My stepfather remembers, and he's been rooting for the criminals ever since."

"That's pretty dark, Houston," said Chris.

He shrugged. "It's just the truth."

"Oh, come on." Garrett crushed his can. "Stop trying to make Rae feel sorry for you. At least you have parents."

Houston's face turned to stone as he shot me a glance. "Yours can't be all that great 'cause you rarely talk about them."

I examined a thin spot on the head of the snare. The session had gone from perfect to nasty in three seconds flat.

"My parents were the best." Garrett whipped out from behind the keyboard. "They were really worried when I went into law enforcement."

Chris gave him a sidelong look. "Your parents? Don't you mean your mom? You told me your dad died when you were a little kid."

"No," I said, twisting a screw on the tom-tom, "Garrett told me they died a few years ago."

But instead of clearing the confusion from Chris's face, my comment only seemed to make it cloud more.

Garrett smacked the keyboard. "I know when my own parents died, Chris." He stormed out of the room.

Houston called after him, "Now who's trying to get Rae to feel sorry for him?"

"Back off, Houston." Chris leaned his bass against this chair.

One long stride brought Houston a little too close to Chris. "Just because you're my landlord doesn't mean you're also my boss."

"I know." The confusion had smoothed away, and Chris looked as he always did, fierce and just about impossible to read. "But we have a guest. We can poke holes in each other later."

He stepped toward the foyer. "Weren't you leaving, Rae?"

Grateful for the opening, I snatched up my sticks. "I'd better. The caffeine isn't working anymore."

"Oh, perfect, Houston." Garrett strode in, opening another beer. "You scared Rae off."

"You killed the mood."

I gathered my jacket and backpack in the dining room, and Chris opened the front door. We stepped out onto the creaky porch.

"Sorry." Chris closed the door, but Houston's and Garrett's insults came to us clearly. "Every once in a while, we get on each other's nerves. Houston's got certain issues, and Garrett knows this, and sometimes pushes his buttons." Shoving his hands in his jeans, Chris looked at the pouring rain. "Do you want to come back for another jam session?"

A pleading note seemed to underline his question. I couldn't imagine anybody with his composure ever needing to plead. Just wishful thinking.

"I'd love to. How long can you keep the drum—"

Chris's whole body snapped to attention, his black eyes thinning to slits. "I think -- I think somebody is hiding beside our cars." He ran off the porch. "Tell the guys."

My lungs balling up, I dashed into the house. Was it the stalker? What idiot would leave a threatening note on my truck when three cops were within shouting distance?

"Chris needs help!" I skidded on the scarred floor of the foyer.

Standing a few inches from each other, Houston and Garrett wheeled to face me.

"He thought he saw somebody sneaking around the cars."

In two strides, they hit sixty, almost knocking me over. I followed them onto the porch.

Houston motioned to Garrett with his right hand and then raced to the left. Garrett ran to the right end of the porch, leaped off, and the dark swallowed him.

The rain picked up tempo, pounding away like a kettle drum player searching for a beat.

I pulled on my shoulder strap. Could someone have a grudge against one of the guys? That made more sense than the stalker tailing me to a house full of cops.

Gliding between the two county SUVs, Chris detached from the night. "I didn't find anybody." He jogged up to me, running a hand through his jet black hair. "I might have been mistaken. You can believe you've seen a unicorn when it's this dark and rainy." He wiped moisture from his face. "Did the guys come out?"

"Houston went to the left of the cars, and I think Garrett is circling in from the right."

Chris hollered, "Come on back. Made a mistake." He shook his head. "But for a moment, I could swear I saw a person huddled between your truck and Garrett's car."

A thump on the porch turned us to Houston. "A mistake? In this weather?" His arms wrapped his skinny chest. "Thanks, man."

I peered into the night beyond the shafts of light projected through the windows. "Where's Garrett?"

"He's probably sulking," said Houston, and Chris repeated his shout.

His words died away under the beat of the rain.

Our gazes shifted between each other, Chris's jawline tightening, Houston's arms loosening their grip.

"Rae, you should wait inside," said Chris.

We went back into the foyer, and Chris and Houston ran up the towering staircase two steps at a time.

Don't let it be anything serious, Father.

They dashed back down, wearing winter coats and carrying guns.

Setting my backpack by the bass drum, I stepped around camp chairs and the drum set and looked out the big picture window in the bay.

If it was my stalker, and if the guys caught him, it would be all over. I wouldn't have bothered Mal at all.

I turned off the floor lamp by the fireplace, making it easier to see into the night. The Rust Bucket's bumper was the only visible part of my truck. No way to see if a note had been left on my windshield.

A door opened at the back of the house, spinning me around and into the cymbal. It hit the floor like an entire cupboard of dishes had shattered at the same second.

Bursting into the living room, Chris and Houston held their guns at shoulder level.

Choking on a scream, I flung up my hands.

Garrett appeared behind Houston. "Are you all right, Rae?"

Shoot fires, I was never going to break the law, not even the speed limit. Not if there was the slightest chance a cop would pull a gun on me.

Chris laid his gun on a chair. "Sorry, Rae. We were coming through the back door and heard the crash and thought whoever Garrett had been chasing had double-backed and come in the front."

My head bobbing like it balanced on a broken spring, I tried to take a breath, but my lungs were paralyzed.

"You can put your hands down." Garrett shook his head, droplets flying from his caramel hair.

A burn flaring on my cheeks, I lowered them. How big of a moron did I look? I didn't want to know. Opening my mouth, I said, "Are you okay, Garrett?" I sounded like I had strep throat.

"Oh, sure. I never got near the guy. I could just see him moving in and out of the trees. Then I lost him."

I cleared my throat and tried to sound like a normal human being. "Did you get a good look at him?"

"Just an outline." Garrett turned his back to the fire. "It could have been a woman. All I can say for certain is that it was a person."

"Good," said Chris. "We can rule out Bigfoot and the Mothman."

Laughter burst out of me. Gasping, I covered my mouth. It was a dumb joke, and I wanted to laugh my head off. I was way too tired.

Slipping his hands into his back pockets, Houston said, "Can y'all think of somebody who'd want to get even with one of y'all? I can't think of anything that's happened to me lately. But that doesn't mean somebody hasn't been stewing somewhere, nursing a grudge."

We grew quiet, the wind tossing rain at the house.

Garrett shook his head, while Chris smoothed his moustache.

I couldn't let them think someone was out to get them. "Somebody could be mad at me." I ran my finger around the edge of the hi-hat. "A lot of people don't like me because I'm the daughter of Bella Rydell."

Chris cocked an eyebrow. "Enough to harass you when you're

hanging out with cops?"

"But your mom hasn't lived here in twenty years." Houston's small sea green eyes widened. "Who'd hold a grudge that long?"

"People in small towns do." Sighing, I lifted my backpack. "Believe me."

"Well, I don't think the person who was here tonight was after you," said Houston. "If someone wanted to harass you, they'd have a ton of better opportunities in town."

"Unless someone really hates you." Garrett spoke quietly, almost too himself.

Chris frowned. "Nice."

"Sorry." Garrett gave me a smile that matched his apology. "Would you feel better, Rae, if you had a police escort?"

Actually, I would, especially when the three cops were so good-looking. But I'd already made a fool of myself. No reason to keep the performance going. "Thanks. I'll be all right."

"Aww, c'mon, Rae." Houston broke into a good ol' boy grin. "Let us play heroes."

That grin and his drawl stopped my air, but in a good way.

Tossing back his head, Garrett assumed a straddled, heroic stance. "Who's playing?"

I had to laugh.

With Garrett in front, and Chris and Houston behind, our four-vehicle convoy twisted its way through the hills and into Wellesville.

My mood dipping when we reached my place, I got out of my truck, climbed the stairs, and waved to them from the landing. I hated to see the evening end.

Swinging open the screen, I watched a piece of paper slide off the sill and onto my tennis shoe. My heart rocketed into light speed. He must have left it either Friday or Saturday night when he knew I was at the farm.

Forcing normal breaths, I picked up the note by one corner with my gloved fingers, unlocked my door, went in, flipped on the kitchen light, and unfolded the paper.

My heart thudded to a standstill.

YOU ARE NEVER ALONE, BELLA.

Underneath the sentence was a photo. Me, in the woods, carrying my camera. The shot was from a distance, but that was me in the middle ground.

He could have attacked me, out there in the woods. Any moment, he could have run out and done …

Grabbing Mom's urn, I shoved the spool in front of the door.

No, no, it wasn't enough. Anybody could shove aside the spool if they really wanted to get me. I pushed the spool aside. Lifting each end of the couch in turns, grunting, I pressed it against the door.

He couldn't get in now. Could he?

Trembling, I sank into a chair by the card table.

He was getting bolder.

Father, what do I do? Do I tell Mal? I don't want to be a problem, ruin all the progress I've made in getting accepted into the family.

Mal!

My fingers shaking, I swiped his number. "Sorry about the late call."

"Just as long as you're safe." Pause. "You sound out of breath."

I blew out a stream of air. "I'm fine. I'll come out for supper tomorrow. Good night." I clicked off before he could say anything else.

I tried another long exhale. Forget the threat, analyze the problem. I took off my vest and jacket, and, wrapping up in the afghan Gram gave me for Christmas, studied the photo. From my clothes, the picture must have been taken Wednesday, when I was hiking on a backpack trail in Wayne National Forest, taking photos for Mal's birthday present.

The stalker was someone who could have been out in the woods late on Wednesday morning and had an opportunity to leave the note between 8:30 a.m. Friday when I left for work and about 1:30 this morning.

After jotting those conclusions in my notebook, I searched social media for any nasty comments about Mal or me. Then I reviewed my previous research. It wasn't until dawn lit the sky that I finally collapsed on my couch.

Chapter 15

"Well, sure, Rae," said Uncle Hank. "Come on over after supper. You can get a lesson then."

"Thanks." I swiped off my phone, got the keys, and opened the library doors to a Monday morning that could have passed for any evening of the week. Rain poured at a steady, depressing rate, and the sky was so overcast I was almost grateful the library had ceiling fixtures with searchlight-intensity. Almost.

Rubbing an eye, I trudged back to the checkout desk. Only two hours of sleep would make the day last forever. My only breakthrough had come to me in the shower as I tried to wake up enough to finish getting ready: borrowing Uncle Hank's trail cam. If he let me, I could be very close to solving the Case of the Cowardly Stalker.

Mrs. O'Neil marched in, giving me a "good morning" so icy my face was in danger of freezer burn, and headed straight for the balcony steps, probably with another complaint to dump on Barb.

With all the extra people Storytime brought in, and an order from Jill to help her in the local history room, noon arrived when I still thought it should be 10:00 at the most.

Coming down the stairs from the balcony, I found Houston lounging against the post at the bottom. "Hey, Houston. Is it your day off or are you working tonight?"

"Working tonight." He held up a stack of DVDs. "Since Chris can't get any kind of internet at his place, we've got to rely on old-fashioned technology. Chris hardly ever picks something I like, so I decided to come in myself."

"Did you find everything you wanted?"

"Just about." His good ol' boy grin slid over his lips. "I was also looking for someone to have lunch with."

A gasp started to surface, but I caught it in time. I couldn't act shocked that a guy wanted to have lunch with me. But was it a friend lunch or a date lunch? From his grin, I guessed it was a date lunch disguised as a friend lunch.

"That'd be great. but I don't get off for a half hour."

The grin grew. "I can wait. I reckon I can find something to do to kill the time. I might even try reading."

I laughed. "You might."

At 12:30 we fought a strong wind barreling rain into our faces to reach Cervelli's Deli two doors down on Main Street. After placing our order, we took a table by a window.

Patting my wet face with my hat, I sorted the questions I'd crafted during the half hour I'd worked before lunch. I hated dead spots in a conversation, especially when only two people were involved.

"How did you end up a cop in Ohio?" I tore the paper from my straw.

He finished a long pull on his straw. "Well, like every good Texan, I was undone by a woman."

When his high school girlfriend told him she was going to Ohio State, Houston applied and was accepted at the university. They were together until they broke up their junior year.

"After we graduated, Madi went back to Houston, but there wasn't anything there for me. I'd gotten a criminal justice degree and planned on going to law school, but during my senior year, I decided I couldn't take any more school. I bounced around a few jobs and then applied to the police academy and found out that I fit this job like my Glock in its holster."

"Is being a deputy here your first job in law enforcement?"

"Yeah. I interviewed with Mal as soon as I graduated. My first interview and my first job offer."

Mr. Cervelli called our names, and we went to the counter to get our food.

I shouldn't have worried about the conversation lapsing. Houston talked about everything, from the pros and cons of his home city to his love of outlaw country music. I sipped French onion soup, ate salad, and threw in some questions and nods. That accent—it was like listening to my favorite band on replay.

When we returned to the library, Houston asked where he'd find books by David Morrell. I took him to the right section upstairs, then went down two floors to drop off my backpack in the kitchen. Settling behind the checkout desk, I expected Houston to show up any minute with his books. But after a half hour I knew I must have missed him.

My mind wandered all afternoon. Did I like him? Yeah, kinda sorta. Did he like me? He seemed to have made a special trip to the library to see me since the only other time he'd been in the building was to introduce himself right after Christmas. Did I like him more than Chris or Garrett?

I sighed, hooking my hair behind my ear as Miss Danvers approached with her usual truckload of romance novels. No. I couldn't say I liked him any better than the other guys. Maybe I needed to take more lunches with him to make up my mind.

When school let out, I spent most of my remaining two hours reminding the junior high kids what the rules were. Except when I took

Garrett back to the teen/tech room to handle Joe Buchanan, one of our patrons who didn't seem to run on all his cylinders. He was in one of his nasty moods and wouldn't get off a computer when Grace told him his time was up. But shortly after I returned to the lobby, Mr. Buchanan stormed out.

Fifteen minutes later, Garrett came to the desk with several DVDs.

"I thought you'd left." I pulled the stack toward me. "Did Mr. Buchanan cause much trouble?"

"Nothing unusual. He protests about his rights as a taxpayer for a couple minutes, then leaves." Garrett broke into his V-shaped smile, as sharp as his nose and chin. "Sorry about me and Houston fighting the other night. But I never know what will set him off. I can joke around with him sometimes, and other times, I can do the exact same thing and he'll blow his stack."

Garrett hadn't sounded like he was joking when he said Houston was trying to make me feel sorry for him. More like fed up. Better not point that out. "Everybody has their hot button issues."

He took his stack of items from me. "Hope you can come back to jam."

"Me too," I called after him as he dashed outside.

Marcus and Suzanne came back from their supper break, and I was telling them about the trouble with Mr. Buchanan when Walter stalked through the front doors.

My eyebrows climbed high. The library was the last place I'd expect to see him. Marcus and Suzanne stiffened. So they knew Walter's reputation.

Walter scanned the lobby, spotted me, and walked over in his stiff-legged way. "You seen China?"

My eyebrows found room to go higher. "I—uh—no."

He muttered something, then said, "You ain't seen her at all? You been here all day?"

"I've--I've been—uh—here si--si--since—" I cleared my throat for a do-over. "I've been here since we opened this morning, but I leave the desk a lot to help patrons."

"I dropped China off here after school 'cause she said she had to do research for a school project. We ain't got no internet at the house. I told her I'd pick her up at 5:00." He cracked the counter with his fist, and Marcus leaped back into the shelves lining the wall. "If she conned me, she won't be gettin' the car keys until graduation. To use a computer, she has to sign in, don't she?"

"Yes. There's always a librarian there to check people in and to help. I'll take you back to the public computers."

Walter and I passed the local history room. Chris sat at the microfilm machine.

"Hold on a minute, Walter." I entered the room. "Have you been here long? I missed seeing you come in."

He looked up. "You weren't at the front desk when I got here. I thought maybe you were off today."

"I must have been helping somebody." I pointed at a shelf. "We got a few new —"

"You can flirt with him later." Walter's deep, serrated voice grated on my ear.

Reddening, I said, "Chris, do you know my great-grandfather, Walter Malinowski, Jr.? Walter, this is Chris Kincaid."

Chris stood, and Walter said, "Yeah, we've met." From his disgusted tone, I figured it had been when Chris was on the job. "C'mon, Rae. I ain't spendin' all night here at the library."

I gave Chris a quick smile and followed Walter into the hall. I stepped around him, turned right at the children's room, and led him into the combined teen/tech room. Every computer was occupied, and China sat at one with headphones on.

Walter nodded in her direction. "I didn't think she'd be dumb enough to get on my bad side so soon. She skipped school last week, and I ain't lettin' her drive until March first. It'd be like her to lie about needin' to do research and then go wherever she wanted to."

"Grace can tell you how long China was on the computer." I glanced at the thin woman, iron gray hair falling out of her ponytail, seated at the information desk.

"Good." He looked me over with such a penetrating stare I wished I'd worn lead-lined clothes. "How're you gettin' along with Mal?"

"Really good. He really likes me." Boy, those two sentences conveyed just about nothing. "He's the best dad I could have asked for."

"He don't boss you too much?"

"No. He's careful not to treat me like the boys since I'm an adult."

"Huh." He looked down to his wet boots with duct tape wrapped around the toes. "I got more'n forty years on him, and Mal's always tryin' to boss me around."

He took a step toward Grace, and a thought came to me. I touched his arm. "Do you remember my mom?"

"Yeah. I reckon everybody does who lived here when she did."

"Did you ever meet her or did you just know about her?"

"I ran into her a few times. Troy — he's Gyp's and China's dad — was hangin' out with her and brought her to the house every once in a while. I'd've probably seen her more if I was hittin' the bars like I did when I was younger. Your mom always seemed to find where the action was."

"Sorry I'm late." China appeared at Walter's side, shoving her headphones into her backpack. She didn't sound sorry. She sounded like a voicemail issuing a coded command.

I was not going to talk about my mom in front of China. "Good seeing you, Walter."

"Don't lie, Rae." She wore her sweet, irritating expression. "St. Mal wouldn't like it. Was it really good seeing Walter?"

A burn inflamed my ears. I'd said that just to be polite.

"Leave her alone, China. I'm starvin'," said Walter. "We're goin' home and gettin' supper."

I leveled my gaze almost a foot down to meet China's mocking eyes. "Actually, I am glad to see you, Walter. I mean it." I turned around and left them.

It was the truth, but why? He scared me. But I sort of sensed he didn't dislike me. And despite my fear, I didn't dislike him.

Chris was still in the local history room, flipping through one of the new books I'd indicated.

I said, "I thought those might interest you."

"They do." He selected another book.

I had supper and a riding lesson waiting for me and the chance to get a trail cam and catch the stalker, and all I wanted to do was stay in the local history room and stare at Chris.

"Are you ever around Wellesville at lunch time?" The question was so loud I should have hushed myself.

"Sometimes. It depends on where my patrol takes me." He looked up from the book. "Would you like to do lunch?" The last word ended on a high note I didn't know he could reach.

"Yes. Just text me. Except on Wednesdays. I work late that day."

A smile spread beneath his moustache that lasted two whole seconds. "Okay."

It took all my self-control not to skip from the room.

Chapter 16

Gathering the reins, I stretched my mouth and eyes, trying to encourage my brain to focus on the lesson. The feeble rays of the sunset mingled with the spotlight on the corner of the stable.

Uncle Hank turned as I rode Pokey around him. "If you're too tired, Rae, we can call it quits."

"I guess I'd better."

"No problem." He looped the lead line, drawing closer. "You can come over any time you like, as long as it's warm enough. It's better to stop now than have you fall off because you can't pay attention." He rolled his eyes. "Mal would arrest me if one of his kids got hurt on a horse here."

I swung off, my feet splatting in the muddy corral. In the stable, I unfastened the girth on the saddle. "Mal isn't much of a horse lover, is he?"

"Much of one?" Uncle Hank unbuckled the bridle. "He ain't one at all. He's scared to death of horses." He patted Pokey on her forelock. "I take it you ain't heard the story.

Shaking my head, I carried the saddle to the tack room.

"Well, you've got to know it. It's one of the key events in the saga of the Norris-Malinowski feud."

I looked over the top of the stall. "I didn't know there'd been a feud."

"Not like the Hatfields and the McCoys. This one had a happy ending. At least for Jeanine and me, it did. But Mal's first and last riding lesson almost saw my dad and Reuel Malinowski come to blows."

Uncle Hank slid the bolt on Pokey's stall and leaned against it, settling his weathered cowboy hat on the back of his head. I found a seat on a haybale.

He had the right face for a storyteller. Extra wide eyes to show every emotion from joy to terror and an extra broad mouth that could do the same job. When he threw in all the body language, he was as good as anybody I'd watched tell a tale in the South. Maybe he had southern blood somewhere back in his family tree.

"Since I'm an only child and sociable, I was always looking for someone to play with when I was a kid. Lucky for me, the neighbors had a kid my age. Unlucky for me, she had a tagalong little brother."

"Dad!" Amber ran into the stable. "Mom says supper's finally ready. Oh, good, you're still here, Rae. Did Dad tell you? I'm legal!" She squealed the last word, bouncing on the balls of her feet, and handed me a card. With her red-gold hair growing to her waist and a face made for Prince Charming to kiss, Amber looked like a storybook princess.

Uncle Hank put an arm around his daughter. "Now, punkin, you've always been legal. Your mom and me tied the knot three and a half years before you came." He winked at me.

Amber groaned. "Please, Dad. Not everything has to be a joke."

"Congratulations." I gave her the license.

She clutched it between her hands. "Maybe -- maybe I could drive you sometime when you're looking for places to shoot."

I put a hand over my mouth. This gorgeous girl, who had the popularity to match her looks, thought I was cool, and for no reason I could figure out, except I was her cousin and nineteen. If the kids I graduated with knew this, they'd laugh themselves into the ICU.

But with a stalker tracking me through the woods, a hike together would have to wait. "I was planning on treating you to a movie for your birthday. You can drive us."

"Just you and me?" She grabbed my arm.

"For sure."

Squealing like a nest full of hysterical mice, she threw her arms around me. I staggered back a few steps to keep from falling.

"Guess the story will have to wait." Uncle Hank moseyed outside, just like I imagined cowboys out West did.

"Which one?" said Amber.

"The one about why the Big Guy is scared of horses." Hank shoved the stable door shut and latched it.

Amber turned to me. "He fell off a horse and broke his arm when he was little."

He threw up his hands. "Now she knows the ending."

"I'd still love to hear the whole story," I said.

Hank headed to the porch. "One thing you should know about Mal is that his feelings go way down deep. I've busted all kinds of bones falling off or getting bucked off horses, and I always get right back up. But Mal feels that fall like it happened yesterday. It'd take a lot of work to cut his fear from him."

"That's why Uncle Mal doesn't want to date," said Amber. "He was so deeply in love with Aunt Em that he still feels married to her." She sighed, like that was the most romantic thing she'd ever heard.

It was the most romantic thing I'd ever run into in reality. His feelings ran deep ... I pulled on my earlobe. "Does it take Mal a while to get to know people? Or to let them get to know him?" Maybe that was why he hadn't said I could call him "Dad."

The wind threw fistfuls of rain at us, and we hurried to the porch of the little house.

Uncle Hank's huge, brown eyes squinted at me, as if the porch light was too weak. "Do you feel like you ain't gettin' to know Mal? He's crazy about you. He won't shut up about you. Didn't you know that?"

My lips parted in a quick smile. "I know he likes me. I didn't expect him to like me so much right away. I thought he'd have to take time to get to know me."

Shaking his head, Hank took off his cowboy hat. "It don't work like that when you're a parent. You're crazy about your kid the second you know one's a-comin'. Then you go crazy all over again the first time you see them. Huh." He fingered a sideburn. "The Big Guy's excited over you like he was when the boys were born. To him, you're brand new."

Amber said, "Do you want to stay for supper, Rae?"

"I've already eaten. But—" I looked to Hank "—could I borrow your trail cam? The one Aaron used for his Santa trap? I'll take care of it."

Hank burst out with a laugh. "If I let Aaron use it, I ain't too concerned about it. Sure, I'll get it."

Amber's new driver's license triggered a question. Before she could follow her dad inside, I said, "Are you in the same grade as China?"

Her beautiful face soured. "No. She's a grade ahead of me."

"Has she ever bullied you?" Being beautiful, popular, and the granddaughter of Reuel seemed the perfect combination to attract China's nasty attention.

"A couple times. Although I couldn't prove it." Her resentful expression deepened. "Things were swiped from my locker in seventh grade a few times. And last year, I had a coat stolen and things put in my locker, like a six-pack."

"Did you get in trouble for the alcohol?"

"No, because I reported it right away. The principal and the guidance counselor were pretty useless because I couldn't prove China and her hench-girls were doing it. But I knew they were guilty." Her voice grew as tight as her folded arms. "She was always in the hall when I found my locker had been tampered with. So Mom talked to Walter. I haven't had any trouble since."

Uncle Hank returned with the trail cam. Handing it to me, he said, in a quiet voice, "Rae, if you don't think you're gettin' to know Mal, you should tell him. He'd want to know."

I twisted the camera's strap around my hand. "I don't want to bother him."

He laughed. "If he didn't want to be bothered, him and Em wouldn't have had three kids in five years."

I said goodbye and dashed for the Rust Bucket as a memory of my last conversation on the front porch of the Norris's home unwound itself.

Mal apologizing for making me uncomfortable.

Me saying he hadn't.

Mal saying, "You tell me what you're comfortable with, and I'll abide by it."

Did that mean he was waiting on me to decide when to call him "Dad"?

I slid under the steering wheel of my truck. That had to be it.

I cranked my key again and again. He didn't want to be pushy, like hugging me if I wasn't ready for it. A lightness came over me that should have lifted me to the ceiling.

After twelve turns, the Rust Bucket must have realized I wasn't giving up and allowed the engine to catch.

If that was what Mal was waiting for, then I'd have to make the first time I called him "Dad" special, something he'd never forget.

~~~~~

I prayed all the way to my apartment Wednesday morning. The hidden trail camera had to have caught some glimpse of the stalker even if it was just through the stairs, even if it was just a shape. At least I'd have a definite time. He had to have come last night. Tuesday, I'd slept at the farm as usual. It was a perfectly safe opportunity for him.

Leaving the truck on the street, I raced to the trash cans under the stairs. The box I'd set by my can looked like it was in the position I'd left it, appearing like an extra box of trash I couldn't fit in my ... no, it wasn't in the same place.

I clenched my hands. Maybe I'd done such a good job of camouflaging the camera in the box of trash that Mrs. Blaney had moved it. The slightest change could have prevented the camera from shooting up through the gaps in the steps when its motion sensor was tripped. I'd have to wait until I went to the library to check the card.

I dug the trail cam out of the box and unlatched the door that covered the card and the control buttons. Pieces of plastic fell to the wet pavement, and a tightly folded sheet of white paper lay on the broken innards of the camera.

Blood seeped from my face as I fell against the stairs.

Father, I really thought this would work.

A numbing sensation crawling down from my scalp, I unfolded the paper.

YOU CAN'T GET AWAY WITH ANYTHING, BELLA.

Another photo of me, this time at the library. The library?

Bringing the paper closer, I stepped out from under the stairs into a sudden shaft of sunshine as the sun made a break from a cover of charcoal clouds.

He had to have taken the photo on Monday. I was standing at the
~~~~~

checkout desk, wearing my red plaid shirt over a black t-shirt, the outfit I wore that day. To get this angle, he must have been standing in-between the four revolving racks of paperbacks, situated under the balcony. Perfect cover.

A hard grin pushed aside the numbness. He'd messed up. Big time.

I ran into my apartment, bagged the note and the camera, and took out my notebook. He was somebody who visited the library from 9:00 to 5:00 on Monday during the times I was on the desk. Since I hadn't worked at the desk every single minute of that time, that narrowed his opportunities even more.

The light in the photo could have given me a clue as to the time of day, but Monday had been so overcast that 9:00 in the morning pretty much looked like 5:00 in the evening. No one else was in the photo, not a patron or a co-worker, to help me fix the time.

Fine. I wrote down every person I could remember, even the kids from Storytime. Then I crossed off the ridiculous names, like the kids and Houston, Garrett, and Chris. But Mrs. O'Neil had been there as well as Jill and China. In fact, I hadn't seen China come in. Had she ducked behind the racks when she saw I wasn't around, waited for me to come back to take a photo, and then slipped out when I wasn't looking? If I went to Walter's place to ask him what he remembered about my mom, I could bring up China and find out if she signed onto the computer like she was supposed to.

I puzzled over the photo and my list of suspects until my worry about the trail cam made me pick up my phone and search for a replacement.

The prices made me gape. Around $150. After monthly expenses, all I had manage to save from working at the library for eight months was $182. And seventy-three cents. Maybe Uncle Hank would let me repay him in installments.

Pushing back runaway strands of hair, I laid down my phone and pulled my camera from my backpack. I scrolled through photos. Valentine's Day was just a week away, and Mal's birthday was a few days after that. Photo after photo passed without any of them leaping out as the ones I should choose. I didn't dare go out hiking by myself again.

I kicked my heel against the worn carpet. The stalker was trying to trap me. But I wasn't trapped. I was waiting, waiting for him to make another mistake.

Chapter 17

As the road changed from paved to unpaved, my breath quickened. Hopefully, on a Monday morning after school started for the day, Walter would be alone. In five days, the only thing I'd discovered was that Sean Ross had died in a car crash about a year after Phoenix Moore had been stabbed. Maybe a relative held my mom responsible for his death, although I hadn't met anyone named Ross. I still hadn't found out if Phoenix Moore had lived. I needed some fresh leads.

The lead-colored clouds had settled in over the weekend, solidly blocking any view of the sun. They hung so low I kept expecting the roof of the Rust Bucket to scrape against them. Each day grew more depressing. The steady diet of February gray might even depress Aaron.

Walter's dilapidated farmhouse popped into view as I rounded the last bend in the drive. It seemed hunkered down on the small hill as if bracing for an attack.

Leaving my truck, I climbed the sodden slope to the front porch. The humid, chilly air felt as comfortable as a wet quilt.

A thunk from behind the house turned me in that direction. Somebody had to be splitting wood.

I retraced my path and walked past the garage to the backyard. Patches of icy snow dotted the yard like islands in a sea of dead grass, and the ground squished beneath my boots with every step.

Where the yard met the woods, Walter lifted a log onto a stump. A long shelter with firewood stacked in perpendicular layers sat behind him.

Shoving a smile in place, I called, "Hey!"

Dropping the log, Walter spun and held his ax like a weapon.

"Rae Riley?" His harsh voice sliced through the damp air. "What do you want?"

"Is it okay for me to stop by?"

He picked up the log. "Your dad'll have a fit, but I don't care." He levelled cold, pale eyes at me. "Why'd you come?"

"A lot of people in the county don't like me now that they know who my mom is. I'd like to know if my mom did something to hurt them or a relative. I wondered if you knew of any men, for certain, that my mom had a relationship with."

"What do you care if people don't like you? That's their problem." Walter set the log on the stump. "You got a double curse. You're Bella

Rydell's daughter and a Malinowski. Though bein' Lydia's grandkid should give you some respectability." He swung the ax and embedded the blade in the log.

"I'd still like to know if you knew of any specific cases. Like a couple who divorced, and my mom was blamed?" Shivering, I sunk my hands deeper into my vest's pockets. The temperature was above freezing, but the damp air seemed to sink right through my jacket and sweater. "Can I help you?"

"Stack the logs over there." He jerked a thumb toward the shelter, then swung his ax again with the log still biting the blade. The piece of wood crashed onto the stump, and the ax cleaved it in half. "I heard a lot of talk back then. A lot of talk."

Either being eighty hadn't affected his strength at all, or it had and now his strength was merely amazing instead of superhuman.

With a grunt, he heaved the ax again. "Back then, Troy said he'd slept with your mother regular. So did Lee J. Both of them could be lying."

Picking up the split logs, I flipped to a clean page in my memory. "Who is Lee J.?"

"Lily's oldest boy from her first marriage. You met my daughter Lily at Christmas, didn't you? Lee J.'s the same age as Mal. Big as he is too."

"Then I haven't met him." I would have remembered another giant.

"Nope. He hasn't come by for a couple years now. Could be in jail for all I know."

I crossed off Lee J.

Walter went on, "Heard tell of a professor up at Killinnick College who she got a heap of money out of. Don't remember the name."

That would have been Terry O'Neil. Or maybe Mom had conquered more than one professor.

"Also heard about a doctor up in Zanesville that left his family for your mother."

"But he couldn't have." I carried several logs to the shelter. "I mean, my mom never married any of the men she was with."

He shrugged. "Maybe he divorced, thinkin' he'd marry Bella, and she didn't want to." Tipping his head back, Walter rested his big, calloused hand on the butt of the ax handle. "One of ol' Dave Kincaid's grandkids got into some trouble with Bella. Might have been a fight. Man, there was a lot of talk back then. Seemed like almost every guy in town was said to've slept with her, but your mom only set her sights on men with money. She had calculator eyes. I saw that when Troy brought her to the house." He lifted a log onto the stump. "She messed up on Mal, though. For some reason, she thought he could come up with 5,000 bucks."

"Mal thinks Mom thought he had cash from his football scholarship."

"Dumb mistake for a sharp girl."

I collected another load of wood. "Was Grace able to tell you when China signed up for the computer?"

"Yep," said Walter. "She signed up about ten minutes after I dropped her off. If she wasn't lookin' at books or her phone, she couldn't have gone far before she signed in."

But she had enough time to hide in the paperback racks and take my picture.

A voice behind me said, "Where's Gyp?" Stumbling out onto the back porch, one of my many cousins pulled a hand over his scruffy, dirty blond beard and blinked in the drab light. Another cousin appeared behind him, taller and skinnier with shaggy, almost black hair .

My stomach took a dive. Knowing how most of my cousins felt about Reuel's descendants made it wise to leave now. But I couldn't pass up this chance to ask all my questions.

"China's at school." Walter snapped his answer. "At least, she'd better be. Gyp's at work. People do that, you know. Hold jobs and work." He turned to me. "Have you met my grandsons, Jack and Rome? Jack's Lily's oldest boy from her third marriage. Rome's the son of my youngest girl, Venice."

"That makes Rome" —I searched the family tree in my mind— "a first cousin to Egypt and China because Troy and Venice are brother and sister."

"Good memory." Walter might have sounded the tiniest bit impressed.

"I met Rae on Christmas Day." His blond hair sticking up every which way, Jack leered at me as he placed his hands on the splintered porch railing. "You've got a lot of guts, coming here without the almighty sheriff as your bodyguard after all the stories I bet he's told you."

Walter stepped a little too close. "What has Lydia said about me? That it's my fault Reuel got killed?"

It didn't matter how old Walter was. This close, his lineman size made me feel like a mouse facing a bull.

"Maybe they didn't tell her." Rome's smooth words slipped through the moist air. "She'd be too scared to come if she knew their opinion of you."

Forcing my feet to stand their ground, I said, "They haven't said anything about how Reuel died. They just talk about what he was like before."

Of course, one of the first stories I'd heard about the Malinowskis when I moved to the county was how Reuel died in a bar fight saving his father's life, and how Walter and Gram had been at war ever since.

Walter closed in, and I had to stutter back a step. "Get this straight," he said. "I asked Reuel to go to the bar with me. I didn't make 'im. He was a grown man. And I didn't shoot 'im. It was that—" with a roar, he grabbed the ax and flung it toward the woods. It slammed into a thick trunk.

The hollow sound of Jack clapping was as loud as the *thunk* of the blade digging into the bark. "Didn't know you still had it in you, Walter."

Did anybody in the family call Walter something other than his first name?

"You don't know nothin', boy." Walter stalked to the tree and jerked the ax free.

I arranged logs on a shelf. "Did you know somebody named Phoenix Moore?"

"Sounds familiar." Walter stroked his chin. "I think she was related to the Kincaids somehow."

I blinked. "Really?" Hadn't expected that connection.

"Troy might have brought her over to the house a few times." He shrugged. "He brought over so many girls, I couldn't keep track of who they was."

"How about Sean Ross? Did you know him?"

Walter nodded. "Him I remember 'cause he was black and wasn't related to the Langs or the Hamiltons. They're the only black families that have lived in the county for years and years. He was a friend of Troy's, probably 'cause he was a crook. Them's the only kind of friends Troy had."

"Thanks, Walter. I appreciate your help. I'd better go." I took a long stride toward the garage. "I'm meeting Aunt Carrie in Lancaster for lunch."

"She still workin' at that detective agency?" said Walter.

"Yes."

"Look what we done, Rome." Jack flung a hand toward me. "We scared off the sheriff's daughter."

"She must've heard we grown horns and a tail during the full moon." Rome blew on his skinny hands.

I squared myself to them. I couldn't show any nerves. "Yeah, but the full moon is a week away."

As I squished my way to the Rust Bucket, Walter chuckled at the bottom of his cavern voice.

Was Walter right? Was Phoenix Moore a relative of Chris? I'd have to find some way to know for certain.

Starting the engine, I fed the truck plenty of gas and had plenty to think about as I headed west to meet Aunt Carrie.

Chapter 18

Late that night, carrying a framed and matted eight-by-ten photo for Mal under my arm, I looked up the stairs to my apartment.

My door seemed to be waiting for me, perched like a bird of prey. And I was the prey.

Tightening my grip on the wrapped frame, I stomped up the steps. It would be just another note, just another threat, one more piece of ammo I could turn against him.

Yanking open the screen door, I glanced down. Nothing fell on my feet. The landing was as empty as a washed plate.

He'd left a note for me to find the past two Mondays. Why not today? Maybe discovering I wasn't just taking his crap and had set up the trail cam made him lose his nerve.

Please, Father, let that be it.

I pushed open the door, flipped on the lights, and all my blood drained away like water disappearing through sand.

My apartment looked like a bull had stampeded though it. Purple strands of Gram's afghan lay scattered across the couch and floor, a photo album had the plastic sleeves ripped out, and the spool was tossed on its side. Mom's ashes. Where were they?

Dropping the package and my backpack, I turned every which way.

There. In the corner of the kitchen. I picked up the urn. The lid was still on tight. I hugged it to my chest.

Thank You, Father.

How had he gotten in? The little blood I had left leeched away, leaving only numbing pricks of fear. Was he still here? He would have come out by now, wouldn't he?

I spun to the bathroom and closet. Both doors were open. My rifle was in the closet. Focusing on the only two places someone could hide, I set the urn on the kitchen counter.

My fingers felt for a drawer and lifted out a bread knife. My other hand pulled the broom from between the fridge and the counter. Tiptoeing, I approached the bathroom.

A few more feet … I lunged into the tiny room, swinging the broom, swiping back the curtain across the shower stall. Then I turned on the light.

Nothing and nobody.

I released a breath that seemed to deflate both my lungs. I attacked the closet, jabbing with a lot more confidence. My rifle clattered to the floor, but that was all.

I rested the broom against the couch. A sheet of paper lay on the frayed cushions. It had a photo printed on it, but not of me. The abandoned children's home stood like a gutted and forgotten beast against a crystal blue sky.

YOU SHOULD HAVE DIED IN THE FIRE, BELLA.

Fear clawing my gut, I picked my way around the debris to the window by the door. It was still latched. The key had worked like it always had in the lock, so unless he was an expert at picking locks, he hadn't come in that way.

I returned to the bathroom. That window was locked, so how …

I peered out the window and gasped.

The top of a ladder was propped under it. I threw up the sash and leaned out, a gust of wind throwing hair in my eyes.

He brought a ladder? He couldn't have known the window would be unlocked, and it must have been for him to get in so easily. Unless I'd forgotten to lock the door. I shook hair from my face. But I always kept everything locked.

Using the flashlight on my phone, I scrutinized the window, the gap in the siding where rain leaked into my bathroom, and the ladder. He wouldn't have left evidence like a ten-foot ladder with black duct tape wrapped around the ends touching the wall. I fell back into the bathroom.

Of course.

I shut the window and texted Mrs. Blaney.

> Did you set up a ladder to take a look at my leaky window

Sitting on my couch, I rested my elbows on my knees and held my phone with both hands.

That was Mrs. Blaney's ladder for certain. I'd seen it hanging on the wall of her garage, black-taped ends and all, a hundred times. The stalker did not take her ladder out of the garage. He found it already set up, took advantage of it, crawled in the bathroom window, trashed my apartment, left the note, and then went out by the door, locking it behind him.

I gathered up the shreds of Gram's beautiful afghan. She wouldn't be mad it got destroyed, would she? I righted the spool and laid the pieces on it. Then I set Mom's urn beside the spool.

Mom's urn … I fell back on the couch. Why was the lid of the urn still sealed? This guy or girl hated Mom enough to hate me. He was in my empty apartment with her ashes. He had to know that dumping them would kill me. Why hadn't he?

I gazed over the room. He really hadn't done that much damage. Besides the ruined afghan, the top of the spool was split, and one album was torn apart but all the photos seemed to be here, and I had four more albums. He'd even dumped the drawers of my dresser or pawed through the closet and found my rifle. Had he been afraid of getting caught? Heard or saw something that made him leave while he could?

> Yes. I took a look yesterday and have a guy coming out Thursday to give me an estimate on a replacement.

So, coming in the window had been an impromptu change. He must have done it last night when no one would spot him. But something kept him from totaling my apartment.

I started to bag the latest note but stopped before I sealed it. The stalker could have left fingerprints all over the place, and I'd touched everything he had, checking for damage.

Sinking back onto the couch, I clasped the baggie. Should I call Mal? Actually, I'd have to call the town police. But I'd still have to let Mal know.

My breath coming in spurts, I went to the drawer in the kitchen, got out all the notes and my notebook, and spread everything on the card table. After two weeks of research, where did I stand? I had to get it all organized.

Date	Opportunity	Mode of Delivery	Text
Jan. 18	Unknown	Mailed	You don't fool me, Rae. You're just like your mother.
Jan. 22	Unknown	Mailed	Your family is better off without you, Rae.
Jan. 26	1-4 p.m.	On truck	No one wants you here, Bella.
Jan. 31	8:15 a.m. Jan. 30 to 8:10 p.m. Jan. 31	At door	Leave before you ruin your family, Bella
Feb. 4	8:15 a.m. Feb. 2 to 1 a.m. Feb. 5. <u>To take photo</u>—around 8:45 to 11 a.m. Jan. 30	At door	You're never alone, Bella
Feb. 7	8:15 a.m. Feb. 6 to 8 a.m. Feb. 7. <u>To take photo</u>— 9 a.m.-5 p.m. Feb. 5	In broken camera	You can't get away with anything, Bella
Feb. 12	Sometime Sunday afternoon Feb. 11 to 8:27 p.m. Feb. 12. Unlikely after dawn on Feb. 12.	In apt.	You should have died in the fire, Bella

Conclusions: The stalker thinks Mom hurt him or her or members of their family. I'm just like her, so it's okay to get revenge on me. The person has to be fit enough to climb a ladder to a second-story window and thin enough and strong enough to pull himself through the window. He's smart and takes advantages of opportunities he finds, such as sticking a note in the camera, taking a photo in the library, and using the ladder to break into my apartment.

Prime Suspects:
China Malinowski
Egypt Malinowski
Melissa O'Neil
Terry O'Neil
Jill Cerda

My pen hovered over the paper. Should I include Chris, since Phoenix Moore was stabbed and Mom seemed to have been a prime suspect?

I set down my pen. No. The stalker felt my mom had deeply hurt him. I couldn't imagine super-composed Chris wanting revenge for a crime committed against an aunt or cousin. The connection to Mom had to be through a close relative.

And, of course, the stalker could be someone who wasn't even near my radar.

Sighing, I slumped in the folding chair. Now I knew where I stood after two weeks of research — besides losing sleep and being too scared to hike in the state park alone, absolutely nowhere.

It would be impossible to check the times of every suspect and be confident I could eliminate any of them. Only the photo at the library narrowed down the list of suspects to about fifty people. But that group just included the ones I had seen. Anybody could have entered while I was away from the desk, ducked behind the paperback racks, snapped my picture, and exited when I waited on a patron. I'd missed Houston, Chris, and China coming in.

A sigh tried to rise again, but I was too depressed to let it out.

Why had I thought I could solve this case? I hadn't really solved Mom's assault or discovered my dad's identity. I had no clue Rick was responsible until he confessed at the children's home when I set up the three meetings with Terry, Jason, and Mal. I only knew Mal was my dad after we compared blood types.

By an inch, I straightened in my seat. I had solved my mystery because I'd forced a confrontation, sending each man an anonymous note accusing him of attacking Mom and burning the children's home. At each meeting, I'd revealed who I was and asked for the man's blood type to finally figure out who was my father.

I needed another confrontation.

Snapping to model-straight posture, I picked up my pen.

He'd left a note for me to find on Monday evening for three Mondays in a row. He'd done the same thing two Tuesday nights in a row.

The guy Mrs. Blaney hired to check the window was coming on Thursday. Knowing Mrs. Blaney, that ladder wouldn't move until she didn't need it anymore.

In a half hour, I had tomorrow night's trap worked out.

If the stalker stuck to his pattern, it would work. If he didn't, I was done. I'd have to tell Mal.

My stomach knotted so hard I went to the cupboard and took out a pouch of Earl Grey tea.

Funny. Tackling the stalker scared me much less than telling everything to Mal. Why?

I reached for a mug, then dropped my hand to hold my aching stomach.

Because I knew how the stalker would react. I wasn't sure about Mal.

Chapter 19

Tuesday morning lasted longer than all the days Mom and I had waited for test results. With each passing minute, my confidence in my plan shriveled a bit more. I had surprise and my rifle on my side. I couldn't let my nerve leave me behind.

I kept busy, cutting out shapes for Storytime crafts and repairing books in between waiting on patrons. After helping Mrs. Schuster find a legal thriller she wanted, I headed toward the back staircase, past Barb's office.

"Rae, do you have a minute?" she said.

"For sure."

"Close the door," she said in a lowered voice.

Something was up. My strained nerves ratcheting an inch or two more, I did as she asked and sat in one of two taupe chairs facing her desk. She took the other.

"I've been wanting to talk to you since Christmas." She cleared her throat. "But I wasn't sure what to say except thank you. Please pass that on to Mal." She gave me a smile so fragile it fell apart almost before I recognized it. "I really appreciate neither of you broadcasting Rick's crime." Her knuckles whitened as she clasped her hands. "I don't need people to know I was dating a murderer."

"You weren't."

Barb's blue eyes narrowed. "Rick told me how he set up your mother, sending her an anonymous note to meet him at the children's home and then attacking her from behind. That's cold-blooded, premeditated murder."

"I know. But the Rick who did that is not the same Rick now."

She huffed. "Of course he is. Nobody who is that evil could change."

"But he did." I leaned toward her. "When Jason received my anonymous note for a meeting at the children's home, he did what he did twenty years ago—he told Rick. Rick could have done the same thing— tell Jason he'd take care of it and try to murder me. But he didn't. He and Jason came to the home and told me Rick was going to confess to Mal."

Studying her balled hands, Barb said, "Why did you let the statute of limitations run out on the attempted murder?" Her voice shook, like she wanted the man she'd dated for six months to spend the rest of his life in prison.

"Because it's what my mom would have wanted." I stared over Barb's cluttered desk to the beige wall that even colorful vacation photos couldn't improve. "In a strange way, she was grateful to her attacker. Mom said she never would've gotten saved if the attack hadn't scared her into seeing how awful her life had become. She was always terrified the guy would find us and finish the job. But she also felt she owed the guy something. So she forgave him."

"How could she forgive someone who tried to murder her and her unborn baby?"

"Mom said God forgave her for a lot of terrible things. So she had to forgive terrible things."

Barb's fists whitened. A cart rolled by in the hall.

She stood. "Thank you, Rae. Please tell Mal that." The fragile smile came and went.

I took the back staircase down to the first floor. For a full five minutes, I had something on my mind other than my trap. Then I went right back to obsessing about it.

Five o'clock finally crept onto my phone. Devon came back from her supper break and said, "Are you staying at the farm tonight?'

I drew in my lips. I didn't want to lie to my only friend. But I couldn't ruin my trap. "I usually do on Tuesdays."

Before she could ask more questions, I hurried to the back staircase. I snatched up my backpack, went to the Rust Bucket, and drove three streets over from my apartment. I dug out my phone and swiped the farm's number.

Gram answered. "On your way?"

"No. I'm staying at my apartment tonight."

Pause. "Are you sure you can't come? We're going to celebrate Valentine's Day because you'll be working late tomorrow."

Valentine's Day was tomorrow? Finding my apartment broken into and planning the trap had blown away every other thought. "Could we celebrate tomorrow? I can be there by 8:30."

"That's fine by me, but we'll have to watch the weather. Snow's predicted for the evening, which means we could get anything from a dusting to three feet. If there's a storm, Mal won't be here. He'll stay in the office to act as backup to his patrols."

"I'm sorry, Gram. I just can't come tonight."

"I should have told you yesterday. Have a good night."

Tucking my phone in my pocket, I forced out a quivering breath.

Father, let it be a good night.

I loaded my backpack with cans of Coke and snacks I'd bought during lunch, then walked toward Mrs. Blaney's house.

A few flakes fell from the darkening sky. The clouds, turning indigo in the dusk, thinned at the western horizon, allowing magenta to seep along the edges of the hills, as if the sky was already decorating for Valentine's Day. Wiping melting flakes from my face, I walked at a normal pace, like I was just strolling home from work. I stopped at the corner of the garage to let a red car pass and then ran behind the garage to the ladder.

Once I made it to the backyard, I stared up at the bathroom window. This was the tricky part—climbing the ladder without being spotted. I couldn't wait until dark and risk missing the stalker. I had to get into position as soon as possible. If someone saw me and asked what I was doing, I could say I was looking at my leaky window.

I scanned the backyards that looked onto this side of the garage. No one was out, and no lights were switched on in any of the windows at the back of Mrs. Blaney's house. I scurried up the ladder, took a brief look at the leak, dug my fingers into the crack I'd open under the window, lifted it, and swung my backpack onto the floor. Then I gripped the edge of the toilet tank and pulled.

Like threading a needle with a hotdog, I scraped myself over the sill and landed in a heap on the closed toilet. Wow. Now I knew how a scaled fish felt. One thing was for sure: Jill could not have squeezed through the window Sunday night. Mrs. O'Neil and Terry probably didn't have the strength. I needed to reevaluate my suspects by weight and age.

I shut the window, then crawled to the front door. Cracking it open, I looked for a note, but no paper had been left between the door and the screen door.

Perfect.

I grabbed my backpack and scampered to the nest of pillows and couch cushions I'd made in my kitchen corner. I laid my rifle in my lap, opened a can of soda, and dug into a box of cereal.

Don't disappoint me, coward. Try to terrorize me one more time.

The apartment grew blacker, the night filling in any pale patches with an almost solid darkness. Only a couple streaks of light from the lamp outside my door stole through the window blind, marring the dark. My fears grew with the night, digging into my gut until I couldn't take another sip of soda or mouthful of cereal.

As the courthouse chimed 7:00, my phone vibrated for a text. Shielding my screen with blankets so it didn't give away my position, I checked the message.

> Are you okay?

Despite the pain in my stomach, I smiled. Mal hated to text, but he may have thought he'd interrupt something if he called. And if he'd already arrived home before he decided to check in with me, he had to drive back toward Wellesville to get a signal. He'd gone to a lot of trouble to see if I was all right.

> For sure talk to you in morning

I clicked off my phone. Maybe sooner than the morning if I caught the stalker.

Mrs. Blaney's car chugged into the garage beneath me. I shifted my stiff legs and numb hind end.

Now the night was complete. It didn't grow any darker, and my eyes couldn't see any better.

All the soda dammed up inside of me, and I had to crawl to the bathroom, carrying my rifle. I knelt on the lid of the toilet and raised my head just enough to clear my eyes above the sill. The ladder was—no, a black mass moved near the bottom rung.

Ducking, I clamped back a scream, every nerve in every muscle tearing at me to run, the soda and cereal churning. I clutched the rifle in both hands, the trigger guard embedded in my fingers. By millimeters, I lifted my head for another peek.

The mass was gone, each rung of the ladder empty and faint but still visible as they collected a skim of tiny snowflakes.

Hoisting myself higher, I scrutinized the ladder and the narrow strip of grass running between the garage and the neighbor's fence.

Had I imagined it? Was I that scared?

A meow drifted up to me. I squinted until my eyelids cramped, but I couldn't see it. The cat must have been sitting on the ladder, and when it moved, I thought the surrounding shadows were part of it.

I dropped onto the toilet lid.

Nearly had a nervous breakdown over a stupid cat. And I was trying to catch a stalker.

I pressed my hand against my forehead. Maybe I should follow the stalker's threats and leave the county. Aunt Carrie would probably let me share her apartment while I looked for a new job in Columbus. I could visit Mal and Gram and the boys on my days off and the weekends.

That's what Mom would have done. I'd dreaded hearing Mom tell me over a special treat of ice cream or slushies, "Well, it's about time we were outa here." Although now I knew she was trying to protect us from a killer, back then, each move was harder than the last.

I stared past the doorway to the black apartment, imagining Mom standing there, her hand on one hip, her face stern with her most critical

Mom look. She'd be so angry and worried about me putting this plan into action. But maybe if she had tried to solve the mystery of her attack instead of running, she would have stopped being so scared.

Confronting the mystery had led me to my dad. And —*please, Father*— another confrontation would let me keep my dad.

My hands coiled around my rifle, tightening their grip. Mal and all the Malinowskis would see I wasn't a manipulator like my mom had been. I took care of myself and solved my own problems. They'd never regret accepting me into the family when I worked so hard not to bother them.

In one swift move, I stood, turning, and took one more look out the window. No one. I went to the bathroom, then scurried back to my nest. Rearranging the cushions, pillows, and blankets, I got comfortable but not too much. I placed my back against the hard cupboard, my spine at marching-band attention, and fine-tuned my senses to pick up any hint of someone climbing the ladder.

This was going to end tonight.

All time seemed to stop. With the black remaining the same solid shade, I couldn't tell if it was 10:00 or midnight or the darkness before the dawn. My phone stayed tucked under a couch cushion. Couldn't afford the distraction.

I waited, waited as minutes grew to hours and hours to eons. He had to come, he had to—

What time was it?

I sat up, and pain shot through my shoulder. I'd fallen asleep in a weird position on my nest.

The dark seemed a shade duller.

The clock on the microwave said 6:30.

He hadn't come. I'd have to tell Mal. There was nothing left I could do.

Father, why?

Swallowing tears, I curled up on my nest.

Chapter 20

Ashen light leaked around the blinds as I squinted through lead-lined eyelids. Must not be too late. My alarm hadn't gone off yet. I staggered to my feet, muscles aching in the oddest places, and took a mug from the dish strainer by the sink. And almost dropped it.

The microwave clock read 11:22. My shift started at noon. I dug through my nest and found my phone buried under a couch cushion. I must not have heard my alarm.

Moving like a whirlwind, I made tea and toast, gulped it all down, and ran for the bathroom. Soon, water drumming from the shower head massaged my aches and pains.

Why hadn't the stalker come? Had he figured out my trap? The only way he could have done that was if he'd seen me climb in my bathroom window. But no one had been in sight. Unless he lived in one of the houses that looked onto that side of the garage and had spied me from the privacy of his home.

I blew water off my lips. How was I going to tell Mal? Fear clamped onto my gut so sudden I was afraid it'd force my toast out.

Toweling my hair, I inhaled slow and deep to ease the grip on my stomach. My phone vibrated on the milkcrates. I swiped to answer.

"Happy Valentine's Day. How's my girl?"

The smile in Mal's voice lightened it, but I couldn't find one in myself. "Okay."

"You should walk to work today. There's a snowstorm coming. Have you heard?"

"Gram mentioned it. She said you'd stay in town tonight to help patrol."

"Yeah. Ma also said you were coming out to the farm after work. I don't think you'll make it. Call me when you get off at 8:00, and I can tell you what road conditions are like."

A new worry punched my stomach. "Is it very dangerous to patrol in a snowstorm?"

Mal laughed. "Not like doing a normal patrol. I'm always careful."

"I'll be praying for you and all the officers out tonight."

"Thanks, kiddo. When's your dinner break?"

"4:00."

"If I'm not busy, I'll call you and you can eat with me. If you want to."

"I definitely want to."

"Okay. Have a good day, Rae."

We hung up.

I threw on an outfit, braided my hair, tucked it under my hat, pulled on my jacket and vest, and snatched up my backpack.

My hand on the doorknob, I stopped. Since he hadn't come last night, he might try tonight. Or today if the expected snow kept people off the street. The ladder was an open invitation, and I wouldn't get home until well after dark. When he found the window locked, would that stop him if he was confident I wasn't here?

I couldn't take the chance. I'd leave my valuables in the Rust Bucket.

Gathering my research and evidence, I slipped them around my towel-wrapped camera. I placed two photo albums on top and zipped my backpack shut. I put the other three albums in a plastic grocery bag and Mom's urn in another one. Walking down the street with an obvious cremation urn in my arms might attract attention.

I stuck all of the rifle's ammo in a pocket in my backpack and then shoved my rifle and the gift into the back of the closet. I couldn't carry everything to my truck in one trip, and that's all I had time for.

Loaded like a pack animal, I checked the latches on the bathroom window and the window by the door and locked the front door behind me.

Patches of snow clung to the stairs. It must have accumulated overnight but melted some, judging from the wet steps. The air held the scent of a fresh chill, which always made me think snow was on the way.

Maybe it was a good thing I had to bring all the evidence with me. I could tell Mal the whole story on my break. My air came short, and it wasn't from the weight pressing against my back. Maybe I should wait until he wasn't so busy.

The thin layer of snow hid some of the Rust Bucket's ragtag appearance. The snowplow had piled snow against the driver's side, and I had to step into a short drift as I pulled the door open. I stretched across the seat to get the snow scraper, and my mouth flopped open.

My windshield was a mass of fractures.

Grabbing the scraper, I cleared away the half-melted layer of smooth snow from the windshield.

The wiper didn't hold a sheet of paper. I reached into the well. Nothing.

Brushing away more snow, I uncovered two broken headlights, four flat tires, and one smashed rear taillight.

But no note.

I stepped back from my truck and onto the sidewalk. After taking the risk of breaking into my apartment, he vandalized my truck. This was a serious de-escalation. Had he chickened out? The breaking and entering had worked on his nerves, so he didn't want to go a step further. And the only step further was physically attacking me.

But he would have left a note on my truck. He had every other time. Could it have blown away? Not much wind now, but there might have been strong gusts overnight, although I hadn't heard any. The snow on my windshield had been undisturbed. It was snowing when I parked last night. If he left a note, he would have had to wipe back snow. Then the wind would have to blow the remaining snow smooth.

I tugged at my earlobe. None of this made an ounce of sense.

The courthouse clock struck noon.

Spinning in its direction, I fumbled for my phone and then the keys on the keypad. I texted Devon to tell Barb I had truck trouble, but I was coming.

I picked up my bags, locked the Rust Bucket, slipped the keys in my vest pocket, and, adjusting the shoulder straps digging into my jacket, began the trudge toward Main Street. I couldn't risk leaving my things in the truck, even during daylight. If I lost Mom's ashes, it'd be worse than telling Mal that, on top of someone hating me so much he was stalking me, I now had no wheels. My car insurance probably covered just about nothing. I'd bought the cheapest plan that let me drive legal.

Father, how much worse can one day get?

As I crossed Main Street to the library, someone honked at me.

Egypt and Harley drove by, grinning like demons, and flicked me off.

How nice. They'd made up. Now they could torment people as a couple instead of facing that job all alone. Those kind of shared activities were what every couple needed to maintain a close relationship.

I headed for the kitchen first, where I put the bags with the urn and the albums in the cupboard and placed my backpack in a corner under the stand for our coats. My camera should be safe for one day sitting on the floor. I hoped.

Flying up the back staircase, I raced for the main level. As I reached the landing, Barb and Mrs. O'Neil walked down from the second floor.

"Barb, I'm so sorry I'm late." My words came out as a harsh whisper between gasps.

"Take it easy, Rae," Barb said. "Anybody can have car trouble. Devon told me why you were late." She glanced at her phone. "Take fifteen minutes off your supper break, and we'll be good."

"Thanks." It came out in an exhale.

Mrs. O'Neil arched an eyebrow. "Don't you expect your employees to arrive on time?'

Pushing up the deep blue glasses that matched her sweater, Barb faced her. "Of course. But for exceptional circumstances, I make exceptions." The warm tone she'd used with me had been replaced with a crisp clip.

Raking me with a glare, Mrs. O'Neil said, "Do you make exceptions often?"

"If you wish to discuss personnel, we should go back to my office." Barb's voice crackled. "Rae—" she turned to me and smiled "—don't let us keep you."

I hurried into the lobby.

Devon was helping Mr. Jesky with his bags of books. Once he was on his way, she said, "You'll have to junk that truck."

Somebody had done that for me. "I'll have to do something."

More patrons than usual came in the afternoon, and nearly all of them checked out stacks of DVDs. They must have thought the snowstorm would last for days.

All the extra patrons didn't give me much time to analyze the stalker's latest move. Trashing my truck made no sense unless he knew I was waiting for him in my apartment and wrecking the Rust Bucket was the best he could do. But he would have left a note.

I waited until five after 4:00 for a call or text from Mal, but none came. He must have been busy. Was I disappointed or relieved? Bending my head as icy rain pelted me, I hurried to the deli. Both, I guessed. Part of me wanted to tell him the whole mess and get it over with, while another part wanted to pretend none of this had happened.

Once I had my Italian sub, corn chips, and Coke, I headed back to the library. The sleet or hard rain or whatever you called it was coming down faster, making the sidewalk slick. I stayed on the concrete edge, avoiding the slippery bricks that decorated the middle.

Cars crawled by as their tires crunched through the refreezing slush on the streets. If this ice kept up, no one would be out by the time I walked home at … I fell against the door of an empty building, my throat closing to the width of a pinhead. That was it, why he'd trashed my truck. To put me on foot. He already knew my schedule. Now he knew exactly where I'd be at 8:00 tonight, and the bad weather would make me even more vulnerable.

Dazed, I somehow made it to the employees' kitchen. I ate, but my sandwich and chips had no flavor.

If Mal was too busy to eat supper with me, he was probably too busy to pick me up. Gram, Uncle Hank, and Aunt Jeanine couldn't make it in. Could I take a long route to my apartment, a route he wouldn't expect?

The chips almost reentered the world, and I swallowed several times to keep them in their place. I couldn't spend one more night in my apartment, even with my rifle. I just couldn't.

I barely noticed cleaning up my bag and papers and empty soda can. What I could see, crystal clear, was myself heading out from the basement door into the parking lot tonight and a dark figure racing toward me.

"Rae, are you all right?" Devon asked when I joined her at the checkout desk. "You're very pale."

"I—uh—I … did you drive today?" My question came out as a shout, but I'd just spotted a lifeline.

"No, I walked. I like to save gas. I also didn't know what the roads would be like tonight."

"Could you—" I gulped "—could you come pick me up at 8:00 and could I stay the night with you?"

Devon's dark eyebrows lowered. "Are you in trouble?"

I nodded. "But if you can come and get me and let me stay with you, it'll be fine."

"Is this something you can tell me?"

I bit my lip. Could I? "Yes. Maybe - -maybe you could give me some advice when I get to your place tonight."

Devon broke into a reassuring grin. "I'll be here at 8:00. The girls will be excited to have you sleep over."

She left for home, and I went over to the holds shelf behind the desk. It seemed so obvious, now that Devon had offered to help. Why hadn't I asked for her advice before? She was the one person in the county I knew had no connection with Mom.

Sliding a book into place, I blew out a sigh. I hadn't asked because, like with a dad, I had no experience with a good friend and hadn't the first clue about the proper operation of one.

At 7:00, Jill sent the rest of the staff home when she learned Mal had declared a second level snow emergency. She asked if I could stay to close, in a tone that implied I'd better, and I said sure.

For an hour we worked in the lobby in a silence more icy than the sidewalks.

A hundred times, Devon's advice about calling Jill on her bad attitude came to me, and a hundred times, I tamped it down.

We closed without exchanging a word, except when Jill snapped out an order to make sure the patron terminals were logged off. She locked the front doors, then we turned off the lights and went downstairs.

As I collected my backpack and bags, Jill said, "Did you go shopping on your break?"

"No." The weight of my backpack reawakened sore muscles from my hike at noon.

Outside the door to the parking lot, Jill punched in the security code. The ice had turned to snow, accumulating in a deeper layer than I'd seen from the lobby windows.

Devon hadn't arrived in her small, green car.

Wrapping her scarf over her mouth, Jill stepped away from the door.

I *did not* want to be left alone. I took Devon's advice. "I know you don't like me, Jill."

Instead of worrying about her reaction, the words seemed to free something in me. Pleasant surprise.

She turned in the glare of the lamp by the door, her tiny eyes shrinking in her heavy face.

"If my mom hurt you," I said, "or someone in your family, she would be very sorry. She really did change."

"Your mom has nothing to do with it." She marched up to me, forcing me back to the door. "You're a liar. We can't trust liars, and Barb's stupid to employ one."

My jaw worked loose. "You--you mean because--because ..." my words dried up.

"If all you were doing was looking for your dad, why didn't you say so? Why did you hide you were Bella's daughter? Instead of telling people the truth, you went through all that nonsense of leaving roses at the children's home like somebody had years ago, melodramatic kids' stuff to get people talking about your mom without your interest in her disappearance appearing out of place. Why?"

Because I had to find out if my father was a murderer. I ground my jaws shut against the urge to release that sentence.

She got closer. "I know why, even if the Malinowskis are too dumb to get it. You were checking them out, seeing if it was worth finding your dad. You must have decided that between Mal's salary and his mother's, you could make out pretty well."

Jill's cloudy breath reached my face. "You're trouble. You'll pull something here at the library eventually. So I'm watching you. Barb will regret the day she hired you."

Whipping away from me, she skidded a few steps but caught herself, waded to her car, and drove away.

Chapter 21

The snow fell and fell, and I stood where Jill had left me against the locked door.

It wasn't Mom. It was me.

And there wasn't a thing I could do about it. To change people's perceptions of me, I'd have to reveal Jason's affair with Mom and how Rick tried to murder her. I couldn't wreck their lives on the slight chance that someone might like me.

My mood crashing like a linebacker had tackled it, I stepped out into the lot, the snow falling so thick it was like an active fog.

Where was Devon? How long had I been standing here?

Peering at the entrance to the lot and the street running past it, I fished my phone from the pocket of my vest. Devon had sent me some texts that I hadn't heard ping. How could I have missed—I thumbed to settings. I still had the ringer on vibrate from last night when my trap had gone up in flames.

> Car slid into gutter. Can't get it out. Girls and I will meet you at Elm and Morrison.

My muscles snapped to attention as numbness stole over my skin.

Could I make it? I'd walk in the opposite direction from the one I'd take to my apartment, nearly eliminating the chance of the stalker finding me.

> On my way

Transferring the bags into my right hand, I freed my left one in case I slipped. My breath led the way in rapid puffs as I followed the tracks Jill's car had made.

At the sidewalk, I glanced up the hill. And dropped the bags.

A figure, backlit by the streetlamp, stood at the corner.

Spinning, I fell to my knees. I snagged the bags and, stumbling across the lot, reached the guardrail at the opposite side.

I scrambled over it and fell five feet down the retaining wall into the little yard behind an empty building. Panting, I raised myself into a hunched stance and ran, scrambling over snow-encrusted chunks of crumbling asphalt.

Please, Father. It can't end like this.

Behind the deli, I slipped, and the urn rolled out of its bag. I squinted against the flakes. No silhouette. Nobody.

I needed to get out on Main Street and head for Mal's office. I slapped piles of snow until my palm smacked the urn. I shoved it into a bag and ran into the alley beside the deli. A streetlight illuminated the end that came out on Main Street, welcoming me like a lighthouse.

Bent under the weight of my backpack, I struggled toward Main Street, gripping and regripping the sagging bags.

A figure ran across the entrance to the alley.

My throat closed as my feet froze to the icy pavement.

What ... what do I do?

Wheeling, I fell against the deli's rough brick wall and glanced back.

No one was coming down the alley. He hadn't seen me.

I slipped and slid behind another empty building and the antique shop, heading for the raised parking lot behind the newspaper office. At the retaining wall for the lot, I threw my bags over the guardrail, then grabbed it, and heaved myself up. And slipped back down.

Ripping off my backpack, I looked behind me. Had he come down the alley from Main Street? Without any light shining between that alley and me, I squinted against the pouring snow.

Yes. Something dark was moving along the dumpster by the deli.

I hurled my backpack over the rail, then myself, and fell, panting, in the fresh snow.

Had he seen me? He couldn't have seen me. Should I hide here or run out of the lot and onto Sugar Street?

My phone vibrated. I fumbled it out of my vest pocket. Maybe Devon could call the cops. If any were available.

"Devon." I stole a glimpse over the guardrail. The shadow was moving down the slope of the alley, heading to where it came out on Elm Street.

"No, it's Mal. Are you home?"

"Dad!" I screamed into the phone.

The figure whipped around.

"Rae, what's wrong?"

I ran out of the parking lot to the street. "Someone's chasing me. Come get me!"

"What?" He gasped the question.

"Can you come get me?" I skidded across the sidewalk and slammed against a streetlamp.

"Where are you?" His cop tone rang my eardrum.

"On Sugar Street." I turned every which way, my back against the lamp. Where was he?

"I'm driving along Elm. If you head straight down Sugar, I can meet you."

I took off downhill. "I'm coming. Hurry!"

"Stay on the phone. If he comes near you, tell him your dad's coming and if he touches you, I'll resign on the spot and rip his head off!"

Through the flakes attacking my eyes, I saw the intersection of Elm and Sugar. But the stalker could race down the alley, come out on Elm, and be waiting for me as I reached the intersection.

If he was laying for me, I wasn't going to make it easy for him.

Digging in with the toes of my boots, I picked up speed, forgetting the snow and ice. Dad was coming, and nobody was stopping me from getting to him.

Shooting off the corner and into the middle of Elm Street, I whipped around and flung up my arms in defense.

Headlights plowed through the dark and mounting drifts.

I ran toward them, yelling into my phone. "I see you. I see you!"

"I see you too."

Snow melted on my teeth and my breath scraped my throat as I ran toward my dad.

The headlights stopped, and I fell against the hood.

Mal jumped out. "Are you okay?"

I dashed around the hood. My feet flew out from under me, pitching me headfirst into Mal's leg. It crumpled, and I hit the snow-covered pavement with a 250-pound sheriff on top of me.

Chapter 22

Grunting, Mal struggled to his feet. "Where is he?'

I pushed myself up into a sitting position, clutching for the air that had been knocked out of me. "Don't know ... lost him."

Mal towered above me, scanning the street drowning in snow. "I don't see anybody." He held out a huge hand. "Are you all right?"

Grasping his hand, I stood and grabbed him in the strongest hug I could give him.

He kissed me on the head. "You're safe now. I'll drive you to your apartment."

I shook my head against his coat. "I don't want to be alone."

"I'm staying with you."

"Don't you have to—"

My phone vibrated. I put it to my ear. "Devon, I'm—"

"Where are you? Are you okay?"

"I am now." I pressed my head against Mal's thick coat. "I got chased by somebody, but Mal called and I got to him okay."

Devon took a quick inhale. "Was that the trouble you wanted to talk to me about?"

"Yeah, but I'm gonna tell my dad now."

"I'm glad you're safe. Can you stay with Mal tonight?"

I told her I could, and Devon sighed. "Good. If you want to tell me anything about this, I'll listen."

"I'm sorry you and the girls had to go outside."

"They're outside?" Mal motioned for my phone, and I handed it to him. "Ma'am, are you driving?"

He listened. "We'll head over your way to make sure you and your daughters get home safely. Whoever chased Rae may be looking for someone else to ... no, ma'am. I mean Devon. It's my job."

"The guy won't bother Devon." I took back my phone. "He was only after me."

"Did he say so?"

Hunching my shoulder, I flinched against a jab of pain and jammed my hands in my vest pockets. "It's a long, long story."

"Okay." Mal squinted at me, then turned and took hold of the driver's door.

I edged around the hood, opened the passenger door, and slipped into the seat. All the extra police equipment and computer in the middle forced me to sit close to the door.

Mal fell into his seat. After closing his door, he gave the SUV gas and turned the vehicle around by backing into a driveway. "Rae, what's going on?"

"Someone's been leaving me anonymous notes." I turned under my seatbelt. "As soon as we know Devon and the girls are all right, we have to go back to the parking lot behind the newspaper office and get my backpack and the bags with Mom's ashes and my photo albums. I had to leave them behind. My backpack has all the notes and my notebook with my research in it."

Mal peered through the whipping wipers. "Why did you have all that stuff with you at the library?"

"Because I was scared the stalker would break in and ruin more of my things."

"What do you mean?" His question was so sharp I jumped. "Why did you call him a stalker? Has he chased you before? What other things has he ruined? Are you sure it's a man?"

Taking a deep breath, like I was diving into a bottomless pit, I started with finding the first note mailed to me, and my words fell faster than the snow.

In profile, Mal's jaw dropped lower and lower, and his eye grew wider and wider.

I'd just told him about the first note with my photo on it when Devon called, saying she and the girls were safe at home. Clicking off, I said, "Can we make it back to the newspaper office?"

Without a word, Mal turned into the parking lot of the Baptist church. We crept back along Elm until it hit Woodward. Climbing the steep slope, the SUV's speed grew slower and slower until we ground to a halt. We were well below the library's parking lot, nowhere close to Main Street.

I leaned forward, like I could pull the SUV after me.

The tires spun, but we didn't move another inch.

"We'll have to get your things in the morning." Mal spoke through his teeth.

I twisted to him in my seat, my ribs sending a painful protest. "But that's where all the notes are and my research and my camera. Can't we park here and walk over?"

"I can't." The SUV slid backwards as Mal passed the wheel through his hands, turning it. "When you fell into me, I landed on my weak knee. From the way it's feeling, I'm gonna have a hard time getting up to your apartment."

"Is it very bad?" I bit my lip. "I'm sorry."

"It's not your fault. Hazards of the job. I just can't patrol." He sighed, aiming the SUV downhill. "Hopefully, it's bad enough now that only a few idiots will be out, and my deputies won't miss me."

"You could wait for me while I—"

"I am not letting you"—his roar reverberated through the cramped cab—"out of my—" he snapped his mouth shut.

I pressed against the door as the snow piled on the ledge below the window.

He swallowed in a loud gulp. "Rae, I'm sorry. I know you don't like my yelling. You flinch or jump every time I do it. I've been trying to control it." A tired smile broke his concerned expression. "I know you're too polite to tell me it bothers you." We eased back onto Elm Street. "Your mom would not want you to risk your life for her ashes and pictures."

"I know she wouldn't. But what about all the evidence and my camera?" The camera Mom blew most of her money on when she was dying.

"You're worth more than your camera or any evidence. We can get all of it later. When you were telling me what the notes said—was that verbatim?"

"Yes."

"Then as soon as we get into your apartment, write down everything you can remember. If a town cop can come to us tonight, we'll have something to give him right away. I don't think the cold will damage any of your things much. It's not going to melt and get them wet overnight."

We crept along Sugar, across Main Street, and then almost glided past the intersection of Sugar and Wyandot. But Mal piloted the SUV through a wide turn and we plowed our way to Mrs. Blaney's garage.

Mal glanced out the windows. "Where's your truck?"

"That's more of the long story." I told him the rest, everything, up to when I met him on Elm Street.

His eyes and mouth grew huge all over again. He almost shouted out several times, slapping his hands over his mouth. When I'd finished, he was clutching the wheel, his forehead pressed against it.

Braced against my door, I said, "You can yell if you want to."

"I'm too horrified to yell. You could have been killed last night. And tonight." Dragging in a barrel of air, he sat back. "Why didn't you tell me? Are you scared of me?" He looked to me, his face in the dim light of the dash such a mix of pain, shock, and total confusion that I wanted to tear out the computer between us and hug him.

"No. Not at all. You're … you're—" Everything I'd come to feel for Mal exploded out of me. "You're the best dad God could have given me. You're better than any dad I ever imagined, and I've been wanting a dad since I was a preschooler and saw other kids with their dads and wondered where mine was."

"Then why didn't you tell me?" His baritone sounded strained, like his vocal cords were unraveling.

"Because I didn't want to mess things up."

"Mess what things up?"

A tap came on Mal's window, making us both jerk in its direction. Mrs. Blaney's pinched face peered into the SUV.

Mal rolled down the window.

"Is something wrong, sheriff?" She pulled together the halves of her coat.

"Fell on patrol and hurt my knee." The command of the cop returned to his voice. "I'm staying the night with Rae."

Staying the night … "Mrs. Blaney, I don't have enough sheets and blankets for two of us. May I borrow some from you? I'll wash them before I return them."

The corners of her mouth dipped down. "All right, I guess. Come on."

Unbuckling my belt, I said, "I'll help my dad up to the apartment first."

Despite using me like a crutch, Mal started to wipe out at the foot of the stairs, but we were close enough for him to grab the railing and save himself. We staggered into the apartment and collapsed on the couch.

Alternating between wincing and gasping, Mal said, "That was only a little harder than climbing Everest."

He propped his leg on the cracked spool, and I went to the kitchen and made an icepack. The cold stung my hands. I washed my skinned and scraped palms, then filled a glass of water, and shook a couple of painkillers onto a saucer. After I gave those to him, I hurried outside and slip-slid to Mrs. Blaney's backdoor.

She handed me a pile of blankets and comforters. "By the way, I don't appreciate being woke up at 2:00 in the morning. But I do appreciate the noise only happened that once. What was going on? It sounded like furniture breaking."

Flakes collecting on my lashes, I stared at her. "Excuse me?"

"That wasn't you? The noise came from this direction."

Excitement fired tingles all over me. "Was this Sunday night? Early Monday morning?"

"Yes. So it was you."

"No, ma'am. Somebody broke into the apartment and damaged some of my things. He or she didn't hurt the apartment," I added as Mrs. Blaney opened her mouth. "I've told my dad about it. Do you know exactly what time it was?"

"2:17. That's what the clock on the stove said. I'd gotten up to take cold medicine and heard the noise and then waited by the back door to see if you kept at it. But that was all."

"Did you turn on your porchlight or step out?"

"I think I did. Why?"

"I think you scared the guy off. He saw the light, knew you were up, and left before you caught him. Thanks. That probably kept him from totaling my stuff."

"Oh. Well. You're welcome." She pointed at the pile of linens. "Wash all of this before you give it back to me." She shut the door.

As I trudged into the apartment with my load, Mal swiped off his phone. His utility belt and coat were draped over the back of the couch, his body armor leaning against the spool.

"Mess what things up?" he said, like my landlady had never interrupted us.

Laying the bedding on the floor, I sat beside Mal, my reason snagged on my tongue. I was such a moron. "It seems pretty stupid now that you came out in a blizzard and crippled yourself to rescue me."

"I'm not crippled." He repositioned the icepack on his knee, grimacing. "Temporarily maimed, yes. Crippled, no. But I'm dying to hear your answer."

A burn raced from my ears to all over my face. Undoing my braid, I focused on the edge of the spool. "I knew you liked me. Driving back from Walter's, you told me how great you thought I was, and I didn't want to do anything to make you change your opinion of me or make you regret that you acknowledged me."

"But you're my daughter." Bewilderment made his voice hoarse. "I'd never regret having you in my life."

"Even though people treat you badly because of me?" I turned to face him. "Mrs. O'Neil said you might lose the next election because people think it's terrible that you're a Christian and sheriff and had a one-night stand with the town tramp. I've cost you your reputation and I could cost you your job. I just didn't want to cause you any more trouble."

My voice started to shake. "Mom and I learned we couldn't count on anybody when we really needed them. When Mom got sick, we tried to get help from our church family, but we had to beg." The scene in the church flashed into my mind, and I made fists. "So I was afraid you and Gram and the rest of the family might be like them. Everything was okay as long as I didn't cause problems for y'all."

All the confusion disappeared, but now Mal looked startled. "Holy smoke," he murmured, "you don't realize how bad your own flaws are until you see them in your kids." He held out his arms. "Come here."

In a millisecond, my head was resting on my dad's shoulder, his arms wrapped around me, and all the days and weeks of fear melted from my soul.

Mal said, "Do you remember how I told you I was a complete jerk in high school because I let being a star lineman go to my head?"

"You said you were drinking and partying and fighting with Gram."

"Right. I started to rebel against Ma my sophomore year, and I was totally unmanageable when I began my senior year. Then I got with your mom after my first home football game. Sobered up the next morning, and I was sick to my soul.

"I had to change. I begged God to forgive me, stopped drinking and running wild every night, and started listening to Ma. And a funny thing happened." His voice softened.

"I could tell Ma was pleased with me, and that made me want to please her more. I'd fought her for so long I'd forgotten how much I'd missed her approval. So I behaved better and better and thought this was a sign God had forgiven me. Then, in the middle of December, your mother told me she was pregnant with my baby and wanted $5,000, or she'd abort you."

The icepack slipped. I caught it and took great care as I replaced it on his knee.

"All my peace of mind was shattered. I was desperate to save you. But I was afraid to tell Ma. After thinking well of me for three months, she'd know I was still a loser."

"Gram wouldn't have thought that."

"I know that now. I don't know why I didn't know that then. At least you have the excuse that you don't really know me. I knew Ma, and I was still terrified of losing her good opinion of me."

Our eyes met and locked. Something passed between us. A connection. A bond. Stronger than chromosomes or our rare blood type.

"You are my daughter." He brushed back a mass of my hair. "You can't do anything to mess up our relationship. I don't care if people throw rocks at me every time I walk down the street. Or I lose the next election and end up digging ditches on a road crew. I thought you were dead for twenty years. You've come back to me alive. How could I regret that?"

Thoughts and feelings spinning into each other like debris in a hurricane, I sat up. "But you don't know me. I -- I could have done anything. Like, well, killed somebody back in North Carolina."

"Rae, I don't have to've raised you to know you aren't a murderer."

"But what if I ... what if I got drunk and killed somebody in a hit and run?"

"You didn't."

"But what if I did?"

"Okay, if you insist on playing out this fantasy." Mal rubbed his forehead. "If you confessed to me that you had killed someone under those circumstances, I'd have to arrest you, which would kill me." He said this as a matter of fact, the way he would state his name. "Then I'd find the best lawyer I could. If you were convicted, I'd visit you whenever I could because you'd still be my daughter, and this is never going to happen, so why are we even talking about it?"

"What if I hurt one of the boys?" I moved to the edge of the couch.

"Accidents happen, Rae."

"I hurt them deliberately because … because I'm jealous."

"You aren't, and you never will be."

"But what if I was and I hurt one of them?"

Clenching his jaw, he moved the bag of ice. "All right. Then I couldn't let you around the boys without Ma or me to watch you, but I'd still see you by yourself and help you find a therapist because you'd still be my daughter and you'd need psychological help." He reached for my face, hesitated, and I guided his hand to cup it.

"You can't mess up our relationship, Rae. Not now, not in twenty years, not in forty years." He pressed his thick fingers against my cheek. "You've been my daughter since the night you were conceived, and you'll be my daughter until forever. So get used to it."

He meant it. From the way his eyes never left mine, I knew he wasn't just being nice. My heart swelled so big it was in danger of flying free.

I clutched him in a hug tight enough to make my shoulder ache where he landed on it and he almost returned the favor. Then we rested in the quiet of our connection.

Mal whispered, "Promise me you'll come to me if you have a problem. Or if it's something you only want to share with a woman, promise me you'll talk to Gram or Jeanine or Carrie or even your friend Devon."

"I promise."

"I could have lost you tonight. Again."

His hug edged toward spine-snapping.

To save my vertebrae, I pulled back. "But you didn't. You won't. I'll never be that stupid again."

Taking a deep breath, he said, "One good thing about tonight, you felt comfortable enough to call me 'Dad'."

I stared at him. "I did?"

"Didn't you mean to?" Mal looked like I'd just kicked him in the knee.

My mind replayed our conversations. "When you called. That's when I said it."

"Rae, if you didn't mean to, it's okay. I want you to want to call me that."

"I do. I really do." I squeezed his hand that rested on the back of the couch. "It's just that I had this plan about how I would make it special the first time I called you that." I huffed a sigh. "I guess screaming it when I was being chased by a stalker in the middle of a snowstorm made it pretty special."

"Got that right."

"But I had it all worked out." I stood. "Would you like your birthday present early?"

He broke into his lit-from-within grin. "I'd love it."

Digging into the back of the closet, I pulled out Mal's gift and card. I filled out the card with the sentence I'd been working on for weeks and then went back to the couch, handing him both items.

He opened the card first.

Dad,
I love being your daughter because I love you.
Rae

He leaned toward me but stopped, biting his lip as his knee shifted. I bridged the distance. He kissed me on the forehead. "I love you too. Maybe I should have said that sooner. But I didn't want to—"

"Make me uncomfortable. I finally figured that out." I laid the gift on his lap, my self-consciousness igniting my face. Would he like it? "Gram told me to frame a photo that's special to me. I picked one I think is special to both of us."

His grin growing brighter, Dad tore off the gift wrap.

A sleek, black metal frame with a cream mat surrounded the eight-by-ten photo of the children's home that Rusty thought looked like a mouth.

Dad held it out as I fiddled with a tear in my leggings. "I picked this one because—uh—well, I think it's a symbol of"—how goofy did this sound?—"our relationship."

"Really? How?" His blue eyes getting damp, he blinked several times.

"The black walls are a symbol of our ..." I cleared my throat and pointed. "A symbol of our past. We were in the dark about each other. But now the past is opening up to the future, which is the sky, and since we're together now, there's no limits."

I dropped my gaze to my socks. It had sounded pretty bad in my head, but I never imagined it could sound so much worse out loud.

Staring at the photo, Dad gripped my shoulder, nodded, swallowed, blinked, and released a shaky breath.

He probably wanted to be alone to collect himself. I picked up the icepack. "I'll get some fresh ice."

In the kitchen corner, I turned my back to him and busied myself in the freezer.

Gram was right. Big pile of mush.

Chapter 23

When I handed Dad the replenished icepack, he was telling dispatch to send over a town cop when they weren't tied up with emergencies.

I brought over steaming mugs of tea as he frowned at his phone. "What's wrong?"

"Ma and the boys, especially Rusty, will be relieved to know I'm not out on patrol. But I'd have to explain I hurt my knee, and I don't want to worry them."

I sipped the tea. "I know Rusty worries, but I can't imagine Gram ever worrying about anything."

"Having kids in law enforcement isn't easy on the nerves. Ma's had to put her worries on God because there was nothing else she could do. I don't like to add to them if I don't have to."

"But she's your parent, and you've got a problem. You should tell her."

The left side of his face contracted. "I said that, didn't I?" Releasing a short growl, he swiped a number. "Hey, Ma … no, nothing's wrong. Not really. I just wanted to let you and the boys know I'm not patrolling any more tonight. I fell and hurt my knee, so I'll be at Rae's place the rest of the … no, Ma, it's not. You know it's weak. I'll wear a brace for a few weeks and be fine." He paused a moment, then, "Oh, uh, sure." He passed me his phone. "Ma wants to talk to you."

I set down my mug and took the phone. "Hey, Gram."

Her voice was as pleasant as ever. "Rae, how seriously is Mal hurt?"

Dad snatched the phone from my hand. "You cannot use my own kid to narc on me."

"But, sweetie …" I lost the rest of her words.

"Yeah, it's painful, but it's no big deal. I'll just …" Rolling his eyes, he shoved the phone at me.

Gram said, "Rae, if Mal can't walk well, make sure he stays off his left leg as much as possible tonight."

"Don't worry. I will."

"I won't, sweetheart. See you tomorrow. Tell Mal to take it easy."

"Yes, ma'am."

I hung up. "You didn't mention the stalker."

"It's not something I want to go into it over the phone with Rusty or the other boys hanging around." He removed the icepack, bent his bad knee, then fell back, groaning. "Could you help me get my shoe off?"

After I untied his shoe and removed it, my phone lit up with a text notice from Houston, and I finally turned up the ringtone.

Heard on radio your apt broken into

Long story tell you l8r

I scrounged around the apartment for scraps of paper to write down the text of the notes and my research, jotting down everything I could remember. Any item I was less than completely sure about, I drew a star beside. I also removed the broken trail cam from a kitchen cupboard. Maybe a town cop could find prints on it that weren't mine.

Taking the sheets from me, Dad placed his mug on the milkcrates. "You know, this tea isn't bad."

Perched on the edge of the couch, I said, "The whole campaign seems like something China would invent. But I don't know why she'd always bring up my mom, unless that's just camouflage, making me think the stalker is someone Mom hurt, and it's really a relative who hates me because I'm your daughter or Reuel's granddaughter."

As he scanned the pages, I told him what I'd learned from Mrs. Blaney. "That's the smallest time window yet. The stalker is someone who was definitely free at 2:17 Monday morning."

Nodding, he kept reading.

Maybe it was my imagination, but he looked paler to me.

"Is your knee hurting more?"

Another slight shake, and he flipped over a sheet.

"One thing I can't figure out is vandalizing my truck. He broke into my apartment and then goes for my truck? And doesn't leave a note? He's left a note every other time."

Dad paled to sheet white.

"Are … are you okay?" I gripped his arm. "Are you going to pass out?"

"No, I'm not okay. It's hard reading these notes." He turned coaster-sized eyes to me. "He wrote that you should have died in the fire at the children's home, and you decided to trap him?"

I twisted the hem of my sweater. "Well, it worked Christmas morning with you and Jason and -- and Rick. I can see now it was pretty stupid."

"Not pretty. Completely." He looked back to the sheets. "You have a remarkable memory."

"I wrote it all down only two nights ago."

"Still remarkable. And, I have to admit, you are very thorough and organized in your research. You have dates and sources for almost everything you've written down." The color washed back into his face.

"Well, it was kinda like doing a research project at school." I finished my tea. "Or when the reference librarians answer questions. You've got to cite your sources. That's how I researched you and Jason and" — I took a breath — "and kept track of all my information." That was the second time Terry's name nearly slipped out. I loved being comfortable with my dad, but I had to keep that particular fact to myself.

"Since you like investigating, you wouldn't want to be a cop, would you?" His words crept out like they were afraid of being heard.

"Shoot fires, no."

"Good. Great." He patted my leg a little too hard. "We'll both live longer that way." His face tensing, he removed the icepack. "Phoenix Moore. I know that name."

"She's related to the Kincaids somehow. Didn't I write that down?"

Dad snapped his fingers. "That's it. And no, you didn't. But that's the connection. She's Chris Kincaid's mother."

I fell against the back of the couch, my mouth working without sound for a moment. "But--but she can't be. I mean, if Phoenix Moore is Chris's mother, then she can't be related to the Kincaids. Chris must be related to his great-grandpa, Dave Kincaid, through his dad and grandfather because his last name is Kincaid."

"No. Phoenix Moore is Dave's granddaughter. There's no father listed on Chris's birth certificate. Chris changed his name to Chris David Kincaid on his eighteenth birthday."

I gawked at a hole in the carpet as if it could help explain this development. "But why? How do you know all this?"

"It came out during my background search of Kincaid when he applied for the deputy's job. I remember Phoenix Moore because when you have an awful name, you notice awful names. I never asked Chris why he changed his because I figured I knew. His birth name is even worse than his mother's."

Phoenix Moore was Chris's mother. "So she survived the stabbing?"

Dad nodded.

Phoenix Moore was stabbed, and my mother was a prime suspect. I tried to work out some calculations, which was never a good idea at night, much less when I was exhausted.

"Chris turns twenty-three in April," I said, "and the stabbing was twenty-four years ago."

Dad caught my gaze. "You're not thinking it was Chris who was chasing—"

"No, no. No, that's ridiculous." I covered a yawn and stretched my eyes. "Now that I have time to think about it, though, I'm sure it was a man who chased me tonight. The build seems right for a man. So if China is behind this, could she have gotten one of her male cousins—our male cousins—to help her?" The image of Jack and Rome standing on Walter's back porch flashed through my mind.

"Possibly. If it isn't Egypt and China, and there's a good chance it isn't, I think your conclusion is right about his motive. Bella hurt this guy and his family. He can't get back at her, so pretending you're like your mom allows him to take revenge. First, he wanted to scare you into leaving your family. When that didn't work, he decided to go after you directly."

I shivered. Dad put his arm around my shoulders, and I scooted closer, resting my head on his shoulder and pulling a comforter over me.

His phone rang. As he talked, his words grew fainter and fainter …

"Rae? Rae, someone's at the door."

I clawed my way to consciousness.

"We're coming," Dad called. "Kiddo, you gotta get the door. It's probably a town cop."

I stumbled around the spool, unlocked the door, and fell back on the couch.

Garrett hurried in, shaking off snow.

Was I dreaming? Why had I let Garrett Matthews into my apartment in the middle of the—oh, that's right. I'd been chased by the stalker tonight. Or last night. I asked Dad for the time. 2:57 a.m. Yep, last night.

Dad offered his hand. "Sorry I can't stand, Matthews. Fell on my weak knee. Things must have settled down."

Now that my brain had switched totally on, I gave Garrett a big smile. "I'm glad you answered our call. Can I get you something?"

"Coffee."

"This is a strictly tea-drinking household," Dad said. "But Rae has some stuff with flavor."

Unzipping his jacket, Garrett said, "As long as it's hot."

After setting a teabag to steep, I showed Garrett my pages and explained the whole mess to him. Scribbling sheet after sheet of his own notes and firing question after question in his machine-gun style, Garrett looked almost as horrified as Mal, his hazel eyes widening.

"You kept six of the seven notes?" he said.

"They're in my backpack." I lifted my jacket and vest from the arm of the couch. "Can we get it and my other things?"

"Don't bother. I'll get all of it." He wrote on his pad. "Then I'll come back and dust for fingerprints, but I doubt I'll find any." He lifted his razor-edged face to me. "I know you've had a bad night, so I don't want to make you feel worse, but you should have contacted us after the second note. I get that you tried to ignore the first one, but after the second, and especially the third, you should have called us."

Dad said, "She knows that now." He tugged on my arm. I leaned to one side, and he kissed me above my ear.

I buttoned my jean jacket. "I want to come with you, Garrett. You might need help finding my stuff."

He was staring into the kitchen but with unfocused eyes, like he was viewing something inside his head.

"Garrett?"

Shaking himself, he snapped his notepad shut. "Sorry. I was just considering your list of suspects. You've done some first-class detective work, but you should leave that kind of job to the professionals."

"I will from now on. Dad, do you need anything before we go?"

Garrett started to tuck his notepad into his belt. "You're coming with me?"

Wow. He really had been deep in his mind. "Yeah. I can show you exactly where I left everything."

Dad asked me to place the folding chairs in a line to the bathroom so he could use them for support. Once I got the chain set up, Garrett and I finished dressing for the storm and went out.

The snow had petered off to a fine spray, but the wind had grown stronger. The first gust in my face stole my air almost as effectively as Dad landing on me. I jammed my hands into the pockets of my vest and flinched as the pain in my sore shoulder flared.

"How much snow do you think we got?" I skittered across the concrete pad to the side yard.

"Over six inches," Garrett said from behind me. "We'll drive as far as we can. If we get stuck, we'll walk the rest of the way."

Walking probably would have been faster, but the patrol car made it to Main Street. Garrett parked in front of the bank. High-stepping like we were in a half-time show, we marched through the snow into the newspaper's lot.

By the guardrail, I dug. Holding a flashlight, Garrett squatted beside me. In a few seconds, my fingers scraped over something hard, and I threw snow like a mole tunneling for his life, uncovering Mom's urn.

I clutched it against my vest.

Thank You, Father.

Digging with one hand, Garret revealed the grocery bag holding three of my albums. The snow was powdery and brushed off easily. Probably none of the photos had been damaged.

We returned to our excavation.

Any minute now, we'd find my backpack. Any minute now. Any ... minute ... now ...

"My backpack's not here." My voice quavered as if the cold had made it brittle. "It had my camera and the six notes and my notebook with my research."

Garrett sat back on his haunches. "You're sure you left all your stuff together?"

"Absolutely sure."

"I've got a shovel in my cruiser. We'll dig up the whole lot if we have to."

We did. No backpack, no camera, no evidence.

I dropped onto the guardrail, numb from the inside out. Snowflakes wandered between us and mixed with the clouds climbing from our panting mouths.

My pouch containing my license and credit card. The notes and my notebook. Two albums.

I squeezed my eyes against tears.

My camera. All of it in the hands of the stalker.

Chapter 24

"It's not the end of the world," Garrett said for the third time, accelerating to a crawl as we crept onto my street. "I can still investigate with what you wrote down from memory."

He'd been rattling off assurances since we'd given up looking for my backpack.

I didn't believe a word of it. He was just being nice.

Carrying the urn and albums, I stumbled into the apartment.

Dad put aside his phone. "What took you so — what's wrong, Rae?"

"My backpack." My voice seemed to come from the end of the street. "It's gone."

"You found everything but your backpack?"

Nodding, I set the urn and the bag of albums beside the couch, and I sank onto it.

Garrett explained what happened. "But I told Rae I can still investigate. The letters probably didn't have any prints on them. I'll dust for prints here, and tomorrow, when it's light, I'll check out your truck. Don't tow it or change the tires until I'm done with it."

He busied himself with tools and techniques.

My camera. All those photos. My license and credit card were in a zippered pouch in the backpack. Could he steal my identity? How could I fix it if he did? And the notes. The stalker had to be throwing a big ol' party for himself.

"Rae, it'll be all right." Dad spoke with a soothing tone. "We'll call the credit company to alert them to the theft of your card. You can get your license replaced. We can issue a description of your camera in case the creep pawns it or tries to sell it. I can help you buy a new camera. It won't be from your mom, but —"

"No," I said like a robot. "It's my mess. You don't have to clean it up for me."

"I'm not. I'm helping you clean it up. The whole family will help you. That's what families are for."

Mom, I am such an idiot. Wish you were here to tell me that, and I could apologize to you. A tear crawled down my cheek. *Wish you were here.*

"Your mom did a nice job with your albums."

My head swiveled. Dad had opened one. How long had he been looking at them? Garrett had moved out of the bathroom and was dusting objects in the main room.

"Printing photos was one thing Mom would splurge on," I said.

"Where were you living in this picture?" He turned the album to me.

He was just trying to get my mind off what a miserable mess I'd made of things.

"That's it." Garrett closed the trail cam. "I'll take your prints, Rae, and compare them to what I've found but I bet they'll all match yours."

After inking my fingers and pressing them onto a slip of paper, Garrett asked for the make and model of my camera. I pulled the operator's manual from the end table made of milk crates and passed it to him.

Jotting down the information, Garrett said, "Was your name or some identifying mark on your camera?"

"I scratched the date Mom gave it to me into the grip."

"That'll help." He shut his pad. "Mal's probably already told you this, so I'll just say it to be official. You shouldn't go anywhere alone."

"That's not an issue," Dad said, "since Rae's moving to the farm."

A flicker of surprise wavered in me. "I am?"

Dad's eyebrows rose. "You don't think I'd let you live here alone anymore, do you? I know I can't make you, but you either move out to the farm or" —he shifted his left leg, wincing—"your poor, crippled father and his poor, crippled leg will have to spend every freezing cold night trying to sleep in his freezing cold SUV."

I could see it—Dad trying to get comfortable in his patrol vehicle like a St. Bernard attempting to sleep on a cat bed.

A smile tried to form on my lips. "I'll move. I don't want to add permanently injuring you to my list of screw-ups."

"You made mistakes. We all do that."

"As backup," Garrett said, "in case you don't have a relative available, I'll text you my schedule."

"Thanks." I opened the door.

Stepping out onto the landing, Garrett zipped his jacket to his chin.

I held the edge of the door. "I really am glad you were the officer to get our call. You said when you've got questions, you keep asking until you get answers. I think that's a great quality for a cop." I sighed. "You'll need it since I lost the evidence."

The light by the door made his caramel hair glow. He broke into his V-shaped smile that should have melted all the snow and ice in a 100-yard radius. "Don't worry. I like a challenge. And I won't give up."

He descended the stairs, and I shut the door. But I didn't need to barricade it now.

I turned to Dad. "Do you think there's any chance I'll get my camera back?"

"I'll be honest." He looked up from the album. "No. But we can help you save for a replacement."

Tears pushed high in my eyes. "Thanks for telling me the truth. Don't worry about helping me buy another one. I'll pay for it." I collapsed beside him on the couch, noticing a hundred little aches and stings. "After I pay Uncle Hank for his trail cam."

"Hank isn't going to care about his camera after he hears why it got broken." He lifted the album closer to his face. "You were an awful cute baby."

Glancing at the album, I sat up. It held my earliest pictures.

"You look a lot like your mom with a bit of Ma and Jeanine thrown in."

My dad had never seen me before nineteen years old. He didn't just look at the photos. His deep blue eyes drank in every detail.

I scooched closer, and he put his arm around me. "I'm a year old in that picture. We lived near Mammoth Cave in Kentucky, and Mom said I liked to …"

~~~~~

Wow. I'd taken more of a beating last night than I thought.

In the shower the next morning, trying to put two thoughts together and have them make sense after only a few hours of sleep, I took inventory of my injuries.

Cut and bruised right knee, scrapes on both palms, sore ankle, sore neck, sore shoulder, bruised left shin, and—I twisted from side to side, flinching—no bruises, but my ribs did not appreciate Dad landing on them.

I dried off and dressed and found Dad staring into a cupboard, his short hair almost dry from his shower.

"No wonder you're so skinny." He shut one cupboard and opened another. "You barely have enough food to feed Micah."

"I get by. Sit down, and I'll fix you breakfast." I took two mugs from the strainer next to the sink. "What would you like?"

Removing two boxes of cereal from the cupboard, he told me toast would be great. He'd polished off what little remained in one box and was emptying the other into his bowl when I set the mugs, a plate of toast, and a jar of pickles on the card table.

The loaded spoon stopped in front of his mouth. "You eat pickles for breakfast?"

"I eat pickles any time."

"You must have a steel-clad stomach." He poured milk into his bowl. "Is your friend Devon up yet? I wanted to know if she needed help with her car."

"You can't help her. Gram told me to make sure you took it easy."
~~~~~

"I wasn't planning on getting out and pushing. But this morning should be quiet. One of my deputies could help."

Chewing a bite of toast, I wiped my fingers on a paper towel and texted Devon the question.

Her answer returned within a minute.

"She says Jason Carlisle is coming over at noon to pull her car out." I took another bite. "I thought of something in the shower, which didn't occur to me last night. I have a contract with Mrs. Blaney until June. I bet she won't knock anything off my rent for the days I don't live here. So I'll have to pay her instead of you. I can pay you what I normally pay for food, but that's not near as much—"

"My own daughter is not paying me rent!" Dad's shout probably woke Mrs. Blaney and the neighbors across the street. It jolted me better than the Irish Breakfast tea I was drinking.

"Sorry." He squeezed my arm. "Rae, if the boys were nineteen and living at home and working, I wouldn't charge them rent."

"But I should pay something. I'm not a user."

"I would never think that, and neither would Ma." He drained his mug.

My phone pinged with a text. "Garrett wants us to meet him at my truck. How long will it take you to get ready?"

"Normally five minutes." Dad frowned at his leg. "Tell him we'll be there in twenty." As I typed my answer, he said, "Do you have something I could wrap around my knee? If I could wrap it tight, it wouldn't hurt as much."

Using a pillowcase, safety pins, and the tie to my bathrobe, I wrapped Dad's badly swollen knee and tugged his pant leg over the makeshift bandage.

"Are you sure you don't need to go to the emergency room? Your knee looks pretty bad."

"I've had a whole heap worse." Gripping the back of a chair, Dad tried to put weight on it. "Could you bring me my shoes and my coat? And get the picture."

"Your birthday gift? Why?" I handed him his coat.

"I want to hang it up in my office. A lot more people can appreciate it there than at home."

A tingle of happiness skittered through me. Then it dissolved. "Are you going to tell people why I gave it to you?"

He watched me. "You don't want me to tell them why?"

"Well, I—uh"—I hooked wet hair behind my ear—"I guess it's your gift, so you can say anything you want about it."

His eyes narrowed. "What would you like me to say, Rae? I don't have to say anything more than it's a gift and I think it's great."

"That … that would be perfect. The other stuff—the symbol—well, I don't know if other people will get it."

"Then it'll be just between you and me."

The tingle came back, stronger.

We climbed down the steps from my apartment like it was a sheer cliff in the Alps. I tested a step first to see how hazardous it was, then Dad, using the railing for support, hopped onto it. The morning had thrown off any signs of the gloomy storm clouds from yesterday. The sun dazzled in a pure blue sky, and the snow sparkled under its cold brilliance.

Climbing into the patrol vehicle, I received a text from Houston. He asked if I was up and if he could stop by. I texted back where to meet us at the Rust Bucket.

Dad waited in the SUV while Garrett conducted his investigation. Yawning, he wrote in his pad.

"Can you go home to sleep after this?" I pulled my scarf higher on my face.

"As soon as I file the paperwork." Garrett smothered another yawn and stretched his hazel eyes open. "I switched to the night shift this week and haven't gotten used to it. You said you couldn't find a note?"

"Yes. Which is weird. He left a note every other time."

"Wind must have blown it away."

"The windshield didn't look windblown."

Another county SUV pulled up and Houston got out, extending his long legs to hike over drifts to reach us. He said, "The internet is going to blow up with the way people are gossiping about the burglary at your apartment. I've read about twelve versions, and one of them may actually be true."

My forehead creased. "But the only people who know are me, Dad, and … I bet it was Mrs. Blaney."

"It only takes one," Garrett said.

I explained to Houston what happened, and his mouth fell open. Then Dad called him over, and they discussed his shift from last night.

Between the snowstorm and the twenty hours since I'd discovered the crime, Garrett couldn't find any clues. "But with the description of your camera, we've got a shot of recovering it," he said. "Let's hope this guy is greedy as well as crazy and won't pass up the chance to make a buck."

As Garrett drove away, Houston said to me, "You took an awful risk, setting up that trap. Where would we find another drummer?" His tone was light, but his smile showed a concern that warmed me clear through.

Smiling back, I said, "I won't do it again. Can't let the band down."

Houston left, and Dad drove us to Main Street, parking almost beside the front door of the sheriff's office. He looked past me to the sidewalk and the door. "This may be harder than getting down from your apartment."

Snow trucks had piled thick banks against the curb. Strips of ice and clumps of salt crusted the sidewalk. We were facing an Olympic-caliber obstacle course and had to compete like we were in a three-legged race.

I shoved against a drift to get my door open, then stomped a path to Dad's side, making it easier for him. He leaned on me, and we were just a couple steps from the sidewalk when he lost his footing and fell across the hood.

"Are you all right?' I pulled hair from my lip.

"Just give me a minute," he said through his teeth.

A county SUV parked behind Dad's, and Chris climbed out.

"Garrett just told me what happened last night." He waded through a snowbank to us. "I'm really sorry to hear it, Rae. I'm glad you're okay."

"Thanks. Are you coming off your shift?"

"No. I didn't work last night. I was coming through town on my way back from a call." His thick eyebrows rose a fraction. "Mal, do you need help?"

"Of course not. I hang out on my hood every morning."

With Chris under Dad's left arm and me under his right, we struggled through the front door. Janice and Liz, sitting at their desks in the reception area, stared.

"How much have you heard about last night?" Dad said.

"A ton, but we weren't going to believe any of it until we talked to you," said Janice.

"I'll have to check with you two to see how long it took the county gossips to spread the story around."

Once Dad got settled at his desk upstairs, I returned to the SUV and grabbed the photo. As I walked into the office, Chris placed a chair beside Dad's desk, and Dad lifted his left leg onto it. Then he directed me to take down a couple of citations and a photo of him receiving some kind of medal. I hung the picture smack in the middle of the wall of photos.

"Rae's birthday gift to me," Dad said with a big grin.

His black eyes fixed on it, Chris stepped closer to the picture.

"Can I get you anything else, Dad?" I said.

"An icepack and lunch would be nice."

Chris backed up beside me. "You're a very good photographer, Rae. Have you thought about going to an arts school to major in photography?"

"Not really. I'm not college material."

"What?" Dad looked about as shocked as when I told him I was receiving threats. "Of course you are. You're one of the most intelligent people I've ever met."

Somewhere in Heaven, God has a book of things good parents should say to their kids, and contained in an early chapter is the line, "You're one of the most intelligent people I've ever met."

I had to smile. "You can't tell that from the grades I got my senior year." I stepped toward the door. "Where's the kitchen?"

"I'll go," said Chris. "What do you need?"

He must have been totally absorbed in my photo to miss Dad's request. Maybe I was a better photographer than I thought.

Dad told him about the icepack and gave me his order for lunch.

When Chris returned with a plastic bag full of ice cubes, Dad gave him a sidelong look. "I'd like to ask a favor of you, Kincaid. As the father of your friend. Not as your boss."

Except for a slight tremor of his right eyebrow, Chris showed no surprise at his words.

"Would you walk with Rae to the library? The cop side of me knows it's perfectly safe to walk along Main Street on a weekday morning. But the dad side doesn't want to take any chances." He looked to me. "Okay, Rae?"

"For sure." I pulled on my gloves. I didn't mind having such a good-looking cop as a bodyguard. "I'm not sure when I'll get lunch. I bet we're short-staffed today because of the snow. But I'll text you when I'm coming."

"Text me when you leave the library and when you leave the deli. I mean" — he cleared his throat — "I'd appreciate it if you did that. And don't forget to call your credit card company."

"Will do." I stepped over to him and hesitated. Then I kissed him near his ear. I hadn't kissed a guy, not even Grandpa Willis, since Noah Halstead dared me to kiss him in second grade. I rubbed my lips. Dad needed to shave.

He beamed as Chris and I left his office.

"Should Mal go to the emergency room?" said Chris as we passed out the front door, blinding, freezing sunshine smacking us in the face.

"He says he doesn't need to. But his knee looks awful."

Chris bent his head to watch the sidewalk. "You aren't carrying your backpack."

"Didn't Garrett tell you?" I skirted a slick spot and told Chris how I lost it.

"I'm really sorry," he said. We stopped in front of the library. "It's important to have things to remember people by."

Ignoring the twist in my stomach, I said, "I'm sure it's important to you that you have your great-grandfather's house."

Gazing down the shining street, he nodded. "When you get off for lunch, text me. Maybe I can accompany you."

The pain melted from my stomach. "That'd be ... that'd be —" I had to come up with something not lame. "That's so thoughtful of you." I wanted to groan. I sounded like Gram.

But a smile came and went over his fierce face. "I'll come if I'm available." Chris jogged back across Main Street without slipping once.

Chapter 25

I knocked on the library doors. Devon unlocked them, and I darted inside. Liberty and Serenity, seated at a table near the fireplace, dashed over to me.

"You look okay." Serenity scrutinized me from head to toe with eyes the same shade of green as her mother's.

Liberty said in her shy voice, "We're glad you didn't get hurt."

"There's nobody here in the lobby but you and me." Devon folded her arms. "You can talk in front of the girls. What happened last night?"

As we opened for the day, I told her everything, from the first note to Dad spending the night. "I don't know why I was so worried about telling Dad. He was only concerned about me staying safe."

"You don't know him. That's why." Devon gave me a thoughtful frown. "But why didn't you come to me? You knew I couldn't have a past with your mom."

Stooping to a low drawer, I let my hair hide the burn that flooded my face. "Because …" If Devon was really my friend — and braving a blizzard pretty much proved it — she could take an honest answer. I said in a rush, "Because I've never had a real friend before and don't know how to act with one." I crouched even lower.

"Oh." The longest pause. "I'm the best friend you've ever had?"

I nodded. "I've got no talent for making friends."

"You've got some talent, or you wouldn't have me."

"You're not mad I didn't tell you?"

"I wasn't mad. Just curious. You don't have to tell me anything you don't want to. Friends should take each other as they find them." Her voice quieted. "I'm very sorry about your camera and those albums. I've had to sell a few of Shayne's paintings to make ends meet. It nearly killed me every time."

"That's awful."

She shrugged. "Shayne would understand that I had to do it for our girls. It hurts me more than it would've hurt him."

Once we opened at 9:00, kids who could walk to the library dribbled in. They usually showed up because hanging out at home on a snow day was not as much fun as harassing the library staff.

About an hour later, Barb came down from the balcony carrying two thick books.

She plopped them on the counter. "These are yours, aren't they, Rae?"

"My albums!" My shout turned the head of every person in the lobby, and two tweens shushed me.

But Barb didn't. "Even if all these pictures hadn't been labeled, I would've recognized you and your mom."

I turned pages. "All the photos seem to be here."

Devon looked to Barb. "Where did you find them?"

"Bean Oller clears the library lot. He found them and brought them to me."

"Is this all he brought?" Hope surged in my heart.

"Yes." Barb tilted her head to one side, resettling her wire-rimmed glasses on her nose. "Are you missing something else?"

I caught my lip in my teeth. Telling Devon about the stalker was one thing. Telling my boss was completely different. Dad seemed to think telling people plainly how we discovered he was my father killed rumors, so I released my lip, and I explained what happened, although in an abbreviated form.

"How terrible." Barb shook her head. "But if Bean had found anything else he would have brought it with the albums. I'll tell the custodial staff to watch out for your backpack." She glanced over the lobby. "We're not busy. Why don't you check our dumpster?"

"I'll help." Serenity ran over from the table, her chubby face alive with interest. "Libby, do you want to come?"

The expression on Liberty's delicate face appeared torn as she drew circles with a crayon. She must have been weighing the choice of being bored inside or being bored outside, but finally set down her crayon and slipped on her lavender coat.

We trooped downstairs and out the basement door. One glance in the dumpster killed my hope. Only two bags lay hunched in one corner.

Serenity scrambled up the side. "I'll see if your stuff is in those bags."

"He wouldn't have wasted time climbing in the dumpster and opening the bags to put my things inside," I said.

But Serenity had swung half her body over the lip of the opening before I grabbed her around the waist and hauled her off.

Leading the girls back inside, I said, "The weird thing is, why did he throw out the albums? He hates me and tearing them up would have really hurt me."

"Maybe he didn't have time." Liberty took off her knit hat and shook out her long, black hair.

"Then why not take them with everything else in my backpack?" I started up the stairs. "I left my backpack behind the newspaper office. He found it and must have decided he couldn't get to me and gave up the chase. But he opened my backpack, dug around in it, and threw out the albums. It doesn't make sense."

"The albums were too heavy." Serenity hung on the railing in the stairwell. "He's carrying your backpack, and it's too heavy, so he takes out some stuff."

"It wasn't that heavy. I only took off my backpack when I couldn't climb the guardrail into the parking lot."

I put the question to Devon. She mulled it over but couldn't come up with any better answer than her daughters.

We were still discussing it when Jason walked in carrying Sylvie, Allison and Richard trotting by his side. All of Jason's kids shared his brown eyes, and Richard was practically his clone.

"Rae, I'm so glad you're all right." Jason sat Sylvie on the counter in front of me, his eyes filled with concern. "Rick told me somebody chased you last night, and then Mal put in a call for a town officer to come to your apartment."

"I'm fine now." I checked my messages and frowned.

"Something wrong?" said Devon.

"Chris can't walk with me to the deli and over to Dad's office."

"I can go with you if Jason will watch the girls."

"I don't want to delay you two."

"Don't worry about that." He scooped Sylvie off the desk. "I'll go, Devon, if you'll keep an eye on Alli and Richard."

Barb and Marcus came to the desk to cover for Devon and me, and I stepped into the frigid afternoon with Jason.

Helping Sylvie with her hood, Jason said, "Rick told me your truck was vandalized last night too."

"Not last night." Once again, I launched into my abridged version of the stalker's campaign.

When I told him the stalker stole my backpack with my camera, Jason skidded to a halt short of the door to the deli. "That's ... that's—I can imagine how you feel. My dad gave me a Mustang for my sixteenth birthday. He died a year after that. I've always kept it." He held open the door.

While waiting for my order, Jason said, "You know, I have a camera with a zoom lens that I don't need since Rick gave me a new one for Christmas. I'd like you to have it."

"That's very nice of you, Jason, but you don't have to—"

"Yes, I do." He allowed Sylvie to slide to the floor while still gripping her hand. "I owe you so much for allowing the statute of limitations to run out on Rick's crimes," he whispered. "I told you to think of me as your fairy godfather. Let me do this for you."

His expression was taut, willing me to accept his gift.

"Okay. I really appreciate it. Can Dad and I swing by after work to get it?"

"Absolutely." The tense lines melted under his smile.

Jason and Sylvie said goodbye on the stoop to the sheriff's office. Loaded with a drink carrier and a bag filled to capacity with sandwiches, chips, and containers of soup, I went upstairs to Dad's office.

He started as if shocked to see me, covering the receiver of his phone. "You didn't text me."

"Jason walked with me to the deli and here."

I unpacked the sandwiches and soup while Dad finished his phone call. His eyes looked droopy, and he kept rubbing them when he wasn't flinching.

"Carlisle's a good guy." Dad took a long sip of coffee. "I'll have to thank him."

"You can do that tonight when we drive over to pick up a camera he's giving me."

"Why is he giving you a camera?"

"Because he knows mine got stolen, and he feels he owes me and wants to help out."

Chewing a bite of a Reuben sandwich, Dad studied a corner of his desk. "You can't accept, Rae. I know you and Jason didn't think of this, but accepting an expensive gift from him could launch an ethics investigation against me."

My spoon stopped halfway to my mouth. "What do you mean? Why would — because you're elected?"

He nodded. "Someone could misunderstand and think Jason is buying my influence by giving gifts to my daughter."

I fell back in my seat. "You're not serious."

"Completely. There's about half a dozen people in this county, influential people, who think it's a crime I beat Simcox by two votes. Any of them would understand it was an innocent gift but still use it as an excuse to get an investigation started."

My eyes widened. "We can't have that."

Dad reached for his phone. "I'll call Carlisle and explain." His hand rested on the phone, but didn't lift it. "No. We'll stop by after we pick up your stuff from your apartment tonight. I've got something else I need to talk to Carlisle about."

Between sips of soup, I described how my photo albums had been found and how strange it was that they weren't damaged. "Why risk stopping in the lot and searching my backpack? That's stupid. After all these weeks, I know he's not that."

"Criminals can do the dumbest things, but this guy or gal doesn't fit that mold." He blew on his chicken noodle soup. "I've got news too. Both good and bad."

"I'll take the bad first."

"Actually, it's one piece of news that's both good and bad. Egypt and China couldn't have chased you." He indicated a sheet of paper in front of him. "I was going over the reports from last night, and at 7:53 p.m., my chief deputy, Harris, found them in their truck where it had slid off Devil's Creek Road about a mile from the intersection at Mason-Inger Road. From that time on, they were with Harris. She was driving them home when she met Walter, who was out looking for them. That was at 8:39. I know you're sure it was a man chasing you, but it doesn't hurt to cross off our prime suspects."

I munched on a chip. "Did they say why they were out in a blizzard?"

"They told Harris they were heading to a friend's house and didn't realize how bad the roads were. That could be true, but most Malinowskis have a reflex to lie whenever they talk to law enforcement."

"Could they have been going to meet a guy to jump me? Like one of their cousins. When they didn't show up, he went ahead alone with the plan."

Footsteps thundered up the stairs like a herd of spooked cows, and my brothers burst into the office carrying crutches and a brace that looked like one of Iron Man's more powerful accessories. Aunt Jeanine brought up the rear.

"The roads must not be too bad." Dad took a hug from Micah and a punch from Aaron.

"I felt a bit like an ice road trucker." Removing her fuzzy winter headband, Jeanine fluffed her long, red-gold hair.

Plopping himself on the desk, Micah brought his nose within inches of Dad's. "Your face looks okay."

"He landed on his knee, Micah." Rusty crouched besides Dad's chair with the brace. "When Rae wrecked into him."

A bite of Italian sub got hung up in my throat.

"Rusty." Dad's tone was stern. "It was an accident. It could've happened with any call I was on."

"Which Ma and I have both explained to him." Her pearly pale face hardening, Aunt Jeanine arched an eyebrow at him, and Rusty became fascinated with helping Dad put on his brace. She put a slim arm around my shoulders. "We're all glad you're safe, Rae."

"You'll be safe when you move out to the farm." Aaron spread three sheets of copier paper on the desk. "We've been working on a plan all morning."

A wary expression crept over Dad's face. "What plan?"

Aaron's light blue eyes shone. "I've worked out a way to set off a trebuchet with a trip wire. So the guy who chased Rae comes to the farm.

He walks into the breezeway, he walks through the trip wire." Aaron pointed from drawing to drawing as a stickman enacted his plan. "The trip wire pulls on the trebuchet and bam! He gets hit with a rock."

"Do you like Gram's room, Rae?" Micah rummaged in the bag I'd brought the food in. "She's giving it to you."

I stared. "I thought I'd sleep in the playroom."

"Without a door to give you any privacy?" Dad grunted, tightening a strap on the brace. "I wanted to give you my room, but Ma said you need your own bathroom."

"She does." Aunt Jeanine looked down to me. "You'll still have to share the bathroom with Ma, but that's world's better than sharing one with four males."

"Excuse me." Aaron glared at us. "I was talking."

Once he had our full attention, he went on. "I'm gonna build a bunch of trebuchets with trip wires. I can put them any place I can string fishing line between two points. We were gonna dig pits, but the ground's too frozen." He grinned at me. "That weirdo won't ever bother you again."

"He'll never make it out alive." Micah dug around Dad's bag of chips.

"Of course he will." Rusty stood. "The trebuchets are only launching rocks at him."

"But if we killed him, he'd be stopped. Right, Dad?" Micah put his hand on Dad's shoulder.

I didn't know whether to feel loved or alarmed.

Dad glanced from Rusty to Aaron to Micah. He opened his mouth, closed it, and looked around at the three of them again.

Her huge, blue eyes twinkling, Aunt Jeanine made a noise that might have been a suppressed giggle.

Then Dad rubbed Aaron on the back. "I'm glad you boys are on my side."

Shuffling the papers together, Aaron beamed.

"But you can't set up trebuchets around the farm to hurt people. It's illegal."

"That's what Ma and I told them." Aunt Jeanine searched through her baggy purse.

The glow in Aaron's face faded. "How come? It's our property."

"If someone trespasses," said Rusty, "aren't we allowed to defend our property?"

"Boys." Dad rubbed his forehead. "I can quote from the Ohio Revised Code, or you can just take my word for it. You can't do it."

Rusty's narrow face grew long with a frown, Aaron's shoulder's slumped as he fingered his drawings, and Micah asked Dad if he was done with his sandwich.

"Rae, if you'd like, the boys and I can get your truck towed and load what we can from your apartment into my truck." Jeanine handed me a piece of paper she found in her purse. "Not personal items, if you don't want us to. List what you want us to take. And write the address of where your truck is parked."

I wrote down the items they could pack and gave her my keyring. Aunt Jeanine headed for the door. Rusty hugged Dad but didn't even glance at me as he left. If he saw me as a threat to our dad, no amount of help with his writing would get me back on his good side.

Taking the last sip of soda, I sighed.

Aaron trudged past me. I touched his arm. "Thanks for looking out for me."

A smile managed to break through the gloom.

Micah said, "Do you have any chips left, Rae?"

"Nope."

"Okay. See you later." He leaped from the desk and ran out.

Chapter 26

After picking up my clothes and the rest of my personal stuff at the apartment, Dad drove us over to Wilmot Avenue, where the oldest, fanciest houses in Wellesville lined the street.

Draped in snow, Jason's solid, three-story house looked posed for a Christmas card photo, even without a wreath on the thick wood door or lights wrapped around the sturdy posts of the porch. Spotlights beamed onto windows upstairs and down. The manicured house didn't flaunt the Carlisle fortune, but it didn't hide it, either.

Dad parked beside the broad stone stairs that led up the little hill to the porch. Hanging his arm over the steering wheel, he studied the cleared steps. He'd only looked tired at lunch. Now he appeared exhausted. "I think I can make it up those steps." He opened his door.

I shoved my door against a snowbank, tromped through it and around to Dad's side, and pulled his crutches from the back seat.

We reached the porch without a single slip. One ring of the bell brought Jason to the door.

"Hey, Rae." He held a navy blue camera case. "Everything you need is in here." His million-watt smile was more dazzling than the spotlights.

Shoot, I hated this. "I can't accept, Jason. I'm really, really sorry. It's because Dad's the sheriff. He can explain."

His smile vanished as Dad said, "May we come in?"

"Of course." Jason swung the door wide.

We stepped into the finest room I'd ever entered, not counting a field trip to a plantation mansion. The rich, dark-stained wood floor and matching paneling gleamed under the light cast by a silver chandelier. A grandfather clock ticked in one corner, and a huge, round rug with a red and blue sunburst was thick enough to lose a shoe in.

High-pitched young voices drifted to us from the back of the house, but not a single toy, not one plastic brick, was in sight. Would my wet boots do more damage to the floor or the rug? Not sure, I remained just inside the door, blinking at the brilliance.

Jason studied Dad. "You don't look well, Mal."

"Good. I'd hate to feel this awful and keep it all to myself." Leaning on his crutches, he went on. "I really appreciate — and Rae does too — your offer of your camera. I know you feel like you owe her and you —"

"I don't feel like it," said Jason. "I do."

Mal explained how my acceptance of the camera could trigger an ethics investigation.

Jason's eyes grew rounder. "You think Eric Simcox would make trouble for you?"

"Or Melissa O'Neil or Mayor Teague. Or any other big shot in the county who thinks 'sheriff' and 'Malinowski' shouldn't go together."

Jason shook his head. "It never occurred to me that my offer might look questionable."

"Of course it didn't," said Dad. "You were being a nice guy. But I can't afford to take even the slightest chance of looking less than totally honest and transparent."

"I had no idea your position was so precarious."

"Two votes don't make it comfortable." Dad heaved an exhale and dredged up a weary smile. "If you want to pay Rae back, you can help us right now. Do you have time to talk?"

His forehead wrinkling, Jason nodded.

Dad looked down the hall in the direction of the children's voices. He nodded at the room to our right. "How about we talk in there?"

Adding wrinkles around the corners of his eyes, Jason called, "Rick, keep the kids in the family room. I have to talk to Mal and Rae."

He slid aside a pocket door, and Mal and I entered an office that continued the dark wood from the foyer, even across the ceiling.

Gesturing toward two high-backed chairs, Jason clicked on the lamp sitting at the corner of a heavy, wooden desk, the kind you'd expect an executive to sit behind as he commanded his family's company.

Dad dropped into a chair. "I need to ask you about Bella." His voice had gone quiet. "I know it's painful, and I wouldn't ask if I didn't think it was necessary."

He explained our theory that the stalker had been hurt because of Mom's connection to him or someone in his family. "How long did you have a relationship with her?"

The lamp illuminating only one side of his face, Jason flinched. "About six months."

"Do you have definite knowledge of any other guys she was involved with?"

Jason offset his jaw. "I heard all kinds of stories, but Bella always talked me out of believing them. However, I do know, personally, of two men. I think one was a relative of yours."

"Big surprise," Dad said. "Who?"

"I think it's a cousin of yours. I saw him running from the children's home one evening—it was fall of our senior year. I usually met Bella at the home, so no one would know we were together. There was just enough light to make him out as he ran into the woods. He looked like a California surfer dude. Still does, the few times I've seen him lately, although now I'd call him a well-used surfer dude."

"That's gotta be Troy, my dad's half-brother."

"Then it can't be him. He was around our age."

Dad made a noise, like a suppressed growl. "I'm sure it's Troy. He's only five years older than I am. I'll find a photo and send it to you to confirm your identification. What's your number?"

They exchanged phone numbers, then Dad said, "Who was the other guy?"

Jason straightened a glass-blown paperweight. "That was at the children's home too, right before our senior year started. Bella and I had set up a meeting there in the evening. We were walking inside when a man rushed out of the darkness. He threw me to the floor, then grabbed Bella, shaking her, pleading with her to take him back." His words sped up. "I tried to pull him off her, but I was built like a stick then, so he kept knocking me down.

"He said over and over he'd given up everything for her, she was all he had now, she had to take him back." A shiver stole through Jason's shoulders. "Until that day, I'd never heard anyone so agonized.

"I finally got a good hold on him, and Bella wiggled free and ran out of the room. The man flung me to the floor and kicked me, and I was trying to get out of his range when Bella came in with a gun. She must have had it hidden in the home."

Mom leveling a gun at a crazy ex-boyfriend? The picture wouldn't gel.

"Bella told the man to get out and leave her alone, or she'd shoot him dead, but he started toward her and only stopped when she fired a bullet near his feet."

Jason shook his head slowly, as if he couldn't quite believe this story had happened to him. "The man froze, stunned, like she'd actually put a bullet in him. He tried pleading again, but Bella told him it was over, and if he didn't leave her alone, it'd really be over.

"The man said, kind of in a daze, that it would never be over and left. I never saw him again. I'd never seen him before, either."

"So he wasn't from the county?" Dad said.

"I don't think so, but he was older, so I wouldn't have noticed somebody that age unless he was a parent of a friend of mine."

"How old do you think he was? Do you remember anything else about his appearance?"

"When you're getting clobbered by someone, you remember everything about him." Jason's smile had a brittle edge. "He had a little gray at the temples. I thought then he had to be ancient, but he could have been as young as forty. He was well-dressed—khaki pants, light blue button-down shirt open at the collar, gold chain necklace, heavy gold pinkie ring, expensive tan loafers. As soon as I saw him, I thought he looked like a Mafioso from a Scorsese movie with the dark brown hair, brown eyes, olive complexion. Or he might have had a deep tan."

"Could he have been Latino?"

Jason offset his jaw again. "Possibly. I can't say for certain."

"Bella never told you his name?"

"No. She would only say he was an ex-boyfriend. I tried to talk to her about him a couple times, but she'd change the subject." A sigh pressed him lower into his well-cushioned desk chair. "I always believed whatever Bella told me."

I gazed at a large globe in a corner. Mom said she'd been a terrible person, hadn't tried to sugarcoat it for me, but it was still hard to hear. Jason was an even nicer guy than I thought for not holding my mom's actions against me.

"We appreciate the help," Dad said. "If you think—"

A knock sounded on the pocket door, and a man's voice said, "May I come in?"

Jason gave us a questioning look, and Dad nodded, trying to leverage himself out of the chair with his crutches.

I came over to him. "Do you need help?"

"No," he said through his teeth.

I put my hand under his arm. "Let me—"

Raising his eyebrows, Dad gave me an expression harder than concrete.

Okay. I dropped my hand. So there's a male equivalent of the mom look. Didn't know that.

Jason called, "Come in," and Rick entered, closing the door behind him. He had Jason's dark brown hair and eyes but was taller, thinner, grimmer than his brother. Batman to his Superman.

Rick said, "Rae. Mal."

Dad notched his head forward a fraction. "Carlisle." He stood at attention, not supporting himself on the crutches anymore, using them just for balance.

The bookcases, the desk, the rich, coffee-colored paneling and floor, all thrown into shadows by the low light of the lamp, seemed the totally wrong backdrop for the tension that had stiffened the atmosphere in the room. A better one would have seen dust blowing between the sheriff and the outlaw under a setting sun with a tumbleweed bouncing by.

Rick said in a husky voice, "I — I wanted to tell you and Rae I'm going on a mission trip to Haiti for three months. Father Keir arranged it." His hands clenched and unclenched at his sides. "I need to get away, where people don't know me. To think." He swallowed like he was trying to get down a melon whole. "I never thanked you, Rae."

"You don't have to." Heat crawled up my face. "Thank Mom and God, not me." His gratitude was a world harder to handle than his running from me.

"I have. Every day." Another painful swallow. "I also want to thank you and Mal for keeping my crimes to yourselves. I don't want to hurt Jason and the kids and Barb."

"Not our story to tell." The response was little more than a growl from Dad.

"Perhaps, someday, you can forgive me, Mal."

My head whipped to Dad. Where had Rick gotten the idea that Dad needed to forgive him for attacking my mother? When Dad called after Christmas?

"I'm trying," Dad said. "My God expects me to, and I'm trying my hardest."

What was going on?

Rick gave us a short nod and slipped out of the room.

Wiping an eye, Jason said, "Hope you recover soon, Mal."

Dad's stance lost its steel-straight rigidity, and, leaning on his crutches, he said, "Thanks, Carlisle."

We made it to the SUV without a stumble and headed out of town. I replayed the scene between Rick and Dad. Why did Dad need to forgive Rick? His crime was against Mom. And me, since she was pregnant with — oh.

I turned under my seatbelt. "You haven't forgiven Rick for trying to kill me."

Shifting his left leg, Dad sucked in a breath. "I know I need to. But he tried to murder one of my kids. That's not easy for a parent to forgive. And if Rick hadn't attacked Bella, I might have been able to pay her and raise you."

"I wish I could have known you my whole life too, but if Rick hadn't attacked Mom, she never would have gotten saved. She was sure she wouldn't have turned her life around without almost dying."

"I know." He widened his eyes, probably wishing he could prop them open. "That's the reason we Christians are here, to help other people find salvation. I just wish I could have had you all these years and your mom still got saved." He released a sigh and seemed to shrink against the bucket seat. "But it's my fault. I messed up that night at the children's home, so I've paid for it by losing so much time with you."

He'd never sounded so depressed before. Maybe looking at my albums had shown him what he'd missed.

"We'll make up for it." I put my hand on his as it gripped the steering wheel.

He gave me a smile so sad it seemed weighed down with all the sorrow from when he'd mourned for me. "You don't have any hard feelings toward me. I can't believe it."

"You think I should be mad at you because you weren't around when I was a kid? You thought I was dead."

"I've been in law enforcement for over fifteen years. I've seen middle-aged adults blame their parents for everything from their addiction to why they tried to shoot a cop."

"On Christmas morning, I told you I don't blame you, and I quit blaming Mom. I was so mad at Mom for telling me about her past only two weeks before she died. She was dying, and it was hard to question her. Then she was gone, and I was mad that I couldn't learn any more. But after a few months, I had to give up being mad because it hurt too much. I just wanted to love my mom and remember all the wonderful things we did together and what a great person she was."

"You have a very kind heart, Rae."

I squeezed his hand. "I guess I get it from both sides."

A little sadness seemed to lift from his expression as we drove deep into the country, the lights from the farms as distant as the stars sparkling in the jet sky.

Chapter 27

"Half the drawers under the sink are empty now," Gram called from the little bathroom connected to her bedroom. "Does that give you enough room?"

"That's plenty." I carried an armful of toiletries and unloaded them onto the sink. "Are you sure you want to sleep in the playroom?"

The second story couldn't compare to Gram's room. The walls were a light blue, the wood furniture was old but not fussy and intricate, and the four lamps guaranteed I'd never need to turn on the ceiling light. If I could move the half-moon window down from the playroom, it'd be perfect.

"Yes." She shook out a blanket. "You're used to living on your own, so you need a space of your own. We'll try this for a while, and if it doesn't work, we'll come up with another arrangement."

I hung three shirts in the huge walk-in closet. "Thanks for understanding about your afghan getting torn up." I started to hang a pair of pants, but my arms dropped. In two days, I'd lost the last gift from my mom and the first gift from my grandmother.

Gram glanced up from the blanket she was tucking in on the double bed. "Now, if I recall correctly, I gave you that afghan on Christmas Day, so I believe that was *your* afghan, unless you stole another one from me, and that's the one the thug ripped apart."

I would have laughed if I hadn't been bone-weary.

She came over to the closet. "I want you to go through my yarn and pick out the kind you like. I'll knit you another afghan."

Tears sprang into my eyes. Shoot, I was way, way more tired than I'd realized. "That'd be perfect."

"Gram." Rusty poked his head in the door from the living room. "Dad's asleep on the couch. Do you want me to wake him up?"

"I'll do it before I turn in." Glancing at the clock on the nightstand, she said, "You should go to bed, Rusty."

"Okay. 'Night, Gram."

He disappeared from the door, but Gram called him back. "You didn't say goodnight to your sister."

Rusty toyed with the paper bookmark protruding from his fantasy novel. "'Night, Rae," he said to the floor and slunk away.

I tried to sigh, but it came out as a yawn.

"Don't let Rusty bother you." Gram patted my back. "He's upset Mal got hurt because he worries that Mal or I will walk out the door and die, like Em did. Give him a few days to think over what's happened. Rusty worries too much. But so does Mal."

"You don't. You said you pray."

"I'm not a worrier by nature. But after Reuel was killed, I found myself worrying more and more, especially about Mal when he was in high school. Then he and Carrie went into law enforcement. I realized the only way I'd be able to live happily was to turn every worry over to the Lord. It's not easy, believe me. But after years and years of practice, I know it does absolutely no good to worry and every good to pray." She gathered her bathrobe and pajamas. "I'll let you get settled."

After she left, I filled drawers with clothes, debating with myself, which isn't a good idea when you're exhausted. Should I tell Dad about Terry? He could be in the same position as Jason, having certain knowledge of other men my mom had seduced. But Mrs. O'Neil couldn't find out. I didn't like Terry, but I felt sorry for him.

I went upstairs and told Gram I'd wake Dad if she wanted to go to bed.

"Aren't you going to sleep now?" She untied the leather strap holding back her long hair. "You look ready to fall over."

"I want to talk to him before I go to bed."

Downstairs, I shook and shook Dad by the shoulder until I was afraid a molar would jiggle loose. Eventually, groaning, he heaved himself into a seated position, swinging his bad leg onto the coffee table. Taking a nap had done nothing to erase the fatigue from his face.

Crouching beside him, I whispered, "I know of somebody else who might be able to help the case because he had an affair with my mom, although I'm dead sure he's not the stalker. Can we talk in your bedroom?"

Attention lifted his sagging shoulders and features. I helped him downstairs and into the finished part of the basement.

I was glad Dad hadn't offered me his room. Although the walls were painted a sandy color and the wood furniture was blond, the basement room still felt claustrophobic with only one decent-sized window looking onto the backyard.

Hunched over his crutches, Dad said, "Who is it?"

I took a deep breath. "My mom blackmailed three men when she was pregnant with me, not two." I bit my lip. "I hope you don't think I lied to you, but I didn't want to get this man into trouble."

"You didn't lie. It was none of my business until now. It's Terry O'Neil, isn't it?"

My gasp sounded as loud as a scream in the quiet house. "How--

how—"

"I noticed a few things. Several times when you mentioned the letters or the meetings at the children's home on Christmas morning, you stuttered over your words or paused, like you had to make a readjustment. And you told me you talked about movies with Terry. That sounded like a similar tactic to the ones you used to get to know Jason and me. Then you said Terry quit speaking to you. That seemed a natural reaction if you confronted him at the children's home, and he was afraid his wife would find out." His voice softened. "The meeting—it didn't go well, did it?"

The same scorched feeling that had tried to hollow my gut Christmas morning flared. "At first, Terry said I couldn't be his kid. Then he said, even if I was, he couldn't acknowledge me because of his wife and his position. If I told anybody of his affair, he'd say I was lying." I held my hand against my stomach.

Dad slumped against the chest of drawers. "I am so sorry you went through that. Now I understand why you thought I was upset about being your father when I almost passed out from shock."

I gave him a big smile. "But then you said you were blessed to have found me."

"I was. I am."

Somehow, my smile managed to grow bigger. I said, "Terry O'Neil can't be the stalker. Leaving nasty notes seems like a perfect fit for his personality, but he couldn't pull himself through my bathroom window."

"I agree. I just want to talk to him like I did Jason. I think he still teaches a few classes at the college, so he must have an office number. I'll try to get a hold of him that way, and his wife will never know." He motioned for me to come closer and enveloped me in a hug. "Thanks for trusting me with this."

Back in Gram's room, I threw on my pajamas and collapsed onto the bed, snuggling under a thick comforter and a hunter green quilt.

Forty-eight hours ago, I was waiting for a stalker with a rifle on my lap. Twenty-four hours ago, I was running for my life through a snowstorm. Now I was going to sleep in my grandmother's room under my great-grandmother's quilt surround by my dad and my brothers.

Thank You, Father, for getting me—

My alarm went off. I slapped for my phone, knocked it onto the floor, and grabbed the little lamp on the bedside table before it toppled to the rag rug. Dawn gave the bedroom a fuzzy appearance. I'd slept better than I had in a month.

Chapter 28

When Uncle Hank dropped me off at work Thursday morning, he said, "Now if that stalker corners you in the library, just grab the biggest book you can find and read it to him. Should put him to sleep in a couple pages. Always did me when I was in school."

"I'll keep it in mind." I grinned as I retied the scrunchy holding my braid. "But nothing's happened in a week. Since I'm living at the farm, maybe he's given up."

"Unless he's as mad as a rabid dog, he should give up. The Big Guy'll pound him into the ground if he catches him."

I waved as Uncle Hank pulled away, then I headed inside, shouldering Aaron's old backpack that held my new pouch with a new credit card and new license and a new lunch bag. I would have liked a bigger backpack, but Dad said I should wait until I found one I really liked before buying. At least this one was plain black. When Aaron offered it to me, I was afraid it would have superheroes or cute bears or something on it.

The clock on the courthouse struck noon and began to play the state song of Ohio as I pushed through the outside doors of the library ... and stopped dead between the double sets.

Mrs. O'Neil stood planted by the checkout desk, looking down on Devon like a vulture analyzing its dinner. Devon met her gaze with one that should have scorched her eyeballs.

Juggling books and CD cases, Mr. Schuster held open an inner door, so I had to enter.

"You're prejudiced," Mrs. O'Neil said in a dismissive tone. "You feel you must defend your friend."

Devon's voice rose above acceptable levels for a library. "I'm defending her because I know that theory couldn't hold water if you lined it with steel."

"Devon, if you hope to keep your job here, I advise you to treat me with something other than contempt."

"I'd be happy to if you weren't so contemptible."

The old lady recoiled like Devon had spit on her.

"Hey, Devon." I sauntered over to the desk like I hadn't heard anything. "I have to drop my stuff off in the kitchen, then I can cover lunch for you." I threw on my professional smile. "Hello, Mrs. O'Neil."

An eager gleam came into her sunken eyes, like the vulture had just spotted a tastier target. "Things have worked out rather well for you, haven't they, Rae? I understand you are quite comfortable at the Malinowski farm."

"Rae, go ahead to the kitchen," Devon said.

"Some people say the stalker has been more a friend to you than an enemy." Mrs. O'Neil's tone was casual, but her pinning gaze was anything but.

I lowered my eyebrows. "What?"

"Oh, just say it." Devon flung a long, dark braid over her shoulder. "I don't suppose you've heard, Rae, because you're not a gossip, but some people are saying you invented the stalker so you can live with your dad and have him foot your bills."

The backpack slid off my shoulder and hit the floor.

Devon continued, "But I just told Mrs. O'Neil that theory is impossible. You asked me to pick you up after work that night. If you concocted the stalker story to make Mal feel sorry for you, you wouldn't have done that. You couldn't have known my car would get stuck and you'd have to walk to meet me. Besides, when you asked me for a ride, you were terrified. You weren't pretending."

"It's still very convenient." Mrs. O'Neil's words slid through the quiet of the library. "Rae has gained so much from this unfortunate circumstance."

My lungs seized up. Dad would believe me, wouldn't he? He'd know I wouldn't make up a story like that so I could live off him. If I hadn't dropped my backpack, if I still had the notes—

"Devon," Mrs. O'Neil said, "I know you think your job is safe because Barb and Jason Carlisle favor you for some unfathomable reason. But you are completely ..."

Jason Carlisle. Mrs. O'Neil's words faded as the scene at the children's home on Christmas morning filled my mind. Rick sobbing on the ground because he wouldn't have to face prison, Jason and Mal and I comparing blood types.

I burst out laughing.

Mrs. O'Neil whipped around to me. "Do you think I'm being funny?"

The laughter poured out of me so hard and fast I could barely shake my head.

If I was the same greedy manipulator Mom had been, I would have conned Jason Carlisle into believing he was my father. Or blackmailed Rick for his crime. I would have targeted the richest men in the county, not the sheriff.

And Dad knew this.

Leaning onto the counter, I rested my head on my arms and gulped in air to sober up. When I stopped sounding like a drunk hyena, I straightened. Mrs. O'Neil was gone.

"She burned a trail to Barb's office," Devon said to my questioning look. "Mind telling me what you found so hilarious?"

I wiped my hand over my forehead. "I wish I could. It's private. But I know my dad will never, ever believe that theory, and that's what matters."

In between patrons, Devon and I scanned new books into the computer.

"Has anybody else brought up this theory to you?" I said.

Devon held a coffee table book about bridges under the laser. "I'm sorry to say Melissa O'Neil was about the seventh or eighth person who's mentioned it to me."

I stared. "Then it's all over the county."

"You know it."

Garrett texted that he wanted to meet with me about the case on my break. I responded that I'd packed my dinner, but if he brought a meal to the library, we could eat in the kitchen.

At 4:00, he hustled into the lobby with a sack and several DVDs. "Houston recommended an author to me. Can you help me find him?"

I showed Garrett the books by David Morrell, and then we went down two flights to the kitchen. Once I'd reheated my container of chili, we sat at one of the round tables squeezed into a corner of the room.

"I'm sorry we haven't gotten anywhere." Garrett placed his burger and fries on the table. "We alerted pawn shop owners about your camera, but nothing so far. That's why I wanted to talk to you."

He really was handsome. Houston's charm and Chris's unique features had snagged my attention first. But Garrett's razor-edged face, caramel hair, and hazel eyes could have qualified him for a less buff Captain America. No. He'd make a better Spiderman, when Peter Parker was out of college and working—

"Rae?"

"Sorry." I gave myself a shake to bring my focus back to the cute officer I was sharing supper with.

"Have you thought of anyone else who might be a suspect?" He held his pencil above his pad. "You said you haven't dated since you moved here, but maybe there's a guy who asked you out, and you turned him down, and he can't handle it."

My face flamed hotter than the chili I'd just swallowed. "No, nobody like that." It'd been hard enough to admit my zero-sum love life once. Did he have to bring it up again?

"Not at all? But you're so ..." Glancing away, he grabbed his burger and took a bite.

I shoveled in more chili.

He fired question after question at me about who I'd met and had interactions with, from patrons to relatives. He proved what he'd told me when I dropped off his birthday pie. Once he had questions, he kept asking until he found answers.

When he finally paused to sip soda, I said, "Have you heard the rumor that I made up the stalker?"

His sharp features contracted, like he'd felt a sudden pain. "Yeah. Don't worry. I don't believe it. I know how seriously to take gossip." He took another sip.

"How did a city boy like you end up a cop in Marlin County?" We didn't have to stick to a strictly business conversation.

His body went stone still. "Why do you ask?" His tone was on guard.

What had I said wrong? Tearing off a chunk of Gram's whole wheat bread, I made my words light. "I'd asked Houston when we had lunch a few weeks back. I just wondered since you have no ties to southeast Ohio. Neither does he."

Running his hand over his crewcut, he leaned back. "I just saw an ad for the job with the Wellesville agency when I finished the academy." All wariness had left his voice. "I'd wanted to get hired near Toledo, but I couldn't find anything. So I applied here. When did you have lunch with Houston?"

"A few weeks ago. The week before Valentine's Day, I think."

"See? You had lunch with a guy, and you didn't even remember it."

My eyes flew open. "You don't mean—"

"No, not at all. I'm just saying that's an interaction you didn't think of before. There could be more that come to you if you try to remember. Let me know when you do." He glanced at his watch. "Gotta go."

"I guess you guys have really been busy." I closed the lid on my empty container. "I was hoping we'd be able to jam again soon."

Gathering his paper products, he gave me his V-shaped grin. "It might take another miracle, now that I'm back on nights, but if we find a time, we'll let you know."

We returned to the lobby, and, with his stack of novels under his arms, Garrett hurried outside without a goodbye.

Frowning, I stared after him. Why had he become alarmed?

"Oh, Devon, Rae." Puffing, Leandra laid a tall pile of books on the counter. "Barb wants you two to stop by her office before you leave for the day."

My teeth caught my lip as Devon's small face turned cynical. This request had to be the result of Mrs. O'Neil talking to our boss.

We climbed the curving stairs to the balcony, Devon muttering under her breath.

Father, I can't lose my job.

Barb's door stood open, and Devon marched in. I dragged my feet, like one of my brothers having to face Dad for discipline.

Turning from her computer, Barb swiveled to face us. "Mrs. O'Neil expects me to talk to you two. So I am." She looked directly at Devon. "I am talking to you, Devon." She shifted her gaze. "I am talking to you, Rae. If Mrs. O'Neil asks, you can tell her I talked to you. Have a great evening." She spun back to her screen.

Devon and I glanced each other. I put a hand over my growing grin.

"You too," said Devon.

Rushing to the stairwell, we exploded with laughter.

~~~~~

After all my brothers had gone to bed, I asked Dad if he had heard the rumor about me inventing the stalker.

Sighing, he set the manuscript he'd been reviewing for Aunt Jeanine on an end table by the couch. "I'd hoped you'd hadn't heard, which was ridiculous. You work with the public." He eyed me. "You know nobody in the family believes it, don't you?"

"I know you don't." I paused to listen for Gram coming out of the basement. "Because if I was going to con someone, it'd be the Carlisle brothers. But nobody else knows about them."

"Believe me, Rae, after living with you this long, the family knows you're honest."

I straightened the shade of the lamp on the table. "But I wasn't honest about the stalker."

"You didn't lie about it. You just didn't tell me. There's a big difference. Ma, Hank, Jeanine, and Carrie understand that." He lowered his voice. "No matter what people are saying, we keep the Carlisles' involvement to ourselves. Right?"

I nodded.

"I'm sorry you have to put up with this." He took my hand.

"You do, too. If people think I'm a crook, then they must think you're an idiot for believing me." I bit my lip. "Could that hurt your chances at reelection?"

Dad launched a guffaw that made me jump.

"Sorry, kiddo." He squeezed my hand. "But reelection is so far from my mind right now, that it never occurred to me until you mentioned it. But I don't care. If I can't get reelected, I'll find some kind of job. The important thing is I've got you and your brothers. We'll be fine."
~~~~~

Chapter 29

On Friday, Garrett texted me right before my lunch break.

Can you see Chief at lunch

Had there been a break in the case?

For sure

I'll tell the Chief Don't let him get to you

Why would Chief Simcox get to me? Because he didn't like Dad? A knot formed in my gut.

After I'd grabbed Aaron's backpack—I'd have to buy one of my own soon—I left the library by the door to the parking lot. I took two steps toward the Beast and stopped. I'd had such a, well, beastly time getting that elephant parked that I hated to move it.

Cars swooshed up and down the steep slope of Woodward Avenue. If I walked to the Wellesville police station, it would be the first time I'd been in town by myself in over a week. Elm and Sugar were busy main roads. I'd be safe.

Hitching my backpack higher, I hiked down from the library to Elm and turned right. The mounds of snow from last week's storm had grown smaller, the day's warm winds from the south eroding them. Dusty blue clouds quilted the sky, sunlight rimming their fuzzy edges. I quickened my pace to Sugar Street and turned left, following another slope down past the butter-yellow Victorian house that held the funeral home and the tan, brick firehouse.

On a street of light-colored Victorian mansions and bungalows converted into businesses, the police station leaped out. A sharp, block building with a low roof and long, tinted windows, the station fit into the neighborhood about as well as a Tesla in a used car lot.

In the lobby, I told the receptionist my name.

The dark-haired women looked over her reading glasses at me. "So you're Rae Riley?"

Her hazel eyes examined me from head to foot, and she didn't make any attempt to hide her analysis. "The Chief is expecting you. Last door on your left."

Pulling off my hat and gloves, I followed the gleaming tiled floor to the back of the building. The door was shut, but the narrow window showed Chief Eric Simcox was on the phone, his back to me.

I waited and waited, shifting from foot to foot. When he finally turned to hang up, I knocked.

Glancing up, he motioned me in with a quick wave.

His office was perfectly square, every edge sharp—the metal desk, the framed photos and citations, the arms and backs of the chairs, even the cushions on the chairs had piping to prevent a rounded appearance.

Chief Simcox fit right in. His chestnut hair was sculpted in a flat top, his broad shoulders looked sharp enough to slice salami under his pressed white shirt, and his jaw could have been used to measure corners in shop class.

His light eyes—grey?—bored into me, and the knot tightened in my gut. I wiggled a toe through the hole in my right sock and noticed a chip in my thumbnail.

"Sit down, Miss Riley." He pointed at one of the square chairs situated in front of his desk. He looked older than Dad, maybe forty or forty-five.

I lowered myself into it and, knowing I couldn't get comfortable on such a seat, remained on the edge.

The phone rang.

"Excuse me." He took the call, said a few words, then hung up. "I'll be right back, Miss Riley."

"You can call me Rae, sir."

He acknowledged that with a nod and left.

I sat, looking straight ahead out the skinny windows behind his desk. Then I shifted in my chair and winced. Everything else had healed nicely from the chase, except my ribs, which zapped me when I twisted the wrong way. The photos on the wall on my left were mostly of Chief Simcox when he was a Marine. Lots of them seemed to have been taken in Iraq or Afghanistan. A shadow box displayed medals.

Bouncing my leg, I resisted the urge to get up and walk around. How long was this going to take? I couldn't be late getting back to work. And I still had to eat lunch. If I'd known it would take—

"Do you know it's a crime to file a false police report?"

The question, fired as he strode in, jerked me around, making my ribs send out a nasty protest. The Chief perched on the corner of his desk.

"Y--yes, sir."

So he'd heard the rumor and had brought me in for questioning, not as a victim, but as a suspect. The knot tightened so hard I didn't want lunch anymore.

"If I discover you created a stalker and vandalized your own apartment and truck, I will arrest you."

His voice was as crisp and cutting as his jawline, his gaze sawing me down until I felt about four feet tall and seven years old.

"I'm not like your dad. He let you off for trespassing at the children's home." His voice grew harsher. "I won't allow you to escape punishment for a crime. Unless you tell me now, right now, that this is nothing but a game you're playing with Mal."

Hoping to ease the pain in my stomach, I gulped. "Everything I told Garrett is true, sir."

"But nothing has happened since you moved to the Malinowski farm." He tipped his head a degree or two from perfectly straight. "Seems odd to me."

Drawing in my lips, I looked to my knobby hands in my lap. I couldn't say anything. He seemed to have bought the rumor completely.

"If Mal is too blind to see through you, that's a personal problem. If you want to manipulate him or any other man in the county, that's a character flaw. But I will not let you waste my agency's time or resources. Just because you can make a fool out of Mal doesn't mean the same con will work on me or my officers." He slapped down the last sentence.

The knot loosened as a little spark of anger ignited in me. "My dad's not a fool."

His eyes *were* grey, cold as winter seas. "We'll see when this case is solved."

The anger bursting into full flame, I found myself on my feet. He stood too, and I fought a grin as the Chief had to tilt his head back to meet my eyes. "I'm telling the truth, sir."

"I gave you a chance." Turning his back on me, he picked up some papers.

Snatching up the backpack, I marched out. I hit the sidewalk, ready to sprint and burn off the fury roaring inside.

But Garrett was waiting beside his car. He rushed over to me. "How'd it go?" His quick question was loaded with concern.

"He thinks I made up the stalker."

Swearing, Garrett shook his head. "I was afraid of that. He kept asking me how credible I thought your story was."

His sympathy extinguished part of the fire in me. "I've got to get back to work." I started up Sugar Street.

"Do you want a lift?"

"I'd better walk." I couldn't be this mad and wait on patrons.

"I'll go with you."

As we hiked toward Main Street, Garrett kept up a staccato beat of reassurance. "No matter what the Chief thinks, I'm still investigating your case. You don't have to worry about me disbelieving you."

I nodded, walking as fast as I could without breaking into a run.

When we reached the tall windows to the lobby, I said, "I appreciate having you in my corner."

His V-shaped grin glowed. With a wave, Garrett jogged back the way we came.

Devon could tell something was wrong, but she couldn't ask until I'd come back from a quick lunch, and we were alone in the lobby.

As I told her, she gasped, then snapped her mouth shut, pressing it tighter and tighter.

"This is … I can't believe—well, yes I can believe he's that stupid. He's a cop." She grabbed the phone on the desk.

"He's not stupid," I said. "He made me wait to make me uncomfortable and then asked the first question when I didn't know he'd come back. Each tactic was calculated." I tucked long strands of hair behind my ear. "I wonder if he really believes that story about me, or he called me in because he hates Dad."

"It doesn't matter what his motive is. Barb?" She spoke into the phone. "It's Devon. I have some information about Rae's case I need to give to the cops right now. Can I make up the time I'm gone on my next shift? Thanks." She hung up.

"What do you have to tell him?"

Devon looked at me like I'd caught the Chief's case of stupidity. "About how scared you were the night of the storm and how you asked me to pick you up. If he's not stupid, or trying to make trouble for your dad, my story should at least make him reconsider his assumptions. Barb said to phone her if you get too many patrons."

To watch Devon tackle Simcox, I'd have given a year's pay. "Tell me all about it when you get back."

"If we were in a public place, I'd stream it."

For the next half hour, I found it hard to give patrons my full attention. I kept listening for an explosion from the south end of town.

When Devon returned, she was breathing hard, her green eyes so fierce that Ms. Zollars hesitated to approach the desk with her books.

Once I had checked her out, other patrons came. Devon couldn't tell me anything until we closed at 5:00.

"Chief Simcox did nothing to change my opinion of cops." Turning off a terminal, she called, "Girls, it's time to leave."

As Liberty and Serenity gathered their backpacks and coats, Devon said, "I told him how you asked to stay at my place that night. He told me I could very well be lying, covering for you. So I told him, without filters, my opinion of cops in general, and him in particular, and he said he'd give me three seconds to leave, or he'd arrest me for trespassing."

The cold, grey eyes lifted in my memory. "He'd do it too."

We walked with the girls down the back staircase.

"You should tell Mal, Rae. This is more than putting up with gossip. The chief of police has accused you of a crime."

"I was planning on it." I fiddled with the hem of my shirt. "It's just … I'm not sure when to tell him. My uncle and aunt and cousins are coming over for supper, and Dad's giving the kids and me a self-defense class. I don't want to ruin his evening. But I don't want to wait until bedtime either. He'd never sleep."

"He's an adult and a cop, Rae. He can take it."

"Not if his head blows up from pure rage."

Chapter 30

As I hurried into the cozy kitchen, Dad took one look at me, Micah hanging on his back, and said, "What's wrong? Did you get bad news from Simcox?"

I took off my vest. "How'd you know I went to see him?"

"Kincaid told me. He probably got it from Matthews."

Couldn't put if off now. "Will you come to Gram's room?"

"That's your room, Rae." Gram rolled the cutter across a bubbling pizza.

Shutting the bedroom door, I told Dad exactly what happened.

He went from his usual dull beige to slightly flushed to deep red, his big hands working at his sides. When I finished, he stood so rigid I was afraid a sinew would snap. Then with a roar they probably heard in Columbus, Dad flung open the door and limped into the kitchen, his brace squeaking as he tried to walk fast.

Aunt Jeanine's huge eyes grew huger. "What in the world is going on?"

"Simcox has gone too far," Dad said between heaving breaths. "It's one thing to hate me and make work difficult for my deputies. But he can't go after my kids." The volume of the last two words made Amber drop her slice of pizza, Coral bobble her glass of juice, and the rest of the family freeze over their food.

Except for Gram. She got out of her chair and touched his arm. "What exactly did he do?"

"Treated Rae like a perp instead of a victim." He reached around her and unplugged his phone from the charger on the counter. Then he set it down. "No. I should talk to him in person."

"Well, sure." At the far end of the table, Uncle Hank hung one arm over the back of his chair. "You can't peel a guy's hide over the phone. Want some help?"

"Mal isn't going to peel Eric's hide," Gram said. "Calm down and have supper, Mal. Then you'll be able to think straight. Besides, he doesn't usually stay in the county on the weekends."

"How do you know that?" I slipped into the empty chair beside Rusty.

Draining his glass, he didn't even glance at me. In the past week, he had spoken a total of about twenty words to me.

"It's just one of the things you hear when you're out and about. He spends a lot of time in Columbus on the weekends."

"He thinks we're all hillbillies here in southeast Ohio." Gripping the counter, Dad drew in some slow breaths.

"But he's from Zanesville," I said. "That's as much a part of southeast Ohio as Marlin County."

Dad jerked his chair out from under the table. "He claims he's lived all over the world and evolved out of any hillbilly tendencies."

"What did Chief Simcox do, Dad?" Aaron balanced on the edge of his seat.

"In a minute, Aaron."

We said grace, and then Dad began to repeat my story, but when he turned red again, I took over, ending with how Devon went to defend me.

"I'll have to thank her." Dad took a long drink of water, and the red faded.

Amber wiped tomato sauce from the corner of her mouth. "Your friend should tell more people about you asking her to come get you. That should prove you're telling the truth."

"Chief Simcox accused Devon of lying."

"Oh, for Pete's sake." Uncle Hank dropped his fork. "Pretty soon he'll be saying the whole Malinowski clan is in on it."

"No." I placed a breadstick on my plate. "He'll tell people Dad's a dope, who isn't smart enough to see through my scam."

"So what? Plenty of elected officials are dopes, and they can still get the job done."

My brothers and cousins whipped their heads toward Dad.

He reached for the spatula on the pizza platter. "Norris, you're lucky you're sitting down there."

"Hey, I've been in this family long enough to know my place."

As we cleared the table, I went over to Uncle Hank. "I know you said I didn't have to pay for the camera, but I would like to give you something for it." I took several bills from the pocket of my shirt. "Here's twenty dollars."

Hank recoiled like I'd offered him a copperhead. "Mal, your daughter's insulting me by offering me money."

"Is that all it takes?" Dad leaned around the basement door. "Where's my wallet?"

Gathering up his dishes, Uncle Hank said, "When the Big Guy catches this creep, I'll see if I can get him to pay for it since he's the one who broke it." He winked at me.

Blinking, I half-smiled and pocketed the bills. I would have felt better paying for some part of it, but Uncle Hank was trying to be nice.

I followed my brothers and cousins to the basement. Amber and I picked up the table Gram used for sorting clean clothes, and she said, "When will your truck get fixed?"

"As soon as we can find a used windshield and parts for the lights."

We carried the table to a wall, opening up the space in front of the washer and dryer, and helped Dad move his bench and weights under the stairs.

Dad said, "I was hoping we could total it, but no such luck. Aaron, Micah, don't get in the way. I'll teach you two after I show Rae, Amber, Rusty, and Coral a few things."

They took seats on the steps like spectators at a ball game.

Leaning against the door that led to the backyard, Dad said, "Some of this will be a refresher for Rae and Amber since they've taken self-defense classes before. But you can't go over these tactics too many times." He hollered up the steps. "Hank, I thought you said you'd help. Stop running your mouth and get down here."

When Uncle Hank joined us, he acted as the attacker, grabbing us in the ways Dad instructed. Then Dad showed us how to break free. None of this was new to me, and I'd been practicing with Dad for over a week now. But I still enjoyed reviewing the techniques. Really, I just liked spending time with my dad.

Whenever I finished my turn, I found Amber watching me with glowing eyes. Since surviving the stalker on Valentine's Day, I'd moved even higher in her admiration. She'd probably put up a poster of me in her bedroom between the ones she had of Wonder Woman and some warrior princess from *The Lord of the Rings*.

Rusty kept as far away from me as he could manage in a space that contained a washer, dryer, a table big enough to sit six people, and a hutch with canning supplies. I couldn't stand my brother treating me like the school bully.

"One very important thing to remember," Dad said as Rusty twisted loose from Hank, "is to follow your instincts. If someone is making you uncomfortable, get away. Don't dismiss your feelings. If you're wrong, you can apologize later."

Dad worked with all six of us until Gram called down to ask if the kids still wanted to watch a movie. As Rusty moved toward the stairs, I whispered, "I want to talk to you."

He glanced everywhere but at me, then jammed his hands into the front pockets of his jeans.

As soon as Dad was out of earshot, I said, "I didn't mean to hurt Dad."

"I know." He toed a chip in the concrete floor. "But if you had told him about the first letter, he wouldn't have been out in the storm. You wouldn't have been either."

"I wish now I'd shown him the first letter, Rusty." I dipped my head and caught his gaze. "I know what's it's like to lose a parent."

Pressing his lips out of sight, he brushed past me.

I stepped in front of him. "I'm not gonna let anything happen to our dad. That's why I went with him to Walter's that night. I wasn't sure how I could help him if there was trouble, but I felt better going with him. Can we make a truce?"

Rusty's thin frame stiffened. "I'm not at war." He ran upstairs.

That was progress. I slumped against the hutch. Maybe.

Chapter 31

"I'll get that for you." Jill held open the door from the cataloging room.

"Thank you, ma'am." I pushed the cart of new books into the hall.

She nodded and went into the room.

Devon's story about me asking for a ride home on Valentine's Day had had some impact on people's opinions of me over the past month. Jill still wasn't friendly, but she wasn't hostile anymore.

I rolled the cart into the elevator. When the doors slid open, Jason walked past.

"Oh, hey, Rae. Any news on your case?"

"Not that I know of." Sighing, I pushed the cart out of the elevator.

No news from any pawn shop about my camera. No leads on anyone my mom might have had an affair with. Dad had gotten nowhere trying to talk to Terry O'Neil. After he'd explained why he had called, Terry hung up on him.

"The only information added to the case," I said, "is your positive ID of Troy as the guy who ran out of the children's home. And I don't see how that helps us any."

"Don't give up hope."

"How's Rick doing in Haiti?"

"Pretty well." He glanced up and down the hall from the lobby to the children's room, making me do the same. We were alone, and the only noise I heard was Leandra chatting at the checkout desk. "Rick needed to get away to a place where he's a stranger, where he doesn't have to pretend" — he lowered his voice — "nothing's happened."

"Glad to hear it. Do you need help finding anything?"

Jason said he could handle it and went back to the children's room. I guided the cart into the lobby. Garrett was waiting by the desk, his sharp face so grim I knew he hadn't stopped by for an update or pep talk.

Before I could say hey, he said, "I was driving by the library parking lot and saw a piece of paper tucked under one of your wipers."

Every fiber in every muscle pulled taut to screaming tension. "But-- but it's been over a month since he chased me."

"It's probably nothing. But we should check. Can you come outside with me?"

"Go ahead, Rae." Leandra tore a due date slip off the printer. "If I need help, I'll call the reference desk."

We took the back staircase. I walked like a statue might if it was trying to figure out what movement meant.

Let this be nothing, Father.

In the parking lot, the wind was so damp it felt like getting hit in the face with a soaked towel every time it gusted.

A piece of paper fluttered against the windshield of the Rust Bucket. Dread hit my stomach like a pickaxe.

Garrett slipped on latex gloves and, lifting the blade, removed the sheet and unfolded it. The way his face got wiped clean of all expression— I forced my legs to carry me over to him and looked at the paper.

A rush of fear sucked away all my blood so fast I tottered against Garrett.

There was a photo. But not of me.

It was Dad, wearing a button-down shirt like he did for church, standing in front of the IGA. A red target with a bullseye over his chest circled him.

ANYTHING CAN HAPPEN TO YOUR FATHER, BELLA.

I had to call Dad. I had to call Dad.

I reached for a pocket that wasn't there, then ran for the basement door. Garrett said something, but he sounded like he was talking from the county line.

Taking the stairs two at a time, I raced to the children's room, dodged parents with preschoolers, and flew to the checkout desk.

Leandra said something. I fumbled around a shelf under the counter and pulled out my phone. My fingers trembling, I swiped Dad's number.

Let him be okay, let him be okay.

The phone rang and rang and rang. Then the message came on.

He was in a meeting. He couldn't answer.

I tried to text, but my fingers were still shaking. Steeling myself, I stiffened them long enough to type:

> R U OK got another note

Gripping my phone, I stared at the screen, willing the little dots to appear to let me know a message was on its way.

Nothing.

A surge of adrenaline fired into every cell, and I shot out the front doors.

He's fine. He's just too busy to answer.

I pounded to the corner of Sugar and Main. Horns honked as I dashed across the intersection to the dingy white building that held the sheriff's department.

Jerking open the door, I said in a gasp, "Where's Dad?"

From behind her desk in the reception room, Liz jumped to her feet, knocking her swivel chair into Janet's desk. "What's wrong, girl?"

I dragged in air, but my lungs had shriveled. "I gotta see Dad. I got another note."

"He had lunch at the high school. He should be back soon. Rae, sit down. You look ready to faint."

Falling back against a wall, I attempted another inhale to combat lightheadedness. I called Dad again.

"What did the note say?"

Putting the phone to my ear, I said, "'Anything can happen to your father.'"

Liz's dark eyebrows disappeared behind a fringe of golden bangs. "Instead of threatening you, he threatened the sheriff? He's gotta be crazy."

The phone message came on again.

Father, why won't he pick up?

"Rae, I'm sure he's fine." Liz spoke in her usual perky tone. "Mal likes to drive around the county when he has time. He probably took a long way from the high school, and he's driving in a dead spot."

My lungs seemed to expand an ounce, and I snuck in some air. "Do you really think so?"

"You know it. This county has more dead spots than a graveyard."

My phone rang. Dad.

"Rae, I saw you—"

"Are you all right?" I shouted.

"Holy smoke, what's wrong?"

He sounded absolutely normal. *Thank You.*

Gulping air, I collapsed into a chair, blood rushing into my face as I told Dad about the note.

He listened without interruption, then said, "Why would he threaten me? I'm the least vulnerable member of your family. Why wouldn't he threaten Ma or the boys? He'd have a more realistic shot of actually hurting one of them."

"I don't know. I'm just glad you're okay."

"Thank you, kiddo," he said in a quiet voice. "But you shouldn't worry. He can't chase me like he did you and not come out on the short end of the stick. He probably did it just to scare you."

I gulped again. "It worked."

"I'll be at the office in thirteen minutes. Wait for me, and I'll walk back to the library with you."

We hung up. I called the library, got Leandra, and told her I'd be delayed getting back.

She said, "That young cop wanted to know where you were. If he's still here, I'll tell him you'll be coming back with the sheriff."

I set my phone on the arm of the chair and held my head in my hands. Why couldn't he leave me and my family alone? Hadn't he learned they weren't going to turn against me and he couldn't scare me out of the county?

"Here ya go." Liz stood over me, holding out a steaming cup of coffee.

I opened my mouth to say I didn't like coffee, but thanked her instead and took it.

He'd taken a big risk, sticking the note under the wiper at lunchtime. Since I'd moved to the farm, it might be the easiest way to deliver a message without mailing it. But why now? What had happened to make him start again?

The front door flew open, and Chief Simcox strode into the reception room. "I thought I'd find you here, Miss Riley. Is Mal in?"

Liz said, "He'll be here soon." Her voice was still upbeat, but a trace of granite ran through it.

Looming above me, the chief took out a pad. "Tell me exactly what you did this morning, Miss Riley. We need your statement."

Taking a miniscule sip of coffee, I stood. He wasn't as intimidating when I could look down on him, even if it was only by an inch. "I work noon to 8:00 today, sir, so I didn't get to the parking lot until 11:50. The stalker only had about fifty minutes to leave the note." I'd been so panicky I hadn't realized that.

"Did you go back to the truck any time between when you parked it and when you and Officer Matthews found the note?"

"No, sir."

The chief stepped a few inches too far into my personal space. "This is the first note in five weeks. Is there anything else you'd like to tell me?" The winter grey gaze seemed to probe me.

Obviously, he wasn't buying Devon's story any more now than when she spoke to him a month ago.

I met the scrutiny without blinking. "No, sir."

"Something wrong, Simcox?" Dad appeared out of the hall that ran to the back of the building.

Seeing him allowed my lungs to recover, and I took a normal breath.

The Chief wrote in his pad and didn't bother to glance at him. "I'm getting Rae's statement."

I edged around Simcox to Dad. Sliding my arm along the small of his back, I gave him a squeeze. "Good to see you."

Dad did his own one-arm hug, then said, "Do you have the note, Simcox?"

"Matthews has it. He's going over the scene."

"Good. I got ahold of Phelps, and she'll meet him at Rae's truck."

Simcox finally looked to Dad. "You don't think my people can analyze a crime scene?"

Under my arm, Dad's posture shifted, his spine straightened, his shoulders pulled back, his whole stance solidifying. "We're two small agencies. We should help each other. Phelps is my deputy with the most CSI training."

"Thanks, but no thanks." The Chief snapped his pad shut.

"The threat was against me." Dad's baritone grew tougher. "My agency is involved whether you like it or not."

"Of course. You're the sheriff." Simcox spoked in a monotone.

"Got that right."

Dad hadn't provided any details about his conversation with Simcox when he'd defended me against the accusation that I'd made up the stalker. Whatever they'd said, it hadn't led to kinder feelings or cooperative attitudes.

"I'm going to the library." Simcox turned and strutted out the front door.

"We'll be over soon," Dad called after him.

Watching the Chief pass a front window, Liz rubbed her arms. "I'd better turn up the heat. It got a little frosty in here."

Dad barked a laugh. "C'mon upstairs, Rae, and tell me what happened."

He took down my story, then sat back in his swivel chair, scratching an eyebrow. "Why me? I don't think it's random. He's had over a month to think about giving up or going on. His choice of me has some significance." He moved forward in his seat. "Don't say anything about this to the boys. I don't think it will bother Aaron or Micah, but Rusty—" He heaved a sigh. "He doesn't need to know something that will only worry him." He stood. "Did you pack your supper?"

"Yeah." Strange change in topics.

"Good. Once I walk you back to the library, don't leave the building until you close. Then I'll follow you home or one of my deputies will."

I got to my feet. "But you were the one who was threatened."

Reaching for his coat, Dad stood too. "I'm taking no chances."

Chapter 32

That night, Deputy Zagoric drove behind me and parked at the head of the drive. He introduced me to a deputy from Muskingum County, who was volunteering to act as guard at the farm until midnight. Then Houston or Deputy Zagoric would be there the rest of the night unless they got a call.

I drove up to the garage and parked beside Aunt Jeanine's green pickup. I found her sitting on the couch in Dad's usual position. Rusty was stretched out beside her, but instead of reading a hefty fantasy novel, he was flipping over sheets of copier paper.

"Hey, Rae." Aunt Jeanine's tone was a little too cheerful. "Would you read my short story when Rusty's done? I'd like your opinion."

"Is it one of your mysteries with the deputy? Or the U.S. marshals?"

Her pale face brightened. "I didn't know you'd been reading my stories. It's about the marshals."

"I've borrowed Gram's copies of your books. I usually read fantasy or sci-fi, but your mysteries are good reads. I like learning all the details about how law enforcement works.

Rusty hid behind the manuscript like a barricade. He had to know about the latest threat.

The backpack falling off my shoulder, I trudged to Gram's room.

It'd taken all of the last five weeks for Rusty to thaw enough to ask me if he could look at my photos for setting inspiration. Now he was back to acting like I carried the plague.

Gram slipped into the room behind me and closed the door. "Rusty found out about the note. He was near panic until Mal got home and assured him he has a lot of protection from all those extra officers donating their time to help out." She smiled. "That's one of the great things about cops—very supportive. Especially when one of their own is threatened. Mal's already called in BCI for more help."

"BCI? What's that?"

"Bureau of Criminal Investigation. It's a department of the state that helps local law enforcement agencies. Especially small ones like the Marlin County sheriff's department."

"Why isn't Dad reading with Rusty?"

"He's downstairs talking to Carrie. When she heard about the threat, she called to discuss the case with him. She's in L.A., working on a case, or she would have driven here as soon as Jeanine told her."

After changing out of my work clothes into sweats, I sat at the computer and reviewed the photos I'd taken with my phone. There wasn't one I wanted to keep.

I set my jaw. It just wasn't the same, pointing and shooting with a phone camera, and I didn't want to dress up the shots with a bunch of filters.

Dad came up from the basement and put his arm around me. "How's my girl?"

"Okay." I forced a smile, but it probably looked more like a grimace.

Aunt Jeanine vacated her spot on the couch, and she and Dad discussed her short story with Rusty. Gram joined them, and it all sounded like a normal family conversation. Well, normal for a family who helps one member figure out things like what is the most dramatic way to stab someone: overhand or underhand.

The tension between Rusty and me was thick enough to choke on. Finally, Dad told him to go to bed.

Once my brother was done in the bathroom and had shut his bedroom door, Dad said, "Carrie and I were talking over a theory about why the stalker's shifted his focus from Rae to me." Glancing back toward the boys' room, Dad walked into the kitchen.

Gram, Aunt Jeanine, and I followed him.

Jeanine said, "What's your theory, Mal?"

"Bella hurt this guy's father somehow." He leaned against the counter by the backdoor. "She could have ruined him personally or professionally. Or this guy—"

"If Mom had done that," I said, "she would have written a note apologizing."

Dad went on, "Or this guy thinks she did. The goal of his previous notes seemed to be to ruin Rae's relationship with us. 'Nobody wants you here.' 'Your family is better off without you.' That didn't work. In fact, it backfired. Rae's closer to us now than before. So he takes the threats to a new level. He identifies Rae with Bella. Bella hurt his father. So he'll hurt Rae's father."

My throat constricted, and Aunt Jeanine said in a hushed voice, "Do you think he'll attack you?"

"Not necessarily." Dad looked straight at the worn linoleum.

Gram's voice was quiet. "You do think that."

"I'm so sorry about all of this." The sentence burst from me.

The three of them couldn't have looked more startled than if my words had actually sprayed them.

"None of this is your fault, Rae." Gram took hold of my hand.

"Of course not." Dad squeezed my shoulder. "He chose to harass you. Now he's dragging me into it. In a way, it's good he's targeted me. He's got a serious issue, and he might have taken his anger out on someone much less capable of handling it. We'll get him."

Tilting her head to one side, Jeanine watched me. "We didn't feel any better when you were the target, Rae."

I tried to swallow, but nothing doing. Maybe they hadn't felt any better, but I did.

Dad said, "Ma, Jeanine, do you know definitely of anyone Bella might have been blamed for hurting?"

Both of them shook their heads, and Aunt Jeanine said, "Tell me what you've uncovered so far, Rae, and where you've searched so I don't waste time in the same area."

I raised my eyebrows, and Dad said, "Jeanine has a lot of experience researching her stories. If I need additional help conducting research, Jeanine assists the department, free of charge, with anything that isn't sensitive."

Once I'd gotten paper from the computer desk and written down everything I thought would help her, Aunt Jeanine left with several sheets of notes. Gram hugged me and took a cup of tea upstairs.

Dad gave me a one-armer. "No more apologies. You're a victim of a crime, not the perpetrator."

I looked up at him. "Do you think Egypt and China could be stalking us for something my mom did to Troy? We know he was involved with her somehow."

Dad snorted. "Troy didn't need any help to ruin himself. And Egypt can't stand him. She wouldn't risk her breath yelling 'Watch out!' if a truck was about to hit him, let alone jail. China doesn't care enough about anybody to put herself on the line. If they are the stalkers, they're doing it for some other reason than avenging Troy."

"What about Sean Ross? He died in a car accident a year after he and Mom found Phoenix Moore stabbed. Gram and Walter don't think he's from around here, but maybe he was, and he has a kid who holds Mom responsible for his death."

"I can dig into his background, but I doubt I'll find anything. Ma or Walter would know if he had any connections to the county."

We said goodnight, and I went to Gram's bedroom. I took off my sweatshirt, letting it slip from my hands. If this psycho did attack Dad, I was pretty certain Gram, Aunt Jeanine, and Aunt Carrie wouldn't hold it against me.

But Rusty would. And maybe Aaron and Micah.

Tension tightened like a noose.

And I wouldn't blame them one bit.

Chapter 33

The next evening, I waved to Uncle Hank from Chris's weathered porched as he pulled away. The opportunity to jam couldn't have come at a better time. I needed something to get my mind off the stalker.

The front door was unlocked, and I hung my jacket and Aaron's backpack on one of the heavy chairs in the dining room. A hot, beefy aroma wafted in from the kitchen, and my nose followed it. A big pot of beef soup or stew simmered on the stove in the crisp, nautical kitchen, but no one was around. Where were the guys?

Faint thuds pulsed through the ceiling. I mounted the old staircase. The thuds grew louder the higher I went. Somebody was probably working out in the third-floor exercise room.

I climbed the steps to the top of the house, and my head had just cleared the floor when I saw Chris pounding the punching bag.

With sharp jabs, he hit the bag, his fierce face looking scary as he concentrated on his technique. He stepped back, his bare chest heaving. I opened my mouth to call to him when, roaring, he attacked the bag again.

But this wasn't a workout. Punch after punch, kick after kick, Chris assaulted the bag like it was his most hated enemy. But not like I'd seen in movies. Chris's blows flowed, like his body had turned to liquid, each move streaming into the next, relentless, like flood waters. This person trying to beat a punching bag into submission didn't look like the quiet, composed Chris I was used to.

Over the continuous thuds came the crack of splintering wood. A section from the beam the bag hung from broke loose, and the bag crashed to the floor.

Chris didn't even pause. He kicked and kicked until he sank to his knees, breathing like a drowning man before he went down for the last time.

Shoot fires, what was wrong? I ducked my head below the level of the floor. What should I do? I backed down two steps. A big ol' creak shot out from under my left foot.

"Houston?" Chris called. "Garrett?"

Pretend I saw nothing. I trotted up to the top floor. "Hey. Are you the only one home?"

Nodding, Chris wiped his face with a towel. "Houston and Garrett texted they'd be late." He looked at the punching bag lying on the floor.

"The beam broke. I thought Houston screwed it in deep enough."

Probably for a workout, not an assault. I peered into the rafters, like the break absorbed all my interest. "Is that an important beam? I mean, do you need to fix it right away?"

"I don't know. I hope not. I've got enough things to fix around here without repairing structural damage. Not much broke off. I think it'll be okay." He pulled on a t-shirt. "Have you had supper? I've got stew warming up."

"I've eaten. Thanks."

We headed downstairs.

Where had all that anger come from? More like rage. But what did I really know about him? Or any of the guys?

As we came to the second floor, I took a deep breath and said, "When I was researching the stalker, I found out that your mom and my mom knew each other." Throwing out the sentence was like casting bait into an unknown stream, but I needed to find out.

Chris stopped on a step like someone else had hit his brakes. "You know who my mother is?"

Was that annoyance in his deep voice?

I kept my tone light. "Dad told me. I mentioned the name Phoenix Moore, and he recognized it."

"It's impossible not to recognize it." Chris hurried to the first floor.

I had to jog to keep up, and we entered the kitchen almost at a run. Chris took the lid off the pot and stirred. Then he opened the stove and looked inside. Didn't say a word.

I hovered by the fridge. The silence was beyond awkward. Ramming around my head for something to say, I came up with, "Why are Houston and Garrett late?"

"Houston went to see some guys who are musicians in Columbus and got caught in rush hour traffic. Garrett said he lost track of time while he was meeting an old friend in Zanesville."

"Somebody he knew in the police academy?"

"No. I got the idea it's someone he knew when he was a kid in Zanesville."

"But Garrett grew up in Toledo."

Chris shut the oven door. "Partly. He was born in Zanesville. I think he moved to Toledo when he was in elementary school."

My gaze dropped to the floor, and I tugged on my earlobe.

The front door slammed, and Garrett bolted into the kitchen, wearing civilian clothes. "Dude, I am starved. What's cooking?"

Houston arrived a few minutes later, and the guys carried bowls, bread, and drinks into the living room.

Once they'd finished eating, we picked up where we'd left off from the last session. But as great as it was to jam with the guys again, my mind refused to focus on music. Chris's fit and Garrett's lie made it impossible. And it was a lie. Garrett had deliberately given the impression he had no connection to this part of Ohio. Why?

I rolled on the snare and went back to the steady beat. Did Chris have it wrong? He'd been wrong about when Garrett's parents died. Unless Garrett was lying about that too. But there was absolutely no reason for him to do that.

What was biting Chris? A bad day at work? The fury he'd unleashed on that poor punching bag seemed to indicate something a whole lot worse than spending twelve hours answering demanding calls. At least he hadn't grabbed one of his knives to finish off the bag.

"Hey, Rae." Houston quit strumming. "If you lost the beat, we can help you look for it."

Garrett glared at him. "Back off. She's been through a lot in the past twenty-four hours."

Houston's skinny frame went rigid. "It was a joke. I think Rae can take a joke even if you can't."

"Use your manners, if you have any." The growl came from Chris.

From their wide eyes, Houston and Garrett were as surprised as I was at his remark.

Chris plucked a string and twisted a screw on the neck of his bass.

Houston drew himself up, as if readying to return fire.

I said, "I'll look under the bass. Maybe the beat rolled under there."

A tight little smile cracked Houston's round face while Garrett exploded with a nervous laugh. Chris continued to tune.

I suggested we go back to the chorus, counted two bars, and we played. But the atmosphere had changed. Garrett seemed uneasy, his hazel eyes darting every which way. Houston's voice was as tight as his smile. Chris's back was to me.

"Sorry." I leaned to one side to reach for the stick I'd dropped.

"Rae, if you aren't in the mood to play, that's cool," said Houston. "We can just hang out. If that note you got yesterday is on your mind, forget it. Mal can take care of himself."

Garrett said, "I don't think it means anything. The guy's just trying to get at you. He wouldn't have the guts to actually take Mal on." He yawned. "Hate to be the one to call it quits, but I still haven't adjusted to working nights. I gotta turn in."

We all said goodnight, and Garrett headed upstairs. We couldn't play quietly enough not to disturb him, so we packed our instruments away, selected songs from our playlists, and talked. But while Chris participated, he barely spoke. Something was on his mind.

When I said I should call Dad to come get me, Houston offered to drive me home.

"Or I can." Chris leaped to his feet. That was the first time all evening he'd sounded anything like himself since I'd mentioned his mother.

Houston threw him a scowl.

If I hadn't seen the attack on the punching bag, I would have had a tough time choosing. "Well, since you asked first, Houston, I'll go with you."

Houston gave me his good ol' boy grin, making my heart skip every other beat. His grin turned smug as he glanced at Chris, and my heart slowed to a normal rhythm.

We pulled away from the house in Houston's maroon hatchback, which was almost too small for him. His head scraped the ceiling.

Walls of black woods lined the road and not a glimmer of light allowed us to see beyond the beams from the headlights. Tree trunks popped out of the night and then vanished, as if the dark had snatched them back.

"Maybe you can clear something up for me," I said. "I thought Garrett was from Toledo, and Chris says he was born in Zanesville but grew up in Toledo. Do you know which one of us is right?"

Houston drew a finger down his nose. "I thought he said at some point he was born around here, but I can't be certain. Garrett doesn't talk much about family. Chris doesn't either, except for Grandpa Dave, and if he mentions him one more time, I may have to move out." Aggravation strained his tenor voice.

At the spot where the road ended by the drive, the headlights revealed a patrol SUV. Its lights turned on, and Houston stopped, rolling down his window and calling, "It's me, Houston, with Rae."

The beam of a flashlight hit him full in the face, and Houston shielded his eyes. A chuckle came from the deputy holding the flashlight as he approached the hatchback.

"You two been on a date?" said Deputy Zagoric, an ornery grin lengthening beneath his thin, graying moustache.

"I'll only answer questions with my lawyer present," Houston said. "Quiet night?"

He nodded. "Haven't had a call in two hours."

"When I get up to the house, I'll have a look around."

"You don't have to—" Deputy Zagoric's bright, black eyes flicked between Houston and me. "Sure. Go ahead, kid." Chuckling again, he left us.

Heat streamed up from my neck. Houston was trying to impress me. Me. All he had to do was be nice. Did I like that he was trying to impress me?

I scrunched down in the seat. Maybe I would be if I was sure I liked him.

Houston drove the hatchback into the little valley. His headlights picked out Knight nibbling grass by a fencepost in the pasture.

"Is that your horse?" Houston said.

"My Uncle Hank's. I'm surprised he's still here. He and Dad must have had trouble fixing the leaky toilet in the main bathroom. Or they got to talking."

At the garage, we got out, and Houston said, "Tell Mal I'll be—"

A shout to our right cut him off and spun me around. My heart bolted into my mouth, and I took off. "That was Dad!"

The night was so dark, I couldn't see where to put my feet. Every step was like falling into a pit, slowing my speed. I ran along the lip of the valley the house sat on toward the woods.

"Aaron!" The bellow could have shaken the moon if there'd been one.

I skidded to a walk. Houston, carrying a flashlight, caught up to me.

I raised my voice. "Dad, Houston and I are here."

"Just what I need: an audience."

We followed his voice into the woods, just past the first line of trees. The flashlight illuminated Dad shaking his right leg, water droplets flying from it, and Uncle Hank, collapsing with laughter, beside a hole.

"I told them. You heard me tell them, Rae." Sliding his pistol into a holster on his belt, Dad ranted at top volume, but outside it wasn't as jarring. "I told them not to booby trap the farm. And they did it anyway."

"Worked pretty well," Hank said between gasps.

"You mean your sons?" said Houston. "Why would they do—oh, to catch the stalker."

"They dug a pit." Uncle Hank crouched and shone his flashlight into a hole about two feet long by a foot deep. "It's been here long enough to collect rainwater."

Dad wrung a sopping pant leg. "Really? I hadn't noticed."

I touched his arm. "Did you hurt your bad knee?"

"No, I hurt my good knee. Of all the—Houston, you had better be keeping a straight face."

Houston's head bobbed up and down. "Dead straight, Mal. Do you need help getting up to the house?"

Dad flexed his leg. "No. I just need to walk it off. I didn't know you were bringing Rae home."

"She was about to call you when I offered to drive her."

Hank patted Dad on the shoulder. "You're lucky, Mal. The only reason it didn't have sharpened stakes in it, I suspect, is because your boys hadn't gotten around to it."

"I'll find out all the details in the morning." Dad's words came out in a snarl.

Houston said he'd conduct a quick patrol around the house and barn, and Dad, Hank, and I walked back to the house. By the time we entered the kitchen, Dad wasn't favoring his right leg.

He shook his head. "It's not like the boys to defy me."

"Could it be a natural hole?" I said.

"No," said Hank. "I studied it. It was dug with a shovel, and fairly recently too."

I said goodbye to Houston when he was done with his patrol. After Uncle Hank went home and Dad went to bed, I turned on the desktop computer and tried to find proof of where Garrett was born. I would have searched for why Chris had thrown a fit in the exercise room, but there were some things even Google couldn't answer.

I got nowhere. The satellite connection was so slow that it strained my patience, and any time I found a promising hit, a box would pop up demanding me to sign on for a six-month trial before it would give me access.

As I crawled into bed, the question that ate at me wasn't what was the truth, but why I cared so much about who was lying. Was it because I liked Chris and Garrett? I pulled my great-grandmother's quilt under my chin. Or was it because there seemed to be no reason for either of them to lie?

~~~~~

The next morning, Dad delayed going into work to conduct his interrogation. Aaron and Micah sat side by side on the couch while I rinsed breakfast dishes.

Towering over them, he said, "I told you boys you couldn't booby trap the farm."

"No, you didn't," Aaron said. "You said we couldn't set up trebuchets with trip wires. You didn't say anything about pits."

"Rusty wouldn't let us put sharp sticks in them," Micah said.

"Yes, he told me that before he went to school." Dad looked to me. "You were there, Rae. What did I say?"

Turning from the sink, I tugged on my earlobe. "I'm pretty sure you told them they couldn't set up trebuchets. You didn't mention any other kinds of traps. What did Rusty tell you before he went to school?"

"Not much." Dad rubbed his forehead. "Just said he was sorry and that he'd fill in the holes with his brothers."

Looking to Micah, whose mouth had formed an "O," Aaron said, his eyebrows rising, "You want us to fill in the holes?"

"Of course," said Dad.

"All of them?"

Dad lowered his hand. "How many are there?"

Frowning, Micah looked to the ceiling as if the answer was painted
~~~~~

there.

Aaron said, "Well, you see, Dad, there's a lot. When the ground thawed, we started digging. But sometimes a rock got in the way or a tree root. And sometimes the ground hadn't thawed enough. So we'd find another spot. So there are some … I guess you could call them depressions. And then there are some holes, and then there are some pits. But none of them are in the yard." He broke into a sunny smile. "If you don't go in the woods, you'll be safe."

Gram came out of her room. "Rae, I'm done in the bathroom if — oh, dear." She must have read Dad's face, which was flushing crimson.

But he swallowed and spoke at his normal volume. "I don't care what you call them. If you dug dirt out of a place, I want you to put the dirt back in. Since you have spring break next week, you'll have plenty of time."

"If we can find them all," said Micah.

"You'd better." Dad stalked into the kitchen.

Chapter 34

Wednesday morning, I woke up with a sick stomach. One week since the stalker left the note threatening Dad. He was a creature of habit. Was he going to leave another note today? Rolling over, I buried my face in my pillow.

Please make him stop, Father. Make him stop.

Someone thumped on the bedroom door. The locked bedroom door.

I staggered to my feet. In the six weeks since I'd moved in, I'd learned that although a locked door gave me privacy, it didn't give me peace. Aaron and/or Micah would knock until they got some kind of reaction. Or until Gram caught them.

I flung open the door, making Aaron and Micah jump, which was pleasant to see.

"Do you want to help us find the holes?" Micah said. He was already wearing boots and his camo winter coat.

"And the depressions and the pits," Aaron said.

My shoulders slumped. For four days, I'd been the good big sister and helped them find and fill in their holes. But I was sick of playing that role, especially after they kept me from sleeping in.

They looked up at me, wide, hopeful smiles on their small faces.

Gram descended the stairs from the playroom. "Morning, Rae. I made—" She studied the three of us. "Boys, did you wake Rae when I told you not to?"

Seated at the computer desk, Rusty looked away from the desktop monitor. "I told them they'd get into trouble."

"It's okay." I couldn't have all my brothers hating me like Rusty did. A sudden idea lifted my shoulders. "Since I'm working today, I don't want to get all muddy. So I can't help you."

"But you could get cleaned up before you have to go," Aaron said.

"You heard your sister," Gram said. "Leave her alone and go outside."

Micah charged out the front door while Aaron, his lively face pulled down in a pout, trudged out of the house.

Gram turned to Rusty. "You're supposed to be helping them."

He concentrated on the screen. "I will in a minute."

I said, "Do you need any new settings for your book? I can hook up my phone for you."

"I'm good," he said without looking at me.

At least he'd responded instead of acting like my words were static.

My phone rang as I was filling a mug for tea. I went to Gram's room and answered it.

"How fast can you get to my office?" Dad said. "I think we've found your camera."

I clutched my phone. "How?"

"We got a hit on that database I told you about. From a pawn shop in Lancaster. I called the pawnbroker, and she's holding it until you can get there and identify it."

"Can we get to Lancaster and back by noon?"

"Probably not. Ask Barb if you can come in late."

"Will do. See you in half an hour."

I washed fast and dressed faster. When I told Gram the good news, she hugged me. But driving for twenty minutes into Wellesville gave me time to think and knocked the legs out from under my high hopes.

Dad was waiting for me in the reception area.

"Barb was okay with you starting later?" He led me to the back of the building.

"She said I could make up the time tomorrow or Saturday." I trotted to keep up with him. "I don't think it's my camera. The stalker hates me and knows that camera is from my mom. He'd destroy it, not pawn it and take the risk of me recovering it."

"I was skeptical too." Dad opened the door to the parking lot behind the building. "But the owner said the camera is marked up where you scratched in the date when you got it, exactly where a thief would try to obliterate the identifying mark. And she told me the name of the guy who pawned it."

I whipped around to him. "You know who the stalker is?'

"Slow down, Rae. Pawning the stolen camera is a long way from proving he's the stalker. It's a first step." Dad jogged to his SUV.

I followed him. "Who is it?"

"Harley Stokes."

I blinked at him over the top of his vehicle. "Egypt's boyfriend?" I stared at the light rack. "So Egypt and China are behind the stalking."

"You're jumping the gun again. Get in." He pulled out of the lot. "First, you have to make sure it's your camera. Then I get a warrant to search his residence and car for your other stolen items. We'll have to search his phone to see if we can place him near your apartment at the times you figured out the notes had to be left. And we'll bring Stokes in for questioning. After all that, we may be on our way to tying Egypt and China to the stalking."

Gazing out my window, I processed Dad's words. "Harley can't be the stalker. The stalker is smart and pawning a stolen camera under your real name is one of the dumbest things I've heard of."

"After you've been in law enforcement for fifteen years, you learn never to underestimate the stupidity of criminals."

In Lancaster, we parked across the street from a store so small we might have missed it, except for the giant sign soaring way above the roofline. Ohio was having one of those bipolar days that seemed the most common in early spring. The sun and clouds fought for dominance, the morning switching from hopeful to depressing and back, hour by hour. The sun broke loose from a clot of clouds and shot a streak of light down the patched street we crossed.

Inside the store, a tiny woman waited behind the counter. All the musical instruments, jewelry, watches, firearms, and electronics lining the walls and cramming the display cases nearly camouflaged her.

"Sheriff Malinowski?" she said. "I have the camera right here." She pulled it off a shelf and gave it to Dad.

Father, let this be my camera.

He passed it to me.

As soon as I cradled it in my hands, I knew. "It's mine."

Dad put his hand on my shoulder. "You're sure?"

"The scratches are right where I put the date. And it just feels right. And there's a little scratch on the edge of the lens when I fell and hurt my ankle."

"You didn't tell me about that scratch when we filled out the report."

"I guess I forgot." I held the camera up to him. "See? It's pretty small. You only notice it when you hold the camera close."

Dad paid for the camera, thanked the woman, and we left the store. Clouds dimmed the morning sky to a dirty gray.

"I don't suppose you'll let me reimburse you for what you paid the pawn shop owner." I hugged the camera against my vest.

"Absolutely not," Dad said.

I'll never forget this, Father.

Pulling away from the curb, Dad said, "You can't take the camera home, Rae. It's evidence. Nothing will happen to it in the evidence room."

"Oh." My spirits deflated a little. "But it's found. That's the main thing. And we know who's involved in the stalking."

"We *think* we know who's involved in the stalking." Dad frowned. "But it doesn't quite add up. Graduating from harassing you to threatening a sheriff is a huge step. Neither China nor Egypt is a dope. I see a lot of Troy in China. He's a con man because he can steal a lot more money with a lot less risk than a typical thief could. I can't see China taking such an enormous chance of getting jailed just to scare you."

"And there's another thing that doesn't make sense," I said. "Why wasn't there a note on my truck when he or they or whoever trashed it? And why trash my truck after breaking into my apartment? If he knew I'd set a trap, he must have been scared to take me on. And I don't think he's scared of me."

Dad shook his head. "We should stop spinning our wheels and wait and see what we can get out of Stokes."

Maybe he could, but I couldn't. If Egypt and China were the stalkers, why would they call me "Bella"? To hide their real intent? What was their real intent? To make me miserable because I was from the branch of the family they hated? So were Amber, Coral, Rusty, Aaron, and Micah.

Dad parked behind the sheriff's office. I got out slowly, trailing my hand across my camera as I left it on the seat. "When will you get the warrant?"

"As soon as I can get Judge Pollock to sign it. I'll keep you posted."

A picture flashed in my mind—Harley the Stalker seeing Dad at his door and deciding he had only one chance to make good on his threat.

I rounded the hood, opened Dad's door, and hugged him. "You aren't going by yourself to Harley's house, right?"

He laughed. "I'll take Kincaid and Houston. They need experience with this kind of job. You can tell people we think we found your camera but nothing else. No names. Got it? I don't want anyone warning Stokes."

"Got it."

I drove the Rust Bucket to the library. After dropping off my coat and Aaron's backpack in the kitchen, I went up to Barb's office to tell her I was back, and she said I could make up the half hour tomorrow. At the checkout desk, Devon pounced on me with questions. "Is it your camera? Do you know who pawned it? Has Mal made an arrest?"

Now I knew why Dad didn't want me to say anything. Probably the majority of the county knew by now that I had come to work a half hour late because Dad thought he'd found my camera.

I repeated what Dad told me to say, adding, "I can't tell you anything else."

"Why not?"

"It could jeopardize the case and my dad."

Devon frowned, but a mischievous glint lightened her expression. "What's the advantage of being best friends with the sheriff's daughter if I can't get the inside scoop on crime in this county?"

We had a lot of patrons for a Wednesday afternoon, especially kids because the county schools were on spring break. But all the work couldn't keep me from wondering how Harley fit into this whole mess. Maybe Egypt and China weren't involved. Maybe my mom had hurt his mom or dad, and he was getting revenge. My mom and his mom …

I handed Mrs. Reynolds her picture books and middle grade novels.

Why had mentioning his mom rattled Chris so much? Why had Garrett lied to me? If Garrett hadn't, why had Chris? Even if Dad solved the stalker mystery, some questions I wanted answers to would remain mysteries.

My mom and his mom. Garrett didn't talk about his late parents. Could Chris or Garrett be …

"Rae."

I looked to Devon.

"You haven't given Shelley her due slip."

I jerked my head as if to knock my focus back to the present. I tore the piece of paper from the printer and gave it to her. "Sorry, Mrs. Reynolds."

Just because a guy acted weird about his background or parents didn't mean he was guilty of a crime.

"Did Mal have to be in court today?" Devon said.

I followed her gaze. Through the two-story window, I saw Dad jogging down the steps of the courthouse.

"No." I blew out a big breath. "But I might get some good news pretty—"

Something exploded, rattling the library windows. His hand on his holster, Dad whipped around, staring wide-eyed down Main Street in the direction of his office. Then he took off.

"Was that a gas main?" Devon said as we hurried outside with several patrons.

The sun freed itself of a cloud bank as the sidewalks along Main Street filled with store owners and customers rushing out of the buildings along it. At my height, I had an advantage over most of the people craning their necks. But I didn't see flames anywhere or smell smoke.

Then sirens screamed to life, and a town cruiser shot past us.

"What is going on?" Devon said to the world.

I took out my phone. Should I text Dad? He was probably too busy to answer if it was serious.

A text pinged. I opened my phone and swiped to it. A scream rose up, but my throat closed off, suffocating it.

The text had a photo of a burning patrol SUV.

NEXT TIME BELLA HE'LL BE IN IT

Chapter 35

Over the next few hours, time sped by as cop after cop questioned me, then crawled as I paced in Dad's office, waiting to hear what happened when he and about every deputy he had went to serve the warrant on Harley Stokes.

When had the stalker planted the bomb on Dad's SUV? Last night? In Lancaster?

My throat shrinking again, I dug through Aaron's backpack. I had to do something to keep from going ... Dad had my phone. It was evidence.

Throwing the backpack on the floor, I spun around to the wall of photos. My gift right in the middle. My first gift to my dad. It couldn't be my last.

I flipped my mop of hair out of my face and clamped my hand on top of it.

Have mercy, Father. Keep my dad safe. Keep me from going crazy with worry.

I went to Dad's desk and pawed through drawers, looking for paper. All these clues were jumbled in my head. A bomb seemed completely out of character for Egypt and China, no matter how much they hated me or Reuel's kids and grandkids or Dad being a cop. I had to organize my information.

I drew a sort of flow chart and filled in the shapes.

"What ya workin' on?"

Uncle Hank and Aunt Jeanine had entered the office without me noticing.

I kept writing. "Harley Stokes isn't the stalker."

"Harley Stokes," said Aunt Jeanine. "Is that Rhea Stokes's son?"

I laid down my pen. "I gotta talk to Dad. If he thinks Harley, Egypt, and China are behind the stalking, the real stalker will be free to do" — nausea churned my stomach — "something worse."

"I'll get him if he's here." Aunt Jeanine left.

Uncle Hank came around to my side of the desk. "What ya got?"

Pointing to the chart, I explained.

Uncle Hank's bushy eyebrows almost reached his wiry hair.

"What do you think?" I watched his face.

"I think the Big Guy should swear you in as a special deputy." Hank sat on the corner of the desk. "By the way, no one is saying a word about the bomb to the boys. With it being spring break, Mal told Lydia he figures we can keep it from them until they go to church on Easter. He thinks he'll have made an arrest by then."

"Not if he thinks it's Harley."

A few minutes passed while I reviewed the chart. Then Aunt Jeanine and Dad walked in.

"Have you arrested Harley?" I fired the question.

"Yes," Dad said, "because we found your backpack and zippered pouch dumped in a closet in his mom's house. He lives with her."

"But no notes?"

"No. He must have destroyed those or thrown them away." Dad scratched at an eyebrow. "But why he pawned … What are you so excited about?"

I grabbed Dad's hand and pulled him around to my side of the desk. Uncle Hank gave him a big grin. "Wait'll you hear this."

I pointed at the sheet of paper.

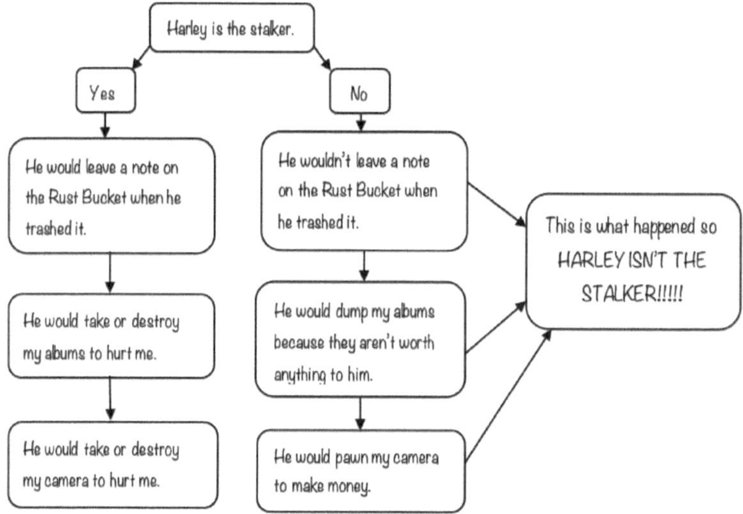

"There are two sets of criminals," I said. "Harley, Egypt, and possibly China were driving around the night of February 13th, found my truck, and decided to have some fun. That's why no note was left. Then Harley and Egypt saw me walking to work the next day. They got the idea of scaring me when I headed home that night.

"I don't think they were going to do more than try to scare me. Egypt and China were on their way into Wellesville when their car got stuck. So Harley carried out their plan on his own. At some point, he gave up chasing me, maybe when he found my backpack. He dumped the two albums because they weren't worth anything to him. If the stalker had found my backpack, he would have destroyed them. At his house, Harley kept the camera, waiting over a month before he pawned it, and hung onto the backpack and pouch probably because he thought he could use them. My research wasn't useful, so he pitched it."

Dad stared at me, then the sheets, then whispered, "Holy smoke."

A thrill of satisfaction shot through me. "You agree with me?"

"It makes perfect sense. It also explains something that's been bugging me since the bomb went off. Even somebody as thick as Harley Stokes wouldn't pawn the camera in his own name on Tuesday and set off a bomb on Wednesday."

Aunt Jeanine said, "What's his story about why he had Rae's backpack?"

"He said he found it, and there was no ID in it, so he kept it. Then we found your license in his wallet. So he had to change his story. He said he found the pouch with your cards in it today, tucked in a pocket in the backpack he hadn't noticed before. And he was going to contact you."

"After he pawned my camera?"

"I said it was his story, not a good story." Dad gave me an apologetic smile. "We didn't find your credit card, so I'm afraid he sold that. He must have had trouble figuring out how to get money for your license. Or he was waiting, like he did before pawning the camera."

"If Rae is right," said Aunt Jeanine, "then the stalker is someone whose father was hurt by Bella." She sighed, brushing back her red-gold bangs. "I've done a lot of searching and calling in the past week. Lots of people remember rumors, but only one gave me a name—Terry O'Neil. Though he has a reputation as a philanderer, I don't know if he actually had an affair with Bella. She certainly didn't ruin him."

Dad kissed me on the ear. "Thanks for your help, kiddo. Hank and Jeanine'll drive you home."

I glanced at the clock on Dad's desk phone. "I've got almost two hours of my shift left."

Aunt Jeanine's blue eyes widened. "You want to work after all this?

Yes, and no. "It'll keep me from worrying. Although I don't know how well I can focus."

"You don't need to worry," said Dad. "There are so many cops around that anyone not wearing a uniform will instantly arouse suspicion." He added, "I'm sure your friend Devon will want a full report. But I need you to keep your theory to yourself." He looked to Hank and Jeanine. "Do you mind coming back for Rae?"

I said, "You don't think you'll be done by 8:00 to drive home with me, Dad?"

"I don't think I'll be home tonight."

"We'll wait." Aunt Jeanine slipped on her sheepskin coat. "We'll have supper."

Uncle Hank looked stunned. "Is that legal? I'm mean, married people who have kids ain't allowed to go out to eat by themselves." He turned to Dad. "Ain't there some law against it, Mal?"

Rolling her eyes, Aunt Jeanine pushed him out the door.

I took hold of Dad's arms and looked straight into his blue eyes. "If I had come to you right away with the notes, you wouldn't be in danger now."

Dad pulled me into a hug. "There's no way of knowing if we could have caught the guy with only two or three notes. But we are going to nail him now." He lowered his head to meet my gaze. "The county is clogged with law enforcement. Officers from Loyal, Muskingum, and Athens counties are volunteering to help protect me and the rest of the family. BCI agents are combing the crime scene. I'll have one of my deputies follow you and Hank and Jeanine home."

He zipped his coat, and we started back toward the library. "What I can't figure out is if he actually plans to attack me, why warn me? Blowing up my SUV has me on guard. How does he think he can get at me now?"

"Maybe he's just scaring me." My tone was hopeful, but I didn't feel it.

"Maybe." Dad didn't sound hopeful at all.

Our walk took five times as long, as people along the sidewalk stopped Dad to ask him about what was going on. As politely as possible, he deflected their questions.

Devon had already gone home for the day, so I didn't have to tell her again that my lips were sealed. But I did have to say that to the rest of the staff and every patron I waited on.

I was explaining it to Mrs. Bates when a sudden thought made me drop two of her cookbooks.

The stalker was somebody who thought Mom had ruined his father in some way, someone who had father issues.

I knew three guys with father issues.

My fingers fumbled as I gathered the fallen books.

They were officers of the law. They wouldn't break the law. I knew them.

Fear congealed in my gut. How well did I know them?

Chapter 36

I drove the Rust Bucket home, Aunt Jeanine riding with me. Uncle Hank followed in their pickup, and Chris brought up the rear. After Chris checked our trucks for bombs.

Gram had ham and sweet potatoes left over from supper waiting for me, but I could only choke down a few bites. Fear took up the rest of the room in my stomach.

With Gram and the boys, I played a card game Aaron invented and lost every time. My mind kept straying back to the guys.

Houston resented, maybe even hated, his father and stepfather.

Chris never spoke of any family except his great-grandfather, had a definite anger issue, and was disturbed when I mentioned his mother.

Garrett went on guard if I asked about his past. And what was the confusion about where Garrett was born and his father's death?

"I love your game, Aaron," Gram said. "It's so different from other card games." She collected the cards spread across the dinner table. "Boys, time for bed."

Aaron and Micah galloped off to their room while Rusty followed at a more mature pace.

I held my head. What would they think if they know about the bomb?

Laying her arm across my shoulders, Gram said, "How're you doing?"

"I'm doing—" *Okay* wouldn't come out because tears rushed in. "This is all my fault. I should have come to Dad with the first note."

"It's definitely not your fault." Gram tightened her hold. "Whoever the stalker is, he could have chosen to stop after every note. He didn't. Now he'll get caught."

I studied her face. Her eyes held a calm I wanted to borrow.

"You're not worried?"

"Oh, yes. But I pray." She released me. "Let's pray together."

She slid into the chair beside me and interlaced her right hand with my left, and we bowed our heads.

Father, we all need Dad so bad. Please protect him. Mom, I wish you were with me to tell me everything is going to be all right.

I pleaded and prayed, almost forgetting Gram prayed with me.

The landline rang, sending me to my feet.

Gram got up more slowly and answered it. She listened, frowning.

But she didn't look alarmed.

She hung up. "That was Deputy Corliss. He's watching the house tonight. He wanted to let us know he's just let Walter through."

"Walter?"

In a minute, pounding rattled the front door.

Gram opened it. "You don't have to break it. We can hear you." All warmth had evaporated from her voice.

"I ain't here to talk to you." Walter glared over her head. "Rae, can you come out here? I got a feeling I ain't welcome inside."

"This is Rae's house," Gram said. "She can invite in whoever she wants."

Their gazes met, and I could feel, almost *see*, the anger and dislike, maybe even hatred, firing between them.

I grabbed my jacket. "We can talk outside."

Joining Walter on the porch, I hadn't even shut the door when he said, "Look, I've got a deal for you. I ain't sayin' Egypt and that idiot she calls a boyfriend wrecked your truck. All I'm sayin' is they might have. If you drop the charges for vandalizing it, I'll make sure Egypt pays you for half the damage. The idiot'll have to cover his half. I'm guessin' you could use the money more than my granddaughter sittin' in jail."

I blinked several times, as if the action would help my brain process the offer. "Dad arrested Egypt?"

"No. But after the cops got done questioning them, the girls told me what they asked. The cops think them and the idiot are the stalkers, but right now they don't got nothin' on them 'cause it's the idiot's word against theirs." He jabbed a thick finger at me. "Egypt ain't got the patience to spend weeks and weeks writin' notes, and China ain't gonna take the risk of plantin' no bomb. What'd that get her? China don't do nothing that don't help her somehow. I got a feeling they'll arrest my girls for the vandalism, thinking it'll protect you and Mal from any more stalking."

I gulped. He really was big, nearly as big as Dad. As he loomed over me, with the night so dark it looked like a black wall had dropped around the house, he seemed gigantic.

As much as I agreed with him, I had to ask, "Could they have planned the stalking together? China thought up all the notes, and Egypt left them and broke into my apartment and trashed my truck. I thought the kids and grandkids of your second and fourth marriages hate everybody descended from Reuel."

Walter's broad shoulders shrank a little. "Yeah, a lot of 'em do. But not enough to come up with writin' notes and plantin' a bomb, like they was goin' to war. They wouldn't bother."

The door creaked open, and Gram slipped out. "Walter, I have three grandsons trying to sleep. Keep your voice down."

He kept his eyes on me. "How much did it cost you to fix your truck?"

"$648. I'm still waiting on the insurance money, but it doesn't cover much."

He sucked in a breath that might have contained a curse. "If you don't press charges for vandalism against Egypt, she'll pay you half that. If she damaged your truck, and I ain't saying she did."

Gram crossed her arms. "You should discuss this with Mal before you decide anything, Rae."

Walter stepped close, so close I could finally tell his deep-set eyes were green with a burst of yellow around the pupils. "She's an adult, Lydia. She don't need her daddy to tell her what to do."

"The police wouldn't suspect Egypt and China without some kind of evidence."

"Yeah, the evidence that they're Malinowskis."

I had the strange sensation I had wandered into somebody else's story. Everybody is the main character of their own life, but watching Gram and Walter's standoff made me feel like a supporting character in a story that had more chapters than I had read.

He turned to me. "Egypt's got a good job being a maid at the lodge at the state park. If she gets arrested, even if it's only for a few days, she'll lose it."

A good job, especially in this county, was rarer than a straight road.

"Stop pressuring her," said Gram. "You can't know Egypt and China aren't the stalkers."

"I ain't raised them kids all these years" — his voice rose to a roar, and I backed up — "and not know what they're like. They ain't no angels, but they got more sense than to blow up Mal's car." He waited, watching me.

"I need ... " The words came out in a squeak, and I cleared my throat. "I need to talk to my dad first."

Snarling, Walter lurched toward me, his hands clenching into fists.

I swallowed all my air and all my courage, forcing my feet to not give an inch.

Gram inserted herself between us, her arms still folded. How she expected to protect me when Walter was a foot taller and 100 pounds heavier than she was, I had no clue.

Walter glared from her to me. Then he stomped off the porch and slammed into his truck.

As he spewed gravel turning around, Gram said, "You did the right thing."

"I hope so. I know Egypt and China aren't stalking us. I just wasn't sure if I should drop the charges on the vandalism. But I don't want Egypt to lose her job."

I opened the front door. Rusty swayed by the foot of the stairs, his narrow face bleached. "Somebody blew up Dad's SUV? Is he okay?"

Gram rushed to his side. "Your dad's fine. He's just working late."

"But was there a bomb?"

Pressing her lips together, Gram put her arm around his bony shoulders. "Rusty, come upstairs with me, so we can talk."

He jerked out from under her arm. "Dad's dead, isn't he? And you won't tell me."

"Sweetheart, you talked to him at supper. You can call him right now."

"But somebody planted a bomb?" His voice cracked.

Gram drew a deep breath. "Yes, and the person who planted it sent a note that said he deliberately set if off when your dad wasn't in his SUV."

"But why would —" Rusty looked to me, and his narrow blue eyes blazed through welling tears. "It's the stalker. Dad's gonna get killed, and it's all because of you!"

He bolted for the front door. Gram grabbed his arm, following him onto the porch, and closed the door after them.

Heaving deep breaths, I tiptoed to my brothers' bedroom and peeked in. Aaron and Micah, wrapped in quilts in their bunkbeds, were already asleep.

Without a sound, I shut their door and pressed myself against a wall, staring at the ceiling.

I was friends with three great guys, guys who had decided to put their lives on the line every time they wore their uniforms. Three guys who had some hang-up with fathers or father figures.

Murmurs and crying drifted through the windows that looked onto the porch.

Our dad was in danger.

Feeling like someone was pulling a belt tighter and tighter around my gut, I sat down at the computer, fired it up, and pulled some sheets of copier paper from a drawer. Fighting through the slow satellite connection, I searched and scrolled and wrote, searched and scrolled and wrote …

Chapter 37

The next morning in the shower, water drumming on my hair, I hung my head, rivers running down my face like tears, mimicking the dread I felt.

Father, let me be wrong. Let my theory be wrong.

My brothers and Gram slept on as I ate pickles and toast with apple butter and watched the morning change from light black to drab gray. A few fat flakes wandered down. Scattered lumps of snow were all that was left of the last snowfall. The weather was as bleak as my mood, perfect for a photo—

I slammed my hand on the table. I didn't even have a phone to take one crummy picture.

Aaron and Micah woke about an hour before I needed to leave. Fixing them bacon and waffles and chatting with them was a welcome distraction.

Gram and Rusty were still asleep by the time I left. One of the Wellesville town officers drove behind me to the library.

As Devon and I opened, she said, "Can you tell me anything about the case today?"

"If I knew anything, no. But I don't know anything."

I worked at 100 miles per hour, checking out customers, repairing books and scanning discarded ones, anything to keep busy. Using the phone Gram let me borrow, I texted Dad about seeing him at lunch. He said he couldn't and reminded me not to leave the library for any reason without a police escort.

At noon, Garrett came in. "How're you doing?"

I turned to stone. Talking to him like I had no suspicions seemed dishonest. But letting him know I had suspicions seemed stupid. "I'm okay. I'm glad I'm working today, so I can keep busy."

"Don't worry, Rae. All the cops in the county, and the extra ones, are working around the clock to solve this case and keep you and your family safe." He lifted a hand, maybe to reach for mine, then dropped it. "I'll see you later." He rushed out.

During lunch, I whipped through newspapers on the microfilm reader, searching for evidence to disprove my theory. I so wanted it disproven.

At 5:00, Dad trudged in. He looked as worn out as the day after he hurt his knee. Every adult in the library came up to him to say how sorry or concerned they were about the explosion.

Demonstrating more patience than I thought possible for someone who looked dead on his feet, Dad thanked them and fielded their questions.

Finally, he made it to the counter and, somehow, managed to give me his special grin. "How's my girl?"

I found a smile of my own, but it felt feeble. "Better now that you're here."

His grin actually grew. "Houston and Chris are waiting for us in the library lot."

"You'd better get down there fast, Mal," said Devon, "before you fall over."

He leaned against the desk. "I can hold myself up until I can fall over in the privacy of my own home."

I collected my jacket, vest, and backpack, and we left the library by the basement door.

Houston and Chris hurried to us, and Houston said, "How are you, Rae?"

I smiled. My research had pretty much cleared him. "Okay." I couldn't look at Chris, though, not with what I was thinking.

Dad said, "Chris, you're staying at the farm until you get off at 7:00, right?"

"I can stay longer."

"No, get a good night's sleep. You're working tomorrow."

Houston slapped Chris on the shoulder. "Besides, I'm coming on after you. They'll be a lot safer then."

I prayed that wasn't true.

Dad and I climbed into the Rust Bucket. Turning onto Woodward behind Chris's vehicle, I said, "Can you tell me anything?"

His eyes closed, Dad sank into the bucket seat. "BCI agents are analyzing the evidence they've gathered from the bomb and my SUV. Simcox and the special agents are convinced the stalker is a relative because Harley Stokes had your camera. They think the reason I'm not buying it is because it's family." He tilted the seat back. "Ma told me about Walter's visit."

"Have you arrested Egypt and China?"

"No. Simcox wanted to, but he can't based solely on their connection to Harley. Anyway, some of the volunteer officers from other counties are watching Walter's place." Turning his head, he cracked an eye. "Are you going to drop the charges for the vandalism of your truck?"

"Do you think I should? I'd rather have the cash, and I don't want Egypt to lose her job. Having a good job when you only have a high school diploma is a gold mine."

"She broke the law, Rae."

"Yeah, but by paying me, she'd be punished."

"You trust her to do that?"

I shook my head. "I trust Walter."

Dad yawned, and I let him doze as I followed Chris to the farm. When could I tell him my theory? I couldn't wait until tomorrow morning.

Houston and Chris stopped on the road as I went on up the drive. When Dad and I walked into the kitchen, Aaron attacked, wilder than usual.

As soon as Dad released Aaron from a hug, Gram took hold of him and held on.

"Ma, I'm fine."

"You're not." Her voice trembled, and she placed her hands either side of his face. "You look terrible."

"Just tired."

Turning toward the living-dining room, I slid off my jacket. Rusty stood by the dinner table.

I bit my lip. What could I say?

Dad said, "Have a good day, Rusty?"

He spun and ran. A door slammed.

Dad released what I thought was a sigh, but he was so weary it came out as a long hiss. "I'll talk to him, Ma. Don't wait supper for us."

I followed Dad through the living room, dragging my feet. It was going to be a very, very long—

"Gotcha!" Micah popped out from beside the piano.

I screamed, and Dad jumped back, his right arm flying up as if to ward off an attack.

"What do you think you're doing?" Dad's shout stole the grin from Micah's face, leaving it bewildered.

"Scaring you," Micah said, like it was obvious.

A smile tried to form as Dad lowered his arm. "Yeah, you did, buddy." He rubbed Micah on the head with a weak hand, then went into the boys' room, and closed the door behind him.

The rest of us sat down to eat.

Aaron snatched a slice of whole wheat bread. "How come Dad and Rusty aren't eating with us?"

"Rusty's upset." Gram ladled mushroom soup into his bowl. "Mal's talking to him about it."

"He's been mean all day." Micah blew on his soup.

Aaron said, "Maybe he'll be nicer when we go hiking tomorrow."

A knife poised over her bread, Gram blinked. "Oh, my. I forgot Mal was taking tomorrow off so you could go to Hocking Hills. Boys, I'm afraid that can't happen. Your dad is working on the stalker case, and he has some new clues he has to follow up."

Micah's happy expression fell, and Aaron made a face.

I stirred my soup. The rich smell of broth-drenched mushrooms should have whetted my appetite so much that I was close to finishing my first helping. But my desire to eat was squashed under a load of tension. How was I going to avoid Rusty all day tomorrow, which I took off so we could hike with Dad?

Aaron tapped his spoon against his bowl. "If Sunday is Easter, then what's today?"

"Maundy Thursday," said Gram.

"Do we have to go to church after supper?"

Micah said through a bite of bread, "I just go to church on Sunday."

"We would be going," Gram said, "but since your dad is so tired, we'll skip tonight's service and go to the one on Good Friday." She looked to Aaron. "Maybe you can go hiking next weekend."

While the boys and I filled the dishwasher, Gram carried plates into the bedroom for Dad and Rusty. Once the kitchen was clean, I helped Aaron and Micah build a city with plastic blocks. Not my favorite evening activity, but it passed the time. We'd gotten Main Street in good shape when a door downstairs opened.

Standing at the bottom of the stairs, Dad called, "Boys, do you want to watch a movie?"

"Sure." Aaron ran down the steps with Micah right behind him.

I followed more slowly, watching for Rusty. The living room was clear. I went to Gram's room and shut the door.

A few seconds later, a knock came. "May I come in?" Dad said.

"For sure." I twisted around in the desk chair.

Plodding into the room, Dad said, "Rae, you don't have to hide."

"I think it'll be easier on Rusty and me if I stay in here tonight. How's he doing?"

Dad fell back against the door. "I've explained what I could about how the investigation is progressing, and all the security measures we've put in place. That seemed to reassure him a bit."

"When the boys go to bed, I've got something to tell you—a theory about who the stalker is."

For the first time since he'd dragged himself into the library, an alertness came over Dad, raising him from the door. "You've remembered something?"

"No, but it's an idea I need to talk over with you."

"The movie can wait."

"No, it can't. The boys should hang out with you this evening."

He kissed me on top of my head. "You're a good big sister."

I fought the urge to hug him. If I latched on, I might not let go.

Chapter 38

I had to develop some new hobbies. Without my camera and my phone, the evening crawled along like it was starved, stabbed, and dragging two broken legs.

Finally, finally, the house got quiet, and Dad came into Gram's room. He sat on the bed. "What's your theory?"

Holding sheets of paper, I took a seat at the foot of the bed. "You said we should concentrate on finding anybody whose father might have been hurt by my mom. I think I have two candidates we've overlooked."

"Who?"

Feeling like I was shoving knives into their spines, I said, "Chris Kincaid and Garrett Matthews."

Dad's mouth dropped open, his eyes flew open, his whole face seemed to fall apart.

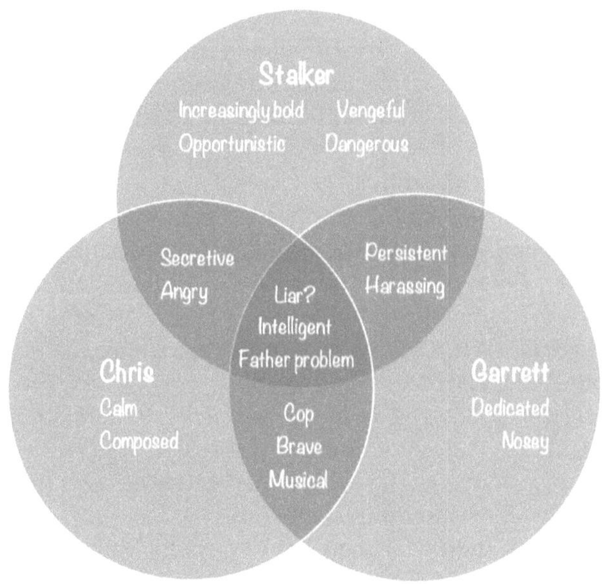

I spread my notes and diagram on the quilt. "I was suspicious of Houston too, because he seems to have major dad issues. But last night when I was researching him, I found out his father is a U.S. congressman. He doesn't sound ruined to me. And it doesn't seem likely with his Texas roots, Houston would have a connection to Marlin County from twenty years ago."

Dad's mouth snapped shut. "This is crazy, Rae. These guys are sworn officers of—"

"Could you hear me out before you bite my head off?"

"I'm not biting your head off." He gripped my hand. "I'll listen, but I can't believe it."

Fighting an urge to shake him, I pointed at my diagram.

"Neither Chris or Garrett say much about their parents, and both are the right age to have had a father who had an affair with my mom. You said Chris has no father listed on his birth certificate. He never talks about any family except his great-grandfather. When I told him I knew our moms knew each other, he became very uncomfortable. The stalker is also someone with an anger issue."

My chest growing tight, I described Chris's assault on the punching bag.

"So what?" Dad said. "He was mad, probably had a rough shift, and took his frustrations out on something appropriate."

"I know the difference between someone working off stress, and someone so angry he's exploding." I leaned toward him. "I thought maybe he blamed Mom for his great-grandfather's death. He seems to have been the only father figure Chris has had. But a newspaper article I found at lunch said Chris's great-grandfather died in a fall almost six years after Mom left."

"Then Chris has no motive."

Against my will, I shook my head. "There's the stabbing. I know Mom didn't do it. She would have written a letter apologizing for it if she had. But what if Chris's father is Sean Ross and he stabbed Chris's mother because she was fighting him about leaving her for Mom? Or maybe Chris holds Mom responsible for Sean Ross dying in that car accident. Have you found out anything about him?"

"Not much. Ross was born in Kentucky, seems to have moved around a lot. Had a few convictions for possession of narcotics, but he was never arrested in Marlin County. He died in that car wreck because his blood alcohol level was twice the legal limit."

"Okay. What about the man who attacked Jason and Mom at the children's home back when they were a couple? Maybe he's Chris's father, and he left Chris and his mother. That's why Chris never talks about his family except for his Grandpa Dave."

"I think I know why Chris was disturbed when you brought up his mother," Dad said. "I found out something about her when he interviewed for his job. But I'm not certain, and it's obvious he doesn't want people to know, so I won't say. But it's a very good reason." He stared at the floor. "How could Matthews be guilty?"

I swallowed and said, "There's this weird discrepancy about where he was born and when his parents died. The first time I met him, he said he was from Toledo, and his parents died a few years ago. Chris says he was born in Zanesville and raised in Toledo. Gram thought so too. Chris also says Garrett's father died when he was little and only his mother died recently. One of them is lying."

"Or Chris is just mistaken."

"He doesn't think so. I've watched his face. I asked Houston and he can't remember, but he thought Garrett said he was born in Zanesville."

"So you think Garrett doesn't want you to know he lived in the area when your mom did."

I nodded. "Some other things make sense too, if he's the stalker. All the notes and crimes have taken place in Wellesville, Chief Simcox's jurisdiction, keeping you out of the investigation."

"I can investigate if I think I should."

"But you waited so you wouldn't tick off Simcox, and Garrett would know that. He was also working day shift until the week of Valentine's Day, when he switched to nights. That explains why he didn't do anything the night I set my trap."

"And you think something happened to his father that he blames Bella for?"

"It's possible, don't you think?"

"Sure, it's possible. But it's much more likely there's a non-criminal explanation. Rae, you didn't take into consideration that Kincaid and Matthews are cops. A cop threatening to kill a cop is just about unthinkable. Our lives depend on working with each other. We support each other in ways no one but a cop can. That's why I can't turn around without stumbling over officers from other agencies. I'm in trouble, and they want to help."

Patching together a respectful tone, I said, "Is Chief Simcox helping?"

Dad shot me an irritated look. "Some cops are more helpful than others." He gestured at the pages. "Rae, none of this is evidence."

"I know that." It came out harsher than I intended. "That's why I'm giving it to you. I thought you could check Chris's and Garrett's work schedule against the times the stalker left the notes and took pictures of me. If there's one time they were tied up with work, they're eliminated. Or you can check on Garrett's birth certificate and his parents' death certificates to see who's right."

"If Garrett's version is correct, and that's most likely, it doesn't mean Chris lied."

"Or it could mean he did, and he was trying to throw suspicion on someone else." I hated airing those words, souring my stomach. "Like at his house, the first time we jammed. Chris said he saw someone hiding between the cars. He could have said that just to freak me out. Or Chris really thought he saw someone, and Garrett pretended to chase someone to freak me out."

I pushed a tangle of hair out of my face. "If the stalker is a cop, it also explains why he didn't care if he put you on your guard with the bomb. He knows he can still get at you."

Dad's eyes darted to mine. Then he picked up a paper. "I'll think this over. But you should know that Chris is one of the finest young officers I've ever worked with. He hasn't been on the force two years yet and shows enormous maturity."

"But he's still human. He has a mother and a father and a past like everyone else." I pressed my hand against my stomach. "Don't get me wrong. I don't want the stalker to be one of the guys. I feel like Judas, telling you all this. But I'd rather be Judas than lose you."

"You're not going to lose me." Dad pulled me close. "Would you like your Valentine's Day gift?"

I drew back. "On Maundy Thursday?"

"I'll explain after you open it."

He led me into the living room. One lamp glowed on an end table. A large, red gift bag with white and pink tissue paper poking out of it sat on the couch.

Removing the paper, I lifted out a backpack, straps dangling, its heaviness surprising me. I unzipped the main compartment. A long lens lay nestled among thick padding.

I gasped. "It's a camera backpack!"

Dad grinned. "This should work better to protect your camera than your towel. Which we also found at Harley's. He wasn't wasting anything he might use."

I removed the lens and held it under the lamp. "It's a zoom. This-- this had to cost—" I turned huge eyes to him.

"Doesn't matter. I knew you could use it."

"You gave this to me now" —I studied the lens in the light—"because we found my camera."

"I couldn't very well give it to you after your camera was stolen. Talk about rubbing salt in a wound. So I waited. The family was pooling money to get you a replacement camera, but we were waiting to give it to you when we thought you were ready. Now we don't have to."

I hugged him, and he held me strong. But not as tight as I held him.

"Rae, we'll catch this guy. Nothing will happen to you or me."

I looked up at him. "I still haven't messed things up between us?"

His lit-from-within grin erased his weariness. "Never, kiddo."

Chapter 39

Knocking. Someone was knocking. I lifted my head from my pillow. But it wasn't at the bedroom door.

I went to it and looked out. Gram hurried down the stairs and opened the front door.

Chris's bass rumble reached me clearly. "I wanted to introduce the other deputy who will be on duty with me this morning. He's from Loyal County. Deputy Cantrell, Lydia Malinowski."

"Why don't you boys come in for coffee and something to eat?"

I shut my door. No way I could face Chris.

I opened the blinds to the two windows in Gram's room. Fog filled the little valley, the barn rising above it like an island. I pressed my head against the window frame. And I didn't even have a phone camera to capture the moody scene.

After the deputies left, Gram tried to keep all of us busy, assigning Rusty and Aaron to work in the barn while Micah and I helped her bake. I mixed cake batter, checked the time, poured it into pans, checked the time, slid it in the oven, and checked the time. How long did it take for Dad to look up Chris's schedule? He'd probably have trouble getting Garrett's from Simcox. Couldn't Liz or Janet check on the birth and death certificates? If I waited much longer, my impatience would reach lethal levels.

Gram showed me how to make a pie crust and the cherry filling, and I washed and folded two loads of clothes and changed all the bedding in the house by the time noon came and a town officer stopped by to say he was now on duty with Chris.

I couldn't wait any longer. I took the landline into Gram's bedroom and called Dad.

As soon as he picked up, I said, "Have you cleared Chris and Garrett?"

"No." The word sounded strained, like he was suppressing a yell. "But I didn't expect to. Chris wasn't working any of the times the notes were left, so he still has opportunity. Garrett was born in Zanesville."

A numbness stole over my skin. "So he lied."

"Yes, but I think I know why. His father committed suicide when he was" — papers rustled — "when he was seven. His mother died of cirrhosis of the liver. Alcoholism is listed as a contributing cause. His father killed himself the day after the divorce was finalized, so it had to be nasty. Garrett probably lied because he doesn't want people bringing up something so painful. Believe me, Rae, the relatives and friends of suicide victims have a horrible time dealing with it. One woman in the county still insists her son didn't commit suicide because the note he left didn't contain the word 'suicide'."

"Did the suicide happen in Zanesville?"

"Yes."

"If Garrett was seven, then it occurred almost four years after Mom disappeared. If his father killed himself because he lost Mom, it took a while. If she broke up the marriage, you'd think the wife would commit suicide."

"It's tragic, but not incriminating. I haven't found anything new on Sean Ross, but I haven't had much time to—I gotta take this call, Rae. If I find anything that will ease your mind, I'll let you know."

My heart heavy for Garrett, I clicked off. When he talked about his parents worrying about him going into law enforcement, it was like Micah telling me how much his mom loved him. Garrett seemed to be pretending he knew how his dad would have felt about his career choice to make himself feel better.

I stared out the bedroom window, the fog still shrouding the valley. That was the most pathetic thing I'd ever heard.

I returned to the kitchen. Aaron and Micah were chomping on pepperoni rolls at the dinner table. Rusty straightened from looking in the fridge.

Our gazes locked.

I opened my mouth, but words dried up. Carrying a glass of juice, Rusty picked up his plate and brushed by me. A door shut.

Aaron said, "Why's Rusty eating in our bedroom?"

If my heart grew any heavier, I wouldn't be able to move. "He doesn't want to eat with me."

"How come?" Micah popped in a grape.

"I'll tell you later."

Another deputy, this one from Athens County, stopped to introduce herself, and Gram invited her to lunch.

After we finished eating, Micah and I washed dishes, and Aaron suggested we look for more holes to fill in.

"No," said Gram. "You can play in the barn or here in the house, but your dad wouldn't want you wandering in the woods."

The fog thinned but still enveloped the afternoon, fraying every edge of the landscape. I vacuumed all the rugs and carpets in the house, mopped the kitchen floor, and, as Gram got supper ready, decided I had to get out of the house.

"Can I borrow your phone, Gram?" I buttoned my jacket. "I want to take pictures of the fog. I'll stay on the drive and walk down and get the mail."

Gram set aside her knife. "That should be okay. The Kincaid boy should be parked near the mailbox. I think he's the only one on duty at the moment. That nice deputy from Athens County said she had to leave around 4:00."

Chris. Was waiting. In the fog. I unbuttoned my jacket to take it off. No, I had absolutely no proof against him. I buttoned my jacket back up and went to the screened porch.

Micah stood in the open doorway to the kitchen as I shoved on my boots. "I'm coming with you."

A scream tried to free itself. We'd been together all day. Why did he feel a need to come with me now?

He grinned, the kitchen light making his strawberry blond hair shine and giving his cheeks a rosy look.

My scream converted to a resigned sigh. "C'mon, but you have to stay right with me." I was such a sucker for a cute face.

Micah chatted while I stopped at various spots on the drive to take photos. Gram's camera wasn't very good, and it certainly didn't look like what my eyes saw, but it felt so good to be taking pictures again, like working a limb that just lost its cast.

We'd almost reached the mailbox when Micah slipped his hand into mine.

"Kinda creepy, isn't it?" He stole a peek over his shoulder. "Like Halloween."

"Yeah, but there's nothing in the fog that wasn't there without the fog." I hoped.

Twigs snapped to our left in the woods lining that side of the drive. I couldn't see past the first row of trees.

Sidling right against me, Micah said, "You scared?"

I bent down to him. "It's just a—"

A crash and a shout from the woods made us jump.

Dragging Micah behind me, I tore up the drive.

A curse word followed us, and I slid to a halt on the wet gravel.

"Garrett?" I called, peering through the mist.

Leaves rattled, twigs broke, and Garrett stumbled onto the drive, carrying a rifle with a scope, brushing debris from his jeans and hooded jacket with his free hand.

"Are you all right?" I said.

He kept brushing. "Oh, yeah. I fell in a hole that had water in the bottom of it."

I looked down to Micah. "Did y'all dig a hole in the woods by the mailbox?"

"I told Rusty and Aaron we hadn't filled 'em all in up here, but they didn't believe me."

"Why were you guys digging holes?" Garrett squeezed moisture from his pant leg.

Micah said, "We were trying to catch the guy scaring Rae."

I explained how my brothers had set booby traps around the farm and had already caught Dad in one.

Garrett chuckled. "I think you guys will have to change your plans. Your holes only seem to catch cops."

He was taking it better than Dad had. I said, "When did you get here?"

"A few minutes ago. I was going to tell Chris I could take over for him when I thought I saw someone in the woods."

Micah leaned toward him. "Did you get him?"

Garrett broke into his V-shaped smile. "No. I'm pretty sure I made a mistake." He gazed about. "This fog plays tricks with you."

Chris had said that about the weather the first night we jammed.

An uneasiness stole over me like the mist that blurred everything.

An engine started, and we turned toward the house. I could just make out the red SUV heading down the drive.

When Gram reached us, she rolled down her window. "Oh, good. Are there still two officers on duty?"

Garrett said, "Chris is parked where your drive meets the road."

"That makes things easy. I have to go to the church. The sisters who were supposed to get the sanctuary ready for the Good Friday service can't now because one's husband had a heart attack. So I'm meeting another friend to get the work done. I knew Deputy Kincaid would feel torn about following me or staying with the kids. But since you're here, if he wants to follow me, I don't have to insist he stay."

She turned to me. "I'll be back as soon as I can. I told Rusty you're in charge. If he doesn't listen to you, tell me. Check the chicken's temperature in ten minutes." Her easygoing blue eyes move to Garrett. "Please stay for supper. There's plenty."

Gram rolled up her window, drove to the road, and stopped. Faint voices managed to work their way through the fog.

We followed the drive, Garrett asking Micah about the pits, and Micah telling him in detail how he had wanted to put in stakes.

Funny. Why hadn't Garrett called out to Micah and me when we came down the drive? He had to have heard us. Micah had talked practically the whole time. And Garrett had to know popping out of the woods like that without warning would scare us.

All my suspicions about him roared back. And now my brothers and

I were alone with him. My lungs clamped shut. I forced them open with a deep breath.

I had no proof, not a crumb.

We clomped onto the screened porch and removed our boots.

But Dad said to follow my instinct if I felt uncomfortable. I definitely did.

Micah darted into the house, and Garrett was about to follow.

I said, "Could you unload your rifle and leave it here? I don't want my brothers messing with it."

Garrett tilted his head sideways, then shrugged. He removed the bullets from the gun and put them in the pocket of his jacket.

As I stepped into the kitchen, another thought halted me. "Are you carrying your pistol?"

The corners of Garrett's hazel eyes crinkled. "I can't very well patrol without one." He pulled back his jacket to reveal a holster on his belt.

"Oh--oh, for sure."

Thumps vibrated through the ceiling of the kitchen.

Glancing up, Garrett said, "What're your brothers doing up there?"

"Playing or fighting. It sounds the same."

He took a big sniff. "That chicken smells great. Better than anything I can cook."

"Nobody cooks like Gram."

The landline rang, and I answered it.

"Hey, Rae," said Jason with road noise behind his cheerful voice. "Is Mal home?"

"No. He must be on his way, or he would have called to say he was going to be late."

"Then he must be in a dead spot. I tried his cell, and he didn't answer. Would you please have him call me as soon as he gets in? I can't believe he found him."

"Who?"

"The man who attacked your mother and me at the home. Mal sent me a photo this afternoon, but I was tied up in meetings until now and just saw it."

My fingers clutched the phone. "Who is it?"

"The caption under the photo—it's from a Zanesville paper—says Dr. Brian Matthews."

Chapter 40

Every function in me froze. Except my eyes. They flicked to where Garrett sat on a stool by the counter, reading the back of a book somebody had left there.

"Rae? Can you have Mal call me?"

"Uh--uh—yeah. Hold on." Turning my back to Garrett, I held my forehead. He hadn't been patrolling the woods. He'd been waiting with a rifle and scope to murder Dad. Then he could sneak home or come running out of the woods, saying he chased the killer and lost him. And he'd have a front row seat to watch me fall to pieces. And my brother. *My brothers!*

"Rae, is something wrong?"

"No. No, not all." I glanced back at Garrett.

He was watching me, a polite expression on his pointed face.

"No. Gram had to go to the church, but she didn't mind leaving because Garrett Matthews is here for supper. Do you know him?"

Jason gasped. "Garrett Matthews? You don't … isn't he … Rae, are you afraid to talk in front of him?"

"For sure." Act natural. He suspected nothing yet. I went to a cupboard by the sink and lifted down plates.

"You and your brothers are alone, and you think Garrett is the stalker?"

"Absolutely."

"You--you have to get out of there."

But if I left Garrett alone, he might try to hide again and kill Dad. How could I keep Garrett busy until Dad got home *and* protect my brothers?

Father, I need help right NOW.

"I'll call 911," Jason said. "I'm about halfway home from Columbus. The dispatcher can give Mal the message that you're with the stalker."

An idea lit up my mind like a lightning strike.

"Of course, Jason. The boys can come over and play with Richard. I know it gets boring for him while Alli's having her riding lesson."

Leaving the kitchen, I yelled for my brothers. Aaron and Micah thundered down the stairs, but I had to knock on the door of their bedroom to get Rusty to come out.

"What?" His thin face was blank.

I glanced over my shoulder. Couldn't see Garrett. He was probably still sitting at the counter. "Alli's having a riding lesson, and Richard wants to play with you guys. You should leave now."

"Great." Aaron ran to the kitchen.

Rusty said, "I don't want to go."

"You have to." I kept my back to the rest of the house in case Garrett left his seat. "You need to walk over with Aaron and Micah. I'll stay here with Garrett to take out the chicken when it's done and wait for Dad. I'll come over with him." I mouthed, "Please, please, please."

Rusty's blue eyes widened.

Into the phone, I said, "They're heading over now, Jason. I'll wait for Dad with Garrett."

"Rae, leave with the boys."

"We'll be over soon."

"You have to—"

"I have to wait for Dad."

"Rae, I'll call you right back after I call 911." Jason panted between words like he was running home instead of driving. "I'll call Hank and Jeanine too. Then I'll call you."

"That's fine." Since the hole had tripped Garrett up, maybe he'd shelved his plans to kill Dad today. He'd wait until he could set up another situation that would give him an alibi.

"I'll just be a minute." Jason hung up.

My gut tensed like it'd taken a blow as my line to the outside world was cut.

I returned to the kitchen, Rusty behind me. On the screened porch, Aaron and Micah pulled on their boots.

Rusty stepped onto the porch. "Are we having supper over there?" he said, his words groping. "I thought Gram was making something."

"She was. She is. But if Aunt Jeanine invites us, I'll just put the chicken in the fridge before Dad, Garrett, and I come over." I bent close to Rusty's head. "Just go. Please," I whispered.

Confusion creasing his face, Rusty pulled on his black winter coat and followed Aaron and Micah into the breezeway.

"I don't think this is safe." Garrett stepped off the stool. "We should go with them."

I spun to him. "I've got to take the chicken out. The boys'll be fine. They're not walking along the road. They cut across the fields and through the woods."

I crossed to the window over the sink. All three of my brothers disappeared into the fog as they headed down the hill toward the Norris farm. I lowered my head. At least they were safe.

Watching me, Garrett's hazel eyes had narrowed to slits.

Had to say something. "We'll catch up to them quick when Dad comes. Should be any minute."

I tried to smile, but its tightness made me give it up. Searching for something to keep my nerves from shattering, I pulled out a drawer next to the stove and rummaged in it.

"What are you looking for?" Garrett said.

"The thermometer."

"It's on the cooktop."

I giggled. "That was dumb." I opened the door to the oven, pulled out the roasting pan, and set it on top of the stove.

He took a couple steps. "I think I'll patrol around the house."

I dropped the thermometer. "You--you don't need to. I--I—" I stooped to pick up the instrument. "I'd feel better if you stayed with me."

Cocking his head to one side, he said, "It's safe for your little brothers to be out in this fog, but you don't want to be alone in the house?"

My mouth dried. "Well, uh, the stalker's only threatened me and Dad."

He looked to the floor, as if thinking, and I inserted the—

A crushing grip around my right wrist jerked me into the pistol Garrett held.

"Who was on the phone, Rae?" His razor-sharp face was an inch from mine. "That stupid lineman finally figured me out?"

He didn't look the same at all. Hate carved his face into a nightmare.

I couldn't outfight him, despite my height advantage.

"It was Jason Carlisle. He wanted my brothers—"

"You're lying." He flung me against the counter, still grasping my wrist. "You're just like your mother. Lying, conning. You went after Houston, Chris, and me just like she would have, and then you played us all off each other, having lunch with Houston and then making sure I knew it."

Shivers rocked me. *Father, he's crazy. Completely crazy.*

He dragged me to the dinner table, glancing back and forth. He now had clear shots at both doors.

"You can't get away with killing my dad now." I panted the words.

"But I can watch you watch me kill him." He jammed the pistol under my chin. "Hard as it was to grow up without my dad, at least I knew Bella was dead. Then you show up and say she got fifteen more years than he did." The muzzle dug deeper. "Fifteen years. Then I see you parading around with Mal like you won the lottery. If I can't have a father, Bella, you can't either."

Father, help me think.

"I'm -- I'm sorry about your dad. But he killed himself long after Mom had disappeared from Marlin County." Maybe if I kept him talking,

Dad could take him by surprise.

He twisted my wrist. "She ruined him. How could Mom take him back after he left her for Bella? He was no good to us. Mom couldn't take him back. She had no choice."

The landline rang.

Our gazes moved to the phone on the counter.

"I've got to answer it," I said. "Whoever's calling will think it's weird if I don't."

"Doesn't matter. If it's Mal, he'll just get here faster."

Dad's words from last night rang in my mind. "But he's a cop. You don't want to kill another cop."

Garrett blinked. "I told you to leave if you cared about your family." He gave his head a violent shake. "I warned you."

He'd cracked, just a sliver. "But you'll hurt a lot more people than me if you kill my dad. My brothers already lost their mom. They're twelve, nine, and seven. You can't make them orphans."

He blinked again. "Your little brother is seven." The pressure from the muzzle under my chin backed off a bit.

The same age he'd lost his father. "Yes, the one who was with me at the mailbox. My brothers are innocent. You can't hurt them because they've got me for a sister."

"Seven." A tremor fired through him.

"I know you don't want to hurt some kids the way you were hurt."

The landline started ringing again, but I kept my focus on Garrett. "And you're a cop. You can't shoot down a fellow officer."

"Shut up!" The muzzle embedded itself in my skin as he bent me back over the dinner table. Tears tried to escape from his eyes, but he squinted against them. His arms shook as they gripped me and the gun.

The air in me froze, but I had to keep talking, had to make him doubt his plan. "You said your mom had no choice. But you do. You don't have to kill another cop."

He threw me to the floor, his gun still trained on me, but his other hand grabbed his bangs. "It's not fair. It's not fair!"

"No, it's not fair to live without a dad." I rolled to my knees. "I know what that's like."

He yanked me to my feet, the gun shoved into my chest. "You don't know anything."

Better to agree with him. "You're right. That was stupid. But I do know you have a choice. Not to murder a cop. Not to orphan some kids who are just like you."

He shoved me to the floor again. Tears leaked down his cheeks despite his gritted teeth. His free hand clasped his forehead.

The screen door creaked open.

Garrett spun toward it and swung his gun away from me.

"Dad!" I screamed and threw myself at Garrett's legs.

We hit the floor, and the gun fired as Garrett's hand cracked against a chair at the dinner table.

He sprang clear of me and raised his gun.

Toward his head.

I kicked at him with all my strength.

His legs flew out from under him, gunfire exploding again, and the back of his head slammed through the edge of the dinner table.

I scrambled onto my knees.

Lying in a heap, he didn't move.

Gasping, I crept forward.

The screen door banged open, and an unsteady voice yelled, "I've got you covered! Rae, are you okay?"

Snatching the pistol from Garrett's limp fingers, I said, "Rusty?" and staggered to my feet.

The barrel of a rifle was thrust through the open kitchen door. "What's going on, Rae? Are you okay?"

"I--I--I'm fine." Rusty was here? He couldn't be here.

But he edged into the kitchen, toting Garrett's rifle.

"What in the world are you doing here?" I screamed. "You're supposed to be with Uncle Hank and Aunt Jeanine!"

His eyes rounded as huge as pie pans. "I didn't know you could get that loud. What's going on?"

Pointing the gun at Garrett, who lay as still as roadkill, I peered down at his head. No bullet wound, no blood, although a reddish stain was smeared along the ragged edge of the dinner table where his head broke it. I couldn't tell if he was breathing, but I wasn't getting close enough for him to grab me if he was playing possum. "Garrett Matthews was the stalker. He's unconscious now."

Rusty's jaw about hit the linoleum. "But he's a cop!"

"He's also a guy who really missed his dad." A rush of pity loosened my muscles a fraction. "Why are you here?"

"You were acting so weird, I thought maybe I should come back and see what was going on."

I backed to the basement door, pistol leveled at Garrett, my wrist aching where he had held it. "You came to check up on me after I told you to leave?"

"Well, yeah." Rusty pointed the rifle's barrel toward the floor. "Gram said I had to listen to you, but—well, I knew something was wrong."

I took my first deep breath and broke into a shaky smile. "You had my back." Maybe someday I'd tell him the rifle wasn't loaded. "Thanks."

Rusty reddened darker than his hair and looked away with a grin.

Blood oozed out from under Garrett's head. "Rusty, call 911 and say we need an ambulance. Dad should be here any minute."

"Did somebody shoot a gun?" Aaron banged into the kitchen.

Rusty whirled to him. "What're you doing here? I told you guys to go on to Aunt Jeanine's."

"If you had to check on Rae, we thought we should too. Where'd you get the gun?"

I drew a hand down the side of my face. "So you didn't listen to me either."

"Oh, hey, Dad." Micah waved from the screened porch.

"Micah, don't go in." Dad's shout almost rattled the roasting pan on the stove and made me jump.

Aaron leaned out the open door. "How come, Dad?"

Pistol drawn and ghost white, Dad burst into the kitchen. His gaze swept over all of us. "You're okay," he whispered. "Where's —" He quick-stepped to me and looked down at Garrett, who still hadn't moved.

"We're fine, Dad." I wiped a trembling hand over my mouth.

Dad bent over the inert body, snapped on handcuffs, and spoke into the radio on his shoulder. Then somehow he scooped all four of us into one giant hug. His heart hammered beneath his body armor. I squeezed him like I was afraid he'd escape.

Aaron groaned, and Rusty said, "We're all okay, Dad."

Gulping, he loosened his hug enough to look at us. "I know. But I got the call from dispatch, and Gloria told me what Jason had told her. And then I called and no one picked up. All the way here, I was thinking … I was thinking …" Another hug and, swallowing, he waved a hand. "You don't want to know what I was thinking."

A siren whined in the distance. Every cop in the county had to be converging on the farm.

Dad hugged us all again, and I tried to do the same to my four guys.

My dad was safe. My brothers were safe. *Thank You forever, Father.*

Chapter 41

"Rae, you here?" Uncle Hank called from outside.

Dad released us, went to the back door, and hollered for him to come in. Hank jogged in with a rifle, took us all in, then sagged against the counter. "Thank You, Lord. When'd you get here, Mal?"

Stooping over Garrett, Dad said, "Just a few minutes ago." He straightened. "Hank, would you — where are your shoes?"

Uncle Hank rubbed one bare foot over the other. "Jason Carlisle calls me hysterical, saying my niece and nephews are in the hands of the stalker, and you think I'm gonna look for my shoes?"

As Dad asked Hank to go to the basement with my brothers, Chief Deputy Harris and other officers poured through the front and back doors. I got a freezer pack for my wrist, then Dad and I moved to Gram's bedroom, where a BCI agent took my statement. When she had everything she needed, she joined the rest of the officers clogging the living-dining room.

Lowering himself onto the corner of my desk, Dad said, his voice tight, "Maybe I should take you to the emergency room." He glared through the open door, as if his gaze could incinerate Garrett.

The ache had graduated to a throb, but I shook my head. "I'm not leaving home tonight."

Dad had me go over the story again from when Micah and I walked down to the mailbox.

"You're sure he decided to kill himself instead of you or me?" Dad said.

"The gun was going toward his head." The action was spring water clear in my mind as I sank onto the bed. "He hadn't thought about how he'd have to kill another cop. I guess he just saw you as my dad. And he hadn't thought about orphaning the boys. When I pointed all that out, he couldn't go through with it. I kept telling him he had a choice. I never thought he'd choose to kill himself. Like his dad."

Weariness poured over me like a cloudburst. "How'd you find the photo of his father?"

"I asked Jeanine to hunt for it. The husband killing himself the day after his divorce was finalized, and the wife dying of cirrhosis of the liver got me to thinking. I've seen enough divorces go wrong to know the husband might have wanted to reconcile and the wife didn't. When he killed himself, she couldn't live with it and drank herself to death. But not before she did her best to offload her guilt onto Bella Rydell and convince her son your mom was to blame."

Dad stepped over and kissed me on the forehead. "You should have left with your brothers."

I shook my head. "He would have come with us, and I had to protect the boys. Or he would have gone back to the woods to snipe you."

"And he revealed himself because he fell into one of the boys' pits?"

"Yeah."

Dad grimaced like he'd just fallen into one himself. "Aaron will never let me forget that." He brushed back a tangle of my hair. "You know, I was right Christmas morning. You do have some kind of guts."

I found the energy to smile.

Sirens signaled more cops on the way. We bypassed all the officials working the crime scene by going out the front door and around to the breezeway and took the steps down from there to the outside door to the basement. Before we crossed over the sill, Gram grabbed us.

"Oh, Rae, Mal, I am so sorry I left." Gram's cheeks were wet.

Dad pulled her close. "Ma, you couldn't have known."

Houston and Chris raced down the steps. They looked like someone had pulled a rug out from under them and they were still falling.

"We had no idea, Mal." Houston's tenor was high, pleading, as if he needed to convince Dad. "Things had been getting tense at the house. Garrett and I always seemed to find something to fight about. I thought he was having trouble with his girlfriend. He said he had one in Columbus, though he never said much about her. But Chris and I were talking, and we think the nights he stayed out real late or never came home—"

"He was leaving notes for Rae." Chris's deep voice was husky. "I had a criminal living under my roof and never suspected a thing."

"Why should you?." Dad used the tone he reserved for reassuring my brothers and me. "Strange behavior can indicate all sorts of problems, and most of them aren't criminal. When you guys have had time to absorb this, we'll go over Matthews's behavior, see if there were any red flags. But there might not have been any."

Chief Deputy Harris called down the basement stairs, "Hey, Mal. Can you come up here?"

"Coming." He looked to me. "Everybody'll be asking you to tell them what happened. Just give them the basics and don't alter your story. I don't want a defense attorney questioning your credibility as a witness. If someone gets too nosy, tell them to talk to me."

He delivered more hugs to my brothers before returning to the main floor.

Houston shook his head. "I just can't believe it. A cop stalking a citizen and threatening to kill another cop."

"Garrett was a son long before he was a cop." I set aside the freezer pack and motioned them to follow me to where the backyard dipped to the first slope that eventually rolled all the way to the fields.

Most of the fog had disappeared, blown away by a fresh breeze that tossed the ends of my hair into my mouth. The uniform gray of the sky lightened toward the west. Warming my hands in the pocket of my jeans, I told the guys how Garrett had made me suspicious with his lies, leaving out my concerns about Chris. Although an urge to come clean gnawed at me, I'd have to tell him that in private.

My story did nothing to wipe the sick, lost looks from their faces.

"So Garrett lied to you about being from Zanesville because he didn't want you to know his family lived in the area when your mom did?" Houston said. "But he'd only sent you one note when he did that."

"Panic." Heat crept into Chris's voice. "He hadn't expected Rae to ask him, and he lied to cover himself. Once he'd said that to her, he had to keep it up, which wasn't that hard because he rarely talked about his past."

I said, "But you remembered that he'd mentioned his dad had died when he was a kid."

"Rae!" called Aunt Jeanine.

She ran down from the breezeway with Amber and Coral, and they caught me in a triple hug.

While the police and other county personnel invaded the upstairs, members from church and friends of Gram and Mal stopped by the basement, expressing their shock and support.

I propped myself against the washer, too tired to do anything but nod as people spoke to me. The boys had run outside with Coral. Gram and Jeanine took turns working the landline, which wouldn't stop ringing. Dad, Houston, and Chris came in and out, though Dad seemed focused on making sure my brothers and I were still all right.

Uncle Hank appeared at my side, offering me a root beer. "Hope everybody clears out soon."

I took a long drink. "Me too." All the commotion annoyed me, but I didn't want to be alone. I looked down at his feet. "You found some socks."

He wiggled his toes. "Yeah, Mal's shoes are way too big for me, but his socks'll work."

Devon walked in from the backyard with Liberty and Serenity. "So you took out a cop?"

Just seeing her, as blunt and confident as ever, washed away some of the weariness.

I told her what I could, explaining that Dad said not to go into details.

Irritation wrinkled Devon's attractive face. "Your father should work for the CIA, as closely as he guards his information. What will happen to that cop?"

"Since he tried to commit suicide, I guess some kind of psychiatric help. I don't know how many charges he'll face. I hope he gets the help he needs."

"You care?" The last word went high in disbelief.

The jam sessions at Chris's house replayed in my mind, churning up so many feelings I couldn't identify them. "Maybe it sounds crazy. And if he'd hurt my dad or my brothers, I'd've killed him." I knew that like I knew my height and weight. I flicked the tab on my can and looked to her. "But I know what it's like to want a dad."

Jason rushed into the basement. "You're all right." He aimed his Superman smile at me. "I nearly drove off the road when you said you thought the stalker was sitting in your house. And then when you told me your idea for getting your brothers away and how you'd be alone with him ..." Swallowing hard, he put a hand against his chest. "I'm so glad you're okay."

"You broke the case." I explained how Dad had asked Aunt Jeanine to find a photo for him to identify.

Jason sighed. "If I hadn't been tied up in meetings all afternoon, I would have seen it earlier and saved you from such a horrible experience."

The memory of cold metal against my chin made me shiver, but I put on a smile for him.

Chris had returned to the basement without Houston, scooting past Gram and the pastor.

"Excuse me, Jason." I crossed to Chris and said, "Can I talk to you?" I didn't want to heap more misery on him, but my unfounded suspicions pushed me.

He followed me outside. My brothers played tag with Coral, Liberty, and Serenity. The sunset washed over the top of the house in gold as the kids chased each other down the hill in the damp grass. I led Chris up to the far side of the garage. I couldn't imagine any reason for anyone, friends or cops, to come over here.

I said in a lowered voice, "I want to apologize to you."

His eyebrows contracted. "I should apologize to you for having a stalker living with me, who's a cop, and I never suspected a thing." Chris rubbed his moustache with the end of his thumb. "He'd sworn to uphold the law and protect citizens."

"I don't blame you or Houston. Why should you think a friend is a criminal?" I bit my lip. "You'll maybe think I'm not much of a friend after you hear what I have to tell you."

Rolling and unrolling the hem of my t-shirt, I told Chris why I'd suspected him, leaving out that I saw him attack the punching bag. I couldn't admit to spying on him. "Dad said he thought he knew why you never talk about your past except about your great-grandpa. He didn't tell me the reason, so you don't have to worry about me blabbing anything. But I -- I felt like I should say I'm sorry. I hope we can still be friends." I met his astonished, black eyes. "Hanging out at your house is the best times I've ever had."

He looked to the ground, smoothing his moustache.

Gulping, I stepped back. Had I just smashed our relationship? Maybe I should leave. Tears stinging my eyes, I turned away.

"My mother's an addict." He blurted the sentence. "She was high when she got pregnant with me, and my father could be any guy of color who passed through southern California or Marlin County the summer before I was born."

I turned back to him as he said, "She can stay fairly sober when she's working — she's an actress — but when she can't find a job, she starts again. The ten years I lived with her were a disaster. I like it here because no one knows about her. I'm known as Dave Kincaid's great-grandson, and Mal's deputy, and that's who I want to be." Some of his composure had crumpled, leaving an expression aching with sadness.

He'd confided in me. I felt so privileged, like a king had handed me the keys to his treasury. "I won't tell anybody."

The sadness disappeared for a second as an ornery grin flashed by. "You're a girl who can keep secrets."

My ears caught fire. Was I pleased or embarrassed or both?

"It'll look better if we talk to the reporters together." Dad's penetrating baritone seemed to reach us from inside the garage. "Show them and the citizens that our agencies are cooperating. We'll explain how you'll examine Matthews's behavior on duty and I'll interview my officers who worked and lived with him and see if there were any red flags we missed."

"'We missed'?" Simcox packed more nastiness into those two syllables than most people could in six sentences.

Dad sighed, loud enough for us to catch it. "You know how one bad cop makes a lot of people think we're all bad. So we should reassure citizens that we're working together to make sure it doesn't happen again."

"Don't be magnanimous, Mal." Simcox's words fell like blows. "I know you're overjoyed that you didn't hire a nut job and then put him in charge of the investigation into his own crime. No one will believe Matthews didn't persuade me to suspect Rae faked the stalker." He paused. "You do know what magnanimous means, don't you?"

The question was so patronizing that a sudden spurt of anger gave me an energy boost. Chris began to march around the garage, but I grabbed his arm, bracing myself for the explosion.

It came, but in a burst of deep laughter. Dad said, "Simcox, the only thing I'm overjoyed about is that I didn't come home to find all my kids murdered. I'm rounding up all of my officers who are still here and going down to the road to talk to the reporters. You and your officers are welcome to come with us."

Chris and I hurried around the back of the garage to the breezeway and found Dad mounting the steps to the screened porch. "Kincaid. I'm going to issue a statement to the reporters massing on the road. As soon as I tell everybody else, I'll ride down with you."

Chris nodded, gave me another fleeting smile, and left.

I went into the kitchen as Dad took Houston and Deputy Zagoric out the front door, emptying the house of cops.

Gram was cutting up the roast chicken. "I'm making sandwiches, enough for everyone."

The mention of food made my stomach lurch, and I covered my mouth. "I can't eat."

"Of course, you can. You need to." She set down her knife. "You should be proud of yourself, Rae. You kept your head in a horrible situation. You shouldn't celebrate—you've lost someone you thought was a friend. But you should feel satisfied."

Gram had summed up perfectly all my conflicting feelings. I hugged her and picked up a sandwich.

Only Jason and Devon remained from the invasion of well-wishers, along with the Norrises. The kids took their plates loaded with sandwiches, chips, and fruit into the living room, avoiding the broken dinner table.

Setting aside my meal, I crossed to the couch where my brothers sat. "Y'all should be proud of yourselves too." I kissed Rusty, Aaron, and Micah on their heads. Aaron made retching noises. "You should have listened to me, but you showed a lot of guts coming back. And you saved Dad by digging those pits."

Rusty's eyebrows fell in confusion as Aaron said in a gasp, "What?"

"You don't know?" I figured somebody would have told them by now. "If y'all hadn't dug that hole by the mailbox, Garrett wouldn't have fallen in it. If he hadn't fallen in it, he could have stayed hidden in the woods with his rifle. Micah and I never would have known he was there. Y'all ruined his plan."

Rusty looked to Aaron, and Aaron looked to Micah, proud grins spreading among them as my family and friends cracked up. Uncle Hank laughed so hard he choked and had to drain his can of soda to stop coughing.

The landline rang, and gulping her mouth clear, Aunt Jeanine picked it up. "Oh, hey, Walter. No, he's still tied up. He's talking to reporters … I'll ask." She covered the mouthpiece. "Rae, Walter wants to come over and see you. Is that okay?"

"For sure. If he wants to talk to me about the vandalism, tell him I won't press charges. But I am pressing charges against Harley for stealing my backpack."

Aunt Jeanine relayed the information and hung up. "He'll never admit it, but he sounded relieved."

After we'd cleaned the dishes and the kids had spilled out the front door, chasing each other down the slope to the alpacas' pastures, Walter's truck rattled up to our farmhouse. Egypt, China, and Walter piled out. He stalked straight for me on the porch, but Egypt and China lagged behind.

Stopping at the bottom step, Walter turned to Egypt. "Give it to her."

She thrust her fist at me, and I took a wad of bills.

"That's $125," Walter said. "You'll get the rest in a few months."

"I know. Thank you."

Walter looked at Egypt. A frown cut so deep in her round face, I figured smiling was beyond it. He smacked her on the shoulder. "Thank her."

Throwing back her shoulders, Egypt whirled to him. They glowered at each other for a moment, then she said to her holey tennis shoes, "Thanks."

I kept my voice neutral. "You're welcome."

"What're you doing here, Walter?" Dad banged out of a patrol SUV with Chris and Houston. The rest of the police vehicles had gone. He'd only taken a few steps before my brothers raced up the hill from the pastures and attacked him.

"Came to see if you and your kids were still alive," said Walter. "Lily called and said she'd heard you'd been shot. Then Cal called, sayin' Rae'd been shot. Jeanine phoned to set the story straight, but I figured I'd come over and see for myself. Besides, Egypt had to pay Rae, show she'd hold up her end of the deal."

With Aaron grabbing his arm, Dad glanced at me, and I nodded. He half-smiled, blinking, like he wasn't sure what to make of my decision.

Shoving his hands deep in the pockets of his corduroy work coat, Walter said, "What happened?"

"Well, my kids saved my life." Dad clumped to the porch with Micah attached to his right leg and Aaron fastened to his back. At least Rusty had settled for walking beside him. "Shortened it by a few years but saved it."

Aaron punched him in the arm. "Told you it would work."

Rolling his eyes, Dad said, "C'mon in, Walter. I'll tell you and the girls what I can. I'll have to leave soon, though. My chief deputy is getting a warrant to search the suspect's room and belongings."

Walter shifted his gaze to Gram, who stood with arms folded. "Your mom wouldn't like it."

"I told you. This is Rae's and Mal's house too." Gram turned to the front door. "They can invite anyone they want."

Dad led the way as my relatives filed inside. Jason, Devon, Houston, and Chris remained on the porch, glancing at each other.

"Perhaps we should go." Jason put in words what they were thinking.

"Since it's my house," I said, "I'd like my friends to stay as long as they want."

Devon grinned. "Anything for a friend."

In the living room, Walter dropped into the recliner while Egypt and China stood behind it. The rest of my family and friends found seats and spots throughout the big room, Dad and Gram sitting on the couch. I took the spot beside Dad with Aaron crowding me on the right by propping himself on the couch's arm, Rusty crowding me from above by leaning over the back, and Micah crowding me to my left by clambering into Dad's lap.

Resting my head on Dad's shoulder, I pulled Micah over to me.

Tonight, and for a long time to come, I couldn't have my family too close.

END

ACKNOWLEDGEMENTS

Writing is a solitary art. But publishing takes the dedication, talent, and skill of many people. The journey of *A Shadow on the Snow* to see the light of print is no exception.

Thank you to the writers I met through the Ohio chapter of American Christian Fiction Writers—Bettie Boswell, Carole Brown, Sandra Merville Hart, Sharyn Kopf, Tamera Lynn Kraft, Michelle L. Levigne, Cindy Thomson, and Rebecca Waters, I would not be published without your support, instruction, and encouragement.

Thanks to Cindy Thomson—your advice on how to construct my first chapter and the importance of summarizing my novel in a few sentences was critical to its development.

Thanks to Sharyn Kopf, my freelance editor—you taught me how to apply "show, don't tell" and a thousand other techniques to improve my writing, including informing me that synonyms for "brown" actually exist.

Thanks to Tamera Lynn Kraft and Michelle L. Levigne – you encouraged me to continue the story of Rae and her family, friends, and enemies. That faith in my writing meant so much. Tamera, your cover design captures the mood of my novel perfectly! Michelle, you put the sparkle on my prose and didn't recoil in horror when I proposed adding graphics.

Thanks to you, Michele King, for taking the time to answer my questions about raising alpacas.

Thanks to my beta readers, Holly Bucher, Ellyn Boynton, Joyce Crouch, Kip Krueger, and Camille Leber – your early input was essential in the improvement of my novel.

A very special thank you to all the law enforcement officers I learned from, especially Randy Martz and Carrie Ryan – both of you were always eager to answer any questions related to your profession. Like most citizens, I had no idea how demanding and difficult a cop's job is. Whether I spoke to officers in one-on-one interviews or attended presentations through my local Sheriff Citizens Academy, you were all so helpful. Thank you for your dedication and sacrifice, for doing a job I could never do.

Almost last, but never least, thanks to my family. Mom, Dad, Alicia, Laura, and Ellyn – you have encouraged my writing since I wrote a Scooby Doo rip-off when I was seven. James, Joy, Daniel, Andrew, Anna, and Peter – you always gave me helpful feedback when I asked for it. Will and Cole – it's not easy having a mom who's a writer. Thank you for your patience and interest. Bill – as an engineer, you had no idea what marrying a writer meant. But you've supported me every step of the way, and every writer should have an engineer to critique plot twists and point out gaps in logic.

Last and first, to my Heavenly Dad – You wanted this story to come out into the world. It's been the privilege of my life to write it with You.

ABOUT THE AUTHOR

JPC Allen started her writing career in second grade with an homage to Scooby Doo. She's been tracking down mysteries ever since and has written mystery short stories for Mt. Zion Ridge Press. Her Christmas mystery, *A Rose from the Ashes,* was a Selah-finalist at the Blue Ridge Mountains Writers Conference in 2020. Online, she offers tips and prompts to ignite the creative spark in every kind of writer . She also leads workshops for tweens, teens, and adults, encouraging them to discover the adventure of writing. A lifelong Buckeye, she has deep roots in the Mountain State. *A Shadow on the Snow* is her first novel.

Follow the clues to her next mystery on her pages @ jpcallenwrites on Facebook and Instagram, her website, JPCAllenWrites.com, and her author pages on Goodreads, and Amazon.